The

DEAD
ASSASSIN

ALSO BY VAUGHN ENTWISTLE

The Revenant of Thraxton Hall

The Angel of Highgate

The

DEAD
ASSASSIN

The Paranormal Casebooks of
Sir Arthur Conan Doyle

VAUGHN ENTWISTLE

MINOTAUR BOOKS
NEW YORK

THE DEAD ASSASSIN. Copyright © 2015 by Vaughn Entwistle. All rights reserved. Printed in the United States of America. For information, address St. Martin's Press, 175 Fifth Avenue, New York, N.Y. 10010.

Design by Meryl Sussman Levavi

ISBN 978-1-250-03506-6

To my mother and father, for a lifetime of love...

...and to my beloved wife, Shelley, who believed in me

CONTENTS

CHAPTER 1. MURDER MOST 'ORRIBLE   1

CHAPTER 2. THE MURDERER IN THE CUPBOARD   21

CHAPTER 3. FENIANS, ANARCHISTS, AND DYNAMITARDS   26

CHAPTER 4. THE FOG COMMITTEE   32

CHAPTER 5. RAISING GHOSTS   40

CHAPTER 6. AN ILL-TIMED LETTER   46

CHAPTER 7. SHANGHAIED IN WATERLOO   53

CHAPTER 8. A MASSIVE ATTACK OF HEART   66

CHAPTER 9. JEDIDIAH'S EMPORIUM OF
            MECHANICAL MARVELS   74

CHAPTER 10. A WILDE NIGHT AT THE THEATER   86

CHAPTER 11. AN UNHOLY RESURRECTION   96

CHAPTER 12. A WONDERFUL EVENING ENDS HORRIBLY   102

CHAPTER 13. THE ASSASSIN KILLS AGAIN   112

CHAPTER 14. A DEEPLY DISTURBING DISCOVERY   122

Chapter 15. Check and Mate 141

Chapter 16. Look Upon My Works and Tremble 152

Chapter 17. A Drowned Ophelia 161

Chapter 18. Invitation to an Execution 163

Chapter 19. Right Coffin, Wrong Corpse 181

Chapter 20. An Encounter in a Pornographic
Bookshop 190

Chapter 21. Before Rigor Sets In 198

Chapter 22. Cakes and Corpses 202

Chapter 23. A Dinner Date to Remember 207

Chapter 24. Useless Friends and Dangerous Drugs 220

Chapter 25. Descent Into the Underworld 226

Chapter 26. A Nice Night for a Drowning 243

Chapter 27. A Pleasant Night Cruise upon the Thames 259

Chapter 28. The Fog Descends 265

Chapter 29. The Importance of Being in
Deadly Earnest 271

Chapter 30. Chasing Monsters 287

Chapter 31. A Toast to Death 300

Chapter 32. A Wagnerian Death 302

Chapter 33. A Summons to the Palace 325

Chapter 34. The Sun Breaks Through 336

The

DEAD
ASSASSIN

CHAPTER 1

MURDER MOST 'ORRIBLE

A *murder. Something nasty. Something twisted. Something baffling and bizarre. Why else would the police have sought me out?*

Such thoughts rattled through the mind of Arthur Conan Doyle as he watched Detective Blenkinsop of Scotland Yard step into the Palm Room of the Tivoli restaurant and sweep his blue-eyed gaze across the crowded tables, searching for something.

Searching for him.

Go away blast you! Not now. Not tonight!

Thanks to the fame Sherlock Holmes had bestowed upon him, Scotland Yard often consulted Conan Doyle on crimes that confounded all conventional means of detection. They dragged to his door the most difficult cases. The inexplicable ones. The conundrums. The impossibly knotted yarn balls the clumsy fingers of the police could not unravel. Ordinarily, he was flattered to be consulted on such cases. But on this occasion, he wished he could throw a cloak of invisibility about his shoulders.

Determined not to make eye contact, he reeled in his gaze from the detective and lavished it instead upon his dinner companion. At just twenty-four years of age, Miss Jean Leckie was a ravishing beauty fourteen years his junior. The two had by happy accident occupied adjacent chairs at the November meeting of the Society for Psychical

Research. In conversation it fell out that Miss Leckie shared Conan Doyle's fascination with Spiritualism and all things occult. After the meeting adjourned, she accepted the older man's invitation to supper, where she had just revealed—over a sumptuous repast of boiled fowl a la béchamel, braised parsnips, and crab-stuffed courgettes— that she herself was an amateur medium who had conducted a number of successful séances.

Throughout their conversation, Conan Doyle fought the urge to stare, but when he gazed into those hazel-green eyes, sparkling with fire and intelligence, his knees trembled like a schoolboy's in the throes of his first crush.

But it wasn't just Conan Doyle who found himself under the thrall of Miss Leckie's beauty. She was a radiant presence that coaxed furtive glances from dinner patrons sitting at adjacent tables. Under the Tivoli's electric lights, her dark golden hair shone. Her long face, with its high cheekbones, strong chin, and aquiline nose, evinced the classical proportions of a Greek bust. In their initial conversation, he had been struck by the musicality of her voice, and was thrilled to discover that she was a classically trained mezzo-soprano. And so, with every revelation of her wit, character, and accomplishments, Conan Doyle was drawn in deeper. By the time the bread pudding arrived at the table, hot and steaming in its tureen, he was utterly smitten.

For her part, Miss Leckie seemed as equally attentive of him, for she caught the look of discomfort that flashed across his face when he glimpsed the arrival of Detective Blenkinsop.

"Are you quite well, Doctor Doyle?" she asked. "You seem suddenly quite distracted."

Conan Doyle chanced to dart a quick look across the dining room and locked eyes with the young detective, who now steamed toward them with the dread determination of a mechanical homing torpedo.

"I'm afraid I have just seen someone I know."

A frown upset her perfect features. "Oh? Someone who shall be joining us?"

"Quite the opposite. Someone, I fear, who shall be tearing us apart."

Conan Doyle snatched the linen napkin from his lap, crumpled it in his fist, and tossed it down on the table. It had been a delightful meal, but the intrusion of Scotland Yard meant the evening had just crashed to an abrupt and unwelcome end. He watched Detective Blenkinsop's approach with dour anticipation, the food already curdling in his stomach.

He was not alone. Other diners recoiled at the officer's approach as a wave of shock and horror surged through the room. Women shrieked. Men shouted in outrage and lurched up from their seats. A string quartet had been playing a subdued air in a quiet corner, but now the despairing cellos groaned into silence. A matronly woman clutched her throat and half rose from her chair before swooning to the floor. Several chivalrous gents jumped to their feet to assist the lady, only to leap back as Blenkinsop swept through their midst like a nightmare torn loose of its moorings. When the detective drew closer, Conan Doyle took one look and understood why his approach elicited so much dread.

Blood . . . Blood . . . Blood . . .

. . . and so much of it: an angry, violent crimson under the Palm Room's cheerful lights. The detective's regulation dark blue rain cape was drenched in pints of it, runneling fresh and sticky down his front and dribbling a crimson trail across the elegant marble floor.

As Blenkinsop arrived at their table, Miss Leckie stifled a shriek behind her hand, averting eyes rolling with horror.

Conan Doyle leapt to his feet, outraged. "Detective Blenkinsop! What on earth is the meaning of this? What are you thinking, coming into a public place in such a state? Are you mad?"

The young man stood before the table. Wavering. Unsteady on his feet. His eyes held the stunned look of crushed glass beads. It took a moment before he registered Conan Doyle's words and stammered out: "B-beg pardon, sir b-but I—I require your assistance, sir. I . . . I mean I ain't never . . . I ain't never seen nothing so . . . 'orrible . . ."

As a physician with years of medical training, Conan Doyle rec-ognized the signs of a man going into shock—the ghastly pallor, the sweating brow—and concern swept aside his anger. He sprang from his chair, gripped Blenkinsop by the shoulder, and eased him into the vacated seat.

But the uproar the young detective had caused was far from over. Diners abandoned their tables and milled in confusion. Waiters scur-ried hither and yon, uttering soothing words to calm frantic diners and coax them back into their seats. The Tivoli's maître d' bustled up to Conan Doyle's table, jabbering hysterically. Instantly, the Scot-tish doctor became the calm eye in a swirling vortex of emotion. He was at his best in a crisis, and now he took command. Barking orders, the maître d' was chivvied off to fetch a large snifter of brandy. He had the detective's blood-drenched rain cape bundled up in an old potato sack from the kitchen and hauled away to be tossed into the furnace. And then he corralled two passing waiters: the first was sent to fetch Miss Leckie's hat and wrap; the second he dispatched to alert the driver of the hansom cab waiting for them outside. Poor Miss Leckie, rather overwhelmed by it all, said little as a waiter eased her into her coat, and then Conan Doyle escorted her to the waiting cab.

The doormen held the door for them and they stepped from the light and warmth of the Tivoli into a chill November night miasmic with swirling fog.

"I am so sorry our lovely evening must end in such an ugly way," the Scottish author apologized.

Miss Leckie smiled. "I, too, am sorry that our most elucidating conversation was interrupted."

"Perhaps you would allow me to invite you to another dinner, to make amends?" Conan Doyle blushed as he spoke the words, which had surged from him in an unrestrainable rush of emotion. The first dinner invite had come spontaneously. The two had struck up a con-versation during the SPR meeting and the invitation to continue the exchange over supper seemed natural. But a second invitation smacked of an ulterior motive. He quailed, fearing he had overstepped the bounds of propriety. What he was doing could be seen as highly indecorous. Even scandalous. He was a married man with an invalid wife. Miss Leckie was a single lady much younger than he. But when he looked into those doeish eyes, a trapdoor in his chest dropped open and his heart plummeted through it.

A brief look of uncertainty crossed her face, but then the corners of her mouth curled in a coquettish smile. "That would be delightful."

He fumbled in his waistcoat pocket, snatched free a calling card, and presented it to her. "Here is my card. Please let me know of a convenient time we might meet again."

"I look forward most anxiously," she said, plucking the card from his grip. And then, in an unambiguous sign of affection, touched a hand to his forearm. The press of her slender fingers, elegant in elbow-length gloves, lingered a moment longer than necessary.

"Until then," she said, smiling sweetly, "au revoir."

Crinoline rustled as she swept up her skirts and climbed into the hansom. Before the cab door folded over her legs, Conan Doyle checked to ensure that none of her skirts were trapped, then called up to the driver, "Blackheath, Jim, and drive carefully. The fog is worsening and you convey a most precious cargo."

The cabbie nodded. "The worst I seen this year, Doctor Doyle. But don't you worry none, she'll be safe as houses with Iron Jim."

Conan Doyle handed up a sovereign coin, scandalously overpaying. The cabbie tugged the brim of his rumpled bowler in salute, then shook the reins and clucked for the horse to pull away. Coach lights blazing, the hansom plunged into the murk and vanished from sight before it had gone thirty feet, but the image of her smile hovered eidetically on the roiling gray fog.

And then, gallingly, Conan Doyle remembered he had forgotten to ask for Miss Leckie's calling card in return. Apart from the fact that she lived with her parents in the London suburb of Blackheath, he had no clue as to her address.

The hansom's departure revealed another carriage waiting at the curbside: a Black Mariah, a hulking, four-wheeled coffin used by the Metropolitan police to haul criminals to jail and condemned prisoners to the gallows—evidently the means by which Detective Blenkinsop had arrived. Two uniformed constables hunkered on the seat, mouths and noses muffled with thick woolen scarves to filter the choking air. Even though two large coach lights burned bright on either side of the Mariah, the blinding fog also obliged two additional officers brandishing flaming torches to lead the horses and light the way.

A convulsive shiver shook Conan Doyle's large frame as the fog ran an icy finger down his spine. The November night was too bitterly cold to tarry long without a coat, and so he slipped quickly back inside the restaurant.

In the welcome warmth of the Palm Room, Conan Doyle dropped into his dinner companion's vacated seat and waited patiently until Detective Blenkinsop finished sipping his brandy, the color flushed back into his face, and the spark of intellect burned once again in his eyes.

"Obviously it's a murder," Conan Doyle ventured. "An extremely bloody one judging by the state of your raincoat."

The hand holding the brandy snifter tremored visibly. "It's a murder all right, sir. But not like nothing I ever seen before."

"It must be something truly dire to have distressed a detective used to witnessing the worst of humanity's deeds."

Blenkinsop shook his head. At just twenty-six, he was alarmingly boyish-looking. He had been promoted to detective just six months previously, in recognition of a feat of bravery: a deranged gunman walked into the crowd gathered outside the gates of Buckingham Palace and began firing his pistol at random. Two people had been shot dead as other constables looked on helplessly. Blenkinsop single-handedly tackled the madman to the ground and disarmed him. In recognition of his valor, he had been promoted to detective, the youngest ever on the force. Although he had grown the wispy suggestion of a moustache in an attempt to look older, he still more closely resembled a fresh-faced schoolboy summoned to the headmaster's office to receive a caning.

"I'd rather say as little as possible," Blenkinsop said. "I figured to fetch you so you can see for yourself." He tossed back the dregs of his liquor, nostrils flaring as he exhaled brandy fumes. "You might have a stiff 'un yourself, afore we go. I reckon even a doctor's nerves will need steadying."

Stepping into the chill night was like an open-handed slap across the face. For days, a pestilential fog, known in the popular vernacular as a "London Particular," had suffocated the capital city beneath a yellow-green blanket. Appearing each evening at the mouth of the Thames, the fog oozed up the river and spilled over onto the surrounding streets, submerging all but the tallest church spires. Fogs were common at this time of year, but rather than abating after a few days as most fogs did, the mephitic cloud seemed to worsen with each evening. After a full week of such fogs, the night air was cold and abrasive, a gritty cloud of pumice swirling with ash, soot, and firefly-like embers that burned the lungs and needled tears to the eyes. The fog muffled sound and shrank the sprawling metropolis to a murky circle of visibility, scarcely twenty feet in any direction.

Detective Blenkinsop snatched wide the battle-scarred rear door of the Mariah and gestured for the Scottish author to step aboard. "Forgive the means of transport, sir. Uncomfortable, I admit, but she'll get us there, no bother."

As Conan Doyle climbed into the boxy carriage, a strangely familiar smell assailed his senses—Turkish tobacco smoke—and he was surprised to find that the Mariah already had an occupant.

"Ah," spoke an urbane voice, "it appears I am not the only prisoner tonight. I bid you welcome, fellow riffraff."

It was only then Conan Doyle realized that the shadowy shape he had at first mistaken for a small bear was in fact a large Irishman.

"Oscar!"

Oscar Wilde wore a gorgeous fur overcoat with an enormous fur collar and cuffs. Atop his head perched a muskrat hat—a trophy fetched from his North American travels. Conan Doyle had ridden in Black Mariahs before, which invariably bore an aura of abject despair and reeked like public urinals in the worse part of London, but Wilde's expensive cologne and piquant tobacco smoke bullied the air of its malodorous stink while his insouciant gravitas commandeered the space and made it his own. A small oil lantern swung from a hook in the ceiling, and in the wan pulse of amber light the Irish wit resembled the sultan of some exotic country being carried to his coronation in an enclosed sedan chair.

Conan Doyle slid in beside his friend, and Detective Blenkinsop dropped onto the bench opposite. The door of the Mariah banged shut and a constable standing outside locked them in. The horses were gee'd up and the Mariah rumbled away on wobbly axles squealing for a lick of grease.

"I am always happy to see you, Oscar," Conan Doyle said. "But I confess you are the last person I would expect to meet in a Black Mariah."

The hot coal of Wilde's cigarette flared red as he drew in a lungful and jetted smoke out both nostrils. "Scotland Yard's best have been combing the city for you. Detective Blenkinsop recruited me to assist in the search. We stopped at The Savoy, Claridge's, and then your club. When you were discovered at none of them, given the hour, I plumped for the Tivoli and am gratified to see my guess was correct." Wilde swept Conan Doyle's dress with an appraising gaze and his full lips curled in a supercilious smile. "And now I understand why you were avoiding your usual haunts."

Conan Doyle stiffened in his seat. "I, ah . . . I was supping with a friend. A fellow member of the Society for Psychical Research."

"A fellow member, but not a *fellow*, per se?" Wilde remarked in a deeply incriminating voice. "You are quite the dog, Arthur. I suspect you were entertaining a lady!"

Conan Doyle blanched as Wilde pierced the bull's-eye with his first arrow.

"I . . . how on earth did you know that?"

Had it not been so gloomy, Conan Doyle's companions would have seen him blush.

"Your dress reveals much, Arthur. You are wearing a very fine bespoke suit—beautifully tailored might I add—rather than your work-a-day tweeds. You sport a beaver top hat, a fresh boutonniere, and have obviously spent a great deal of effort on your toilet, including taking the time to wax your extravagant moustaches, which I must confess positively coruscate in the light. Were we actually heading to jail you would be the talk of the prison yard. A man as practical as Arthur Conan Doyle does not take such pains with his attire to dine with an old school chum or a chalk-dusted academic. You have clearly dressed for a lady friend. A young and fetching lady, I would wager. Another good reason to dodge your usual haunts to avoid wagging tongues—"

"Yes, thank you, Oscar," Conan Doyle interrupted. "And I think that's quite enough. I assume you were carousing at The Savoy, as usual?"

The Irishman trilled with laughter. "Au contraire. It is scarcely ten o'clock. Oscar Wilde does not *begin* to carouse until midnight at the very earliest. No, I was visiting the Haymarket Theatre. My new play is in its third week. I look in on the production from time to time. To boost company morale. To thrill my audiences with a personal appearance . . . and to count the box office receipts. Plus I am a great aficionado of my own work. I love the sound of my own voice. And I love to hear the sound of my own voice coming out of someone else's mouth. It is the primary reason for my connexion with the theater; it ensures I am never far from the thing I love most."

"Well now you've found me," Conan Doyle said, and turned his attention to the policeman sitting opposite. "Can you reveal, Detective

Blenkinsop, what has prompted Scotland Yard to search for me so diligently?"

Blenkinsop drew the homburg from his head and held it slackly in his hands, turning it slowly by the brim. "There's been a murder—no, not a murder. That ain't right. I guess you'd properly call it . . . an assassination."

Conan Doyle and Wilde exchanged stunned glances.

"Are we permitted to know whom?" Wilde asked.

The young detective's expression grew tragic. "The whole world will know soon enough: Lord Howell."

Both Wilde and Conan Doyle grunted as if gut-punched.

"The prime minister's secretary for war," Conan Doyle muttered in shocked tones.

Wilde leaned forward, his expression tense. "An assassination, you say? Do you suspect the party or parties responsible for such an act?"

Blenkinsop shook his head. "Not a clue. Right now all we got is the body. But it's not just the murder. It's *how* he was murdered. The murder scene . . ." A gasp tore loose from Blenkinsop, whose eyes lost focus as he stared blankly into space. "I can't tell ya no more. I can't describe it. I seen some dark doings in me days as a copper. But I ain't never seen nothing like this. When I shut me eyes, I can still see it."

With Blenkinsop unwilling to reveal more, the men fell into a tense silence for the rest of the journey. Held to a slow walk by the fog, the horses clop-clopped through deserted streets, at times narrowly avoiding horseless, abandoned carriages that loomed like shipwrecks in the fog. And so the Black Mariah took thirty minutes to travel less than a mile to reach its destination. When Conan Doyle and Wilde finally climbed out, the fog had grown thicker still, caging the streetlamps in tremulous globes of light.

Conan Doyle, who knew London intimately, looked about, utterly lost, and asked in a baffled voice, "Where the devil are we?"

"Belgravia, sir," Detective Blenkinsop answered. He nodded toward the limestone façade of a handsome residence where two constables stood guard on either side of the front gate. "That there is Lord Howell's residence."

As he spoke, a third constable came staggering out of the house. He wobbled a rubber-legged path to the pavement where he doubled over and vomited explosively into the gutter. Conan Doyle and Wilde jumped back to avoid having their shoes splashed as a second wave hit and the officer gargled up the remainder of his dinner. As he sagged to his knees, clutching the railings for support, the young constable looked up at them, his face wretched with horror, and moaned, "Don't go in there!"

Conan Doyle shared a look with Wilde, whose eyes were saucered, his complexion waxen and ghastly in the otherworldly throb of gaslight.

"Oscar, perhaps it would be better if you remained outside. As a medical doctor, I am used to such sights—"

"No," Wilde shook his head. "If I do not see for myself then you shall be forced to describe it to me, and I fear my imagination excels when it comes to fathoming horrible things from nothing."

"Right then," Conan Doyle said. "Let's get this over with."

"Boyle! Jennings!" Blenkinsop called to the two officers posted on either side of the gate. Lend the gentlemen your rain capes," he fixed the two friends with a dire look. "You'll be needin' them, I reckon."

With their fine clothes protected beneath long police rain capes, Conan Doyle and Wilde cautiously stepped up to the front door—or rather, what remained of it. A solid chunk of milled and planed English oak, the door had been smashed violently inward, tearing the mortise lock completely through the doorframe and wrenching two of the three hinges loose. Once painted ivory, the door gleamed crimson with spattered gore. The two friends stood goggling at the site, which bore mute testament to an act of extreme violence. Although the door had been solidly locked—they could see the exposed brass tenon—something with the force of a steam locomotive had smashed straight through it. They entered the house and found the marble tiles

of the entrance hall slippery with blood. The footprints of every police officer that had entered the space tracked in all directions, like
macabre steps in a dance studio from hell. Conan Doyle cast a doubting look at his tall Irish friend. "Really, Oscar, I don't think there's a
need for you to see this."

Wilde, who had yanked a scented handkerchief from his breast
pocket and pressed it over his nose and mouth, shook his head. "No,"
he said in a muffled voice. "Proceed. I have witnessed the dreadful
prologue. I must see how the act ends."

Their feet slithered across blood-slick tiles to a front parlor where
the same maniacal force had also ripped the lighter parlor door to
splinters. Inside the room, toppled chairs and broken furniture testified to a dreadful struggle. The tepid air of the parlor roiled with the
ferric tang of blood. Beside an overturned divan, a body lay on
the floor. Conan Doyle stepped around a broken end table to inspect it.

The corpse had a face both men recognized from the newspapers:
Lord Montague Howell, hero of the battle of Alma and the siege of
Sevastopol—amongst a score of Crimean campaigns. Miraculously,
the handsome features had escaped unscathed; the blue eyes retained
a calm gaze, the lids drooped slightly, a rictus-smile drawing back the
lips, showing strong white teeth beneath a scrupulously groomed
brown moustache. However, Lord Howell's head was unnaturally
kinked upon his neck.

With his years of medical experience, Conan Doyle was used to
blood and death, but as he stepped closer, his gorge rose and invisible needles tattooed his face as he saw, to his horror, that the body
was lying chest down.

The head had been twisted one hundred and eighty degrees, so
that it pointed in the wrong direction.

"Dear God!" he gasped. "His neck has been wrung like a pigeon's."
He crouched down to examine ten finger-sized bruises, five tattooed
on either side of the neck. "And by someone with a demon's grip."

Wilde made a dry heaving sound and gripped a drinks cabinet to steady himself. "I think I shall look for clues outside," he said in a squeezed-tight voice.

"Yes," Conan Doyle agreed. "Detective Blenkinsop, please help Mister Wilde."

The young detective took Wilde firmly by the arm and walked him out of the room.

As they left, two new constables crowded in through the parlor door, gawking at the corpse.

"Lumme! What'd I tell ya, Alfie?" the first said, elbowing his companion.

"Yer right, Stan. Won't nobody be sneakin' up on him from behind now!"

The prospect of the horrifying tableau becoming a macabre attraction struck a nerve with Conan Doyle. He rose to his feet and bellowed at the young constables: "Show some respect, damn you! This man was a hero of the British Empire. He was at the Charge of the Light Brigade and earned the Victoria Cross for valor!"

Detective Blenkinsop stepped back into the room just in time to hear. He threw a scowl at the two constables and jerked a thumb at the door, saying, "Right, you two, hop it!"

The young constables skulked out, heads lowered in shame. Conan Doyle took in a deep breath, bracing himself, and then dropped to his knees and rolled the body over. Once turned upon on its back, he took the noble head in both hands and turned it the right way around. The corpse wore evening dress, the once-elegant tuxedo jacket glutinous with congealing blood.

"Dressed for dinner," he noted. "Lord Howell was evidently about to go out."

He paused and sniffed in deeply. A bitter tang of cordite spooled in the air. He looked down to see the fingers of Lord Howell's right hand still curled about the trigger of a revolver—a Webley Mark IV. Conan Doyle eased it from fingers stiffening with rigor and snapped open the barrel with a practiced flick of the wrist and dumped out a handful of spent shell casings into his palm.

"All six rounds have been fired."

Conan Doyle gripped the corpse's wrist. The body was cold and when he lifted the arm, it bent like a strip of India rubber—the bones had been smashed to fragments. He unbuttoned the tuxedo jacket and peeled open the blood-soaked fabric. A moment's palpation revealed that the sternum and every rib were broken. He concluded his examination by patting down the stomach and legs, searching for bullet wounds. To his astonishment, he found not a one.

And then he looked up and his mouth dropped open in astonishment. One wall bore the bloody imprint of a body. He rose and stumbled closer. Something had hurled Lord Howell's body at the wall with tremendous force, leaving a man-sized dent in the plaster and a ballistic spray of blood.

"What on earth could have done this?" Conan Doyle breathed.

Blenkinsop shook his head, baffled. "Now you know why I fetched you, sir. I can't fathom none of it."

The Scottish doctor finally turned away from his ghoulish task, wiping sticky blood from his hands on a handkerchief. He flashed a grim look at Detective Blenkinsop. "I can find no bullet wounds. Not a single one. That can only mean—"

"All this blood?" Blenkinsop interjected. "It's not his?"

"Unbelievable, but yes."

"There must have been multiple assailants," Conan Doyle speculated. "Lord Howell fired six shots, many of which clearly found their target. If a single man lost that much blood he would have died on the spot."

"If it was something *human* what killed him." Detective Blenkinsop spoke aloud what Conan Doyle had secretly conjectured. The smashed front door, the demolished parlor, the body hurled against the wall and then beaten to a bag of broken bones—all after six shots spilled pints of blood everywhere—defied rational explanation. It seemed more like the attack of a raging monster than a man . . . or men.

"Pardon, Detective, but I must step outside to clear my head."

When Conan Doyle emerged through the ruined doorway, Wilde was lurking by the front gate, smoking a cigarette. The Irishman saw Conan Doyle approach and drew him farther away with a nod.

"What is it, Oscar?"

"I believe I have spotted what your fellow Sherlock Holmes would have referred to as 'a clue.'"

Conan Doyle's eyebrows rose. He leaned close and whispered, "What?"

"Look at the gatepost on the right." Wilde drew out his silver cigarette case, opened it with a practiced flick, and held it out to the two constables standing guard. "Care for a cigarette?"

The nearest constable turned his head, sneaking a subtle look-around. "Very decent of you, sir. Don't mind if I do." As he stepped forward, the gatepost he had been shielding came into view, giving Conan Doyle clear sight of a figure scrawled in chalk:

"Much obliged, sir. I'll smoke it later." The constable grinned as he tucked the cigarette in a pocket and stepped back to his post, hiding the chalk scrawl once again.

Conan Doyle and Wilde casually stepped away, leaning their heads together to confer.

"Just random graffiti?" Conan Doyle pondered.

"We are in Belgravia. A place where the idle scribbler and his ball of chalk seldom make an appearance."

"Quite right."

Something caught Conan Doyle's eye, and he tugged at his friend's sleeve, nodding at the road. "If you look at just the right angle, you can see a trail of bloody footprints leading off into the fog."

The Irish wit peered down, eyes asquint. "Ah yes, I see them now. Should we inform your detective friend?"

Conan Doyle shook his head. "Not just yet. Perhaps you and I should investigate before the London constabulary has a chance to tramp all over them with their regulation size nines." He stepped onto the road and nodded for his friend to follow. "Come, Oscar. Let's see where they lead."

Wilde's face plummeted. "Ah, you expect me to accompany you? I had rather planned on standing sentinel at the front gate."

"I need you to watch my back."

Wilde's expression betrayed a decided lack of enthusiasm. "Which begs the question, who shall watch mine?"

Conan Doyle stepped from the curb into the street and Wilde reluctantly traipsed after. In less than ten strides, the house, the Mariah, and the police officers vanished from sight.

"I do not think we should stray too far," Wilde worried aloud, "lest we become lost in the fog."

Conan Doyle did not reply. He had his head down, eyes scouring the pavement for footprints. They reached a low garden wall daubed with a bloody handprint.

"Look! He put out a hand here to steady himself." Conan Doyle looked at Wilde and spoke in a voice coiled tight with urgency. "Come, the assailant cannot be far ahead."

"That is precisely what I am afraid of."

"Judging by the staggering gait, if the murderer is still alive, he's badly wounded and unlikely to be a danger to us."

They followed the trail of fading footprints as they reeled around a corner into a side street. But instead of petering out, the footsteps carried on. And on. And on. Until finally, in a circle of light beneath a streetlamp, they found the bloody corpse of a large man slumped facedown on the pavement, the staring eyes opaque with death.

"Riddled from front to back with bullet wounds," Conan Doyle said. "I count at least five." He fixed Wilde with an urgent look. "Guard the body, Oscar, I must fetch Detective Blenkinsop at once."

Distress flashed across Wilde's long face. "Come now, Arthur," he laughed shakily. "Dead bodies require little guarding. Who would wish to steal one? I have seen my share of wakes and lyings-in growing up in Ireland and I have found that the dead seldom make for good company. They are poor conversationalists, and should one actually speak, I am sure it should have nothing I would like to hear."

"Very well. You fetch Detective Blenkinsop and I shall remain behind."

Wilde took one step away from the pool of light beneath the streetlamp and recoiled. It was clear he realized that becoming lost in the fog was a real possibility.

"On second thought," he corrected, "you are quite right. It would be better if I remained here whilst you return for help."

As Conan Doyle moved to step away, Wilde death-gripped his arm. "This would be an appropriate time for haste, Arthur."

"I shall not dilly-dally." In just three steps the fog swallowed the Scottish author. Two more and it suffocated even the sound of his footfalls.

Instantly, Wilde found himself totally . . . utterly . . . alone. A solitary figure marooned on an island of lamplight, his isolation was palpable. The street. The houses. London . . . no longer existed.

It was a bitter night. He squirmed his shoulders deeper into his fur coat, large hands rummaging for warmth in his fur-lined pockets. Cold radiated up from the pavement through the soles of his shiny leather shoes. He stamped his feet, setting frozen toes tingling. Reluctant to look back at the bullet-riddled corpse, he gazed instead into the seething grayness, shivering from more than the November chill.

Long . . . long . . . long minutes passed.

"Really," he said aloud to keep himself company, "what *is* taking Arthur so long?" He finished his cigarette and tossed the glowing fag end away, then fumbled his silver cigarette case from his pocket, flicked a lucifer to life with his thumbnail, kindled another cigarette with shaking hands, and gloved them in his pockets once again. He drew in a comforting lungful of warm smoke and let it out. Then, from somewhere, a faint noise caught his ear: *wisssshthump . . . wissssssshthump . . . wisssssssshthump . . .*

It was a noise somehow familiar. He looked around, straining his eyes. The fog curled into arabesques, as though stirred by invisible shapes moving through it. A nervous glance confirmed the body was still there. But then, as he watched, the fingers of the left hand twitched.

Wilde's eyes widened.

The left leg shivered and kicked.

The cigarette tumbled from Wilde's lips.

The corpse heaved; the chest rose and fell.

Wilde's head quivered atop his neck, but he could not look away.

And then, the arm flexed. Shifted. Drew back. A bloody hand grappled for a handhold and the corpse began to push itself up from the pavement.

Wilde took a step backward.

A plume of steam shot out both its nostrils with a pneumatic *hisssssssssssssss.*

Wilde stumbled backward several steps, unaware of the shape looming in the fog behind him.

The arm suddenly buckled and the corpse slumped facedown to the pavement with an expiring wheeze.

Wilde shrieked as a hand clamped upon his shoulder and a ghastly glowing face swam up through the fog. "It's me, Oscar." Conan Doyle was holding a police officer's bull's-eye lantern that lit his face eerily from below. A second wraith materialized beside him: Detective Blenkinsop.

"It moved," Wilde said breathlessly. "It groaned and moved."

"That happens," Conan Doyle reassured. "Dead bodies are filled with gases. They gurgle. They twitch. Sometimes sit up. I have experienced it myself, working the morgue as a medical student. It's simply—"

"No, you fail to understand. It struggled to rise—"

"Oscar, I assure you, the fellow is quite dead."

But despite the reassurance, the Irishman was reluctant to approach any closer. Conan Doyle and Detective Blenkinsop stepped to the body, hitched their trouser legs, and dropped to a crouch for a closer examination. Lit from below, the glare from the bull's-eye lanterns stretched their faces into black-socketed fright masks.

"I count five bullet holes," Conan Doyle said.

"Lord Howell was quite the marksman. He only missed once."

"How on earth did the man stagger this far after taking five bullets? It's almost as if he walked until he ran out of blood."

Blenkinsop shook his head. "Like I said, something awful queer . . ."

Conan Doyle did not respond. The night. The fog. The grotesque murder. Everything conspired to twist minds in an eldritch direction. Determined not to lose his grip on rationality, he asked, "When do you estimate this happened?"

"The neighbors said they heard a row about six o'clock. A lot of shoutin' and yellin'. Then shots. Five or more. A footman from the house two doors down was sent to run and fetch the police. But it took a while for a constable to arrive—what with the fog and all."

"Six o'clock?" Conan Doyle repeated. "That's nearly four hours ago!" He touched a hand to the dead man's throat and looked up at Detective Blenkinsop in amazement. "Impossible! Lord Howell's body was quite cold. But this body is still warm. Very warm. Burning up, in fact, as if the man had a fever!" He grabbed the heavy arm and lifted its dead weight. "No sign of rigor; he could not have died more than half an hour ago."

Detective Blenkinsop leaned closer, sniffed the corpse, and

recoiled. "Ugh! He pongs something 'orrible. Like he's been dead a fortnight!"

Conan Doyle had also noticed the distinctive stench of corruption. "Maybe that's a clue: he could be a tanner . . . or an abattoir worker . . . or a resurrection man." He dragged the beam of his lantern across the body. The corpse was dressed in a motley of tattered clothes picked from the bottom of a rag bin. Clothes too shabby even for a casual laborer. The lank mop of black hair was greasy and matted. The lantern beam swept across the exposed back of the neck and paused.

"Look," Conan Doyle said, pointing. "He has a tattoo of some kind. Let's see if we can't get a better look at it." He scrunched down to turn the head further toward the light.

The young detective leaned closer and shone his own light in the murderer's face, but then let out a shout of surprise and sprang to his feet, backpedaling several steps.

"What is it?" Conan Doyle asked. "Do you recognize him?"

Blenkinsop nodded manically, never taking his startled eyes off the corpse. "Yeah, I know him. I'd know him anywhere. But it ain't possible. It ain't possible!"

"What is it? Speak up, man. Who is this fellow?"

"I know the face. A-a-and that butterfly tattoo on his neck. I only seen a tattoo like that once before. It's Charlie Higginbotham, that is. And no doubt about it."

"A criminal you are acquainted with?"

"Charlie's a petty thief. A dip. A cracksman. Strictly small time. It's him. It's definitely him. But it can't be . . . it just can't."

"What do you mean? Why ever not?"

Detective Blenkinsop fixed the Scottish author with a demented stare. "Two months ago, I collared Charlie for the murder of his wife. I even testified against him at the trial." He paused to lick dry lips. "I watched him take the drop last week at Newgate Prison. Hanged for murder. The last time I seen Charlie Higginbotham the hangman was digging the rope out of his neck. And he was dead. Very dead!"

THE MURDERER IN THE CUPBOARD

When the three men finally navigated their way back to the violated wreck of the war minister's home, they found Death awaiting them. Or more correctly, Death's henchmen: a hearse had drawn up behind the Mariah, and now four funeral attendants in black frock coats and top hats wrapped in black crepe emerged from the ruined doorway, bearing a coffin upon their shoulders. They carried their burden to the waiting hearse with the slow, underwater motion of men walking along the silty bottom of the Thames. The coffin loaded, the grooms clambered atop the boxy carriage while the driver took his place on the seat and gathered up the reins. Before he whipped up the horses, the driver cast a quick look about. Conan Doyle was watching, and by the paltry light of the streetlamps, he saw that the man had a port-wine birthmark that started on one cheek and ran down his neck below the collar. The driver flicked the horse's ears with the tip of his whip, and the hearse swung away from the curb and rattled off into the fog, revealing a four-wheeler drawn up to the curb ahead.

"I recognize that growler," Detective Blenkinsop said. "It's the commissioner's."

Upon entering the parlor, they were met by a tall, thin, ectomorphic man with bushy salt-and-pepper sideburns and a straggle of gray hair scraped carefully over a balding pate: the Commissioner of Police, Edmund Burke.

"Why have you removed the body?" Conan Doyle demanded.

Burke flayed Conan Doyle with an excoriating stare, then looked down at a small, spaniel-faced man who lurked at his shoulder, scribbling notes in a journal. "Who is this *civilian*, Dobbs?" he boomed in a headache-inducing voice. "Remove him at once!"

Blenkinsop moved forward and tugged off his hat, eager to explain. "Beggin' pardon, Commissioner Burke. This here is Doctor Conan Doyle, the chap what writes the Sherlock Holmes stories. I, er, I called him in, sir."

The commissioner frosted Detective Blenkinsop with a look of icy fury but swallowed his rage with obvious difficulty and plastered on an unconvincing smile. "Doctor Doyle, I am an enthusiast of your Sherlock Holmes stories. I confess I had hoped to meet you some day, but not at the scene of an actual police investigation."

Conan Doyle shook the commissioner's hand and launched into a breathless explanation.

"We have found the body of the murderer. Although shot multiple times he managed to stagger several streets away before succumbing to his wounds."

"You have found but *one* of the murderers," Burke corrected. "This crime was obviously the work of more than one man."

"Really? How can you say that? We found no—"

"Doctor Doyle," the commissioner interrupted. "I have been investigating murders for thirty years and I can safely say there is far too much blood for one assailant." Burke looked about the room, nodding at the blood trails sprayed across the walls. "Too much blood by far, and . . ." He eyed the drinks cabinet and stepped toward it. ". . . if you care to take notice, this cupboard appears to be bleeding."

All eyes fixed upon the only intact piece of furniture remaining in the room: a very handsome drinks cabinet where, indeed, drops of blood were weeping from the bottom of the double doors. Commissioner Burke fumbled the latch and snatched them open like a conjurer performing a trick. Inside the cupboard, a man crouched in a contortionist's pose, head tucked between his knees, legs drawn up tight to his chest. His right hand clutched his left forearm, trying to staunch the copious flow of blood from a bullet wound.

"Aha!" the commissioner exulted. "Here is your murderer. Hiding like the craven coward he is." He nodded to the young detective. "Blenkinsop, drag him out of there."

It took Detective Blenkinsop and another constable to pry the man, who clearly did not want to be removed, loose of his confined hiding space. It soon became evident the man had not been idle during his sequester, as a half-drunk whiskey bottle tumbled out with him and glugged itself empty on the Persian rug. Despite his injury, the man was strong and grappled with the officers, but was finally wrestled to his knees before the commissioner. He was a tall, muscular youth with swarthy good looks and a thick head of curly black hair. The young man dissolved into hysterics, gesturing with exaggerated emotion at the shattered parlor door, the toppled divan, the grotesque imprint on the wall, all the while cradling his wounded forearm and wailing with pain.

Conan Doyle stepped forward and gently loosened the man's grip on his injured arm to examine it. "Shot clean through the forearm. Shattered the bone most likely. He must be in considerable discomfort."

"The man is a murderer," Commissioner Burke snarled. "He has assassinated a patriot and hero of the empire. Let him howl all he wants; he warrants no sympathy from us."

The man at once unleashed a torrent of indecipherable words, his face animated with fear and despair.

"And he's a foreigner! Talking in some foreign babble. An anarchist, no doubt."

Oscar Wilde stepped forward and coughed politely to draw the commissioner's attention. When all eyes had fixed upon him, he spoke in a calm voice. "I should point out the young fellow is wearing a servant's uniform. And I happen to speak that 'foreign babble.' The gentleman is Italian. Although he speaks in a dialect I am not entirely fluent in, I can tell you that his name is Vicente, and that he is Lord Howell's personal valet."

"Well, there you have it," Conan Doyle said. "The poor chap likely received the bullet wound trying to defend his master. After which, he crawled into the cupboard to hide."

The commissioner sneered. "Italy is a hot bed of anarchy." He threw a piercing look at his adjutant. "Dobbs, find the servant's quarters. Search the foreigner's room for subversive materials."

"Yes, commissioner, sir." Dobbs shouldered his satchel and hurried from the room.

All the while the Italian tore at his hair with his good hand, weeping and muttering.

"See here, Commissioner Burke," Conan Doyle said, "something extraordinary took place in this room. This man is likely our only witness—"

"Yes," Burke interrupted. "Something extraordinary did take place. Clearly this foreigner has conspired in the murder of his master."

"But he himself is wounded!"

"Proof conclusive I would say that he was a party to the crime."

Conan Doyle could not suppress a grunt of exasperation, but Burke was just gathering steam. "It would not surprise me if the man murdered Lord Howell and then shot himself as a ruse to divert our suspicion. After all, he's had hours to prepare this fantastical tableau."

Conan Doyle threw a disbelieving look at Wilde, who shook his head and discreetly touched a finger to his lips in a *shush* gesture. The Scottish author's throat clenched around the words queued up there, but Wilde was right—the argument was devolving into a wrestling match of egos. Edmund Burke was an unctuous buffoon whose mind was closed to anyone's opinion other than his own.

The adjutant returned, clutching a fistful of broadsheets. He handed them to the commissioner, who gave them a cursory, lip-curling glance, then thrust them in Conan Doyle's face. "As I suspected, subversive literature. The man is an agitator. An enemy of the British nation."

Conan Doyle took the broadsheets and examined them. Most were emblazoned with anarchist slogans and calls for revolution and uprising. He thumbed through them until he found one broadsheet in particular: a sheet of black paper with a simple graphic in white lettering.

He flashed it at Wilde, whose eyebrows shot up in consternation—it precisely matched the symbol scribbled on the front gatepost.

The valet looked at the broadsheet, and then at the faces around him. Clearly, he understood what was being said about him and unleashed an excited torrent of Italian.

The commissioner watched the valet's histrionics with a face drained of empathy and finally swiveled his jaded gaze to Wilde. "Mister Wilde, is it not? Your language skills may prove useful. Please ask our Italian assassin how many of his confederates took part in the murder."

Wilde touched the man's shoulder to corral his attention and said, "*Quanti assassini hanno attaccato il tuo padrone?*"

The Italian valet shook his head, emphatically, "*Solo uno. Solo uno. Ma era il diavolo! Il diavolo!*"

At the reply, Wilde's face hardened to stone.

"What did he say, Oscar?" Conan Doyle asked.

"He said there was only one assassin . . . but he was the Devil."

CHAPTER 3

FENIANS, ANARCHISTS, AND DYNAMITARDS

"We found the body just up here . . ." Detective Blenkinsop said, and added in a muttered breath, ". . . somewhere."

He was leading police commissioner Edmund Burke and his fawning assistant, Dobbs, through the fog-blind streets to the place where they had discovered the corpse of Charlie Higginbotham. Conan Doyle and Wilde trailed behind at a respectful distance.

"And this lone assassin was somehow able to stagger this far with five bullets in him?" Burke quibbled, releasing a skeptical snort. "Highly unlikely."

"No, I'm sure of it, sir. You'll see. And it's Charlie Higginbotham, no mistaking."

But when they reached the streetlamp where they had discovered the corpse, it had vanished.

"It's gone!" Detective Blenkinsop gasped.

"Gone?" Chief Burke exploded. "What do you mean, *gone*?"

"It was right here. I swear it was." The young police detective dashed about, frantically searching a widening circle around the streetlamp, but the corpse was nowhere to be found. "This is the spot. It was right here! These gents will back me up, won't you?" He looked for support from Conan Doyle and Wilde, who hurried to reassure the commissioner that they, too, had seen the body on this very spot.

"Then where is this corpse now?" Burke demanded. "Dead men are not in the habit of getting up and walking away."

"It is difficult to explain," Conan Doyle quickly put in. "But what the detective says is true. Both Oscar and I would verify that this is the location."

The commissioner turned to his adjutant and remarked in a sarcastic tone: "Do you see a body, Dobbs?"

"No, sir."

"And neither do I. Come, let us go."

Conan Doyle interjected, "Might I borrow your bull's-eye lamp, detective?" He took Blenkinsop's lamp and crouched at the edge of the curb shining the lantern light obliquely across the road. Two thin, silver trails gleamed on the cobbles.

"Look!" Conan Doyle said. "See the frost that's forming? If you look at the right angle, you can see hoofprints and the wheel marks of a carriage. Two horses, I'd say." Conan Doyle stood up and looked at the police commissioner, his face animated. "We need a measuring tape. The gauge of the wheels looks quite narrow. By measuring the wheel tracks we could determine what kind of vehicle removed the body: a carriage, a dray cart, a—"

"*Mister* Doyle," the commissioner interrupted in a booming voice. "If you please, this is not one of your silly Sherlock Holmes stories; this is a real investigation. We have no time for dazzling and ingenious explanations. This road sees all kinds of traffic—"

"But the frost is forming even as we speak. These wheel tracks can only have just been—"

"Enough, Mister Doyle!" the commissioner roared, cutting him off.

"*Doctor* Doyle, if you please—"

"Forgive me, *Doctor*," Burke corrected sourly. "Your fictions may be filled with inexplicable crimes that warrant fantastic explanations, but I'm afraid in the real world the explanations for most crimes are quite prosaic."

Detective Blenkinsop stepped forward, his face earnest. "Sir, I know what I seen. I'd swear to it. The dead man was Charlie Higginbotham. No question." He tapped the back of his neck. "Charlie had this tattoo of a butterfly—"

The commissioner silenced Blenkinsop with a raised hand and then crooked his fingers in a beckoning gesture. "Step closer, Detective."

"Sir?" Blenkinsop took a step and the commissioner leaned into his face and sniffed.

"Do I smell strong spirits on your breath? Have you been drinking on duty?"

"No!" Blenkinsop shook his head. "I mean, well . . . I suppose . . . yeah, but—"

"I'm afraid that was my doing," Conan Doyle interrupted, quickly coming to Blenkinsop's defense. "When I first saw the detective tonight, he was in a state of shock—hardly surprising given the horrific nature of the crime scene. In my role as a physician, I insisted he drink a brandy, purely for medicinal reasons. But I can testify that he only had the one—"

"Undoubtedly," the police commissioner snarled, cutting him off. Burke cleared his throat with a sound like tumbrel wheels grinding across cobblestones. When he spoke again, his tone made it clear he believed that the young detective's word was no longer to be trusted.

"Detective Blenkinsop, you are clearly suffering from mental distress that is causing your judgment to be skewed. I am, therefore, suspending you from active duty—without pay, naturally—until your mind clears and you are better able to serve the force."

"But, sir. I know what I saw and it was definitely—"

"Enough!" Burke barked with fury. He simmered a moment before speaking again. "With such a fog as this, it is impossible for anyone to make an accurate identification of a body. It is clear that you are emotionally overwrought. I suggest you return to the other officers. You will ride back to Scotland Yard in the Mariah."

"But, sir!"

"That is quite enough, Detective! Unless you wish your suspension to be indefinite!"

Blenkinsop dropped his head in resignation and quietly muttered, "Yes, sir," and then turned and trudged away into the fog.

"That is a brave young man," Conan Doyle remarked in a voice taut with anger.

"No one doubts his bravery," Burke responded. "It is his judgment I question. His promotion to detective at such an unseasoned age was, I fear, a mistake."

"We witnessed the same thing," Wilde put in. "Both Arthur and I."

"About what you saw or imagined you saw, we shall speak of in the comfort and privacy of my carriage. The Yard is thankful for your, ah, *assistance* gentlemen, but now the case is in the hands of *professionals*. It is a foul night and I do not wish to keep you from the bosom of your family. Come along, let us conclude before anything else vanishes mysteriously."

When they returned to Lord Howell's house, the Italian valet, shackled hand and foot, was being manhandled into the back of the Black Mariah despite his howls and screams of pain. Conan Doyle would have preferred to ride with the prisoner in order to further question him, but Commissioner Burke was adamant that he and Wilde share his carriage.

They stood in the street, watching the Black Mariah pull away and vanish into the fog, and then the commissioner turned his corrosive gaze upon the two friends and said, "Of course, as this matter touches upon the safety of the realm, and as gentlemen, I expect you to say nothing of this matter to the newspapers. Especially, given the current air of unrest."

"There have been threats?" Conan Doyle asked.

Burke barked a laugh. "Scotland Yard is awash in threats. Most are the impotent ramblings of lunatics and the feebleminded. Very few are of any real consequence."

"Threats from whom?" Wilde inquired.

"Bolsheviks. Anarchists. And, of course . . ." he eyed the Irishman coldly and spoke the final word with such emphasis that spittle flew from his lips, ". . . *Fenians*."

Conan Doyle saw the way the conversation was turning, and hurriedly put in, "I am certain the resources of Scotland Yard must be stretched right now, trying to defeat this anarchist threat."

But his words had the reverse effect on Burke, who visibly bristled. "Hear me now, *Mister* Doyle, there is no *anarchist threat*. These people are a disorganized rabble of illiterate thugs. Compared to the sweeping powers of Scotland Yard and the Metropolitan Police Force, they represent a minor irritation. The dynamitards may set off their little whiz-bang's here and there, but they do little real damage—apart from blowing themselves up occasionally." He punctuated the remark with a sardonic laugh.

A bright flash that cut through the fog suddenly drew all eyes. Above the rooftops, a splash of light lit up the sides of tall buildings. Even from this distance, they watched the upward arc of flying masonry followed several seconds later by a rumbling detonation that struck like a fist to the chest, setting diaphragms aflutter.

BOOOOOOOOOOOOOOMMMMM!

The light flared and faded, and the darkness resounded to a brittle symphony of shattering glass followed, moments later, by the mournful shriek of police whistles, calling out the alarm.

"That looked like Whitehall to me," Wilde observed.

"Yes," Conan Doyle agreed. "And something a little larger than a whiz-bang."

At their glib comments, Commissioner Burke inflated with rage. He choked and spluttered but when he spoke again his voice thundered out in a nasal snarl: "I warn you two now, say nothing of tonight's happenings to anyone. Not to the press. Not even your wives and loved ones . . ."

"You may count upon our discretion, Commissioner," Conan Doyle assured, attempting to deflect his ire.

"Discretion, be damned! If I hear about either of you two scribblers playing *consulting detective* or in any way interfering in a police investigation, you will find yourselves in the deepest, darkest, dankest cell in Newgate. And with no official record of your arrest. *Do I make myself clear?*"

Distress rippled across Wilde's face. Conan Doyle pressed his lips tight together, bridling at the naked threat, but neither man spoke. It was clear that their assent was not required.

CHAPTER 4

THE FOG COMMITTEE

It was the wrong side of 3:00 A.M. when Conan Doyle shuffled after Wilde into the smoking room of Wilde's club, the Albemarle, both men drooping with fatigue. The space was furnished with enormous winged armchairs upholstered in buttoned oxblood leather, and now they flopped into adjoining seats and groaned in weary unison.

"Dear Lord," Conan Doyle said. "What a night!"

A waiter bearing a silver salver glided into the room, bowed, and asked, "Would you gentlemen be requiring anything?"

"Ah, Cranford," Wilde said. "We've had a beastly night and the trains do not run due to the fog. Would you have a guest room made up for Doctor Doyle?"

Cranford's mournful expression telegraphed the news before he spoke it. "With regrets, sir, all our rooms are taken—what with the fog and all."

"That's all right," Conan Doyle said. "A large brandy and I could sleep at the top of Nelson's column. This chair will seem luxurious by comparison."

"Bother," Wilde said. "Oh, and I suppose the kitchens are closed at this hour?"

"I'm afraid so, sir."

Wilde fished in a pocket, tugged out a half-sovereign and tossed it onto the salver. "Fortunately I possess the skeleton key that opens all doors."

Cranford stole a glimpse at the coin. "Yes, sir, I believe I can rouse the chef. Anything in particular you fancy?"

"Oh, nothing much: a dozen oysters, some pâté and toast, fresh figs, a good brie and crackers, olives—green, not black—and, oh yes, a bottle of champagne."

"Very good, sir. Vintage?"

Wilde answered with an insouciant wave. "You choose. I'm not fussy," and quickly added, "But nothing that isn't French. Nothing newer than an '86. And nothing cheaper than five pounds a bottle."

"I'll check the cellar." Cranford shifted his gaze to Conan Doyle. "And for Mister Wilde's guest?"

"Your best brandy. Triple snit."

"Ice or water?"

"Ice. Large chunk. Big enough to sink a ship."

"As you wish, sir." Cranford flourished his most obsequious bow and slid noiselessly from the room as if gliding on greased runners.

For several minutes, the two friends sat umbrellaed beneath an enervated silence as they awaited their drinks. Then a thought occurred to both men at the same instant.

"We left the body alone for scant minutes—" Conan Doyle began.

"And he was a big fellow—"

"So it would require two men, perhaps more, to lift him—"

"Even then, they could not carry such a weight very far."

"And yet we heard no carriage come or go."

"Perhaps the commissioner was right. Perhaps he did get up and walk away."

Conan Doyle shifted in his chair and pondered. "How does one move a dead body without attracting attention?"

As he spoke the words, Cranford entered the room, balancing a tray with Conan Doyle's brandy and Wilde's champagne. Although he had undoubtedly overheard the remark, like all good British servants his demeanor betrayed nothing.

"What do you think, Cranford?" Wilde asked directly. "How would you move a dead body about London without attracting attention?"

The waiter paused to set the brandy down on Conan Doyle's end table. "In a hearse, sir," he said mildly. "That's what they're for, is it not?"

Wilde and Conan Doyle shared a look of surprised delight.

"Quite so," Wilde laughed. "And we did see a hearse at the scene of the crime."

"Yes," Conan Doyle agreed, "but that hearse had come to take away the body of Lord Howell."

"Who is to say how many bodies it took away?"

Conan Doyle sat up in his chair, his fatigue suddenly forgotten. "You have a point. And looking back on it now, from the moment he entered the fray, Commissioner Burke seemed in great haste to wrap things up and cinch tight the bow on a murder investigation!"

Cranford popped the cork on the champagne, charged Wilde's flute with effervescence, and returned the bottle to its ice bucket. "Your food will be forthcoming shortly, sir."

Conan Doyle waited until the waiter had gone before saying, "While you were alone with the body, did you see a carriage of any kind?"

Wilde shook his head as he swished a mouthful of Perrier-Jouët.

"Hear anything?"

The Irishman allowed champagne to trickle down his throat before adding, "I did hear something. A very odd sound."

"Oh, really?"

"It was faint, but sounded something like: *hissssss-ka-chung* . . . *hissssss-ka-chung* . . ."

"A steamer? No, it couldn't have been, we were too far from the Thames . . . and no steamers would be running in such a fog."

They were about to continue when Cranford sailed back in with a knife, fork, and napkin, arranging them silently on Wilde's table before nodding a bow and dissolving into the fine walnut paneling.

"The man's a ghost," Conan Doyle muttered as he hefted his brandy.

"Yes," Wilde agreed. "Cranford does not exit a room as much as disparate from it."

Conan Doyle grew serious. "Speaking of servants, you don't believe for a moment—"

"The Italian valet was somehow involved?" Wilde paused to sip his champagne. "No. I believe the young man is entirely innocent."

"What about those pamphlets? Awfully incriminating."

"And awfully convenient. In the space of a few minutes the police commissioner's man has time to locate the valet's room, search it, and return with a handful of damning evidence."

Conan Doyle thoughtfully swirled his brandy. "Careful, Oscar. What you are suggesting smacks of conspiracy."

"And does that not describe most assassinations? I watched Vicente's face as those pamphlets were produced. I am convinced he had never seen them before."

"And then there is the bullet-riddled body of a dead assassin. Three of us saw it and yet the commissioner showed not a jot of interest."

Wilde shrugged. "You know the police: why let evidence stand in the way of a good trial and execution?"

Wilde's comment sprung a frown to Conan Doyle's lips. "If that happens, it will be a grave miscarriage of justice. Surely we must do something?"

"It is no longer our concern. Let us not forget Commissioner Burke's generous offer of free accommodation in one of Her Majesty's least luxurious prisons. I have been known to abandon a first-class hotel on a moment's notice should I find the towels a tad scratchy. I doubt I would find Newgate much to my taste."

Conan Doyle rumbled a grunt and said, "Point taken. I shall think no more on it."

Wilde snatched up the day's newspaper from the end table and vanished behind it, rattling the pages from time to time. But after several moments he lowered the paper and glowered at his friend. "Arthur, that is undoubtedly the noisiest silence I have ever *not* heard. Could you possibly think a little more quietly?"

Conan Doyle shifted in his chair and apologized. "Sorry. Still . . . bad business."

"*Very* bad for business," Wilde agreed. "This fog is caning my box office receipts."

"I meant the murder of Lord Howell."

"Yes, that, too." The paper rattled violently and Wilde emitted a strangled sound. "Listen to this review of *An Ideal Husband*: 'Whilst Mister Wilde's words were filled with light and illumination, the same could sadly not be said of the theater, which at one point was so obscured by fog and the footlights so dimmed that the play took on the aspect of a rather witty séance.'"

Wilde crumpled the paper and tossed it to the floor. "This blasted fog is ruining me!"

The paper landed against Conan Doyle's shins. When he leant forward to pick it up, a large photograph and its accompanying headline caught his eye: "Fog Committee Sees No Solution."

He glanced at it a moment, and then folded the paper back upon itself and held up the article for his friend to see.

"It seems as though the government has already taken your advice, Oscar. They have appointed a 'Fog Committee' to look into the problem."

Wilde squinted doubtfully at the newspaper. "'A Fog Committee'?" he echoed, and choked on an ironic laugh. "Forming a committee is always the best possible way to achieve the minimum in the maximum time. Even the spelling is redundant: two m's, two t's, and two e's. Why not save labor and spell it c-o-m-i-t-e? It would save precious ink and be equally ineffectual. Really, what would the world have gained if the English had not had such a spendthrift attitude to consonants?"

Conan Doyle chuckled as his eyes skimmed the text. The committee had concluded that the unusually dense fogs of recent months were purely a function of the vagaries of the English climate and that the much-bruited theory that the burning of coal in any way contributed to the fog was precisely that, a fantastical theory. The article went on to cite the historical record, with bad London fogs being reported as early as the time of King Stephen.

Wilde dredged the champagne bottle from its bucket, recharged his glass, and waved the bottle at Conan Doyle who, by way of declining, rattled the ice in his brandy. Wilde took a long sip, and wryly observed, "The government invariably forms committees to look into problems they have no intention of doing anything about. It is a classic stalling tactic employed in the hopes that either the problem will resolve itself or the government will eventually be voted out of power, at which point they can use the issue to cudgel the incoming administration."

"Good Lord!" Conan Doyle said, reacting to something he had seen in the paper. "Look at this!" He held the paper up for Wilde to see. Accompanying the article was a photograph of the "Fog Committee." It was a prime example of the kind of formally posed portrait indulged in by minor dignitaries to boost their sense of self-importance. The Fog Committee comprised of a group of well-dressed gents puffing away at pipes or cigars (apparently with no sense of irony) so that a nimbus of smoke curled about them. The majority were well-fed men in expensive suits with double chins strangling beneath starched collars and cinched-tight ties. There were eight in all—sporting an imposing assortment of beards, muttonchops, and mustachios, most veined with gray whiskers. They looked out of the photograph with the humorless glares of busy-men-who-have-better-things-to-do-than-to-interrupt-overburdened-schedules-with-activities-as-trivial-as-posing-for-a-portrait. One could practically hear the exasperated voice of the photographer trying to corral such men in perpetual motion to hold still long enough to allow light to refract through the lens of a camera and burn their images onto a photographic plate. One figure in particular, a man in a tall stovepipe hat, had turned his head at the vital moment so that his features registered as nothing more than an amorphous gray blur of motion. A caption at the bottom of the photograph identified the committee members, and now Conan Doyle read the names aloud.

"Look here, our friend, Police Commissioner Burke."

Wilde snorted. "There's a face badly in need of a fist."

Conan Doyle chortled at Wilde's quip and continued reading. "'The Right Honorable Judge Robert Jordan; Sir Lionel Ransome, financier; Retired Admiral Peregrine Windlesham; Tarquin Hogg, president of the Bank of England; Tristram Oldfield, railroad magnate; George Hardcastle, owner of Oxton Coal . . .'"

He reached the stovepipe wearer, who was listed only as UNKNOWN. Seated next to the anonymous figure was a face he knew only too well.

"'. . . and Lord Howell, Minister of War!'"

Conan Doyle dropped the paper to look at Wilde. "War minister? I could see a reason for the police commissioner, but what has a war minister to do with the issue of fog? It hardly seems a coincidence."

Wilde sighed aloud. "Honestly, Arthur, I know that you and your confederates in the Society for Psychic Silliness do not believe in coincidences, but they do happen. My days are full of coincidences. I arrive at my table at The Savoy and there is always a chilled bottle of champagne and a plate of Oysters on Horseback waiting. You call it coincidence. I call it sterling service."

"You could be right, Oscar. It could be a coincidence. The war minister's photograph appears in the morning paper and by the evening he is assassinated." Conan Doyle's brown eyes swept the pho-

THE FOG COMMITTEE ❧ 39

tograph. "But if another of the committee members were to be assassinated, then the odds of coincidence have just greatly fallen."

Wilde chuckled. "A war minister? A judge? A banker? If you drew up a list of professions most likely to be assassinated they would all top the list. Who has never had a bank manager they would not wish to murder? I myself would happily strangle mine, would it not leave my many creditors orphaned and inconsolable."

There was a long silence, finally broken by Conan Doyle. "I should like to speak to that poor Italian chap, Lord Howell's valet. As the sole surviving witness, only he knows what really happened."

Wilde fixed Conan Doyle with an abject stare. "You speak in jest, I hope. Commissioner Burke warned us in no uncertain terms about being caught meddling."

Conan Doyle nodded grimly and tossed off the dregs of his brandy. "That is why it is imperative I am not caught."

Wilde said nothing for several thoughtful moments, and then he, too, drained his champagne glass, dabbed his lips with a napkin, and set the glass aside. "You mean, that is why it is imperative *we* should not be caught."

Conan Doyle threw his friend a quizzical look.

"I am not asking to be included, Arthur. I am insisting. Your tourist's Italian is clearly insufficient. You are not negotiating the purchase of a gelato from a street vendor in Napoli. You are questioning a man on trial for murder. You shall require my services as translator."

Conan Doyle mulled the offer and finally acquiesced with a nod. "Quite right, Oscar, your language skills are far superior to mine. Very well, shall we go tomorrow?"

"Not tomorrow. Perhaps Friday."

"Why Friday?"

"I have been living at the club of late. I must return to Tite Street to spend a few days in the bosom of my family. I should like to dandle my boys upon my knee one final time before I am tossed into the deepest, darkest, dankest cell in Newgate."

CHAPTER 5

RAISING GHOSTS

The face moves forward through the gloom and presses its forehead to the metal visor, eyes peering through a tiny glass window. One hand gropes the handle of a crank. The other drops a penny into a slot and the mechanism unlocks with a metallic *clunk*. Electricity flows and a bulb within the Mutoscope glimmers to life, illuminating a rustic scene: a lake surrounded by hills. (The English Lake District?) No, the hills are too high, the lake too wide. Not a lake but a *loch* somewhere in the Scottish highlands.

The black-and-white photo is creased from use, but the image is clear. The sun slanting low across the flat water suggests that it was taken in the early morning, scarcely after dawn. The face presses closer, eyes devouring the image. The hand slowly turns the crank. Within the Mutoscope, a drum of eight hundred paper photographs revolves. A brass finger releases, dropping a second photo and then a third, a fourth, a fifth . . . etc. The cranking speeds up. Photographs cascade in a riffling purr, and like a child's flip-book, the scene animates with motion.

A low, rippling wave disturbs the glass-smooth waters. A tenuous veil of silver mist ascends from the surface like a specter rising from its tomb. The viewer draws in a breath. The hand turns faster, and the scene comes fully alive.

An open steam launch puffs across the loch, dragging behind it the expanding V of a trailing wake. Another photo drops and . . .

The scene changes.

The camera, closer now, looks onto a muddy foreshore where two figures stand.

The scene changes.

The camera, closer still, reveals the image of a young woman. Tall. Slender. Dressed in a light summer dress. She has peeled off her black stockings and kicked aside her shoes and now she wades in the shallows. Her shoes and stockings, along with her hat, sit neatly piled on the dry shore. The young woman's hair is so blond it burns luminous as a white flame. The camera delights in her image, one of the Graces caught by human eyes, idling in a moment of unawareness.

The hand ceases turning. The image freezes. The viewer draws in a deep breath and exhales raggedly. The hand resumes its cranking, and the figure in the viewfinder squeezes up from two-dimensions into three. She strolls toward the viewer in dreamy slow motion. When she notices the camera, her coy smile suggests embarrassment and she lowers her eyes demurely. Her hair has come unpinned and her slender fingers sweep back a stray lock that has fallen over one eye. She paddles through water so shallow it scarcely covers her bare feet. Her hitched skirts are gathered up in one hand, revealing to the lascivious camera slender calves and shapely ankles. Distracted by something behind her, she turns to look over her shoulder.

The scene changes.

A little boy stands calf-deep in the loch. He is togged out in a sailor's suit and knee britches. The boy, perhaps four years of age, has the same white-blond hair spilling from beneath the sailor's cap and is almost certainly her child. He holds a toy boat in hands chubby with baby fat. The toy boat—a tin-plate warship—sports a huge key protruding from the top deck and now he winds it, the young face taut with concentration. He lowers the battleship to the water, aims, and releases. The windup ship motors off, trailing a wake churned by a whirling propeller. The large tin rudder has been bent so that the warship sails in a tight circle about the boy's legs. He silently claps his hands and mimes laughter. It is a wonderful moment of childish innocence.

The hand turning the crank stops and the riffling cards cease their tumble, arresting time. The moment hangs frozen. The watching eyes blink tears from their corners, peer deeper, harder, greedy to absorb every last detail. A noise escapes the hunched-over viewer: a sound halfway between a sob of mourning and a keening wail that is a premonition of something dreadful yet to come.

Slowly, reluctantly, the hand tightens upon the crank and begins to turn. Photographs spill from the drum.

The scene changes again.

A long view of the loch. The camera pans to reveal the foreshore and a reviewing stand erected on the loch side. A crowd mills before it.

The scene changes.

Uniformed naval men in plumed hats mingle with bureaucrats in tight suits and top hats. They puff cigars, releasing wisps of smoke. Gesticulate jerkily.

The scene changes.

The crowd parts as a carriage arrives. Dignitaries scuttle to form an honor guard. Bewigged pages snatch open the carriage door and *she* clambers out—the namesake of the age: Victoria Regina. Her image is unmistakable: Short. Squat. Stumpy and obese in her black mourning dress and headdress of white lace. A bearded man in a uniform bedecked with medals and an admiral's plumed hat bows and kisses her hand. He escorts her through silent applause to where a throne-like chair awaits beneath an awning. She acknowledges the crowd with a regal wave.

The scene changes.

A stack of wicker baskets. A hand fumbles a latch and white doves spill out in a blur of fluttering wings. The doves scatter into the skies above.

The scene changes.

Out on the loch, a steam launch cruises swiftly over the flat water. White smoke billows from the chimney. At the tiller is a man in a black topcoat and a stovepipe hat. Something with the shape of a slender metal sardine is strapped to the side of the launch.

The scene changes.

A mighty warship lies at anchor. But no, a camera affixed the gunwale of a boat drifts past revealing that it is a sham: a barn-sized wooden cutout lashed to a raft of barrels. It looks uncannily similar to the child's windup battleship.

The scene changes.

The man at the wheel of the steam launch yanks a lever. A propeller at the rear of the torpedo spins up and the iron fish, steam spouting from a blowhole, drops heavily from the side of the boat. Relieved of its massy weight, the steamer heels alarmingly.

The scene changes.

Churning a bubbling wake, the torpedo streaks toward the battleship target anchored in the distance.

The scene changes.

The crowd in the viewing stands surges to its feet. Men remove top hats, jostle shoulders, craning to see.

The scene changes.

The torpedo speeds unerringly toward its target. It is only seconds away when it abruptly veers left. In the skies above the loch, the flock of doves wheels in an inward tightening circle. Suddenly, the torpedo goes into a wild, tail-chasing spin. Then the lead dove turns and heads for shore, and the cloud of flapping wings follows. The torpedo suddenly straightens. It swooshes past the anchored target, missing by yards and heads straight for the shore. From this distance, the tiny figures of the wading woman and her child can be seen running. Running away. Running for shelter in the viewing stand. But too late. Moving at tremendous speed, the torpedo skims through the shallows and hurtles onto the land, the spinning propeller flinging up a rooster tail of sand and mud. It overtakes the running figures and the young woman and her child vanish in a cloud of steam. Carried by its dread inertia, the torpedo crashes into the viewing stand and explodes.

Although the Mutoscope has no sound, the mind supplies the concussive roar. Bodies and debris tumble high into the sky. The blast hits the camera and the world upends and tilts onto its side.

Feet run past the toppled camera. A top hat falls sideways to the ground and rolls uphill until a trampling foot crushes it. Black smoke swirls and the world dims to darkness.

The scene changes.

Daylight returns. The camera, once again upright, pans across a scene of devastation. Nothing remains of the reviewing stand but jagged splinters of wood, rows of toppled seats, and entangled within, the grotesquely sprawled bodies of the dead.

The scene changes.

Victoria sags in the arms of two men who support her by the armpits and drag her toward the waiting coach. But they must pick their way through wreckage, stepping over fallen bodies and severed limbs. The queen is loaded aboard the carriage, which jerks away.

The scene changes.

A final look at the devastated shore. Hatless and disheveled survivors stumble aimlessly, faces streaked with blood and dirt, eyes spilling shock. A handsome bearded man in a stovepipe hat shambles past the camera, craning to scan the foreshore where the young woman and her child were wading. He calls out for them, his face contorted in a mask of horror. And then his silent shouts become voiceless screams. His face darkens with the rush of blood. Whipcord veins pop from his neck and forehead. He turns away and stares blindly into the camera lens. But then the Mutoscope reaches the end of the drum and the final photograph falls. The coin drops into a metal box with a monetary *ka-chunk*, the bulb extinguishes, and the viewfinder goes black.

As the cooling filament fades, the viewer draws back from the

Mutoscope. His is the same face glimpsed in the final frame, although the once-dark beard is now shock white, the trimmed and pomaded hair is a shoulder-length tangle of gray dishevelment and the handsome face now lined and haggard beyond the normal passage of years. The only thing unchanged is the haunted look of the eyes, which are tunnels receding into an empty, echoing darkness . . . swarmed by ghosts.

CHAPTER 6

AN ILL-TIMED LETTER

"Kiss me," Miss Jean Leckie breathed in a husky voice. "Kiss me!" She and Conan Doyle were seated at a quiet table amongst the potted plants in the Tivoli's fern room. All eyes in the restaurant turned toward them, watching. And yet, Conan Doyle did not care. Miss Leckie was leaning forward in her chair, so that her hazel-green eyes were all that filled his vision. She tugged insistently at his sleeve. "Kiss me, Daddy!" she breathed and Conan Doyle no longer resisted, but leaned into her face and pressed his lips against hers.

"Daddy! Dad-dee!"

Conan Doyle pried open his eyes and groggily dragged himself up from the pit of sleep. He was slouched in his writing chair, the Tivoli dining room jarringly replaced by his study and a desk strewn with pens and notebooks, the delicious dream still evaporating from the surface of his mind while an insistent hand jerked at his sleeve from below.

"Dad-dee. My soldier's broken."

He looked down to see Kingsley, his five-year-old son, yanking at his sleeve. The little boy was holding his very favorite toy: a windup soldier. Conan Doyle could tell from the gleaming red pout of the boy's lip and eyes pooled to overflowing that his child teetered on the verge of hysteria.

"What is it, Kingsley?"

"My soldier's broken Dad-dee. He won't drum."

Conan Doyle sighed and took the mechanical soldier from his son's small hands. It was a tinplate guardsman with a painted red uniform and a black bearskin. When wound with the key in the middle of his back, the soldier would march forward in a grind of gears while a blur of mechanical arms pounded upon a tin drum.

"You haven't overwound him again, have you?"

The little boy shook his blond head emphatically, but Conan Doyle suspected quite the opposite.

"Come, climb upon Papa's knee and we'll see if we can't heal your poor wounded soldier." The small boy clambered into his father's lap. Conan Doyle gripped the key and gave it a gentle, experimental twist. It turned a few degrees, hit a hard stop, and sprang back when released.

Overwound.

"I'm afraid you have wound it too tightly, Kingsley. Daddy has told you before, you have to be careful winding it."

"I need my drummer, Daddy! He beats his drum to scare away the monster who lives under my bed."

Conan Doyle swallowed a grimace. The monster again. As a writer, he was all for encouraging a child's imagination, but "the monster" was the cause of much bedwetting.

"Kingsley, I have told you there are no monsters under your bed. Monsters cannot enter our house. Daddy has expressly forbidden them."

"Can you fix my drummer, Daddy? Can you?"

He hugged the little boy and said, "Well, let's see. Papa will try his best, but I cannot promise."

Conan Doyle rummaged a hand in his pants pocket and withdrew the small silver penknife he kept tucked there. The tinplate soldier was constructed in two halves held together by bent metal tabs. He worked the sharp knife blade under each tab in turn and levered them open. But when he eased the two halves of the soldier apart, there was a *sproinnnnggggg* as the tightly wound spring spat out like a metal tongue, uncoiling a spool of black spring steel that whiplashed across the floor.

"Oh, dear," Conan Doyle said, struggling to push the spring back into the metal body.

"Is it broken, Daddy?"

"I'm afraid it is, Kingsley. But you've got lots of other toys to play with—"

"But I want my drummer!" Kingsley shrieked, his voice ripping on each syllable.

"Shush! Shush! Calm yourself. Daddy will take it to a shop when he goes to London and have it mended."

During this exchange, Conan Doyle failed to hear the door open or footsteps until his wife spoke. "Arthur, I see you decided to return home at long last."

He looked up in surprise. These days, his wife, Louise Doyle, or "Touie" as he affectionately called her, did not leave her bedroom very often. Five years earlier, she had been diagnosed with galloping consumption, the dread disease of the age, which carried off most of its victims within a matter of months. But thanks to Conan Doyle's diligence, moving the family from Switzerland to Egypt to the rural climes of Sussex to find the most beneficent air, Touie had endured, although mostly as an invalid, bedridden and sickly. At times she hovered on the precipice of death, and Conan Doyle made sure his funeral clothes were cleaned and pressed. But at other times, she rallied. Touie had not left her room for a full month, so Conan Doyle was surprised to see her downstairs and dressed, although the apple-cheeked girl he had married was now emaciated, and her gaunt, hollow-eyed features held the deathly pallor of a consumptive. Even now, despite the efforts of her toilet, the smell of the sick room hovered about her.

"Touie, darling! You're up."

"I was concerned when the servants told me you had not slept in your bed last night."

He caught the recrimination frosting her words and quickly replied, "I stayed at Oscar's club. Had to sleep in a chair. Trains weren't running because of the blasted fog."

"Fog? Really?" his wife said, deepening the incrimination with a pause before adding, "We had no such fog."

"Well, the house is in Sussex, darling. It's precisely for the healthful air that I chose to move the family here—"

"Did you attend your meeting? The Society for Psychical Research, wasn't it? The first Monday of the month?"

"Yes, I did, and it was most edifying."

"I am quite sure." She eyed his apparel pointedly. "You do not normally dress in your finery to attend a Society meeting."

Kingsley began to squirm and so did Conan Doyle. "Kingsley, get down. Daddy is trying to talk to Mama." He slid the boy off his lap.

"Daddy, what about my soldier?"

Conan Doyle irritatedly snatched the toy from his little boy's grip and set it down on his writing desk. "Daddy will have it mended. Now go and find out what your sister's up to. Go on." He chivvied the boy from the room with a wave and a paternal look.

Louise Doyle sank wearily onto the edge of a leather armchair. From the look on her face it was clear the interrogation was only just beginning.

"After the meeting, did you go for supper with one of the members?"

"Ahhhh, let me think. Um, yes . . . yes I did."

"A gentleman . . . or a lady?"

At that moment, Florence, the maid, entered the study bearing a letter on a silver salver.

"A letter arrived for you, sir. By *first* post."

"Thank you, Florence." He bade her to place it on the desk with an impatient wave, but she obstinately remained hovering by the door.

"A-a-a lady, as a matter of fact. A medium. Yes, quite fascinating. Our conversation, that is. We discussed séances and—"

"She must be a very pretty lady for you to wear your best suit and take the time to wax your moustaches."

"Pretty? I-I didn't really notice. I—no, I'd say she was, if anything, a little . . . frowsy. You know, the *spinsterly* type."

"A spinster, indeed? I know many of the members of the Society. Might I recognize the unmarried lady's name?"

"No, ah, no. Probably not. She only recently joined. Ah, I believe her name was Jean. Yes, Jean . . . Leckie, or something like that."

"Beggin' your pardon, sir," Florence interrupted. She held up the envelope. "That's who the letter is from, a *Miss Jean Leckie*."

Something deeply wounded flashed across Louise Doyle's face, but she reined it in behind a tight smile. "How interesting. You two had dinner just last evening and here she has already sent you a billet-doux. She sounds very keen."

"Hardly a billet-doux, darling," Conan Doyle said with an uneasy chuckle. "What ever must Florence think? A billet-doux, indeed!"

To make matters worse, the letter had arrived in a lilac envelope, an incriminatingly feminine color. But even as he waffled, Conan Doyle realized he had a possible bolt-hole: he could reveal the fact that he'd been called in to consult on a murder. But then this was no ordinary murder—it was an assassination, and one he had been officially proscribed from speaking about—to anyone. A logjam of sentences crowded Conan Doyle's throat and suffocated there.

Louise Doyle rose unsteadily from her chair, eyes gleaming, her pale features cinched in a broken smile. "Well, Arthur. I'll leave you to read your letter in private. I think I can guess exactly what kind of message it is."

And with that, his wife tottered from the study, helping herself along the way by leaning on every piece of furniture that came to hand.

The maid flushed and fidgeted. She handed the letter to her master, bounced a quick curtsy, and muttered, "I'd best be getting on with the ironing" and fled the room.

That had been a disaster. But now it was over, Conan Doyle felt his spine unratchet a cog or two. Still, his hands shook with excitement as he slashed a letter opener beneath the flap and tore open the envelope. At the sight of exquisite feminine handwriting, his heart quickened and he fought to focus his mind as he read the short missive.

> Dearest Arthur,
>
> I so enjoyed our little tête-à-tête last evening. I was sorry to see it cut short. If you are free today, perhaps we may luncheon together. My train arrives at Waterloo Station at 12:30 p.m., Platform 2. If you are unable to make it on such short notice, I shall understand, although I will be sad not to see your handsome face again.
>
> Yours fondly,
> Miss Jean Leckie

As his eyes tripped over the elegant flourish of her signature, a thrill surged through him. It seemed shockingly forward, but then Conan Doyle reasoned, times were changing and Miss Leckie was of a generation where the old rules of chaste female decorum seemed laughably twee. He rose to his feet, dithering. If he left now, so suddenly, it would be clear that his departure was in response to the letter. But then the image swam up in his mind of Jean's graceful neck, the doeish eyes, and the baying hound of desire slipped free of its leash. Suddenly energized, he rushed from the study and galumphed up the staircase to his room. If he hurried, he might just catch the 10:45 train back to London.

Minutes later, Conan Doyle was pedaling his three-wheeler bicycle along the tree-lined lane that ascended in a long, sweeping curve into Haslemere. He was standing on the pedals, thighs burning, as he muscled up the final hill before the train station, when he was snatched from his reverie by a *wisssshthump* . . . *wissssssshthump* . . .

Suddenly, he was overtaken by a man in a flapping canvas coat, goggles and a backward cap, sitting astride a fiery broomstick—a steam-powered bicycle. Conan Doyle was an enthusiastic cyclist, and had published articles on the benefits of exercise and mental relaxation afforded to him by cycling, but now he cursed his tricycle, which by comparison seemed ponderous and lumbering. The steam cyclist swooped effortlessly up the steep hill dragging a wispy vapor trail of steam. Conan Doyle felt a stab of envy and grumbled to himself, "I shall have to get one of those."

SHANGHAIED IN WATERLOO

Conan Doyle panted into Haslemere station, stiff-legged and red-faced, only to find that he was annoyingly early as the persistent fog made nonsense of railway timetables. Fortunately, this gave him time to snatch up a copy of *The Times*, and during the train ride to London he read with great interest the official version of Lord Howell's assassination. Prime Minister Gladstone expressed outrage at the murder, which he laid at the feet of "International Anarchists" and other shadowy groups (made up mostly of foreigners) striving to topple the legitimate government of Great Britain. Somehow the paper had produced a highly accurate sketch of Vicente, Lord Howell's Italian valet, whom Gladstone thundered, "Would feel the lash of British Justice!"

With just ten miles to London, he tossed the paper aside, flipped open his leather portfolio, and slid out his Casebook: a slim leather volume secured by a strap and a tiny padlock. He reached beneath his collar and drew out a key on a long ribbon. The key sprung open the lock and Conan Doyle took out a fountain pen and turned to the blank first page. For the remainder of the journey, he scribbled an account of his adventure of the previous night and the mysteriously vanishing body of Charlie Higginbotham. When he finished his account, he snapped the cap back on his fountain pen and took out the newspaper cutting tucked between the Casebook's pages.

"Fog Committee Sees No Solution"

His eyes dropped to the large photograph and the cadre of high-powered politicos and industrial magnates seated around the table. He scanned the line of puffed-up faces and stopped at the figure whose features registered only as an anonymous gray blur indentified by the enigmatic caption as UNKNOWN.

A whistle sounded as the London train passed the signal and began its rumbling deceleration into Waterloo Station. He closed the journal in his lap and studied it. Written across the cover in his own neat hand was: *Casebook No. 2* followed by a hovering colon waiting to complete the thought. The man who created Sherlock Holmes considered a moment and then uncapped his fountain pen, touched its gold nib to smooth leather, and penned in a careful, steady hand: *The Dead Assassin.*

* * *

Conan Doyle hurried through the crowded train station, banging shoulders and muttering *excuse-me*s and *dreadfully sorry*s as he jostled through teeming shoals of rail passengers. Finally breaking free of the crowds, he sprinted across the echoing transepts, coattails flying, one hand clamping the gray homburg to his head. Puffing wind, he raced up Platform 2 where a train stood waiting on either side, hissing steam.

He spotted Jean Leckie as she gathered her skirts and stepped down from the carriage. She did not see him immediately, and for a magical moment she looked about herself, unaware she was being observed. She was wearing the same hat and the same violet dress as the previous evening. She stepped to the middle of the platform and paused to smooth her crinolines. It was a delightfully unguarded moment and his heart cartwheeled at the sight. A notion struck him, and he quickened his pace—he would touch a hand to her arm to surprise her. It would not be unseemly. Waterloo Station was a vast, echoing vault of arching steel and glass clangorous with the chuff and hiss of arriving and departing railway stock, the yawps of porters, and the loud-hailer announcements of trains. It was a place a called-out name could not be heard. He had an entirely appropriate excuse for a touch.

A railway engine with a single carriage had drawn up one side of the platform. A porter straining at a luggage cart piled to overflowing trundled toward him. A large ginger man in a black bowler idled on a bench, twirling a pocket watch by its chain. Close by, another large man in a long coat and a matching black bowler hunkered behind his newspaper.

As Conan Doyle sidestepped the luggage cart, Miss Leckie began to turn his way. She would see him at any moment. He had lost the element of surprise. He began to raise his hat, a smile beaming on his face. And then she turned to face him full on, her eyes met his, and he stumbled to a halt.

It was not Jean Leckie. The young woman was a total stranger.

At that moment a train whistle shrieked and the parked railway engine jetted a swirling cloud of steam across the platform. As it engulfed him, Waterloo Station vanished. Suddenly, a powerful hand gripped his right arm. Another gripped his left. To his shock and surprise, Arthur Conan Doyle, a large, athletic man, was lifted off his feet and whisked sideways across the platform, the toes of his shoes scuffing the concrete. The side of a railway carriage appeared. A door opened and he was hurled inside and bounced into a seat with the bowler-hatted bullies dropping heavily on either side of him.

"What the devil! What is the meaning? Who are you people?"

Perched on the seat opposite was a small man with a head the shape of a blown-glass bulb. He was entirely bald on top, apart from a single pomaded forelock, which curled upon his brow like a question mark.

The carriage jerked as the railway engine began to move, accelerating out of the station, iron wheels squealing for traction on the rails. It traveled several hundred feet before an unseen railway switch was thrown and the train swerved off the main track and plunged into the black maw of a tunnel. Out the carriage windows, the perpetual night of the Underground network hurtled darkly past.

"Who—?"

"You may call me Cypher," the little man interrupted before Conan Doyle could spit out his question.

"Cypher?" Conan Doyle grunted. "You must have had very imaginative parents."

The diminutive figure smiled indulgently. "Not my real name, obviously. And given your intellect, Doctor Doyle, you have probably already surmised that you have been duped for a reason. I know that you and your friend Oscar Wilde were present at the scene of Lord Howell's assassination last night."

Conan Doyle shifted in his seat. Was the man trying to somehow entrap him into confessing something?

"I was there at the request of the Yard. Despite that fact, my friend and I were warned in no uncertain terms by the commissioner of police himself to have no further involvement in the case. The fact that you have snatched me, tells me you are not the police. Then who, indeed, are you?"

Conan Doyle eyed the little man up and down. He was short: under five feet, so that the tips of his polished shoes swung free of the carriage floor, like a child's. However, the finely made suit, immaculately tailored down to the last stitch, and the fastidiousness of his dress, complete with boutonniere and round, gold-rimmed spectacles that sparkled in the electric carriage light, suggested a man of power and influence.

"Someone from the government, I presume. A spy master?"

"Not a bad guess, as I would expect from the author of Sherlock Holmes. I confess, I am an enthusiast of your clever fictions but that does not appertain to this—"

"Kidnapping?" Conan Doyle interrupted.

"Summons," the man who called himself Cypher corrected. "I

represent a higher authority. One greater than the government, comprised as it is of grubby politicians who are merely temporary holders of office."

"Who, then, God?" Conan Doyle challenged, his sense of outrage recovering after the shock of being shanghaied in the middle of Waterloo Station.

Cypher's small face attempted to mold itself into something approaching a smile; he flashed a collection of tiny, peg-like teeth, aiming at geniality, but managing instead to convey the menacing look of a playground Napoleon.

"God *and* country," he answered cryptically. "As you shall soon see."

The brakes squealed on. The train shuddered as it decelerated and drew up at an Underground station, where it trembled like a whippet straining at its lead, anxious to be released. By the sparkle of electric lamps, Conan Doyle read the name spelled out on the porcelain tiles: ORPHEUS STREET STATION.

The ginger behemoth flung open the door and stepped out, holding the door. Cypher slid from the bench onto his feet. "Come along, Doctor Doyle. And no heroics, please. I do not wish for an unfortunate accident."

Conan Doyle had been planning a dozen such scenarios in his head. His hands were balled into fists, and he had already decided he would punch the larger of the two thugs first; but at Cypher's words, his fists unclenched. They stepped out onto the deserted platform. He casually eyed the steps leading up into the station, wondering whether to run for it, but up close he saw to his surprise that the steps ascended a mere five feet before abutting a wall. The remainder of the staircase was a painting, like cheap scenery from a theatrical production. And then he realized the stunning implication: the entire station was a ruse.

Cypher caught the bafflement on Conan Doyle's face and smiled. "Quite right, Doctor Doyle, there is no *Orpheus Street* in London and no station. A personal joke of mine." He stepped to the wall and depressed a blank white tile in the middle of the O in Orpheus. It sank beneath his gloved fingers. A sound followed—the clunk of a mechanism releasing—and then a section of wall cracked open and swung inward: a secret door leading to a lighted tunnel. At the end, a staircase.

Cypher sent the ginger mauler ahead and fixed Conan Doyle with an unequivocal look. "If you would follow, please."

At the end of the tunnel they reached a wrought-iron staircase and rang the metal steps with their feet as they climbed two stories to a stout wooden door reinforced with metal straps and heavy iron rivets. It looked like the door to a castle, so Conan Doyle was surprised when it opened and they stepped into a sumptuous room with wallpapered walls, and high ceilings with chandeliers and elaborate plaster cornices.

Cypher nodded for his hulking minotaurs to take a seat on a fussy floral sofa and eyed Conan Doyle coldly. "Everything you have seen and everything you are about to see or hear is a state secret. You will say nothing of this to a living soul. Do you understand?"

The fineness of the room and the cryptic warning kicked over the hornet's nest of speculation in Conan Doyle's mind and set it abuzz. He was finally beginning to suspect where he was. "Y-yes, of course," he stammered.

Cypher flayed him with a final, scorching look. "You would do well to remember that." He stepped to a second door and Conan Doyle followed. The interior door was painted gleaming white with elaborate gilt door handles. Cypher rapped at it with his tiny knuckles and bewigged servants in royal-blue satin uniforms and knee breeches immediately swept the door open.

"Leave your coat and hat," Cypher commanded. A servant stepped behind Conan Doyle and slipped the wool overcoat from his broad shoulders while the other took his hat and gloves.

"Follow me closely."

Conan Doyle shadowed Cypher along a long plush-carpeted corridor. His attention was drawn by the many fine paintings in enormous gilt frames that hung on either side. Most were portraits of English kings and queens stretching back centuries. He longed to stop and study them, but the little man was setting a cracking pace and he hurried to keep up. Abruptly, they turned sharp right into a large room with vaulted ceilings bedecked with plaster frieze works. Dazzled by the opulence of scarlet walls and glittering gilt, his eyes roved wildly, until his focus was drawn, by deliberate intent of the architect, to the far end of the room. Beneath a proscenium arch, a dais of three steps ascended to a throne. Seated upon the throne, still wearing her familiar dress of mourning black and white lace headdress, was a figure whose face was struck into every coin of the realm.

Victoria Regina.

Pike-wielding beefeaters hovered in every corner of the room, while red-tunicked soldiers of the queen's life guard stood at attention on either side of the throne, cutlasses drawn and held ready. Cypher stopped fifteen feet shy of the throne, bowed his head, and uttered in a reverential voice, "Majesty."

Conan Doyle echoed the salutation and by pure reflex fell to one knee and bowed deeply.

"Your zeal is noted, Doctor Doyle," Victoria answered in a quavering, old ladie's voice, "but men have not bowed from the knee since Elizabeth's time."

Feeling foolish, Conan Doyle rose and bowed again, this time from the waist. When he finally summoned the courage to stand tall and raise his head, he was shocked by Victoria's appearance. It had been ten years since the death of Prince Albert. In deep mourning, Victoria had withdrawn from public life and soon became a mystery to her own subjects. People whispered that she had secretly died and that the news was being suppressed to delay the succession of her dissolute son, Edward, Prince of Wales. Other scuttlebutt was far more vicious—the aging queen was stricken with disease: consumption, heart failure, even syphilis (contracted from Albert).

As a trained physician, Conan Doyle could not fail to notice the ailing condition of the seventy-eight-year-old monarch. She had lost weight, he could tell from previously taken photographs, but she retained the pudding-in-a-sock physique. She slumped upon the throne. Her face was waxy and pallid. Her glassy brown eyes protruded like a spaniel's. Her chest rose and fell unevenly—he could hear the leather-bellows wheeze of her respiration. And when she spoke, Victoria's voice was faltering and distant, as though it had traveled a wearisome journey from her lips to his ears. In point of fact, she was barely audible.

"Doctor Doyle, your Sherlock Holmes stories have been a great source of diversion to us during our retreat from the world." She raised a hand in a series of palsied jerks and let it drop heavily in her lap. "Now it is our hope that a mind as ingenious as yours might be employed to save your queen, your country, and the great Empire we represent."

"Indeed, your highness, it is an honor to be asked," Conan Doyle answered, and bowed again, quite unnecessarily.

"The queen's representative, Mister Cypher, will describe in detail the task you are asked to perform. But *we* wanted to meet you personally, so that you do not labor under any suspicion of this being the highest possible service you could render to the nation."

Throughout her speech, Conan Doyle leaned forward, straining to hear. He threw a worried frown at Cypher. "Her Majesty's voice is very faint," he whispered out the side of his mouth. "Might I approach the throne?"

"You may, but at the risk of being skewered on a pike staff," Cypher replied beneath his breath.

"But I am not quite certain what is being asked of me," Conan Doyle whispered to Cypher. "I don't know what to say."

"Simply say 'yes' and bow," Cypher replied. "Your acquiescence to a royal request is a foregone conclusion. Say 'yes,' bow to Her Majesty, and then we shall back away before we turn and leave the royal presence."

* * *

"Do you know what the French term, coup d'état means, Doctor Doyle?"

They were back on the private underground train, the bowler-hatted bruisers squeezed tight on either side of the Scottish author. This time the train was rumbling in the reverse direction, toward Waterloo Station.

"A coup d'état? Yes, I believe so. It is a kind of palace revolution, is it not?"

Cypher's face soured, as if the words left a vile taste upon his tongue. "You have no doubt read in the newspapers of the assassination attempts made upon Her Majesty?"

"Of course."

"There have been eight 'official' attempts. All were the handiwork of lunatics or disaffected outcasts from society. They were not ruthlessly planned, but rather the slapdash bumblings of delusional cretins discharging pistols at the royal carriage and such—more public nuisance than serious assassination attempt. However, there have been four attempts that you have not read about—because I forbade the newspapers from publishing them." Cypher's demeanor grew grim. "And because those four attempts were very nearly successful. By contrast these outrages were masterminded by organized groups: Fenians, anarchists, and in two cases by agents we believe are homegrown."

"What do you mean by *homegrown*?"

"Britain is one of the few European countries never to have suffered a revolution. But now I fear there is a threat to the monarchy from within. Of late there have been a number of carefully targeted assassinations. Lord Howell was the fourth victim." Cypher saw the question poised on Conan Doyle's lips and preempted it. "Yes, the other three were officially described as *accidents*. We believe some shadowy group is planning the equivalent of a palace coup. As a smoke screen, they are stirring up agitators—anarchists, Fenians—to commit random acts of terror. Meanwhile key members of the government and aristocracy are being eliminated. I fear these actions will culminate in a palace coup where Victoria will be murdered and a new government will sweep to power, most likely under the pretense of protecting a nation about to descend into chaos."

"But what of the Prince of Wales? If the queen were to be murdered, would he not accede to the throne?"

At mention of the heir presumptive, Cypher's mouth puckered in a moue of disgust. "There are those who would seek to delay the Prince of Wales' accession for as long as possible. I am one of them. Albert Edward is a frivolous gallivanter who does not possess the temperament required of a monarch. Still, as you say, he is the rightful heir to the throne. And so, as an insurance policy, I have dispatched him on a diplomatic mission to Europe. He should be in Prague about now."

"Out of harm's reach?"

"Hopefully," Cypher grudgingly conceded.

"I am baffled by your interest in me. Surely you have spies, police officers, people more suited than myself?"

"I sought you out precisely because you are *not* of the government. Nor the police. Nor the military. Each of these bodies has been compromised and harbors traitors to the crown. I summoned you because your ability to fathom out the plots of your ingenious stories may help us to fathom out this plot . . . or, at the minimum, provide us with valuable information."

"I am flattered by your trust in my abilities, but I am not sure what I can—"

"I do not believe in *trust*," Cypher interrupted. "Or luck. Or God. I believe in knowledge. I believe in being two steps ahead of my friends and three steps ahead of my foes. I have had you followed for some time, Doctor Doyle. I know your habits. I know your allegiances. I know the barber you frequent for your morning shave. I know which newspapers you read. I even know that you take your tea with milk and three heaping sugars. In short, I do not trust you can be relied upon, I *know* you may be relied upon."

For a moment, Conan Doyle could not speak. The revelation that he was being spied upon chilled him to the quick. Finally, he muttered, with obvious reluctance, "And what exactly is it I am to do?"

"I want you to observe the political climate. Watch the newspapers. Sift every scrap of gossip, rumor and tittle-tattle you overhear and eke from it the inklings of treachery. Conspiracies leave fingerprints. As the author of Sherlock Holmes you are the perfect man to play sleuth and deduce who are the enemies amongst us. Of course, you cannot breathe a syllable of what you have seen today to a single living soul."

"The other night, my friend Oscar Wilde and I were threatened with Newgate by none other than Police Commissioner Burke should we be discovered *interfering* in any ongoing investigation. You will have to contact him to—"

"Out of the question." Cypher interrupted. "As I just said, we do not know precisely which parts of the government have been compromised. Even the police force."

"And what happens if I am arrested?"

"The answer is simple: be sure you are not."

Conan Doyle met the little man's feral gaze squarely and said, "I must tell my friend, Oscar."

Cypher visibly recoiled.

"You most definitely shall not. Oscar Wilde is a man of questionable character—"

"But not questionable bravery—for that I can personally vouch."

A look of irritation swept Cypher's face. "The man's every move is a public spectacle. We cannot afford to risk secrecy—"

"We cannot afford to fail in this mission. If I am to play Sherlock, I need Oscar to be my Watson. Do you wish me to succeed or not?"

If Cypher attempted to conceal his anger, he was unsuccessful. Strawberries bloomed on the little man's cheeks. In the gloomy carriage, with his deeply lined face and bald pate, he resembled a performance-worn puppet from a Punch and Judy show. "I repeat once again, you can tell no one else of this. Not Oscar Wilde. Not your wife. Not your mistress—"

"I have no mistress, sir!"

Cypher swallowed a vinegar smile, reached into his jacket pocket, drew out a lilac envelope, and dangled it in front of Conan Doyle, who recognized the letter and the handwriting instantly. It was identical to the one he had received this morning.

"Our agent in the post office intercepted the original letter. I'm afraid we did have to open the letter so our forger could duplicate the young lady friend's handwriting." He smiled at Conan Doyle's obvious discomfort and added, "Are you surprised to find that your correspondence is being opened and read? It is, after all, the *Royal* Mail."

Conan Doyle's stomach clenched. Blood drained from his face. The use of the word *mistress* made the implied threat obvious: Cypher was threatening to publically expose him. Conan Doyle lunged and snatched the letter from his fingers.

"I'll save you the bother of reading it, Doctor Doyle. The young lady has invited you to meet her at the round pond in Hyde Park at two o'clock." Cypher lifted his pocket watch and glanced at it. "I want you to keep that assignation." The carriage shuddered about them as the private train eased into Waterloo station.

"Say I do discover something. How do I get in touch with you?"

"You must never attempt to contact me directly, Doctor Doyle. Assume you are being watched, because you are. I shall contact you." Cypher drew something from his top pocket: a tiny gray envelope.

He handed the envelope to Conan Doyle. "Only in the direst emergency, open this envelope."

"What's in it?"

"A means of escape that will bring you directly to me. Now I suggest you hurry. You have half an hour to reach Hyde Park, and a gentleman does not keep a lady waiting."

The train drew up at the platform, trembling with impatience to be off again. The bowler-hatted enforcers never twitched as Conan Doyle rose from his seat. He had the carriage door half open when Cypher called him back. "Oh, and you'll need this."

Cypher handed him a bulging paper bag. It was very light and contained something that rattled faintly when shaken.

"What is this? Some kind of disguise? Gunpowder? A signal flare?"

Cypher's face bowled around a smirk. "Bread crusts . . . for the ducks."

CHAPTER 8

A MASSIVE ATTACK OF HEART

As the tall gates of Hyde Park hove into view, Conan Doyle knuckled the cab ceiling and called out, "This is close enough." The trapdoor above his head flung open and he jammed a crown into the grasping hand. The cab drew up at the curb and he leaped out.

Although the day had begun in dense fog, as he hurried through the park gates the wan November sun was gamely burning blue holes in the gray pall. He raced along the paths, dodging dawdling strollers, and at last approached the round pond. It was deserted, apart from the willowy grace of a solitary female figure. The woman was dressed in a long fur coat with a fur cap in the style of a Russian Cossack, both hands plunged into a matching muff. She was intently watching the mute swans whose white wings in the brittle winter light seemed to burn upon the water. They glided toward her, honking and stretching their necks to be fed, while a scrum of ducks quacked and waddled around her feet. For a moment he was half-convinced that it was another of Cypher's tricks and that the woman would turn around and greet him with the face of a stranger. But at the sound of his approaching footsteps, she turned to look, their eyes met, and Jean Leckie's exquisite features fountained with delight.

"Miss Leckie," he panted, doffing his hat. "How lovely to see you again." He drew off his glove and she offered him a cool clutch of gloved fingers and a beguiling smile.

"So pleasant to see you again, Doctor Doyle."

Seeing her this close, in the full light of day, all the clever words he had been rehearsing evaporated from his tongue. There was an awkward silence until she bubbled gaily, "Whatever shall we do? Here we are at the duck pond with nothing to feed the birds."

Suddenly remembering, Conan Doyle scrabbled in his coat pocket and drew out the bag of bread crusts Cypher had given him.

She clapped her hands with delight. "How clever and thoughtful you are!"

He nodded modestly. It was a small lie.

They spent the next half hour tossing bread to the waterfowl. Miss Leckie shrieked with giddy fear and laughter as the greedy swans snatched crusts with their finger-bruising beaks. When the bread ran out, the swans became a little too aggressive, and took to nuzzling at their pockets and pecking the cuffs of their coat sleeves, and so the two decided to retreat from the pond's edge.

"A turn about the park, Miss Leckie?"

She glowed with approval. "That would be delightful, Doctor Doyle."

Together they strolled the mostly empty pathways, the world receding and returning as they wandered through alternating regions of sunshine and fog. As they waded through a cooing flock of pigeons, the birds startled up in a cloud of flapping wings and Jean Leckie stumbled and clutched fast to him.

"I must take your arm, Doctor Doyle. A lady needs the support of a strong man." She leaned her entire body into his, their faces came dangerously close, and her perfume filled his nostrils. It was a moment ripe with desire, but then it was suddenly over. They moved apart. He swallowed. Smiled amiably. And the two walked on as if nothing had occurred.

They reached the bridge over the Serpentine and paused to admire the view. At that moment, a song sparrow landed on the stone railing, flung back its head, and chirruped a melodious tune that seemed too large to be encompassed within such a tiny envelope of life. The bird finished its song and flew off. But then, as if in response, Jean Leckie opened her mouth and trilled up and down the musical scales in an operatic voice both beautiful and clear. Conan Doyle was taken aback and beamed with pleasure. A pair of strolling couples also stopped to listen as Miss Leckie sang a series of trills and arpeggios in a silvery voice. When she finished, the bystanders warmly applauded and she acknowledged them with a bashful giggle and a quick curtsey.

"You are wonderful," Conan Doyle breathed. "Simply wonderful!"

"I am no grand diva, but my voice lessons are progressing. Some day, I should like to sing you an aria."

"I look forward to it."

As they descended from the bridge, Conan Doyle hesitated, choosing his words carefully before asking, "Do you have family in London, Miss Leckie?"

"I live with my parents in Blackheath."

"Ah yes. You told me the other night."

At that moment, they passed a park bench where a homeless beggar woman sat swaddled in a jumble of old coats and ragged clothes, a bag containing her worldly goods nestled at her feet. She hunched over into herself, a bloody rag clamped to her mouth as a jagged-edged cough racked her emaciated frame. It was a cough Conan Doyle knew only too well: the telltale death rattle of consumption. The woman looked up as they approached and her hollow, staring eyes looked deep into his. He drew in a sharp breath and faltered to a stop. His heart clenched painfully. It was his wife, Louise—she had somehow followed him there.

"What ever's the matter?" Miss Leckie asked.

But in the next instant, he realized that the woman was not Touie.

It was not his wife's face he recognized—it was the mask of consumption. Still, the realization scorched his soul for knowing a moment of happiness. He quickly gathered himself and as they walked on Conan Doyle grappled to explain his reaction. "Ah, it was nothing. I merely remembered something I should not have forgotten." He forced a strained smile and insisted, "Really, it is nothing for you to concern yourself."

But she had caught the change in his face and drew him to a stop. "It is obviously not nothing. Tell me, how is your family?"

"I have a boy and a girl. They are well—flourishing. My wife—" He struggled to keep the hitch from his voice. "I have told you about my wife, Touie. About her condition. She endures, but I fear she is not long for this world."

As soon as the words left his mouth, he damned himself for uttering them, for they sounded like a promise: *Be patient, for my wife will soon enough be gone.*

But she saw the truth in his eyes and said, "I have told you a little about my experiences as a medium." She took both of his large hands in hers. "I believe that all lives are part of a One Great Love into which our souls dissolve."

His throat constricted. His eyes welled. Despite his outward appearance of strength and calm, the years of anguish over Touie and personal loneliness had flayed his soul to a thing of tattered threads. He realized for the first time that he, too, was an invalid—an emotional invalid. He had lost what little spontaneity he once had with the opposite sex. He felt clumsy and clueless and stymied. What to say? How to act? The moment drew taut, and Conan Doyle was seized by the terrible urge to lean forward and kiss her. She read the emotions swimming in his eyes and disarmed the moment by letting go of his hands and dropping her head demurely. The tension broken, she turned away and they resumed their slow promenade.

An embarrassed silence clung to them and for several minutes they said nothing. She stifled a cough on the back of her gloved hand.

He said nothing and a moment later she coughed again, a little more insistently.

"Are you feeling well, Miss Leckie?"

"I am quite thirsty. Perhaps a cup of tea . . ."

Conan Doyle finally took the hint and cursed himself for not thinking of it first. "Yes, of course. We could find a tea shop. Would you like that?"

Miss Leckie smiled. "Oh could we? That would be most delightful!"

"There you have it, then. Tea for two, it is."

As they strode toward the park gates, a strange sensation uncoiled in his chest, an emotion he had not felt in years. And then he realized what it was: happiness. His writing successes gave him satisfaction, but what he felt now was a soul-quaking sense of delight that goes by only one name: joy. The walls of the fortress he had built around his heart were crumbling. At times the vivacious young woman at his side made him feel old. Clumsy. Out of date. But she also made him feel terrifyingly alive. She was a being made of grace and loveliness. He also knew that, despite her youth, she was skilled at lovemaking. He realized for the first time—clod that he was—that it had been no accident that she had occupied the chair next to his at the SPR meeting. Rather, it was the kind of chance encounter that only results from careful planning. He was a successful author. He possessed fame and wealth. Had she set about to ensnare him? Was she deluding him? Leading him on? But then, in a moment of soul-searching, he was forced to confess his own culpability. He had noticed the lingering glances of the striking young lady at previous meetings of the SPR. And so, it was no accident that he had chosen to wax his moustaches and wear his finest clothing upon that fateful Monday evening.

They exited Hyde Park at Speaker's Corner where a crowd milled. A man standing on a soapbox called for the overthrow of the monarchy and the establishment of a worker's utopia. Some in the crowd, wearing bright red rosettes, cheered encouragement. Nearby, an Irishman was

braying loudly about freedom for Ireland. Beyond him, a Trade Union-
ist sermonized about the loss of jobs from the rise of the infernal
machine. "Smash the machines, before they smash us!" Shouts, catcalls, and counter calls filled the air, and many curses and vulgarities
were cast back and forth. A lone constable loitered on the corner to
keep the peace, looking sleepy and bored. Conan Doyle flushed to
think he was exposing a young woman to vulgarity and tried to hurry
through the crowd. But then they passed a group of women. An older
lady wound with a sash reading VOTES FOR WOMEN was addressing
the crowd when a stubble-faced man in rumpled clothes, reeking of
gin, stumbled forward and bawled: "Shut up, ya poxy whores!"

Conan Doyle's blood boiled. His large hands balled into fists. "You
vile wretch!" he growled. "Curb your tongue in the presence of ladies or I'll put you on the ground where you belong!"

The man threw Conan Doyle an off-kilter look, smiling slackly.
"Eff off!"

Conan Doyle lunged for the man, but Jean Leckie gripped his
arm and held him back.

"Please, Doctor Doyle. These women are steeled by battle. They
are not frightened by the rantings of a shabby drunk." Jean Leckie
spoke up, addressing the man herself. "Like all small men full up with
drink, you are a bully and a coward. I pity the poor woman married
to you."

"Oh yeah?" the man slurred. His bleary eyes shifted to Miss Leckie
and his face slid into a sloppy leer. "Why don't you and your dolly-
mop go and fuh—"

The man still had the word on his lips, coiled and ready to fire,
when Conan Doyle swung an uppercut that slammed into the point
of the drunk's chin, snapping his head back and laying him out cold
on the pavement.

The crowd cheered Conan Doyle, which awoke the constable who
looked about himself dozily and then began to saunter their way,
dimly aware that something was amiss.

"Quickly, Arthur," she said, seizing his hand. "We must away!"

The two put their heads down and pushed through the press of people until they reached the road.

Conan Doyle was mortified by his outburst of violence and stammered an apology, but his companion erupted in an infectious titter. Conan Doyle could not help but join in and soon was barking with laughter.

"You were magnificent!" he said.

"And you were my brave Sir Galahad, defending my honor."

He saw a line of hansoms parked at the corner and steered her toward them. "Let's take a cab, shall we?"

But Jean Leckie's eyes were following a passing omnibus. "No, let's ride the omnibus."

Conan Doyle frowned skeptically. "Are you quite sure?"

"Oh yes, it is so exhilarating! Come along!"

Conan Doyle let himself be led by the hand as they dashed into the street after a passing omnibus. He had assumed Miss Leckie would wish to ride inside, shielded by glass windows from the elements, but instead she ran straight to the rear staircase, grabbed the railing and pulled herself aboard the moving vehicle. Conan Doyle leapt up behind her. "You wish to ride on top?" he questioned. "It is not considered decorous for ladies!"

"Do come along, Doctor Doyle," she teased and sprang up the steps ahead of him, her flying skirts revealing black lace-up boots and a thrilling glimpse of shapely ankles clad in black stockings. Heart rumbling and face flushing, Conan Doyle tromped up the stairs after her. As they filed between rows of occupied seats, they ran a gauntlet of disapproving stares from a gallery of top hatted, po-faced men. Oblivious, Jean led Conan Doyle to the very front of the omnibus where they squeezed hip-to-hip onto the narrow bench.

"Oh, isn't this supreme!" she exulted. "I feel quite giddy up here."

"It's the altitude. Perhaps we should remove to the lower carriage."

"No," she countered. "It is not the altitude that makes me dizzy, it is the company of a brave and handsome man." She boldly took his hand and squeezed.

Conan Doyle's heart stepped off a cliff . . . and fell weightless.

The November air was cold and smoky. As they turned onto Park Lane, the sepulchral Dome of St. Paul's floated above the rooftops, hanging weightless in the yellow haze. It had been years since Conan Doyle had ridden atop an omnibus and he found himself delighting in the experience. Although only fifteen feet up, from this perch they seemed to be riding in a winged gondola flying low through London's stony canyons. And the great city was a whirring, hissing, steam-driven contraption clanking noisily about them. At eye level, every bus, every building, every shop awning bore a shouting banner that drowned the clop of hooves, the rumble of cart wheels, the cries of street hawkers in a visual cacophony: NESTLE'S MILK, PEARS SOAP, ALLSOPP'S, KOKO FOR HAIR, NESTLE'S MILK, BOVRIL, SANITAS SOAP, AZIL, NESTLE'S MILK, NESTLE'S MILK, NESTLE'S MILK.

At times, falling white ash, like a mockery of snow, swirled in the air about their heads and danced off their shoulders. But Conan Doyle heard nothing, saw nothing but the fine down on Miss Leckie's cheek and the way the corners of her eyes crinkled when she smiled.

"It is chilly," she laughed. "I'm rather looking forward to my tea." She leaned a hip into him and suddenly stiffened, a look of surprise on her face. "Oh!"

"What is it?"

"I felt something . . . hard."

"W-What?" Conan Doyle stammered. He fished a hand in his coat pocket and withdrew Kingsley's windup soldier. "It's my little boy's favorite toy. I'm afraid it's broken. I was supposed to find a place where it could be mended. He is quite distraught."

The two shared an embarrassed laugh and then an idea lit up Jean Leckie's face. "I know of the most splendid toy shop just up the way." She leapt to her feet and tugged at his hand. "Come, we must get off at the next stop. You must see it. It is a wonderland!"

CHAPTER 9

❦

JEDIDIAH'S EMPORIUM OF MECHANICAL MARVELS

The sign above the shop announced JEDIDIAH'S EMPORIUM OF ME-CHANICAL MARVELS. As Conan Doyle and Jean Leckie approached, a half-dozen street urchins scrummaged the windows, runny-noses smearing the glass as they ogled the multicolored toys on display.

Conan Doyle chided a path through the press of children with a throat-clearing *harrumph.* He thumbed the latch and a bell jangled as he swung wide the shop door and stood aside to allow Jean Leckie to enter. At that moment, one of the boys barged past, reached into the shop window, snatched a toy, and bolted.

"You young scoundrel!" Conan Doyle shouted impotently, but the boy was a blur of running arms and feet fast disappearing down the cobblestone street. "Stop!" He looked at his lady friend with concern. "That impudent tyke just pinched a toy right from under our noses."

A rumble from behind made Conan Doyle turn. A large trapdoor in the floor flung upward and footsteps thumped up a flight of wooden steps. The figure that ascended from the cellar had a long white beard that spilled down upon his chest. He wore half-moon spectacles balanced upon his nose and a tasseled and richly embroidered burgundy smoking cap upon his head, beneath which his long white hair was pulled back and braided into a ponytail. With his avuncular demeanor and stained canvas apron, he resembled an emaciated Father Christmas.

"Welcome! Welcome," said the man. "I am Jedidiah, owner of the emporium."

Conan Doyle was about to speak when a mournful whistle interrupted him. He looked for the source of the sound and saw a miniature steam locomotive running on a set of steel tracks set high on the walls. The train orbited the shop in a frenzy of reciprocating motion and then plunged into the maw of a papier-mâché tunnel and vanished.

"I must apologize, sir," Conan Doyle said. "We have inadvertently assisted a robbery. I was holding the door for the lady when a young guttersnipe snatched a toy from the display and took to his heels."

The shopkeeper, a man who appeared to be in his sixties, rumbled with good-natured laughter.

"Do not be concerned. I think I know the boy. He has been staring at that toy for days with the kind of hopeless longing only a poor child can manifest."

"But the lad is a thief! Should we not summon a constable?"

The older man shook his head dismissively. "There is no need. I did not become a toy maker seeking to become a rich man. I did so to make children happy."

"How wonderful!" Jean beamed, and Conan Doyle, who was still perturbed about encouraging theft in the young, swallowed what he was about to say. "Now see here," he said, drawing out his coin purse, "you must allow me to recompense you—"

The shopkeeper silenced him with a raised hand. "No, sir, that shall not be necessary. Perhaps if you find something to your fancy and make a purchase, that will help defray the loss." Jedidiah looked from Conan Doyle to Jean Leckie with a sparkle in his eye and an amused smile. "But I see you are a handsome young couple, come to shop for your children."

Conan Doyle blushed at the comment and quickly mumbled, "Actually, I was wondering if you could possibly mend this." He pried the windup drummer from his deep coat pocket. "It is my son's favorite toy and he is quite upset that it is broken."

"How unfortunate. Let me see what I can do." Jedidiah wiped his hands on his apron and took the toy. His tinkerer's hands, stained with oil that marked every crease, poked and probed and gave the key an exploratory twist. After a ruminating pause he frowned and shook his head. "I am familiar with this make of toys. Inexpensive, but rather shabbily made. They soon break—an unfortunate situation guaranteed to break a child's heart. He indicated the wares of his shop with a careless wave. "Everything in my shop is handmade by myself on the premises. Should a toy ever break, a customer may simply return it for free repair or replacement."

"Ah," Conan Doyle said. "So you cannot fix the toy? I had hoped . . . it is Kingsley's favorite."

Jedidiah raised a placating hand. "Do not give up hope so soon. Let me have a look inside."

The toy maker produced a small screwdriver from an apron pocket and prized loose the tabs holding together the tin body. A black ribbon of coil spring unspooled and dangled. "As you can see," Jedidiah noted, pointing to a gearwheel missing several teeth, "inferior gears. It has been overwound, stripping several teeth."

"I see. Beyond repair. Dash it. Perhaps I can find something to replace it."

"I cannot repair it," Jedidiah said, looking craftily over his glasses, "but I can rebuild it. Properly. I'll just take it to my workshop for a better look. Perhaps you and your pretty wife would care to browse while you wait?"

Both Conan Doyle and Jean Leckie squirmed a moment, embarrassed by the false presumption, but neither said anything to correct the mistake.

"Yes," Conan Doyle agreed. "That would be splendid."

The shopkeeper nodded. He left the counter and tromped down the steps into the glowing cave of his cellar workshop.

"Isn't it a dreamland?" Jean Leckie said, wandering the store, fondling toys hanging from the ceiling on cords and crowding the busy shelves. She touched a tinplate monkey in a red fez and it came to life, its arms winding forward and then snapping back as the monkey backflipped. The arms wound up again and the monkey backflipped a second time. "How funny!" she laughed.

Conan Doyle looked around, dazzled by the assortment. The shop displayed a few simple toys, such as stuffed bears, a maniacally smiling rocking horse, a few wooden swords and shields, but most everything was mechanical: windup, clockwork mechanisms of great ingenuity painted in colors to dazzle a child's eye. "I could never bring Kingsley in here," he remarked. "I should have to prise his hands off the counter to get him out!"

As Conan Doyle perused the shop, he found that it was much more than a simple toy store. It was also part museum and displayed a variety of wondrous mechanical contrivances. Then he glimpsed something hanging on the back wall that made his heart leap into his throat.

A steam motorcycle.

And a beautiful one at that. He had never seen such an advanced design. The motor was a compact unit streamlined into the fuel tank. Everything was beautifully wrought of painted steel and machined brass, all held together by shiny bolts. The motorcycle was fitted with a giant brass headlamp and two sculpted metal bucket seats, one for the rider and one for a pillion passenger. For a moment Conan Doyle was possessed by visions of swooping along a winding country lane on such a machine, gauntleted hands gripping the handlebars, cap on backward, eyes goggled against the rushing wind. And, of course, Miss Leckie would be seated pillion behind him, arms hugging about his waist, her long tresses tucked beneath a handsome bonnet, a silk scarf fluttering around her neck.

In all his life, he had never lusted so strongly after a material possession. He was at heart a Scotsman, cursed with the Caledonian habit of thrift. But, gripped by a mad impulse, he resolved on the spot to buy it—no matter what the expense. But then he noticed to his crushing disappointment a printed card affixed to the wall beside it: Display Only. Not for Sale.

"Blast!" he muttered as the bubble of his fantasy burst.

Meanwhile, Jean had wandered deeper in the shop, and now her musical voice carried from the far back reaches. "Oh, Arthur, you must come and see this!"

Conan Doyle followed her voice to the back of the shop. When he finally found her, she was staring at something that dropped his jaw with surprise.

Sitting behind a low cabinet was a coffee-skinned man in a costume of the exotic east: a plumed turban and a crimson robe trimmed with white rabbit. An inlaid chessboard took pride of place atop the cabinet before him, which had its all of its doors left wide open to display its many brassy cogwheels, pulleys, and mechanisms of diabolical complexity. Atop the chessboard were ivory chess pieces set out, ready for a game. The turbaned man, who on closer inspection, proved to be a simple wooden dummy, held a long-stemmed pipe in one hand. Conan Doyle recognized instantly what he was confronted with.

"Extraordinary! It is a replica of—"

"The Automaton Chess Player," Jean Leckie interjected before he could finish.

He looked at her, mouth agape. "You know of it?"

"Yes, Arthur. Although I am a *mere* woman I have a keen mind and am an active member of three lending libraries." She gave him a cutting look that softened into a playful smirk. "As I told you in the park, I have made a study of all things occult since I was a young girl. It is a replica of Wolfgang von Kempelen's mechanical chess player, one of the most famous automatons of all time. The original was built in 1789 to impress the Austrian court. Although many declared it a fake, no one could prove it so. The automaton defeated some of the greatest chess players of the day. It even defeated Napoleon. The original wound up in America where it was destroyed in a fire."

Conan Doyle bowed, hand on heart. "I apologize and happily stand corrected. Miss Leckie, your knowledge of the arcane is positively encyclopedic."

"Go on, Arthur," she said, nudging him with an encouraging look. "Try it. Let's see if the mind behind Sherlock Holmes can defeat a mere mechanical apparatus."

Conan Doyle vacillated, suddenly reluctant. "But I don't even know if it functions. Or how to turn it on. I don't see a switch anywhere."

"Try moving a piece and see what happens."

Conan Doyle cleared his throat, feeling slightly ridiculous, and also a little nervous should the device actually work and he be defeated in front of the lady. But he stepped forward gamely, studied the chessboard for a moment and then began with his usual opening, pushing his queen's pawn to queen 4. He drew his hand away and waited. Nothing happened. He turned to Miss Leckie. "I don't think it's work—"

He was interrupted by the ascending whine of mechanical gears. The figure of the Turk drew itself erect, the turbaned head lifted, and the eyes sprang open, glowing with an eerie inner light. The Turk's arm lifted the long pipe to his carved wooden lips, as if to take a puff, and then blew out a slender jet of steam. The left arm jerked, swept across the chessboard, hooked the black queen's pawn with its wooden fingers and pushed it forward, exactly matching Conan Doyle's opening gambit.

"Amazing!" Conan Doyle laughed. "It's powered by steam. I must have Oscar take a crack at this." He smiled and looked around for Miss Leckie, but she had vanished. Conan Doyle returned his attention to the automaton. He reasoned it must be a simple mechanical device—a series of gears mathematically determined to play one or possibly two game variations. Conan Doyle had been a bit of a chess prodigy while at Stonyhurst College. He had little doubt he could make short work of a clockwork cabinet full of gears and pulleys, a mechanism little more than an elaborate cuckoo clock. He stooped forward, placed his large index finger atop his rook's pawn, and pushed it forward to rook four. Jean would have a few minutes to explore the shop on her own.

This would not take long.

Miss Leckie had been drawn away by an object of great beauty and even greater notoriety. The Mutoscope resembled a metal snail set atop a trapezoidal stand. Painted in a gleaming cream and red paint scheme resplendent with whorls and flourishes, it was more than a beautiful object—it embodied the allure of the forbidden. Even though she was a well-bred young lady, Jean had heard of such devices and knew of their salacious reputation. Mutoscopes could be found in the arcades of every seaside pier in England, but she had never had chance to personally experience one.

The temptation proved irresistible.

She glanced about. Conan Doyle was busy battling the chess player. The toy maker was tinkering in his workshop. She had no audience. The elaborate gold script painted above the coin slot pleaded for only 1d. She rummaged a penny from her purse and dropped it in. The Mutoscope swallowed the coin with a *clunk*. Instantly, a light bulb glimmered to life. She leaned forward and pressed her forehead to the metal visor, peering in through the glass window.

The bulb glowed, illuminating a tranquil scene: a Scottish loch in early morning, its glassy surface mirroring the surrounding mountains. She gripped the crank handle with a gloved hand and began to turn. A succession of paper photographs peeled from beneath a brass finger and the scene animated to life. An open steamer sped across the loch. And then the scene changed to show a young blond lady of great beauty wading in the shallows. Jean Leckie felt a stab of disappointment. She had expected a scene in a harem, or a butler's eye pressed to a keyhole watching a lady in a state of undress, but the images seemed beautiful and natural and not at all lascivious. The young woman in the Mutoscope combed a long strand of blond hair from her face and turned to look behind her. A young child in a sailor's suit stood knee-deep in the water, clutching a windup toy boat—

A hand clamped over hers with surprising force and halted the crank's rotation. Startled, she pulled her face away from the glass to see Jedidiah looming at her side. His grip relented in its pressure, but he insistently drew her hand away.

"I must apologize," he said. "The machine is here for repairs. Should you turn the handle further, irreparable harm will result."

"Forgive me. I did not mean to—"

"It is nothing. A misunderstanding." He released her hand and straightened, forcing a smile. "I really must hang a sign upon the machine." He was standing very close and his gaze upon her grew vulpine. His head shook with a slight tremor. "But after all, who could resist touching such a beautiful thing?"

He must have realized that his gaze had devolved into something threatening, for he took a step back, and his demeanor became avuncular once again. "But I have something that will truly delight you." He turned and drew her along with a gesture. She timidly followed to a glass display cabinet. She looked inside and gasped.

A doll. But not just a doll: a miniature princess in a silk gown of royal blue. Atop her head a sparkling tiara of semiprecious stones.

"Oh," she gushed. "It is the most beautiful doll I have ever seen!"

"Yes," Jedidiah agreed. He smiled mischievously and slipped the cabinet's catch. After carefully drawing the doll from its crystal coffin, he placed it in her hands.

The little girl in Jean Leckie was enthralled. She had never owned a doll this lovely. This remarkable. This lifelike. As she tilted it upright, the eyes glided open revealing orbs of stunning blue flecked with gold—disconcertingly lifelike under the gaslight.

"She is beautiful is she not? My favorite creation."

"She is breathtaking," Jean said, and added impetuously, "I wish to buy her. You simply must sell her to me." She looked around. "And this also," she added, snatching up the backflipping monkey in his red fez.

"An excellent choice," Jedidiah purred. "Will the gentleman be paying?" He craned to look about the shop for Conan Doyle.

"No. I shall be paying. These are a gift for the children of my gentleman friend. I want it to be a surprise."

"A surprise, eh?" The shopkeeper smiled knowingly. "Everyone loves surprises and the gift of a wonderful toy earns the giver a special place in the heart of any child."

"Yes," she agreed. "I'm sure you are correct. She is the most beautiful doll I have ever seen. I should have so loved to have had her as a child."

"And she has a secret beneath her petticoats."

Her eyes widened slightly at the shocking suggestion.

Jedidiah chuckled at her concern. "A wonderful surprise," he said and urged her to explore with a gesture.

Jean was intrigued, but lifted the doll's skirts to find nothing but the rounded, sexless crotch of a toy.

"At the back."

When she turned the doll around she found a keyhole and, attached to the petticoats by a short blue ribbon, a shiny silver key.

"What does it do?" she asked, fingering the key.

"Wind it and see."

Intrigued, Jean Leckie slipped the key into the hole and wound the doll several times. When she released her grip, the key turned and a hidden music box trilled an enchanting series of silvery notes. It was a melody she recognized.

"I know this music. It is an aria. How wonderful!"

"Yes. She is a very special doll. I do hope she is destined for a little girl who will treasure her very much. Beautiful things must be treasured for always."

"I am certain she will be the pride of her collection." Jean handed him the doll and the mechanical monkey. She followed him to the shop counter where he found a sturdy box and nestled the toys inside. She drew out her calling card and handed it to him.

"Could you please have them delivered to this address in Blackheath, along with the bill?"

"Certainly, Madam," the toy man chuckled. He eased the card from between her slender fingers and tucked it in the breast pocket of his apron. Returning to his task, he tore off a sheet of brown paper from a roll, but then paused in his wrapping as if remembering something.

"But where has your gentleman got to after all this time?"

They found Conan Doyle transfixed before the Turkish Automaton. Most of his white pieces had been swept from the board and he was desperately juggling the position of his queen and king, dodging in and out of check.

The Turk patiently puffed at his long pipe, exhaled a wisp of steam and then slid his queen forward, pinning Conan Doyle's king inescapably.

"Checkmate, I think, sir," Jedidiah observed.

The author's shoulders slumped. He brushed at his moustache in agitation, then reached forward and solemnly toppled his king in surrender. "Beaten by a clockwork mechanism," he moaned in an exhausted voice and cast a sheepish look at Jean. "Of course, I haven't played in years."

"Of course not," she cooed, laying a reassuring hand on his arm.

"And playing against oneself hardly counts as practice."

"Hardly at all."

Conan Doyle caught her mocking tone and had to laugh at himself. He noticed Jedidiah hovering. "Well? Can you fix my boy's soldier?"

"Of course," Jedidiah reassured. "The spring is repairable but some of the gears are broken and I shall have to make new ones."

"Ah, I see—"

"But do not worry. When Jedidiah has repaired your boy's soldier with new gears, he will never break again. Your son will hand down the toy to his son."

"Topping! When might I pick it up?"

"The day after tomorrow?"

Conan Doyle pulled a calling card from an inside pocket and

handed it to the toy maker. "Please send the bill to my home address. I should be able to pop in to pick it up sometime this week."

Jedidiah accepted the card and bowed slightly. A violent tremor shook his head, but his smile remained fixed.

A *touch of palsy*, Conan Doyle quickly diagnosed.

"Very good sir. A pleasant day to you and your lady and thank you for stopping in." Jedidiah escorted them to the door and held it open as they left amid smiles and nods.

In the street outside, although it was barely four-thirty, the sky was a dark swirl of fog. Perched atop his ladder, a lamplighter was kindling a nearby streetlamp to life. Conan Doyle looked doubtfully at the sky and checked his pocket watch.

"Is something the matter?" she asked.

"It's practically dark already."

Jean Leckie's face fell. "And so our wonderful day together is nearly over?"

Conan Doyle thought a moment and said, "No, I was about to say we are late for afternoon tea." He smiled. "But perfectly on time for supper at The Savoy."

"Really? Supper at The Savoy? How wonderful!"

Conan Doyle reached in his top pocket and drew out the tickets Wilde had given him. "And then I have two tickets for Oscar's latest play—unless you wish me to convey you home after supper?"

She clapped her hands together and trilled with delight, "Oh, I should *love* to visit the theater!"

"Yes, I believe they are rather good tickets. Next to the royal box. One of the perks of knowing the playwright." He added in a low mutter, "I suppose there had to be *some* advantage. Wait here, I'll just sort out a cab."

Conan Doyle wandered off to look for a hansom, leaving Jean Leckie to loiter in the circle of light beneath the gas lamp. The lamplighter, having finished, closed the glass shade, slid down his ladder, then tucked it over his arm and moved on to light the next.

Inside the Emporium, Jedidiah turned over the sign in the shop door from OPEN to CLOSED and stood watching Jean Leckie through the glass. From behind came a whish of gears as the Turkish Automaton stirred to life. The glowing eyes sprang open, the turbaned head swiveled. It breathed a jet of steam and then the arm swung over and tapped three times on the chessboard with the tip of his pipe. Jedidiah ignored it and drew the two calling cards from his apron pocket. He scanned the addresses on each, first Conan Doyle's home in Surrey, and then Miss Leckie's in Blackheath. He smiled to himself.

Outside, in the street, Jean Leckie stood alone, marooned within a halo of amber light. A drunken swell staggered past, white silk scarf fluttering loose, top hat askew. He must have said something to her, something disrespectful, because she dropped her head and looked away. Now, she was visibly nervous, as any young gentlewoman would be, abandoned on her own in the gathering gloom. The street dimmed perceptibly as dusk mixed with yellow fog and turned the light a murky green. The daily fogs drove most Londoners indoors early, and cabbies without fares quit for their homes. It was not surprising that Conan Doyle was having difficulty locating a hansom.

Jedidiah remained at the window, watching Jean Leckie with growing interest. "You are as lovely as any doll I have ever created," he breathed aloud. His head tremored violently.

Outside, Conan Doyle had returned with a hansom and was helping Miss Leckie step aboard.

The automaton hissed again, releasing a coiling tendril of steam into the air. The wooden hand lifted and tapped the pipe three times.

"Be patient, Otto," the shopkeeper called over his shoulder. "I shall feed you in a moment."

CHAPTER 10

A WILDE NIGHT AT THE THEATER

Conan Doyle and Miss Leckie left The Savoy shortly after six, filled with caviar, champagne, and bonhomie. Conan Doyle ordered a four-wheeler—expense be-damned—to whisk them to the Haymarket Theatre where Wilde's *An Ideal Husband*, was in its third week.

London traffic was unusually light, the fog having driven indoors all those who were not of the leisure class to cough and wheeze in the privacy of their own parlors. When the two acquaintances alighted from the carriage in front of the theater, they found a cadre of doormen and ushers who had been positioned bearing lighted torches and lanterns to guide theatergoers and burn off the fog swirling about the marquee.

It was the Scottish doctor's fondest ambition to impress his guest, and the tickets Wilde had supplied him with succeeded winningly. From the moment he flashed the box tickets to the second they were escorted to their seats, his companion chattered excitedly about the gleaming marble columns, the glittering gilt cherubs, the plush red velvet seats, and the salubrious ambience of luxury and genteel prosperity.

As they took their seats next to the royal box, a drumroll sounded and an offstage voice announced: "Please be upstanding for his Royal Highness, the Prince of Wales."

A hubbub of anticipation rippled through the audience as a door at the back of the royal box opened and three figures stepped through. First came the Prince of Wales, at fifty-six prematurely old and balding, the once-dashing figure grown corpulent, larded with decades of indulgence. On his arm, like a gaudy decoration, was Daisy Greville, Countess of Warwick, a lady similar in age to Miss Leckie. Tonight, she was dressed in a stunning gown of champagne-colored silk; her waspish, tight-corseted waist pushing up a pneumatic bosom that preceded her into the box like twin spinnakers ballooned by a gale. She wore her long chestnut curls swept up and pinned into place by a tiara sparkling with rubies and emeralds—undoubtedly a token from her royal escort.

The Prince of Wales, elegant in a black evening suit with a red sash slashing from shoulder to hip, stepped to the railing of his box and swept the audience below with a regal look, removing the fat cigar lodged in the corner of his mouth just long enough to acknowledge their applause with an imperious wave. It was then that the prince noticed his neighbors in the adjoining box. His eyes registered Conan Doyle with obvious recognition, and then lavished Miss Leckie with a lascivious gaze, up and down, brazenly assessing her attributes—and this despite the fact that he already had a companion for the evening. To Conan Doyle's mortification, the prince flashed him a jaunty wink and a "boy's club" smile, as if to say *well, done, old fellow!*

The Scottish author blanched, imagining that everyone in the theater must be thinking the same thing. Teeth clenched, he acknowledged the royal presence with a cursory bow while Jean Leckie curtsied deeply.

The third guest in the Royal Box, whom Conan Doyle had at first taken to be a tall young woman, was in fact a slender young man with a pallid complexion, narrow shoulders, and an outrageous mane of red hair that spilled down upon his shoulders in a cascade of fiery copper curls. He was dressed operatically in a long black cape and fiery red cravat. A medallion dangled around his neck on a leather cord. With an unsettling sense of déjà vu, Conan Doyle noticed that the medal was embossed with a pentagram. The youth met and held Conan Doyle's gaze with a mocking smirk.

Following protocol, the prince took his seat first, the countess second and then the youth took the seat on the prince's right hand, flinging his long tresses behind his shoulders with a toss of the head.

"My goodness!" Miss Leckie gushed in a whisper. "The Prince of Wales, so close I could reach out and touch him. I am quite giddy!"

Conan Doyle indulged her with a smile, but said nothing, unwilling to allow his low opinion of the *Heir Apparent* to stifle his companion's excitement.

The audience resumed their seats. After a brief delay, the curtains at one end of the stage flirted open and Oscar Wilde stepped out. He was immaculately dressed in a black evening suit and white cotton gloves, a green carnation pinned to his lapel. Conan Doyle was dismayed to see that Wilde was smoking one of his aromatic cigarettes (which would seem rude on a normal occasion and positively impudent in the presence of royalty). He sauntered to center stage, his lone footsteps echoing in the anticipatory silence. Here he paused, drew deeply from his cigarette, exhaled languidly, and finally addressed the crowd.

"Unaccustomed as I am to being outshone, tonight our performance is graced by the presence of royalty." He turned and bowed deeply to the royal box. "And so I find the meager spark of my wit eclipsed by the full sun of majesty." He began to clap his gloved hands together and the audience joined in, surging to their feet and shouting "Huzzahs!"

The prince rode the surf of applause a moment longer before standing and settling the audience with a gesture, and then spoke in his fruity voice, "Thank you Mister Wilde for your kind comments, but we have all come to be dazzled by *your* wit and wisdom. On this foul and foggy night, we shall require your genius to burn its brightest, so that it may light our way home."

The audience roared with laughter at the prince matching wits with Oscar Wilde, who knew when to let a weaker opponent win and merely bowed and joined in the applause.

"Well played, Oscar," Conan Doyle muttered to himself.

The playwright quit the stage. The play began and soon the theater shook with laughter. But throughout the performance, Conan Doyle noticed that his companion was paying more attention to the prince than to Wilde's witty dialogue, and suffered the pangs of jealously.

But by the end of the first act, it was becoming clear that the fog was creeping into the playhouse through every crack and crevice. In the open space before the proscenium arch, a misty haze congealed and thickened, dimming the chandeliers and causing theatergoers to look about themselves nervously. Conan Doyle knew it was only fog, but at any moment expected to hear panicked cries of "fire." By degrees the fog thickened from distraction to nuisance and murmurs began to rumble when the drifting grayness became so opaque as to render the actors onstage as little more than shadow puppets.

The Prince of Wales suddenly stood up and left his box, followed by the countess and his youthful companion. A rising hubbub from worried theatergoers soon drowned out the actors' voices, and with the tie between audience and actors severed, the illusion of theater collapsed. Theatergoers became aware they were just a herd of people crowded into a large and very foggy room. People began leaving—first in ones and twos, and then whole aisles emptied and scurried for the doors.

The curtains whished shut in the middle of the action. The remaining audience members began to rise from their seats. Some of the ladies uttered tones of alarm. Just as the moment teetered upon the precipice of panic, a lone figure in a black evening suit strode out into the footlights and stood at center stage.

Oscar Wilde.

"Ladies and Gentlemen," he said, raising his arms for attention.

"It appears the fog has succeeded where my worst critics have failed: they have silenced the voice of Oscar Wilde."

A welcome titter of laughter rippled through the audience, and many began to retake their seats.

"As a man of the theater, it gives me great joy to fill the seats of a playhouse. Likewise, it causes me great pain to see them emptied. However, even I must admit defeat in the face of nature's intrusion, and so I am sad to announce that tonight's performance must end prematurely. Should you wish a refund, return your tickets to the ticketing booth. However, if you wish to see true genius, retain your ticket stubs and they will be honored at a future, hopefully, less inclement date. I thank you all."

Wilde bowed and strolled offstage to broken applause. But Conan Doyle noticed the stifled rage in his stiff posture.

"How unfortunate," Miss Leckie said, disappointment dragging down the edges of her words. "I was so enjoying myself."

"Fear not," Conan Doyle said, "there will be other performances. Many, I hope."

She wrung his heart with an adorable pout. "I am sure there will, but I did not want our wonderful evening to end."

"But it need not end. There will be a reception for the Prince of Wales. The stage will be cleared and a buffet table laid out. Champagne. Canapés. Many delicacies. I could introduce you to my friend, Oscar. Perhaps even the prince."

At his words she gasped and gripped his hand warmly.

* * *

When Conan Doyle and Jean Leckie wandered backstage looking for Wilde, a sumptuous table groaning with a celebratory feast had been laid out on the stage. The actors and stagehands stood in a receiving line, bowing and curtseying as the theater manager presented each in turn to the prince and countess. (The prince's young shadow hung back and did not shake any hands.)

However, Conan Doyle was perturbed to find that the playwright himself was inexplicably absent.

The introductions over, the theater manager conducted the royals to the buffet table, where he poured each a glass of champagne. The Prince of Wales had just taken his first sip when he spotted the pair loitering in the wings. He gave the slightest nod of his head, which Conan Doyle took as a command to come forward. Reluctantly, he led Miss Leckie onto the stage to meet the heir to the throne.

"Doctor Doyle," the prince said. "So good to meet you again."

"Your Highness," Conan Doyle said, bowing and shaking the prince's hand, clammy even through his cotton gloves.

"I have not read one of your Sherlock Holmes tales of late," the prince continued. "When can we expect the next installment?"

Conan Doyle squirmed, momentarily at a loss. Apparently the prince did not know that the Scottish author had killed off his consulting detective in "The Adventure of the Final Problem," a move that sent shockwaves through the nation and enraged legions of Holmes fans.

"Ah . . . soon, Your Highness," he lied, "quite soon."

"And who is this ravishing beauty?" the Prince of Wales asked, molesting Jean Leckie with his gaze.

"May I introduce Miss Jean Leckie, a fellow member of the Society for Psychical Research."

"Ah, yes. Séances? Spooks? Goings on in the dark, eh?" The prince turned and addressed his young companion. "See, Rufie, you're not the only one to dabble in the dark side."

Wishing to derail this line of conversation, Conan Doyle quickly interjected, "I had understood that you were traveling abroad, sir?"

"Did you, indeed?" The look of surprise on the prince's face told Conan Doyle that he had just blundered out a state secret. "And how the devil did you come by that notion?"

Conan Doyle groped for a safe rejoinder. "I believe I read it in *The Times*."

Prince Edward shook his head bad temperedly. "There are those in the palace who urge me to journey abroad, what with the damned nihilists setting off bombs everywhere. I, however, prefer to stay in London amongst my friends."

The prince noticed Miss Leckie eyeing his youthful companion. He turned and slipped a thick arm around the younger man's narrow shoulders, drawing him forward. "This is my cousin, Rufus DeVayne, the Marquess of Gravistock. He suffers from a *nervous* disposition, so his doctors packed him off to the countryside to rest. We had to go down and rescue him. Isn't that right, Rufie?"

The marquess tossed his red curls in a bashful nod and gave the meagerest hint of a smile.

The prince went on: "But now we're off to a party at the Gravistock family seat to celebrate his freedom." A thought struck the prince. "Doctor Doyle, would you and your young lady friend care to join us?" He winked suggestively. "I promise an evening to remember."

Miss Leckie gave Conan Doyle's bicep an importuning squeeze, but he demurred, saying, "Thank you, but I must humbly decline. I need to ensure that the young lady returns home safely to her parents before the fog maroons us all."

"Ah, I see. Pity." The prince suddenly seemed to notice an absence and said, "But where is your friend, Mister Wilde? I wanted to congratulate him on the play. Funny stuff—what we saw of it. Where has the fellow got to?"

"I am afraid he is somewhat indisposed," Conan Doyle lied. "He suffers from a rheumatic chest. The fog. You understand."

The prince's baffled expression revealed that he didn't, but the answer seemed to placate him. "Well then, we must be off. Revels await. So pleasant to meet you again, Doctor Doyle"—he lusted after Miss Leckie with one last lecherous look—"and your exquisite young lady."

The prince and countess moved away, but the marquess lingered a moment.

"I, too, had longed to meet Mister Wilde," the youth said in his high-pitched, ethereal voice. His face was narrow, what Conan Doyle would have described as *weasely.* "I consider myself his greatest admirer. Do pass along my regards."

"I most certainly shall," agreed Conan Doyle. He bowed to the marquess, who turned and followed the retreating back of the Prince of Wales. At that instant it struck Conan Doyle that the young man had never once tossed the slightest glance the way of Miss Leckie, as if she, a beautiful and vivacious woman, were invisible. It was nothing he could verbalize but he felt a prickling in his guts. There was something . . . unsavory about the marquess, and Conan Doyle determined he would not say a word about the young man to Wilde.

"But where is your friend?" Miss Leckie asked. "I had so been looking forward to meeting the notorious Oscar Wilde."

"Yes, where indeed?" Conan Doyle echoed. "He has snubbed the Prince of Wales in a most unforgivable fashion." He linked arms with Miss Leckie. "Come, let us see if we can run the rapscallion to ground."

* * *

Conan Doyle found Wilde sulking in a dressing room, slouched in a chair beside a battered dressing table, black tie unraveled about his neck, shoulders slumped. The bottle of Perrier-Jouët chilling in an ice bucket remained inexplicably unopened. Instead, a half-empty bottle of whiskey sat by Wilde's elbow, and he was diligently working to pour the remainder down his gullet.

"Oscar! You're drinking whiskey instead of your usual champagne?"

The Irishman raised a tumbler to his lips, quaffed deeply, and paused to catch his breath before remarking morosely, "Champagne is for a celebration. Whiskey is the appropriate libation for a wake."

"Cheer up, old man. Nothing can be helped. It's the fault of the fog."

Wilde tossed back his whiskey, grimaced, and gurgled himself two fingers more. "Fog? I have seen London fogs before. This is not a normal fog—it is an amorphous beast possessed of an evil sentience.

And for some reason it hates Oscar Wilde and is determined to ruin him." He sighed fretfully, shaking his auburn waves. "The box office receipts are pitiful and now a royal performance reduced to a shambles. What worse can happen?"

"Don't be so glum. You cannot control the weather. I'm sure the prince will return on a more clement day."

"It's not just the lost performances. Much as it pains me to be reduced to the role of a grubby accountant tallying piles of pounds and pennies, there are financial repercussions to consider. Do not forget, although the performances are canceled and the public refunded their money, actors and sceneshifters must still be paid. The theater rent ticks on. There are many outheld hands grasping to be paid and most of them are currently rifling through my pockets."

Conan Doyle cleared his throat. "If you're temporarily short of funds, I am doing quite well at the present time and would be happy to lend—"

Wilde raised a hand to silence his friend before he could say more. "Your kindness is noted and appreciated, Arthur, but I would sooner borrow money from my very worst enemy than from my very best friend. For nothing curdles a friendship faster than indebtedness. I might obtain the loan of lucre from any quarter, but where can I obtain friendship and loyalty?"

"You do live rather extravagantly. Perhaps if you tightened your purse strings."

Wilde recoiled as if from a blow.

"Extravagant? *Moi?*" he said, pouring himself another glass of whiskey from the open bottle. Conan Doyle eyed the label—it was a top-drawer Scots whiskey he personally could not afford to drink.

"I am perfectly at ease with the notion of sacrifice, it's giving things up that I cannot abide."

Conan Doyle shifted his feet and said, "I, ah . . . I have an acquaintance with me. A friend. The young lady I told you of: Miss Jean Leckie. She is waiting outside. My friend had rather been hoping to meet the famous Oscar Wilde. However, if you are indisposed, I suppose I must disappoint her."

Instantly, the scowling, fretting man vanished. The large Irishman rose from his chair. Shot his cuffs. Retied his tie. Then, like a cape, he drew upon his shoulders the persona of Oscar Wilde.

"Forgive my rudeness, Arthur." He seized the champagne bottle, loosened the cork with a twist, and pulled it from the ice bucket. "Pray, bring your friend before me, and I shall give her an audience to be remembered."

As Conan Doyle escorted Miss Jean Leckie into the room, Wilde fired the champagne cork with a flick of his thumb. Bubbly fountained and splashed upon the floor.

"Greetings and salutations, Miss Leckie." Wilde bowed and threw her a *salaam* gesture with his free hand. "Would you do me the considerable honor of joining us in a libation?" He charged three waiting champagne flutes and presented one to her. "Friends of Arthur's must always be greeted with a glass of bubbly, a bow, and kiss upon the cheek." Wilde moved forward and kissed her lightly on both cheeks, in the continental style. Jean Leckie cooed with delight, eyes sparkling brighter than the bubbles effervescing in her champagne flute.

"I offer a toast," Wilde said, raising his glass.

"A toast to what?" asked Conan Doyle.

The Irishman regarded him with a raised eyebrow, as if he were the slow child in the class. "Why, to Oscar Wilde, who else? The luckiest man I know."

"Lucky? Two seconds ago, you were quite in the dumps."

"Yes, but that was two seconds ago. What are you, Arthur, an historian? For Oscar Wilde, there is only the present moment. No, I give you a toast to the most fortunate fellow I know: Oscar Wilde, for a man who has such wonderful friends must always count himself lucky."

The three chinked glasses and said together, "Cheers!"

CHAPTER 11

꾱

AN UNHOLY RESURRECTION

An underground cellar, windowless and dark. The cobblestone walls and arched brick ceiling hold the dank-earth chill of the subterranean. The space is bare apart from a huddle of tables strewn with beakers, surgical instruments, a bone doctor's collection of amputation saws and scalpels. On a second table, glass flasks of colored liquids warm on alcohol burners, chemicals bubble in retorts. A third table holds a brassy scatter of mechanical gears, tiny pistons, flywheels. Dominating the space is a single piece of hideous furniture: a restraining chair built of huge timbers. A human figure sits pinioned in the chair.

Cold. Inert. Dead.

Weirdly, the corpse is strapped in place by iron bands at the ankles, the wrists, the forearms. A heavy metal band encircles the chest while a thinner strap pinions the head to the chair back.

A sheet of frosted glass hangs behind the chair, and now two hideous demons step from behind. They hover over the immobile corpse: their eyes glassy disks, mouths squirming with dangling proboscises. Although no, not demons, but men in rubber devil masks, the kind that might be obtained from theatrical costumers, modified to accept glass lenses and rubber hoses fitted with breathing filters. They lean, heads together, and confer in muffled voices.

"Is it ready?"

"Yes."

"Did you inject the adrenaline?"

"Of course."

"Are you certain? You did not forget this time?"

"The injection *was* given."

"What about the damage? The bullet holes?"

"All repaired. I patched the torn arteries with veins stripped from an ox."

"And the blood?"

"Replaced."

"All eight pints?"

"Of course."

"Where did you obtain so much blood?"

"A patient in the infirmary died."

"Died of what?"

"Lack of blood."

A dark laugh.

"Very well, then, let the reanimation begin."

The taller demon hovers over the corpse. Hands with long, thin fingers, supple in kid gloves, tear open the dead man's shirt (which, like the rag-bin trousers and scuff-toed boots, are beggar's offcasts) revealing a chest that has been surgically violated postmortem—a rectangular opening sawed into the sternum and ribs so that a shiny brass box could be inserted into the chest cavity. The surgery is recent and done without the care shown to a living patient, for the enormous sutures (made with a sailmaker's needle and thread) are angry red and rusty with blood.

The gloved hand slides a finger along the brassy surface of the metal box, searching for and finding a shallow indent. A finger depresses and a metal chute springs open. The other hand brings forward a smoked glass jar and pours in a trickle of white pellets.

"The fuel?"

"Calcium carbide pellets. They react with the water in the reservoir to produce acetylene, a combustible gas."

The hand sets the jar aside on a nearby bench, snaps shut the metal chute, and then depresses a metal plunger. Inside, a steel striker scratches across flint and sparks ignite the acetylene gas with a dull *whumph*. A translucent mica window pulses with an eerie blue flame.

"And now?"

"Now, it is a matter of moments before we achieve the required steam pressure."

There is a rising rumble and hiss of water bubbling to a boil. A pressure gauge is set flush into the face of the metal chest plate and now the needle sweeps across the dial as steam pressure builds and peaks, the needle trembling just shy of the red warning zone. Inside the metal box, pistons rise and fall, tiny flywheels spin, and a sound fills the underground space: *wisssshthump . . . wissssssshthump . . . wisssssssshthump. . . .*

The second figure begins to fumble at the straps holding its mask in place.

"What are you doing!"

"This mask . . . cannot breathe!"

"Stop! You must not remove it. When the creature awakens it will imprint on the first human face it sees. It must not be yours!"

The masked figure hesitates, relents, drops its hands.

Heated blood begins to pump through cold, inanimate flesh. *Wisssshthump . . . wissssssshthump . . . wisssssssshthump. . . .*

The gloved hands hurry to refasten the buttons of the ragged shirt, and both masked figures retreat behind the opaque glass.

Suddenly the body tremors. The chest inflates in a deep drawing in of breath. The head lifts on its thick pillar of neck. The crusted eyes startle open. Wide. Staring. Pupils pinpricked. The whites are a sickly bright yellow.

The head strains against the band clamping it in place, whipcord veins in the neck and forehead engorge and throb dangerously, muscles knot and bunch as the mouth opens and a deafening cry rips out.

"AAAAAAAAAAAAAAAAAAAHHHHHHHHHHHHHIIIIIIIII
EEEEEEEEEEEIIIIIIIIIEEEEEEeeeeeeeeiiiiiiiiiieeeeeeeeeee-
aaaaaaaaaaaaaaaaaaaaaaaah!"

The scream finally dwindles when no air remains in the lungs to push it out.

"Why do they always scream?"

"Because their last memory is of the drop. The rope. The terrible pain and the flash of light behind the eyes as the soul is ripped from its mortal frame."

"So it has no soul?"

"None. It is nothing. It feels nothing. The human spark has fled. What remains is but a puppet of meat and flesh *we* have reanimated. The higher brain functions are the first to die: Memory. Personality. Morality. Only the lower functions remain. The animal drives. It feels no hunger. No pain. No pity. No remorse. It is something for us to train. To mold. Something malleable. Something biddable."

In the hulking chair, the resurrected corpse begins to stir. The muscles ripple and flex, limbs straining against the metal bonds. The slavering mouth opens and a second howl of rage roars out: *Aaaiiiiieeeeeeaaaaah!*

"It is no longer human. Less than a beast. It is a creature. A monster. But it is *our* monster. The mechanical heart pumps four times faster than a human's. The blood pressure is tripled, giving it enormous strength. Muscles like iron bars. It possesses no more than a splinter of intellect. The immense pressure in the brain is what feeds its terrible anger. Its mind is little more than a retort bubbling with hatred and rage. Now we shall give it something to focus that rage upon."

The gloved hand reaches toward a magic lantern set on a nearby table and presses a slide in.

A glowing image splashes upon the large screen immediately in front of the restraining chair.

The taller demon fumbles a speaking tube to its mouth. When it speaks the voice passes through tubes into resonating chambers and emerges from gramophone bells set on either side of the chair. Amplified. Booming. The voice of an angry god.

"You are in purgatory. Neither dead nor alive, but in a place where you suffer for the sins committed in life."

The monster writhes in the restraining chair. Rips a mournful howl.

The second demon leans close and mutters, "Are you sure nothing of the human remains? It sounds . . . wounded. Like a tortured man in despair."

"Nothing human remains. It is a machine. A flesh automaton."

A second slide pushes in to replace the first and the screen burns with the image of a portly gentleman in a fine top hat and suit. He is looking into the camera and smiling a smug, self-satisfied smile.

"This is Tarquin Hogg. Tarquin Hogg is the reason for your death. Tarquin Hogg is the reason your soul is bound in purgatory. You must find Tarquin Hogg. You must destroy him. Smash him. Only then will you be free. Only then will your soul be released from its prison of flesh."

The thing in the chair begins a growl that ends in a spray of spittle. It thrashes violently, straining against its iron bonds with such force that the massive chair creaks and groans, threatening to tear apart.

One of the demons depresses a lever at the back of the chair with the toe of a polished shoe. The metal bands caging the beast snap open. A gloved hand jerks a lever. At the far end of the cellar, an iron-banded door flings open.

Outside, the night seethes with vaporous gray.

Released, the thing in the chair rises up on the trembling pillars of its legs. The gory head pivots as the waiting darkness draws its yellow-eyed gaze. It takes one lumbering step and then another, jerkily locomoting across the room. Then it clumsies up a short flight of stone steps. A broad shoulder caroms off the doorframe as it stumbles across the threshold and outside. Here it pauses to look up at a sky hidden behind a choking blanket of yellow-green fog. The grizzled head turns this way and that, as if sensing currents of subtle energies crackling in the air. Then the thing that had once been Charlie Higginbotham lumbers away and vanishes into the smoky night.

The gloved hand yanks a lever and the iron door bangs shut, cutting loose a surge of cold air that swirls about the cellar, setting the gas jets ajitter. The demons step from behind the cover of the glass screen.

"It is done."

"But how can the creature find its way? How can it know where Tarquin Hogg is?"

"It is a thing neither dead nor alive, trapped between this world and the next. It senses the living, wherever they are, and tracks them unerringly. It is untiring. Indefatigable. Once set upon a target it cannot be recalled until its task is finished. It does not know hunger. It does not sense the rain. The cold. It feels no pain. No pity. No remorse. It is unkillable. Tarquin Hogg's death is irrevocable."

CHAPTER 12

A WONDERFUL EVENING ENDS HORRIBLY

Conan Doyle and Jean Leckie emerged from the Haymarket Theatre to discover that the fog had grown ponderously dense, so much so that the usher's torches stained the fog with a seething crimson glare that made the theatergoers waiting for carriages and cabs appear like well-dressed citizens queuing to enter Hell. Conan Doyle had thought ahead to retain the four-wheeler for the entire evening, and now it drew up at the curb and he escorted Miss Leckie toward it, already practicing what he should say as he bid her good night. The coachman dismounted and held the carriage door.

"I am so sorry the evening proved a disappointment—"

"Heavens, no!" she interrupted. "I have had the most wonderful day of my life! Feeding the swans in Hyde Park. Shopping for toys at the Emporium. Attending the theater and then meeting the Prince of Wales and your friend Oscar Wilde—all on the same day! I am certain I shall not sleep at all tonight."

"I find that a glass of warm milk often helps to—"

She interrupted him with a laugh and took both his large hands in hers.

"But I *don't* want to sleep. I want to remember every last detail." Her smile took on a special quality. "But mostly, I want to think of a dashing and handsome man I have become good friends with." She suddenly bounced up on the balls of her feet and bussed him on the cheek. It was a quick peck. Quite chaste. The kiss of familiar friends.

But it was a kiss that knocked him dizzy.

Conan Doyle watched, rapt, as the young woman climbed into the carriage. She wrung his heart with a final smile and then pulled her skirts clear as the driver closed the carriage door. He suddenly realized he still did not know her address and frantically rapped on the glass. She lowered the window and looked at him inquisitively.

"Have you a calling card?"

She searched in her purse and handed him a card. Even the calligraphied script was elegantly feminine. He smiled and doffed his hat to her.

"Where to, sir?" the driver asked.

"Blackheath," Conan Doyle said, and read aloud from the card: "Number 34 Loxley Avenue."

"Be sure not to lose it," she chided playfully.

"I shall guard it with my life."

The cabbie shook the reins and the carriage lumbered away. She called out "au revoir" and left him with a wave before drawing up the window glass.

Conan Doyle slipped the precious calling card into his breast pocket and patted it reassuringly. The day that had begun so badly was ending on a note of triumph. He noticed Wilde's waiting carriage and strode toward it. Vaguely he registered two large men in bowler hats sauntering toward him, but his mind was bounding in the fields of happiness and the cold hard pavement felt as if he were walking on cushions.

The men parted to pass around him, when OOOF! One of them stumbled into him; at the same moment he felt a blow in the kidneys that drove the wind from his lungs. Stunned, he staggered to keep his footing and threw a shocked look behind at their retreating backs. At that moment, one turned and flashed him a cheeky grin. As they marched shoulder-to-shoulder into the wall of scarlet-tinged fog, he recognized the vaudevillian bowler hats and the long black rain-coats.

Cypher's men.

Was this a less-than-subtle warning that he was being watched? It was an unwelcome end to what had been a wonderful evening, but Conan Doyle shook it off and readjusted his dress as he walked to the waiting carriage.

"I saw that," Wilde said, as Conan Doyle climbed into the carriage and slumped into the seat opposite.

"Saw what?"

"Those two clumsy oafs who collided with you. At first I thought they merely wished to dance, but then I realized my mistake: Arthur Conan Doyle does not dance. You should have informed them your ticket was full."

"Just a couple of drunken swells." He did not want to get involved in a discussion that could lead to revealing his adventure with Cypher.

"I also watched you bid good night to the ravishing Miss Leckie. And I saw the kiss."

"What? Oh, that? Just a friendly peck."

"*Very* friendly. My wife, Constance, no longer kisses me with such ardor." Wilde tapped on the ceiling and called out, "Home to the Albemarle, Gibson."

As the carriage jolted away, Conan Doyle said, "What do you mean about Constance? And why are you always at your club? Why are you not living at Tite Street? Are you two having . . . *difficulties?*"

"No difficulty at all. The simple truth is that I am no longer in love with my wife . . ." Wilde interrupted himself to spark a lucifer and ignite a Turkish cigarette. ". . . and the indifference is recipro-cated."

Conan Doyle's scalp prickled with disbelief. "But you cannot be serious, Oscar. What about your marriage?"

Wilde chuckled ironically.

"What about your sacred vows?"

Wilde chuckled louder. "When it comes to matrimony, there are two types of people: those it is suited to and those it is not; unfortunately, it is the latter who insist on getting married."

"But Constance is a great beauty. An adoring wife. A wonderful mother to your two strapping boys."

"All true. Nonetheless, I feel nothing for her anymore. When Constance and I married we agreed to try matrimony for seven years. We have been ball and chain these thirteen years now. Six more than our original bargain. We remain very fond of one another, but our marriage has run its course. To continue the pretense would be dishonest. And Oscar Wilde abhors dishonesty."

His friend's offhand confession stunned the Scotsman into momentary silence. Finally he spoke up and asked, "But what about your children? What of Vyvyan and Cyril?"

Wilde released a tortured sigh. "Ah yes, children, the barbed wire that binds a man and woman together at the heart."

"No, you cannot divorce Constance. It would be the ruin of you."

But the fact that Wilde could voice such outrageous things out loud set Conan Doyle's mind reeling with giddy possibilities.

Wilde gestured with his lit cigarette as he spoke. "Of course, Constance will keep Tite Street as her domicile and the children will remain with her. I shall visit as regularly as I am able. In truth, I suspect they will notice little difference."

"But what about appearances? What will people think?"

"I have no doubt people will be scandalized. The Great British Public is never truly happy unless it has a scandal to gossip about. But society and appearances can go hang. Society does not care a jot for my happiness."

Conan Doyle sat in stunned silence, heart skipping, brain bubbling over with thoughts he could no longer suppress. He had great affection for his wife. He could never abandon Touie, no matter what. But for years they had lived more like brother and sister. He was a physical man and longed for passion and the sensual pleasures of romance. He could, as many gentlemen did, visit one of the high-class "introduction" houses scattered about London. Touie had as much as given her permission, albeit obliquely. However, as a physician, Conan Doyle worried too much about the ravages of syphilis to risk it. But now, Wilde's confession seemed to give him tacit approval to seek a paramour. What if he pursued happiness with Jean Leckie—discreetly? Would society condemn him for it? Could he ever be like Oscar? Could he not care what the world thought of him?

Wilde used the opportunity to light up an opium-tipped cigarette. He lowered the window to toss the match out, allowing a chill tendril of fog to snake in through the open window and coil above their heads like a question mark. With his next breath, he blew it to atoms by exhaling a stream of his own narcotic fog.

Conan Doyle's brooding suddenly erupted in an outburst of honesty, things he had not allowed himself up until now to say aloud, to even think. "I, too, have something to share. I confess I find myself embroiled in the moral crisis of a lifetime."

Wilde sniffed at the comment. "Moral crisis? I suffer those daily. But please, do go on, it sounds so much more interesting than what I was about to say."

"I'm sure you can guess what I hint at."

"The pulchritudinous Miss Leckie?"

Conan Doyle nodded grimly.

"But I do not see the cause of your dilemma."

"Although I have only known Jean scarcely two days, she has given me certain signs of encouragement—I think you know what I mean—and I believe that something could well come of it."

"I am listening."

"You know that Touie has had the consumption for years. By now the disease is far advanced. Every morning I am relieved to awaken and find that she still draws breath . . ." He trailed off as his throat began to constrict. He swallowed his sorrow and continued. "I know the inevitable will happen. Perhaps soon. Perhaps not so soon. But what am I to do? I made a vow on our wedding day and I must remain true to that vow. And yet I have feelings for Miss Leckie. Powerful feelings. She is possessed of great beauty and a keen intellect. Jean is the type of woman one is lucky to encounter once in a lifetime. But I am morally forbidden from pressing my suit. What am I to do, Oscar? I feel as though my soul is torn apart."

His friend remained sequestered behind the flaring orange coal of his opium cigarette for a moment and then spoke in a low and serious voice: "You must follow the Wildean Maxim."

"And what is that?"

"I don't know. I just made it up. There is no Wildean Maxim. But if there were, it would be this: 'Do whatsoever makes you happy.'"

"That's hardly profound."

"True, but it has worked for me thus far."

Abruptly, the carriage rumbled to a standstill and swayed violently as the driver clambered down. He appeared at the window and Wilde drew down the glass. Gibson tugged loose the muffler that had been masking his nose and mouth and coughed up a plug of fog before he could speak.

"Beggin' yer pardon, master, but the fog's thick as treacle and I can't see no further than the horses' snouts. All this while I been looking for Albemarle Street, only I can't seem to find it. I'm sorry, sir, but I reckon we're lost."

Wilde shook his head calmly. "You misunderstand, Gibson, we are not lost. Oscar Wilde is never lost. We have merely misplaced London."

"Well, that's as may be, sir, but if you wish to proceed, I must ask that you and the doctor step down and walk ahead of the carriage."

Wilde answered the request with a groan.

If the Irishman had reason to complain about the fog while he rode inside the carriage, now as the pair of them trudged the gleaming cobbles ahead of the carriage, a glowing lantern swinging in each man's grip, he had real reason to complain. The fog was at once chill-ingly cold while simultaneously suspended with hot particles of ash and scorching embers. Even with their noses and mouths muffled be-neath scarves, they wheezed and choked on the stifling air. The fog pumiced their faces raw. Soot sifted down from the skies above, speck-ling their white shirt collars and cuffs with greasy black smudges—a rain of filth commonly referred to as "the blacks."

"London is transmuted into Hades and the Thames its Lethe," Wilde moaned. "If we meet a large red fellow coming in the oppo-site direction, do not hail him. It will likely be Mephistopheles mak-ing the rounds of his kingdom."

"Do we even know what street we're on?" Conan Doyle called up to the driver.

"Piccadilly, sir," Gibson called back. "Or, at least . . . I hope we are."

Wilde peered skeptically at the torn-paper silhouettes of trees looming at the edges of the streetlamp's glow. "Unless the Ritz has been demolished to make way for a forest, I would say yonder lies Green Park. Which suggests that we have overshot Albemarle Street by a considerable—"

"Shush!" Conan Doyle urged, and grabbed one of the horses' bridles and jerked so that the carriage rumbled to a halt. "Listen. What's that noise?"

From the roiling fog ahead they heard a faint sound, growing more audible by the moment: *wisssshthump . . . wissssssshthump . . . wisssssssshthump . . .*

Two glowing orbs appeared in the fog ahead. At first Conan Doyle thought they were gas lamps, but as their perspective changed, it be-came clear the lights were floating toward them, accompanied by that noise: *wisssshthump . . . wissssssshthump . . . wisssssssshthump . . .*

Conan Doyle glanced at his friend, who was staring into the fog with a gaze of dread fixity. "That sound . . ." Wilde breathed. "The very sound I heard that night."

Both men froze, listening.

Wisssshthump . . . wissssssshthump . . . wissssssshthump . . .

The sound grew louder. Nearer.

A dim shape appeared. Fog swirled and something with the shape of a carriage tore loose, the two lights its powerful headlamps.

"It's a steam car!" Conan Doyle said.

Wheezing and hissing, the vehicle trundled toward them and drew up in a squeal of brakes. The driver, whose features could not be dredged from the shadows beneath his tall top hat, leaned around the flat glass windscreen and bellowed in a thick Yorkshire accent: "Why the bloody hell are you sitting in the middle of the road? Shift, you daft buggers!"

Without thinking to object, the two friends took hold of the horses' harness and led the carriage to the side of the road.

The way clear, the driver leaned back behind the enormous spoked steering wheel and began snatching at levers protruding through the running boards. The gearbox emitted a teeth-curling succession of *graunch*ing noises until the driver happened upon a gear more to his liking. The steam engine picked up revs and the vehicle rumbled past, curling wisps of steam from the boiler mixing with the fog, giving the illusion of a man riding past on a small cloud.

Both men stood watching, openmouthed, as the steam car merged with the fog and vanished, and the *wisssshthump . . . wissssssshthump* dwindled from hearing.

"How disturbing," Wilde said.

"What? Meeting a motor vehicle on such a night?"

Wilde shook his head. "No, the driver was wearing a stovepipe hat." He threw a doubting look at his companion. "Who wears a stovepipe these days?"

But Conan Doyle's mind was calculating other possibilities. "A steam car," he said. "Perhaps that's what you heard the other night. Perhaps a steam car was used to whisk the body away."

Wilde looked doubtful. "But the noise I heard was not so loud. And that steam car looked as if it could barely accommodate two passengers, with no room to stow the corpse of a large man."

It seemed a cogent observation, and Conan Doyle mulled on it as they turned the coach around and headed the other way up Piccadilly, back toward Albemarle Street. But they had barely gone twenty feet when they heard a familiar sound: *wisssshthump . . . wisssssshthump . . . wisssssssshthump . . .*

"Sounds like our friend with the steam car is returning," Wilde noted. "No doubt he is as lost as we are."

But the sound was quieter this time, and Conan Doyle noticed something missing. "If it's the steam car driver, I see no coach lights."

Up ahead, a wispy filament of fog calved from the gray mass, shifting shape until it coalesced as the tenuous shadow of a walking human form.

Slouching fast toward them.

The walking figure crashed from light back into darkness as it passed by the glow of each streetlamp, accumulating solidity with every step.

Wisssshthump . . . wisssssshthump . . . wisssssssshthump . . .

It reached the glow of a nearby gas lamp that peeled the shadows from it and revealed a man in tattered clothing. A gray cloak fluttered about his shoulders like ragged bat wings—no, not a cloak, but a wispy veil of steam that wreathed about his head and shoulders. He lurched toward them with a faltering, foot-dragging gait.

"Remember what I said about Mephistopheles?" Wilde muttered in a despairing voice. "I wish to retract it."

Wisssshthump . . . wisssssshthump . . . wisssssssshthump . . .

By now, the shambling figure loomed large. It seemed ready to pass them on the far side of the street when, suddenly . . . it stopped. The eyes remained fixed ahead while the whole head turned to look their way, as if noticing the carriage for the first time. The figure was a large man with a bull's chest. His clothes hung from him in rags. A greasy tangle of lank hair fell over both eyes. Thick arms hung leaden at his side. In the ghastly light, he looked like something that had stepped through a portal and arrived hot and smoking from hell. A charnel house reek of corruption shivered in the air.

The two friends stood transfixed, aware of being in the presence of something uncanny and utterly inhuman.

"G-good Lord . . . !" Conan Doyle breathed in a low whisper.

As if it heard, the head tilted back, the greasy fringe parted, and the white marble of a single eye fixed them with its glaucous gaze.

Time elasticated. The moment stretched to a trembling breaking point ready to snap. Wilde snatched aside the scarf wrapped about his mouth, unable to draw a breath. For long, silent moments, the thing studied them as they studied it. Finally, it seemed to lose interest. The lurid face turned away. Abruptly, the thing resumed its shambling walk and slouched away up Piccadilly, dragging a pall of wispy steam with it.

Wisssshthump . . . wissssssshthump . . . wissssssshthump . . .

Its crippled stride carried it beyond the glow of the streetlamps and the fog smothered it up. The *wisssshthump . . . wissssssshthump . . .* grew fainter until it dropped from hearing.

Shaken to the quivering core of his being, Conan Doyle turned to look first at Wilde and then up at Gibson.

"You both saw it, too?"

The driver sat mouth agape, eyes wide. Too stunned to speak, he nodded dumbly.

"I have seen that face before," Wilde said in a quavering voice.

"The man called Charlie Higginbotham?"

Wilde nodded manically. "Not a man . . . a monster."

❦

CHAPTER 13

THE ASSASSIN KILLS AGAIN

"I have flirted with Catholicism in the past," Wilde remarked. "If I were of the persuasion right now I would be worrying my rosary beads to dust."

Conan Doyle regarded his friend archly. "Catholic, indeed? Oscar, you are a skein of contradictions."

"I cultivate my contradictions, Arthur. It is how I remain fascinating to the world."

He and Conan Doyle had decamped to the lobby of the Albemarle Club—a public space chosen because, at that hour in the morning, it was the only room that enjoyed a generous fire of cedar logs crackling in the fireplace. The two friends had paused only to sponge the smuts from their faces and collars, and now sat in adjacent chairs drawn up within pants-singeing proximity to the flames. Despite the heat, their clothes retained the chill of the evening air and the lingering tang of brimstone fog.

"Could we have witnessed a walking ghost?" Conan Doyle asked. "I have read tales of such things."

"It seemed offensively corporeal to me. The thing stank like a dead dog dredged from the Thames."

"Good evening, Mister Wilde."

Both men jumped at the voice. Cranford had silently materialized at Wilde's side. As usual, he had a white towel draped over one arm. "Will you be requiring me to open the kitchens, sir?"

"Not tonight, Cranford. The only thing I shall require you to open is a large bottle of brandy . . . oh and two glasses."

Cranford nodded a bow and looked up at Conan Doyle. "And ice, sir? Is that how you take it?"

"Large chunk—" Conan Doyle grunted.

"Big enough to sink a ship," Wilde finished the thought. "Just go lasso an iceberg, Cranford."

The waiter failed to conceal a smirk. "Very good, sir." And with that, he vanished.

"There was something supernatural about what we witnessed."

"There's something supernatural about that waiter."

"It was dark . . . and foggy . . . but the figure bore an uncanny resemblance to the dead assassin we saw the other night . . . the Charlie Higginbotham character."

"Uncanny is the word of the hour. Anarchist bombs detonating all over London. Hanged men walking abroad. And this accursed fog."

"You don't think—" Conan Doyle started to say.

"Think what?"

The Scotsman shifted in his seat. "You don't think our friend, Charlie Higginbotham—if indeed it was him—was on his way—"

But Wilde was already aboard his friend's train of thought and flourishing his ticket. "To assassinate another victim?"

"Dear God," Conan Doyle said. "I am not a religious man either, but let us pray not!"

* * *

A moonless night starved of its shadows.

Outside fine residences guarded by spike-topped railings, a line of streetlamps receded dimly into the miasma, so that the farthest lamps showed as little more than smudges of titanium white on a palette painted in every hue of silence. From somewhere beyond the visible came the telltale sound: *wisssshthump* . . . *wisssssshthump* . . . *wisssssshthump* . . .

Silvery tissues of fog swirled as a shambling form tore loose of them. Guided by some internal compass, it slogged along the road in its wounded but indefatigable stride, the grizzled head looking neither left nor right.

Wisssshthump . . . *wisssssshthump* . . . *wisssssshthump* . . .

Suddenly the hoary man broke stride. Stumbled to a halt in front of a handsome Georgian house of six storeys. It was an area normally well policed of the poor, the indigent, of beggars and idle vandals. But tonight, someone had chalked a message on the low garden wall of the handsome house:

For a long moment, the horrid yellow eyes fixed upon the graffiti, as if in recognition. Then the head tilted on its muscular stump of a neck, and the glaucous gaze raked up the brickwork to a second story window that pulsed with the telltale flicker of a coal fire burning in the grate. The mouth slackened, releasing a rumbling, feral growl. The nostrils jetted plumes of steam. The figure stirred itself, and limped to the marble front step where it stood looking up. The bedroom boasted an iron-railed balcony, but the building's façade was smooth limestone with few handholds. Impossible for a man to scale.

For a *living* man.

* * *

Conan Doyle rattled the ice chunk melting in his brandy. He looked up to thank the waiter, but Cranford had vanished, leaving only a stir in the air currents. He and Wilde lounged in a bubble of thoughtful silence as his thoughts boomeranged back, for the thousandth time, to Jean Leckie. Quite unconsciously, he fingered his breast pocket for her calling card, withdrew it from his pocket, and gave it a casual glance.

Only to stiffen with shock. Instead of the feminine script and the address in Blackheath, he held a rectangle of card scribbled with a cryptic message: *Stay sharp! The young lady is a distraction. Cypher.*

Wilde noticed his reaction. "Is something amiss?"

Flummoxed, Conan Doyle grappled for an answer. He had carefully secured Jean's calling card in his breast pocket. But then he remembered Cypher's bowler-hatted bruisers outside the theater. The "accidental" collision. The sharp punch in the kidney. Suddenly the truth broke upon him—they had picked his pocket. He felt a gull, a fool, a dupe. The brazen impudence of the man raised Conan Doyle's dander. Immediately, he scorned his half promise to keep the matter secret. Leaning forward in his chair, he snatched the poker from the fire stand and rammed it into the logs, lifting and heaving until the fire roared up, popping and crackling and spitting hot sparks onto the hearth rug. He only settled back into his chair when the press of heat against his face forced him to retreat.

"You certainly gave the fire a damned good thrashing, Arthur. I take it something has greatly perturbed you."

"I have something to confess."

"We are hardly in a confessional box, but at least we now have the purgatorial flames dancing before us."

"I had hoped to keep you out of this, but the world is out-of-kilter more than you know. Or could begin to guess."

"Do not kill me with suspense, Arthur. Ennui is the only death appropriate for a poet."

"This morning I had the most extraordinary meeting . . ."

And then Conan Doyle spent twenty minutes relating his abduction from Waterloo Station, his meeting with Cypher, and finally his audience with Victoria herself. When he had finished, Wilde sat staring at the fire through the refracting lens of his brandy glass before tossing back the dregs and wryly remarking, "After a tale such as that, I will not regale you with the story of *my* morning, which began with a rather amusing incident concerning a misplaced egg cup." He leaned forward and set his glass down on the rug. "So our assassin is involved in these anarchist plots that threaten to bring down England, the Commonwealth, and the Empire?"

"Assassin or *assassins*."

"And who do you think is likely to be the next victim?"

"I am not sure. I cannot help but speculate there is some link to the members of an organization you and I are already familiar with."

Wilde asked the question by raising his extravagant eyebrows.

"Yes, Oscar, the so-called *Fog Committee*."

* * *

The bedroom was large and expensively furnished. An enormous four-poster hung with heavy curtains occupied one half of the room. Seated in a leather tub chair before the throbbing coal fire, his heels resting upon the emaciated form of a tiger-skin rug, was a man who was the living antonym of emaciated: Tarquin Hogg, banker. Aptly named, for with his porcine girth, piggy eyes, pug nose, and dimply assemblage of chins, the banker could have easily ribboned as best of breed in any county fair. As he gripped the newspaper spread across his generous lap with one hand, the other fleshy trotter groped a plate stacked with mince pies. He crammed one into his salivating mouth and chewed juicily. The large man had draped his bulk in a quilted silk dressing gown of peacock blue; a red fez capped his silvery hair. But despite the comfort of his dress and the luxury of his surroundings, Hogg looked decidedly ill at ease. For once, he was griped with more than just gas pains. He gave the paper a vexed rattle and glared at a front-page headline that screamed: "Lord Howell Assassinated" while below an equally menacing subtitle muttered ominously: "Another public figure murdered." The fleshy pillows of his brow knitted in consternation. He snatched the pince-nez from his nose. Chewed his lower lip. A gentle knock at the bedroom door dragged him from his brooding reverie. He crumpled the newspaper double, hiding the story, and called out thickly around a mouthful of masticated pastry, "Come."

A maid slid quickly into the room. Young. White. Starched. Comely. She bobbed a curtsey and said, "Sir, there's someone at the door."

Hogg glared at her with bemusement. No honest person would venture abroad on such a vile night.

"Who the devil is it?"

The young maid shook her head helplessly. "A gentleman. I don't know who, sir." And then she held out something in her hand. "He sends you his card."

The fat banker levered himself up from the chair, tightened the sash of his dressing gown, and snatched the card from the maid's hand.

When he read the name on the calling card, the color drained from his face. "Where . . . ?"

"Waiting outside, sir."

"Very good," he said, handing the card back. He made to leave the room but then paused a moment. "Myrtle, I want you to turn down my bed and close the bed curtains. Then fetch a warming pan." He caressed a downy cheek with the back of his chubby hand. "When I return I shall have you warm my bed."

The young woman dropped her eyes. Her lips quivered as she answered meekly, "Very good, sir."

When Tarquin Hogg stepped out of his front door, a strange vision waited at the curbside. Whooshing and hissing, it sat vibrating on its hard rubber tires, a pall of steam wreathing about it: one of the new horseless carriages. A human form skulked in the shadows beneath the fabric hood: a figure indistinguishable apart from a tall top hat. The glass window let down and a hand beckoned from the gloomy interior. With a grunt of umbrage, Hogg cinched tight the belt of his robe against the bitter chill of the night and waddled down the marble steps in his slippered feet.

"You!" he said, addressing the shadowy figure inside the carriage. "What do you want from me? Why are you here?"

"You read about Lord Howell?"

Hogg went rigid at the name. "Of course. But he was murdered by his valet—"

"Don't bloody believe it. A lie for the newspapers."

"What are you saying?"

"You are in great danger."

"Danger? Me? What . . . what do you mean?"

"The Fog Committee knows that you are Cypher's man."

"They . . . they . . ." Hogg trailed off. Swallowed hard. "Oh, God, no!" he moaned. His eyes grew crazed, his jowls quivered with distress. "What am I to do? I could go to the authorities. Cypher must help me—"

"You are on your own. We all are. Even Cypher cannot protect you now."

"Y-you, m-must help me," the big man blubbered. "Your brother and his mad friends will murder us all."

A hand extended from the steamer, a pistol clutched in its grip. "Take this. Keep it near you at all times. Do not go abroad alone."

Hogg's eyes bulged at the sight of the weapon. "A pistol? No, I cannot—"

"Take it, you daft bugger! And God be with you."

The banker squeamishly took the pistol. Before he could say anything further, there was a grinding of gears, and the steamer chugged away into the fog.

Tarquin Hogg jammed the pistol in the pocket of his robe and panted up the front steps of his home, pausing to throw an uneasy look around at the empty street, his brown eyes probing the shadows for lurkers. Had he lingered longer on the front steps, or looked harder, he might have just made out the vague human form standing in the shadow of the large oak tree opposite. Instead he fled indoors and banged the door shut on the night.

His butler was waiting in the hallway and fixed him with a questioning look. "Sir? Is something amiss?"

"Alderton, I want you to personally ensure that the doors and all the windows are securely locked—"

"But, of course—"

"And then I want you to post a footman at every door. And ensure each is armed with some kind of weapon."

For once, the aging butler's face lost its composure. "W-with a weapon? But whatever—"

"See to it!" the banker snapped. "And Alderton . . ."

"Yes, sir?"

"Before you came into service, you were in the army, were you not?"

"Yes, m'lud. Infantry. Royal Fusiliers."

"So you know how to use a gun?"

The butler allowed himself a modest smile. "I dare say I was a fair old shot back in the day."

"Good," Hogg said. He reached into the pocket of his robe, produced the pistol, and held it out to his servant. "Take it."

The butler's composure broke as his face registered wide-eyed astonishment.

"Sir?"

"Take it!"

The butler numbly complied.

"I want you to guard the front door tonight. Sleep in a chair if you must. No one is to be allowed in. Do you understand? No one. And if someone tries to break in . . . shoot them dead."

Minutes later, the banker slunk into his bedroom, closed the door, and leaned with his back against it, breathing hard. Suddenly he noticed the heavy curtains at the window stir. He froze and watched.

The curtains stirred a second time, as if someone or something lurked behind them. Scarcely able to draw breath, he crept to the fireplace, drew the iron poker and stepped quietly to the curtains.

Once again, the curtains ballooned out and sucked back. Raising the poker high, he snatched aside the curtain.

Nothing.

But then he felt the icy fingers of a chill draft trail across his face and realized what had been causing the curtains to stir. Inexplicably, the French door to the balcony stood ajar, allowing cold night air to waft in. "Who the devil opened this?" he complained aloud. He bumped the door shut and yanked at the handle to ensure that it was latched properly. As he turned back to the room, he heard a bedspring creak and froze. But then his face smeared with a knowing grin. He tiptoed toward the bed and softly called out: "Myrtle, you naughty child. Is that you? Have you a surprise for your master?"

He reached the bed and gripped the bed curtains, ready to fling them wide. But then he paused, sniffing the air as he caught a whiff of something horrid.

From behind came a timid knock and the maid's voice calling through the bedroom door, "Sir, it is me . . . Myrtle."

Puzzled, he snatched open the bed curtains.

He had only seconds to register the grizzled mien, the hideous face with its ghastly yellow eyes, before two calloused hands seized him by the throat, crushing his windpipe. The poker slipped from his hand and thudded to the rug.

At that moment, the bedroom door opened and the maid slid inside. The young woman stood agog for speechless seconds, her eyes wide with terror.

A hulking man had hold of her master by the throat and, despite his bulk, held him suspended so that his feet kicked the air clear of the floor. And then as she watched, the bestial man twisted her master's head violently around. Vertebrae popped with a zippering sound. Myrtle's horrified face was the last thing Tarquin Hogg's bulging eyes fixed upon before the light went out of them and his portly body danced a sick shiver of death.

A scream coiled inside her chest and ripped the air as it burst out. Her cries alerted Alderton, who bounded up the staircase and reached the open bedroom door just as the creature flung the body of Tarquin Hogg across the room, where it crashed into the far wall, shattering a mirror before thudding to the floor.

"Stop!" Alderton shouted at the back of the large figure dominating the room. When it turned to face him, the butler saw the yellow eyes, the kinked neck, and the purple-green hue of the face. And then it took a shambling step toward him.

BANG!

The first bullet hit the monster in the shoulder. A gout of blood spurted, but the creature kept coming.

BANG!

The second shot hit it in the stomach, staggering it momentarily. "Myrtle," he shouted over his shoulder. "Go, lass. Run!"

With a whimper of terror, the maid turned and bolted from the room.

BANG! BANG!

Bullets hit. Blood gushed. Alderton backed away as it crashed through the doorway, breaking loose the doorjamb with a shoulder.

BANG!

Alderton retreated down the hallway as the creature came on.

He fired again, hitting the lower chest. From years in the military, he knew he had only one bullet left. "Make it count, Johnny boy," he muttered to himself. He fought to steady his shaking hand and drew a bead dead center, aiming for the heart.

BANG!

There was a metallic clang. A three-foot gout of blue flame shot from the chest and a moment later: BOOOOOOOOOOOOOOOM-MMMM! The hallway exploded in a ball of fire.

CHAPTER 14

A DEEPLY DISTURBING DISCOVERY

Waterloo Station was just stirring from its foggy slumber as Conan Doyle stepped out of the station into the predawn murk. He had cabbed from the Albemarle to catch the first train back to his home in Surrey. At this early hour, the majority of daily commuters had yet to arrive, but carts rolled in and out of the echoing archways and the platforms bustled with the earliest risers in London: costermongers and barrow men scurrying to unload crates of vegetables and flowers bound for Covent Garden, sides of beef and sheep for Smithfield's Market, fish and seafood for Billingsgate Market.

He was making for his favorite newspaper kiosk when his attention was deflected by a cheerful Cockney voice calling out: "Show your patriotism, sir, buy a ribbon from an old soldier."

Standing in the shelter of a station arch was an elderly man in a battered pillbox hat and worn British army jacket. The uniform was in sad repair, the once-proud scarlet faded with the passing of years. One epaulet dangled loose. The gold brocade of the cuffs was frayed and threadbare in places, although the sleeves still bore the stripes of a sergeant. A Crimean War medal, tarnished and dull, hung crookedly on the jacket's right breast. The man's eyes were hidden behind opaque round spectacles. A white stick dangled from the crook of his arm. Hanging from a strap around his neck was a tray filled with trinkets: Union Jack bunting and ribbons. Up close, the skin of his face was shriveled and marked with a tracery of livid red lines.

Burns, Conan Doyle thought.

"How much, my good fellow?"

"Sam's me name, sir. And a sixpence is all. And gawd bless ya for helpin' an old soldier."

The Scotsman rummaged his pockets, found a coin, and dropped it into the collection box.

"Half a crown?" the veteran guessed, catching the ka-chunk of a higher denomination. "Very generous. Very generous, indeed. Allow me, sir."

The veteran plucked a ribbon from his tray and pinned it to the lapel of Conan Doyle's woolen coat with surprising alacrity. "You usually come to London on the eight thirty train, don't you, sir?"

The Scottish author's mouth dropped open with surprise. Apparently, the veteran considered himself a bit of an amateur Sherlock Holmes.

"Yes, I do. How on earth did you know that?"

"I recognize you by your hair oil and cologne. Very top drawer. Very distinctive."

"Remarkable," Conan Doyle said, "but tell me, how do you find your way about on these foggy mornings?"

"I taps me way around London," the veteran explained, demonstrating by tapping his white cane upon the ground. "Day or night, fog or no fog, makes no nevermind to me."

"Clever . . . and remarkable. I shall have to use that in one of my detective fictions." He dug out another coin and dropped it in the veteran's collection box. "There you go, Sam. That's well worth another half-crown."

"Thank ya kindly, sir. Gawd bless ya, and Gawd bless the Queen."

As Conan Doyle approached the newspaper kiosk, his eye was caught by the hysterical message scrawled upon the reader board: As-sassins Strike Again! He hurriedly purchased a paper and snapped it open only to be flayed about the face by a giant screaming headline: "HOGG SLAUGHTERED!"

The Scottish author grimaced at the tasteless pun and scanned the subheading: "Bank of England president killed by anarchist bomber." As he read the words, images of the previous evening swam up in his mind: the hoary figure they had witnessed shambling through the fog and the steam car and its stovepipe-hatted driver seen shortly before that. He stood pondering. If only he could visit the scene of the most recent assassination—a course of action fraught with danger after Commissioner Burke's blunt threat. He momentarily considered his journalism contacts, but they would likely be fobbed off with an "official" description of events. He needed to somehow slip inside Hogg's residence and see for himself what had transpired. He needed a type of disguise, a mask, and suddenly realized that he already knew an insider who could help them walk straight through the police guard as if invisible.

* * *

The door, which had been a stranger to paint for years, still bore the ghostly silhouette of where a knocker once hung. Conan Doyle was forced to remove his glove and knuckle the fibrous wood. Almost instantly, his knocking roused voices from inside. He caught the light tread of feet and the door was opened by a young woman with a babe balanced on her hip. The mother, barely out of her girlhood years, eyed him quickly up and down and snapped, "If it's about the rent—"

"Ah, no," he quickly put in. "I am an acquaintance of your husband's. My name is Arthur Conan Doyle. I am the author of the Sherlock Ho—"

Abruptly, the woman slammed the door in his face with the force of a cannon blast.

The vehemence of the response rocked him back momentarily. He blinked away his surprise and turned to walk away, but then paused at the sound of raised voices: a man's and a woman's, arguing. In the background, the baby's startled wailing. A moment later, the door snatched open again. This time it was answered by a cowed-looking young man. It took a moment to recognize Detective Blenkinsop so very out of uniform. He was wearing worn trousers gone baggy at the knees and a tea-stained under-vest. His thick dark hair was wildly mussed and it was clear his barber had not enjoyed a visit in days.

"Sorry about that," he said. "A misunderstandin'. Come in, Doctor Doyle . . . please."

Conan Doyle entered a modest room; it was clean, but furnished with a cheap assortment of mismatched furniture clearly on its third or fourth owners. Despite the chill outside, the space was humid and fugged with steam. Evidently, his visit coincided with washday—an iron cauldron bubbled on a hook in the small fireplace; baby nappies and a lady's unmentionables dangled from a clothes rack winched tight to the ceiling. The young woman who had slammed the door in his face, evidently Blenkinsop's wife, kept her back resolutely turned, bouncing the squalling baby in her arms as she glared out a window that offered only a view of a brick wall two feet opposite.

"My apologies," Blenkinsop muttered in a low voice, "but the missus is a bit miffed—"

Overhearing his words, the young wife turned upon them, her pretty face ugly with rage. "Miffed? You nearly got him chucked off the force!"

"I'm just suspended," Blenkinsop quickly countered.

"Suspended with no pay! No pay and us with a new babe!"

"Enough, Fanny," Blenkinsop said. "It ain't the gentleman's fault—"

"I am sorry, I had no idea." Conan Doyle reached into his pocket and drew out a clutch of banknotes, holding them out to Blenkinsop.

The detective looked at the notes hungrily, but shook his head. "I can't take no charity—"

"This is not charity. I am here to interrupt your leisure. I wish to hire you."

"Hire me? I don't— What for?"

"I am still pursuing the Lord Howell case. Albeit . . ." He lowered his voice. ". . . in an *unofficial* capacity. I require the assistance of a professional detective. I could wish for no better than yourself."

Blenkinsop and his wife exchanged a look freighted with meaning. Conan Doyle could almost see her visibly willing him to take the money. For the second time, the young detective eyeballed the banknotes.

"That's too much," he said.

"You do not yet know what I'm hiring you to do."

"Nothing illegal, right? I'm just suspended from the force. I ain't been booted yet."

The hand holding the money did not waver. "I cannot share anything until you are officially in my employ."

With a commingling of reluctance and relief, Blenkinsop took the banknotes, glanced at them, and then crossed the room and handed them to his wife saying, "Here ya go, girl. Mebbe you can pop to the shops and buy the babe some milk and a rusk, and something for our tea."

The young woman snatched up a shawl and wrapped it about her and the babe in arms. "I'll be off, then," she said, and moments later the two men were alone in the room and able to speak freely.

"What's going on, Doctor Doyle?"

"Nothing short of a coup d'état."

"A coo—? You mean the Frenchies are about to invade?"

Conan Doyle chuckled. "Not exactly, but our nation is in crisis. The murder of Lord Howell is part of a plot of programmed assassinations aimed at key politicians and magnates of industry. But that is only the beginning. The plot will culminate in the assassination of the queen and the overthrow of the government."

"Lumme! What can I do, Doctor Doyle?"

"I have needs of your sleuthing skills."

A smile cracked Blenkinsop's face for the first time. "You can count on me, sir. It'll be good to be back in harness and out from underfoot with the wife and little-un."

"There is one thing, Detective."

"Tom. You'd best call me Tom. I'm suspended, remember?"

"Ah, yes. Very well then, *Tom*. I must stress, there will be danger involved. Possibly, great danger."

Blenkinsop sniffed at the possibility. "No different from me regular day job then, is it? I'm your man, sir. Like you say in your Sherlock Holmes stories, the game's afoot, eh?"

Conan Doyle clapped the detective on the shoulder and smiled. "Indeed, Tom, the game is very much afoot!"

* * *

When Conan Doyle and Detective Blenkinsop alighted from the cab, they found a cordon of blue uniformed constables surrounding Tarquin Hogg's house. Three hearses and a black Mariah were already drawn up at the curbside.

"Blimey," Blenkinsop said. "How do we get past that lot? Sneak in the back way?"

Conan Doyle thought a moment and said, "I say we sneak in the front way. You still have your detective's badge, I take it?"

"Yeah, but—"

"Bluff and bluster are often superior to stealth. You and I will march up there as though we are in charge. Flash them your badge. Just make sure they don't have time to read it. Eh, Detective Sutcliffe?"

Blenkinsop frowned with puzzlement. "Sutcliffe? But me name is—" And then a smile broke across his face. "Ah, I tumble it. Very good . . . *Doctor Watson*. Shall we?"

The two men stepped onto the road and walked briskly up to the knot of police officers. But as they drew close, an officer in plainclothes noticed them and threw down the gauntlet.

"Who are you two, then?"

Judging by the man's bushy brown moustache, martial bearing, and flat-footed stance that comes from years of pounding the beat, Conan Doyle guessed they had run into a plainclothes inspector. Blenkinsop flashed his badge, one finger held across it so no one could read the number."

"Detective Sutcliffe."

"Who? What you doing here, sonny Jim? This ain't your manor—"

"Commissioner Burke sent me personally. Told me to get down here sharpish and fetch a doctor." Blenkinsop indicated Conan Doyle with a nod. "Course, you got a problem with that, you could take it up with the commissioner when he arrives."

Invoking the name of the police commissioner worked its magic. The inspector was suddenly all smiles. "Sorry. Didn't mean to sound narky." He extended a hand. "The name's Barnes."

"Good to meet you, Inspector Barnes." The two men shook hands. "So, what's happening?"

"Beggared if I know. We been here all night. No one's allowed to go in until his nibs gets here. He don't want nothing disturbed."

"Yeah," Blenkinsop quickly ad-libbed. "Commissioner Burke wanted the doctor to examine the victims' bodies and have a report ready for him."

Conan Doyle spoke for the first time. "So why three hearses?"

"Three stiffs. The murderer, the fat banker himself, and a butler copped it as well. Old army lad. Put five rounds in the murderer. Only the geezer had a bomb strapped to his chest. Butler found it with the fifth round, didn't he? KA-BOOM!"

"Déjà vu?" Conan Doyle muttered to Detective Blenkinsop.

"Any witnesses still breathin'?" Blenkinsop asked.

"Maid. Name of Myrtle. Saw the murderer doing the dirty. A monster, she called him. Of course, you know women and their hysterics. But he was a big bastard as you'll see from what's left of him."

"Right," Blenkinsop said. "I'd better get the doctor in there before the commissioner arrives and thinks we're all slackin' off."

They made a move to step past, but Inspector Barnes held them back with a gesture. "Wait, before you go in." He lowered his voice to a conspiratorial rumble. "There's something queer about this one. The victim looks like he went ten rounds with a circus gorilla. And you should see the state of the room . . ." The inspector shook his head. ". . . in bits." He squinted up at the second story balcony. "So maybe what the maid said ain't so daft after all."

With that, Detective Blenkinsop and Conan Doyle passed unmolested through the gaggle of constables and entered the house. In the entrance hall, a solitary constable slouched against a wall, but jerked to attention as they entered.

"Oi! No one's allowed in here—"

Blenkinsop flashed his badge. "Detective Sutcliffe. I brought the doctor with me."

"Oh, right. Second floor. Can't miss it."

The two men ascended a grand staircase that spiraled upward in a swirl of polished mahogany balustrades. From behind they heard the constable guarding the door shout up to them: "Hope ya got a strong stomach."

As they reached the first floor, a greasy haze hung suspended in the air and their mouths filmed with the acrid tang of scorched hair and burned flesh. They found the butler's body sprawled close to the stairs on the second-floor landing. His eyes were open, shocked wide, as if surprised by his own death. His right hand still gripped a pistol. The blast had merely singed him, but a weeping hole in the middle of his forehead showed the cause of death. When Conan Doyle bent closer to look he found a brassy bolt protruding from the skull.

"Nasty," Blenkinsop commented.

"Yes. No doubt a component from the bomb."

They stepped carefully around the butler's body. The blast had stripped the fine flock wallpaper from the wall and it hung in peeling curls. Farther up the hallway, the assassin's corpse lay on its back: a hulking form with the mass of a toppled idol, heavy with inertia.

Even in death it radiated menace and threatened to jerk to life at any moment. The yellow eyes were wide, the dreadful gaze scorching the ceiling.

"Charlie Higginbotham!" Detective Blenkinsop hissed from several feet away, his legs unwilling to carry him any closer.

Conan Doyle stepped close and dropped to a crouch over the body. The tattered remnants of the shirt were burned black and crispy. But most remarkable was the perfect rectangular opening in the middle of the chest, out of which a thin gray tendril of smoke still curled.

"You can see he had a bomb strapped to his chest," Blenkinsop observed. "It's blown a hole."

Conan Doyle leaned closer, peering into the smoldering cavity. "No. This hole is far too neat and regular to be caused by an explosion. The chest has been cut open by someone with the skill of a surgeon using a bone saw." He grunted with astonishment and looked up at the young detective. "The heart . . . it's gone!"

Blenkinsop's mouth dropped open. "What? How? How is that possible?"

Conan Doyle looked around the hallway and spotted a twisted metal box lying several feet away. Even from a distance, he judged that its dimensions exactly matched the rectangular hole in the assassin's chest. He arose from the corpse and stepped over to pick it up. The oblong metal box was constructed of machined plates of shiny metal, held together around the edges by precise rows of brass bolts. One bolt was missing—likely the one that wound up in the butler's forehead. An outward-puckered hole in the metal showed where a bullet had punctured the casing. Beside the bullet hole was what appeared to be a gauge, although the face was unreadable behind cracked and blackened glass. Something rattled loose when he shook it and fell out on the hall rug. He snatched it up. The heavy cogwheel had been formed from a solid chunk of metal, exquisitely machined so that it iridesced in the light. Conan Doyle wrapped it in a handkerchief and tucked in his pocket.

"This is not a bomb," Conan Doyle announced.

"What, then?"

The Scotsman shook his head. "Some kind of infernal device."

He turned it over and froze. A sick heat washed through him followed by a chill as sweat dried on the back of his neck. A tangle of rubber hoses dangled from the backside, and a trickle of blood now dribbled from one.

"Good heavens! It appears to be some kind of . . . mechanical heart!"

Before he could speculate further, a booming voice vaulted up the staircase ahead of its owner: "Come along, Dobbs. Don't dawdle, man!"

The two companions shared a look of alarm. Blenkinsop ducked back down the hallway, darted a quick look down the stairs, and quickly jerked his head back.

"Commissioner Burke!" he hissed in a low whisper. "If he finds us . . ."

"Come!" Conan Doyle urged. He set the metal box down where he had discovered it. "There must be a servant's staircase somewhere."

The two hurried along the hallway as the tramp of climbing feet grew louder.

"So no one's been in here?" Burke bellowed.

"No, sir." The voice belonged to Barnes, the inspector they had bluffed their way past. "Just Detective Sutcliffe and the doctor you sent for."

"Doctor? What doctor? And who the devil is Detective Sutcliffe?"

"But. He's upstairs. I thought—"

"You imbecile!"

The thunder of police feet grew louder. Conan Doyle and Blenkinsop ran to the end of the hallway, which branched in two directions.

"If we go the wrong way, we're buggered!" Blenkinsop said.

Conan Doyle noticed what appeared to be a bedroom door nearby.

He snatched it open and the two men ducked inside and pulled it shut behind them.

The bedroom proved to be a linen closet. They stood in the darkness, straining to hear, breathing in the clean aroma of freshly ironed linen. Heavy feet tramped past, grew distant, but soon returned. Both men drew in a breath, and held it.

"Where are they?" Commissioner Burke's voice thundered from the other side of the door. "Tell your man in the entrance hall not to let anyone leave."

Thankfully, after a few minutes, the voices moved away and they were finally able to breathe out. From downstairs they caught the cannonade of the police chief's voice bawling orders, in an obvious state of dyspepsia. Should they be caught, it seemed entirely likely that both would indeed be tossed into the deepest, darkest, dankest cell in Newgate.

Minutes passed. The voices faded from hearing. And then they heard the soft tread of approaching feet. Both men tensed as a floorboard on the other side of the closet door creaked. Suddenly, the door flung wide, spilling in light. The look of astonishment on the maid's face betrayed her surprise at finding two men crouching in the darkness. It would have been comical in less dire circumstances.

"Thank you so much," Conan Doyle said mildly as he and Detective Blenkinsop stepped past her. "We were quite lost in there." He threw a glance up the hallway. The body of Charlie Higginbotham had been removed, but he could still hear the rumble of Commissioner Burke's voice echoing in the entrance hall. He turned his attention to the astonished maid. "Where are your servant's stairs?"

The woman numbly pointed.

"Thank you," Conan Doyle said, and then asked, "Are you Myrtle?"

The maid nodded slowly.

"Excellent. Myrtle, I have a few questions for you."

At Conan Doyle's prodding, the young maid began a halting description of the events of the previous night. When she mentioned the steam car that visited earlier in the evening, Conan Doyle fought to keep his voice steady as he asked her, "And did you happen to see the driver of the steam car?"

The maid nodded. "Just a glimpse, sir—it was quite dark. He was a queerly dressed chap in a great black stovepipe hat. I took his card. It were a funny old name." She suddenly remembered something and scrabbled in the pocket of her pinny, producing a calling card, which she handed to Conan Doyle.

He read the name on the card and gears meshed in his brain: "Ozymandius Arkwright!"

"That's him!" the maid agreed. "Wot you just said."

"Who?" Blenkinsop asked.

Conan Doyle threw a meaningful look at Blenkinsop. "Ozymandius Aurelius Arkwright, one of the nation's best engineers. I've no doubt the steamer he rides around in is his own invention." He was about to continue when the police commissioner's head-splitting voice boomed up in the stairwell from below: "Dobbs! Blast you man. Get over here. Come with me upstairs."

Both men flinched. They had to leave quickly. The Scottish author grasped the young maid's hand and gave it a comforting squeeze. "Thank you so much, Myrtle. Do carry on. You're holding up wonderfully during such trying times."

They fled down the servant's stairs and emerged from a tradesmen's entrance on the side of the house. When they reached the police cordon, Blenkinsop nodded familiarly to the waiting constables and slapped one on the shoulder, saying, "Good job, lads. Stay sharp."

And so they slipped unchallenged through the police line and sauntered back up the road to their waiting hansom. They were just climbing inside when four funeral attendants exited the front door of the residence bearing the coffin containing the body of the dead assassin. The two friends watched as it was loaded into the waiting hearse. And then something struck Conan Doyle as remarkably familiar.

"Tom, do you see that hearse the coffin is being loaded into?"

"Yeah."

"Anything about it seem remarkable?"

"Remarkable?" Blenkinsop squinted a moment. "Nothing that strikes me. I seen a thousand like it in me day."

"Precisely. Superstitious lot that we are, most people see a hearse and look away. One might remember a brewer's dray cart, or a wagon delivering furniture. But to the casual observer one black hearse is very much the same as another: anonymous. As are the funeral grooms with their black frock coats and top hats draped with crepe—a uniform consciously designed to submerge an individual's personality beneath the role they fulfill. Except there is something unique about the driver of that hearse."

Blenkinsop looked again. The driver was just settling himself on the seat of hearse. Although he was dressed identically to the other funeral grooms, he stood out because of the port-wine stain running across one cheek and down his neck.

"I seen that bloke before!" Blenkinsop cried. "But where?"

"Lord Howell's residence, the night of the assassination. I believe it was also the very same hearse."

The young detective glanced at the Scottish author, brows hunched. "Coincidence?"

Conan Doyle's moustaches drooped into a frown. "My friend Oscar Wilde believes in coincidences. Do you?"

The young detective shook his head. "Bein' in my line of work . . . no. Never have. Never will."

Commissioner Burke appeared with his spaniel-faced assistant Dobbs at his side, satchel slung over one shoulder. The commissioner shared words with the driver and then, to their surprise, Dobbs clambered up onto the hearse and took a seat beside the driver.

"What the devil is going on?" Conan Doyle breathed.

The hearse drew away from the curb and turned about in the road before heading away in the opposite direction.

Conan Doyle banged on the cab ceiling. The overhead hatch opened and the cabbie's eyes appeared in the opening, "Yes, guv'nor?"

"Follow that hearse. And don't let it slip away!"

The cabbie cracked his whip and the hansom lurched away in pursuit.

"Where we off to now?" Blenkinsop asked.

"Wherever Dobbs and that hearse go. And I'm dashed interested to find out where."

* * *

Over the next few miles, the houses they passed grew poorer, shabbier, steadily declining from raunchy to ramshackle until they rock-bottomed at derelict. Suddenly, the cab clattered to a halt while the hearse they were pursuing continued on.

"What? Why have we stopped?" Conan Doyle shouted up.

A hatch in the roof flung open and the cabby's white-stubbled face appeared. "We're almost into St. Giles. I ain't going in there no matter how much dosh yer offerin'. I can't spend nuffink if I'm dead."

"What do we do now?" Blenkinsop asked.

Conan Doyle pondered. He looked up the long street and noticed that the hearse had also drawn up and that Dobbs was preparing to climb down. The Scottish writer pulled a half-sovereign from his pocket. "Here," he said, pressing it in Blenkinsop's hand. "Take the cab and go home. I shall proceed on foot . . . alone."

Blenkinsop was incredulous. "Alone? Into St. Giles? Are you bonkers? You won't last five minutes! Especially dressed in them fine clothes."

The young policeman had a point. Conan Doyle made a quick decision. He shrugged off his fine wool topcoat and hat and set them in Blenkinsop's lap. "Deliver my coat and hat to the Athenaeum Club. I shouldn't be too long."

"I can't let you go in there on your own. Not into one of the worse rookeries in London."

"I'm sorry, Tom, but I believe I'll be safer alone than in your company." He smiled archly. "I may look a bit like a toff, but they'd sniff you out as a copper in a heartbeat. Besides, you work for me now, and that's an order."

Without waiting for an answer, Conan Doyle leapt down from the cab and hurried off in pursuit.

As the hansom clattered away, he spotted the adjutant a scant fifty feet ahead. Oblivious to the fact that he was being followed, the small man stood at the curb conferring with the funeral grooms atop the hearse and finally took his leave of them, striding off toward the huddle of squalid houses and frowsy shop fronts that marked the last traces of civilization before descending into the lawless hellhole of St. Giles, one of the most dangerous slums in London.

As Conan Doyle trailed from a discreet distance, Dobbs stopped and went into each of the shops in turn: a green grocer, a butcher, and a shop selling secondhand clothes. Each time, he exited after less than a minute. Puzzled, the author of Sherlock Holmes decided he needed to find out why. He wandered into the second-hand clothes shop where a large lout slouched in a chair rocked back against a motley pile of clothes, paring his nails with a rusty knife. The man glared suspiciously from under a pair of eyebrows the size of hedgehogs as Conan Doyle strode in and made a laughably poor attempt at pretending to be browsing the worn, holed, and ragged castoffs hanging from lengths of twine stretched across the shop.

"See anything to your fancy, sir?" the man asked spikily. "Only I doubt we got nothing your size in here."

Conan Doyle dropped the pretense and spoke directly. "The gentleman who was just in here a moment ago. He is, ah, a friend of mine."

"That right?"

"Yes. You see, I am a doctor and . . . I had wished to consult with him . . . on a matter of some . . . delicacy."

"Oh yeah? What's yer name, then?"

"Ah, Doctor . . . Watson. Doctor John Watson."

"And what's your business coming in my shop, sniffing about, Doctor Whatsits?"

The voice of a woman, well versed in woe, came from somewhere deep behind the piles of clothing. "Bobby," the woman urged. "We don't want no trouble—"

"Shut yer pie 'ole woman!" the lout bellowed.

"I concur with the lady," Conan Doyle echoed. "I also am not looking for trouble."

"Too bad, 'cause you found it." The lout surged up from this chair, which clattered to the floor. He flourished the knife and advanced menacingly on Conan Doyle, who chose the better part of valor and hurriedly retreated from the shop into the street, feeling rather humiliated. Up the road he saw the diminutive figure of Dobbs, striding toward a row of tenements whose walls were propped up by giant wooden beams to stop them from collapse. Conan Doyle hurried on, desperate to keep him in sight. But as he passed the grocer's store he noticed a woman just setting a printed flyer in the shop window:

13/13
The Revolution is Upon Us.
Join the struggle for workers' rights
Meeting: St. Winifred's
Friday, Dusk

So that was what Dobbs had stopped to deliver. Conan Doyle had seen an almost identical flyer the night he and Wilde were called to the murder scene of Lord Howell: the one Dobbs had produced as evidence of Vicente's anarchist sympathies. Only this one featured a date and a call to attend a meeting.

Conan Doyle pressed on, hurrying to catch up with Dobbs, who by now was a tiny figure in the distance. The little man had been busy: 13/13 flyers were tacked onto every boarded-up window. The Scotsman passed an abandoned church, the roof holed and ruined. Nowadays the only churchgoers were gangs of idle boys who gathered on the street corner to fling stones at the few remaining panes of a stained glass. The name carved into the stone lintel above the missing church door read ST. WINIFRED'S. More of the 13/13 flyers had been wedged into crevices in the stone, and many lay scattered on the ground where the wind restlessly tossed them.

By this time, Dobbs had reached the tenements and strode into the midst of a large group of rough-looking men gathered on the street. As Conan Doyle watched, the police commissioner's adjutant moved through the crowd, reaching into his satchel to pass out large handfuls of leaflets.

"What on earth are you up to?" Conan Doyle muttered to himself, watching from across the street. Suddenly, he tumbled to it as the men receiving the leaflets then began to distribute them amongst comrades just arriving upon the scene. Soon a huge mob milled on the street, and it was clear by the rumble of voices they were whipped up and spoiling for a fight. The mob turned and moved as one, marching down the street to a straggle of tenements where suddenly the crude weapons they had been concealing up a jacket sleeve and down a pants leg—iron pipes, cudgels, knives, broken bottles—began to appear, clutched in their hands.

Across an open swath of waste ground a hundred or more navvies were swinging picks, wheeling wheelbarrows, flinging shovelfuls of dirt as they laid the rails of a new stretch of railway. It soon became obvious what was going on: the tumbledown tenements lay in the path of the railway, and now a work gang—protected by a squad of hired brutes and a small force of constables conspicuously armed with truncheons and pistols—had come to tear it down. Conan Doyle realized he was watching two armies drawn up and about to collide. As the opposing gangs faced off, men cursed and spat at one another, but both sides seemed reluctant to strike the first blow. In the midst of railroad laborers stood a man in a fine frock coat and a gray top hat. He clutched a set of rolled-up drawings and shouted orders around a cigar clamped in his jaws. It was a figure Conan Doyle instantly recognized: Tristram Oldfield, railroad magnate.

And, more importantly, a member of the Fog Committee.

Despite the oaths, curses, and threats shouted back and forth, the work gang advanced slowly and steadily toward the first tenement. The building was in an advanced state of dereliction. The roof sagged like a broken-backed horse. The entire structure leaned at an alarming angle, a row of giant timbers propping up the low wall. The work gang edged forward, constables threatening with their truncheons, forcing the defenders to back away until they reached the shadow of the tenement and the navvies fell to work. Using long iron bars, they levered free first one of the giant props and then another. As they loosened the third, an ominous crack sounded, followed by the rumble of shattering masonry as the entire side of the building cleaved and sheared away. Men scattered and ran for their lives as masonry and bricks avalanched down, raising a cloud of soot and dust that engulfed both sides in a blinding cloud of grit. A chill breeze swept the cloud away, revealing that the entire side of the tenement had sloughed off. It was like tearing open a giant termite nest. To his horror, Conan Doyle saw women and children scurrying about the exposed rooms, screaming with terror. And more pathetically, many old and infirm people still lying in their beds, unable to flee.

Chaos erupted. The mob surged forward and clashed with the constables. Skulls collided with truncheons and blood flowed. Rocks and bottles and cobblestones pried up from the roadway whizzed low and lethal through the air. A single gunshot ripped the air and a man fell to the ground clutching his stomach. The fighting paused for a moment, but then a voice screamed "MURDER!" and the mêlée resumed with increased ferocity. Conan Doyle threw himself to the ground and sheltered behind a lamppost as the fusillade crashed down about him. The wind tumbled a square of paper through the air and plastered it against the iron pole he crouched behind. He peeled it loose. It was a simple square of deathly black paper printed with a contrasting design in stark white ink:

CHAPTER 15

CHECK AND MATE

"Does that look familiar?" Conan Doyle asked, tossing the 13/13 flyer down on the table.

The Scots author had run Oscar Wilde to ground in his habitual morning haunt: the domino room of the Café Royal, a favorite spot for London's artists, longhairs and bohemians, a place where the buzz of gossip competed with the clink of coffee cups and the clack of domino tiles being slapped down onto marble tabletops. Wilde looked up from the chair he reposed in. As always, he was smoking, one hand cupping the elbow of the arm holding the cigarette, his chair pushed back from the small table to allow room to cross one leg over the other.

The Scotsman dropped into an empty chair and spoke in a voice both urgent and excited. "I have many new discoveries to share. I just procured that flyer from St. Giles. If you read it, you will see that there is to be a meeting of anarchists. I believe it to be a kind of war council for revolution."

Wilde studied his friend with a doubting expression and then shook his head dismissively. "Revolution? Surely, not in England. Yes, it is possible to whip up discontent and fiery fervor in the English but only until the moment the pubs open. It is difficult to plan, organize, and maintain a revolution around licensing hours."

"Perhaps, but you will never guess who was distributing these leaflets."

"You have a lot of questions for this early in the morning, Arthur. I seldom achieve full awakening consciousness until after my third coffee."

"Dobbs. You know the man. The police commissioner's lackey."

Wilde's eyes widened. "Dobbs? No wonder he was mister-johnny-on-the-spot when it came to locating the subversive literature he claimed to have discovered in the valet's room. But why would the police be distributing anarchist literature?"

"Why indeed? And you'll never guess who else was there."

"More questions, Arthur? I feel a headache coming on."

"Tristram Oldfield."

"Really? Tristram Oldfield?"

Conan Doyle paused a moment, then said, "You have no idea who Tristram Oldfield is, do you, Oscar?"

"I knew I could rely upon you informing me."

"Another member of the Fog Committee. What's more, did you hear that the president of the Bank of England, Tarquin Hogg, died last night."

"A deceased banker. Shall I break out the bunting and celebratory champagne?"

"It's nothing to laugh about, Oscar. The man was murdered, or rather, assassinated."

"Ah!" Wilde said. "Yes, that is rather indecorous of me. In the fashion of Lord Howell?"

Conan Doyle nodded. "And by an assassin you and I know. Only this time he did not get up and walk away."

Wilde grew suddenly serious. "Are we, by chance, talking about the noctivagant, Charlie Higginbotham?"

"The same."

"Good gracious, indeed!" For the first time, Wilde shifted his attention to the figure seated on his left, who had sat silently throughout the whole exchange. "By the way, Arthur, you know my friend, Robbie Ross."

The diminutive art critic—completely ignored up until this moment—occupied the chair directly across from Wilde. He sat in slack-jawed amazement listening to their extraordinary exchange, the domino he was about to play still clutched in his hand.

"Yes, ah, hello, Arthur," Ross looked at them both askance. "What on earth are you two discussing?"

"Ah, just an idea for a play that Oscar and I are working on," Conan Doyle said. He rose to his feet and nodded for Wilde to do the same. "I'm afraid I must spoil your domino game, Robbie. Come, Oscar, we have much to discuss."

Moments later, they spilled out of the café, Wilde still objecting as he pulled his arms into the sleeves of his coat. They secured a hackney carriage from the nearby cabstand and piled inside. As the cab drew out into the thrash and brawl of London traffic, Conan Doyle reached into his pocket and flourished the cogwheel. "Do you know what this is, Oscar?"

Wilde pursed his lips and peered at the object with a frown. "If it's an engagement ring I have to say it is rather clunky looking."

"It is a cogwheel."

"Ahhhhh, a cogwheel," Wilde said, nodding his head. But then added a moment later. "What on earth is a cogwheel?"

"Part of a gear train used in mechanical devices of great complexity."

Wilde cogitated upon that and finally shook his head. "No . . . that still doesn't help."

"As I told you, Tarquin Hogg, the president of the Bank of England, was assassinated last night. This morning, Detective Blenkinsop and I visited the murder scene."

The Irishman's muddy complexion turned ashen. "Tell me you speak in jest, Arthur. Commissioner Burke expressly forbade—"

"I know. This was an unsanctioned visit. And I now suspect that the commissioner is part of an ongoing conspiracy." Conan Doyle went on to narrate their visit to Tarquin Hogg's house, his discovery of the infernal device and their near miss with Burke. He concluded by narrating how he followed his adjutant Dobbs to the scene of a riot at St. Giles.

"Good Lord!" Wilde said. "What is this all about?"

"I'm not sure, but someone is dabbling in unnatural things: the reanimation of corpses using mechanical hearts. This cogwheel is a component. I need to find who has the knowledge to fashion such a thing, and I believe I know who might be able to help us."

*   *   *

The hackney carriage dropped them in the Fitzrovia neighborhood of central London. As he stepped down, Conan Doyle happened to glance back up the stretch of Mortimer Street in time to see a familiar pair of bowler-hatted figures descend from a hansom.

"Damn and blast!"

"Whatever is it?"

"We've been followed by Cypher's bully boys. They must have been lurking outside the Café Royal. Do you see the two large gents in bowlers? I call them Dandelion and Burdock."

Wilde chuckled. "That's very amusing and quite apropos, I might add. These are your erstwhile protectors, sent by the enigmatically monikered Cypher?"

"I believe they are his men—protectors, spies, whatever they may be. But I don't like being followed everywhere. The Emporium is just up the street. We need to give them the slip. I shall attempt to get them to follow me and then hopefully elude them. Oscar, you walk on. Go to the end of the street and then cross over and double back. Lose yourself in the crowd. Dodge into a shop doorway now and again. Try to be inconspicuous."

Wilde flashed a deeply wounded expression. "Inconspicuous?

Moi? Now you go too far, Arthur. Oscar Wilde has many hues to his palette, but *inconspicuous* is not amongst them."

* * *

Conan Doyle had been loitering outside Jedidiah's Emporium of Mechanical Marvels for ten minutes before Wilde finally sauntered up. "What took you so long? I deliberately hurried all the way here."

"Really? I deliberately dawdled. If they were pursuing me, it is likely they overshot."

"Quickly, let's go inside."

The bell jangled as the two friends stepped inside the shop, and were greeted by its dazzling cornucopia of toys, dolls, and mechanical wonders, a place permeated with magic and the lingering odor of machine oil.

"I say," Wilde exclaimed, looking around in amazement. "I must never bring the boys in here. I would leave bankrupt."

The shop proprietor was not manning the counter when they entered, and failed to appear after a long wait.

"Hello?" Conan Doyle called aloud.

No response.

A train whistle moaned and the toy steam train whooshed from the alpine tunnel and circuited the shop on its elevated track before plunging into another tunnel at the far side of the room and vanishing.

The two friends drifted about the shop, poking at things, picking up the odd toy, which whirred or buzzed or jangled as it performed some kind of intricate mechanical motion. As he prowled the space, Conan Doyle's scalp prickled and he had the feeling he was being watched. Then he saw the shadowy figure watching him from the back of the shop: the Automaton Turk.

"What the devil is it?" Wilde asked.

"A mechanical chess-playing device. You should try it."

"You mean it actually works?"

"Very well. Too dashed well! You play chess, of course?"

"*Naturellement.* I was chess champion at Trinity."

"Go on. Have a bash. Play a game."

Wilde studied the elaborate device with a puzzled frown.

"How does it function? I see no switch."

"Simply play your opening move. It somehow activates the mechanism."

"Really?" Wilde tossed Conan Doyle an incredulous glance, but then squared his shoulders and pushed his knight's pawn to knight 4.

Instantly, the Turk came alive in a whir of gears. The dusky head lifted, the eyes opened and glowed. It drew the long-stemmed pipe to its lips, paused, and exhaled a jet of steam. The arm jerked across the chessboard and pushed a black pawn to bishop 4, threatening Wilde's pawn.

Wilde chuckled. "That's the damndest thing I've ever seen. It plays like my old chess master, Shaughnessy. It even pongs a bit like him."

Conan Doyle left Wilde to his game and wandered deeper into the shop. The toy steam train sounded its mournful whistle and burst once more from the mountain tunnel, thundered around the walls in a blur of mechanical hurry, and vanished through the far wall. Beneath the alpine tunnel was a door, presumably leading to living premises behind the shop. He rapped his knuckles on the wood and called out, "Hello? You have customers! Hello?"

He waited a polite moment and, when no one answered, tried the doorknob. It was not locked and he stepped into a small sitting room decorated with horsehide settees bedecked with doilies and fripperies. Fresh cut flowers sat in glass vases. A coal fire throbbed in the grate.

"Are you quite certain we should be in here?" Wilde's voice asked in his ear.

Conan Doyle gave a start. The large Irishman hovered at his shoulder.

"What happened to your chess game?"

A look of discomfort flashed across Wilde's long face. "The machine cheats. Of that I am quite sure. Check and mate in under a dozen moves? Preposterous! Did I mention I was chess champion at Trinity?"

Conan Doyle noticed a framed black-and-white photograph hanging on the wall. Two figures posed on the foreshore of a large and placid lake: a young blond woman in a light crinoline; by her side a small boy, probably a few years younger than his son Kingsley, clutching a windup toy warship.

"Ah, there's life," Wilde said, and nodded out the window.

Like many English properties, the shop had a long, narrow garden. At the far end of the space, sitting in a kind of open pavilion, were two people: a woman in a rocking chair (Conan Doyle guessed it had to be the same woman as in the photograph, but could not be certain as her face was hidden beneath a rather old-fashioned pokey bonnet); at her side was a young boy seated in a bath chair, a cap upon his head and a blanket draped across his lap. His hands worked at the controls of a black box, which evidently threw the switches of the train track and determined the path of the toy steam locomotive. His face was set in a smile of childish delight, and his gaze followed the train's progress as it sizzled along the shiny loops of track.

"Doctor Doyle, is it not?"

Both men jumped. The shopkeeper stood behind them, wiping his hands on a rag.

"Terribly sorry," Conan Doyle apologized. "I knocked but no one answered. We had been waiting some time."

Jedidiah beamed with his usual good humor. "Yes, I was down in the workshop, just putting the finishing touches on . . . a project. Your little boy's soldier has been fixed. I have it under the counter, all boxed up and ready to take home."

"Wonderful."

Wilde nodded at the figures in the garden. "If I may say so, you have a beautiful boy. A quite radiant child."

"Thank you, sir." Jedidiah gazed out the window at the two figures and his eyes misted. "My wife and child are the reason I draw breath. Without them, I would be nothing."

A silence crowded into the room with them and overstayed its welcome. The toy maker drew himself together. "Shall I ring you up, sir?"

They returned to the shop counter. As Conan Doyle settled the bill, Wilde continued to browse.

"There you go, sir," Jedidiah said brightly, tightening the twine fastening the box securely. "And as I promised, a lifetime guarantee."

Conan Doyle thanked him and, seeing an opening, said, "You're a man conversant in all matters mechanical. As a matter of interest, have you ever seen anything like this?" He fished in his pocket, took out the shiny brass cogwheel, and laid it on the counter.

The shopkeeper glanced down at the object and froze. After a long pause he picked it up and studied it, turning it over and over. His head shook from an involuntary tremor. "No . . . no, I have never seen its like. Quite remarkable. The machining is exquisite." He laughed. "I am a mere toy maker. This is the work of a great engineer. A master." He fondled the shiny gear. "Might I inquire where you obtained it?"

Conan Doyle did not want to reveal too much, and offhandedly muttered, "I found it. In the street somewhere."

"In the street?" Jedidiah repeated in a tone brittle with skepticism. "Do you recall which street?"

Conan Doyle shook his head. "I'm afraid not. Just happened upon it in my travels." He held out his hand. "Well, there you are. Thank you for trying."

Jedidiah hesitated. "I'd be very interested in finding the maker of these gears, sir. Their use would contribute greatly to my business."

"Afraid I can't help." Conan Doyle kept his hand held out. With obvious reluctance, the toy maker handed the gearwheel back.

Wilde arrived at the counter. "Might I inquire, sir, which are the noisiest toys in your shop?"

"The noisiest?" the shopkeeper repeated, puzzled by the question. He squinted around. "I suppose the tin trumpet and the drum. Between them they make a fair old racket."

"Splendid," Wilde said, laying his calling card on the counter. "Please box them up and have them delivered to my home address."

The bell chimed as Conan Doyle and Wilde left the shop. As soon as the door closed on their backs, Jedidiah rushed from the counter. He flipped the sign from OPEN to CLOSED and turned his key in the lock, watching through the glass as the two friends stood conversing on the pavement.

From behind, the Ottoman Turk stirred to life in a purr of greased gears. The head lifted, the eyes sprang open and glowed eerily. A jet of steam shot from the automaton's caved lips. The wooden arm lifted, swung across the chessboard, and tapped the tip of its pipe one . . . two . . . three . . . four . . . five times upon the chessboard.

"Yes, Otto, you are right," the toy maker said without turning to look around. "This is a most worrisome development." His eyes momentarily dropped from the men outside to the calling cards clutched in his trembling hands. "Fortunately, the two gentlemen"—he squinted to read the finely calligraphied names—"*Dr. Arthur Conan Doyle, Author,* and *Mr. Oscar Fingal O'Flahertie Wills Wilde, Playwright,* have been kind enough to provide me with their calling cards. Now I know who they are . . . and precisely where they live."

Out in the street, Wilde and Conan Doyle were still arguing over their respective chess prowess, or lack thereof.

"I haven't played chess in ages," Wilde rationalized.

"No, of course not."

"And playing against oneself hardly counts."

"I had precisely the same excuse."

The Irishman was incensed. "Beaten by a, a, a—"

"Glorified cuckoo clock?"

"Precisely! Did I mention I was chess champion at Trinity?"

"This would make the third time."

Wilde fixed his friend with a look of concern. "Are we growing old, Arthur? Losing our faculties?"

"No. Nowadays we play different games. With greater outcomes."

Something up the street caught Conan Doyle's eye. He grabbed Wilde by the lapel of his coat, propelled him into a nearby shop doorway, and pressed him up against the door.

"What? Must we really fight about this? Or are we about to dance?"

"Look." Conan Doyle nodded at two bowler-hatted men standing on a street corner, looking about, studying the faces of passersby.

"Dandelion and Burdock! Not again! Did they see us?"

"I think not."

"What now?"

Conan Doyle reached into a pocket, removed the cogwheel and tossed it in his hand. "The shopkeeper is possessed of a keen mechanical bent, and yet he said he'd never seen the like of this gear. He concluded it was clearly the work of a master engineer. It just so happened that a master engineer visited Tarquin Hogg shortly before he was murdered. I think we need to pay a visit to Ozymandius Arkwright."

At that precise moment a hansom veered around a stationary omnibus and clopped in their direction. "Here comes a cab now, Oscar. Quickly."

They stepped from the shop doorway and flagged the cab. The two friends clambered aboard and Conan Doyle shouted for the cabbie to drive on.

"Did they see us?" Wilde asked.

Conan Doyle turned and peered out the back window.

"If they did, they show no signs. I think we made a clean escape." He instructed the driver to take them to an address Wilde had never heard of, a place on the very outskirts of London.

"Where are we going?"

"Arkadia."

"What's that?"

"Arkwright's factory. This may take a while. I'm afraid it's a bit out of the way."

"Ah," said Wilde, and then took out his silver cigarette case and counted how many cigarettes he had left. "So long as it's no farther than seven cigarettes there should no problem."

The two fell into reverie as the cab clopped through the busy streets. Finally Conan Doyle turned to Wilde and said, "Why did you ask for the noisiest toys in the shop?"

Wilde paused in lighting up his second cigarette of the journey. "My wife, Constance, suffers from the most excruciating migraines."

"What? You can't. You couldn't do that!" Conan Doyle said, utterly scandalized. "Oh, that's terribly cruel, Oscar!"

"As I have told you, Arthur. These days, Robert Sheridan is there to keep her company. He lingers in the parlor like the aroma of bacon long after the breakfast things have been cleared. I feel quite forgot. However, my little gift to our boys will be sure to keep me uppermost in her thoughts."

CHAPTER 16

LOOK UPON MY WORKS AND TREMBLE

"What is this drab and dreary place, Arthur?"

"Arkadia. Spelled with a *k*, not a *c*. Note the sign."

The hackney had traveled north for close to an hour, taking them to the ragged edge of the metropolis, a place where rows of brick houses abruptly transitioned into green fields. Up ahead, like a smudge of soot upon the landscape, stood a huge factory with rows of tall chimneys vomiting smoke.

They stepped down from the hackney and walked through an archway of wrought iron. The top of the arch spelled out a name in black iron letters: ARKADIA.

"Arkadia," Wilde read aloud, and sniffed. "Obviously meant to be ironic. That name conjures a land of rustic simplicity and beauty. Yet all I see is a dark satanic mill with chimneys billowing brimstone and huddled before it a ghastly monotony of identical brick terraces."

"It is a planned village. A model of sanitary and modern living. Arkwright has built a place for his workers to live, complete with a church and town hall."

"Planned dreariness more like it. Why can the English not build villages modeled after those in Tuscany? Are Italian bricks somehow more expensive to make?"

Like the strands of a web, all streets led to the factory and were long and wide. The two friends set off walking at a good clip and it did not take long for Conan Doyle to concede Wilde's point: the houses were indeed drab and anonymous. But compared to the filthy, dilapidated hovels many Londoners lived in, they were palaces.

The two friends had almost reached the factory gates when they heard a familiar sound from behind: *wisshhhhthump . . . wishhhhhhhthump . . . . wishhhhhhhhthump . . .*

They turned to find a steam car bearing down on them. The top-hatted driver did not slow down, but instead squeezed the rubber bulb of a horn and honked impatiently. The two friends had barely time to throw themselves clear as the steam car whistled past and disappeared through the factory gates.

"That's him now!" Conan Doyle grumbled. "Bounder near ran us over!"

Although the steam car was nowhere in sight when they passed through the gates, a figure in a stovepipe hat was. Standing upon a plinth was a bronze statue of a tall thin man with muttonchop whiskers, a cigar clamped in his jaws, and his trademark tall headgear. A brass plaque beneath it bore the inscription: Ozymandius Arkwright, Benefactor.

"Ozymandius, indeed?" Wilde snickered and began to recite in a chest-thumping voice the sonnet by Percy Bysshe Shelley: "My name is Ozymandius, king of kings: look upon my works, ye Mighty and despair!"

"Yes, very amusing, Oscar. I know the poem, too."

"One moment," Wilde said, wrinkling his nose. "Don't you think there's something a little odd about this statue?"

"Odd in what way?"

"The left arm looks a bit off. And the statue is not properly centered."

A moment's closer inspection revealed two cutoff brass stubs in the concrete plinth.

"This statue originally had a companion," Wilde surmised. "A second figure that has since been removed. I would speculate that the pose has been amended. The arm was once draped about the shoulder of its neighbor, but has been cut off and the pose rather crudely changed."

"Yes, you're right, Oscar," Conan Doyle agreed. "How odd. How very odd."

*   *   *

After being left in a small waiting room for the best part of an hour, the two colleagues were then conducted into an even smaller waiting room. After an additional wait of twenty minutes, a balding secretary entered.

"Lord forbid," Wilde muttered. "No doubt he's come to shift us to a closet and from there into a biscuit tin."

Instead, the secretary, muttering apologies for the wait, conducted them into a long, low-ceilinged room, brightly lit by strings of electric bulbs. Men in shirts and waistcoats wearing accountants' visors with elastic garters holding up their sleeves stood at rows of drafting tables, working with pencils, protractors, compasses. Ozymandius Arkwright stood gazing over the shoulder of one of the draftsmen, and Conan Doyle noticed that the man's hand trembled visibly as he drew.

When Arkwright finally noticed the two friends, he fixed them with a suspicious glare, his muttonchop whiskers bristling as he clenched a jaw so square it could have been machined from a billet of steel.

"What the bloody hell do you two want?" he bellowed in a broad, Yorkshire accent.

Conan Doyle removed his hat and spoke in a firm, but diplomatic tone. "Mister Arkwright, I am Arthur Conan Doyle and this is my friend, Oscar Wilde."

There were few names in British society of equal fame, but it was obvious the master engineer was completely clueless. "Who? Never bloody heard of you. State your business and then kindly bugger off!"

"It's about the fog, sir," Wilde put in—rashly, it turned out.

At the mention of the word *fog* the large Yorkshire engineer grew apoplectic.

"Oh, I've seen you bloody London types before! Are you come here to dun me about the smoke my factories release? Ignorance, gentlemen. Mindless piffle! London sits on marshland through which a great river runs. There have been London fogs since Roman times. The puny efforts of man have no effect whatsoever upon the climate."

Rather inadvisably, Wilde chose to argue the point. "But surely it must have some effect. When I smoke in my carriage it fogs the air dreadfully and my wife upbraids me. Of course, I simply must smoke as it is vital to the creative process, and yet still she complains."

"Your analogy is baseless," Arkwright sneered. "The interior of a carriage is a tiny space. By comparison the atmosphere is as vast and limitless as the oceans. Besides, do you know what that smoke represents?"

"Black lung?" Conan Doyle ventured; the man's rudeness had got his dander up. "Respiratory distress, inflammation of the bronchioles, emphysema—"

"Work, sir! Work. Employment. Commerce. The creation of wealth for all. Food on the table for my workers. Employment for colliers. For coal merchants. Warmth for the hearths of millions. Baked bread to feed hungry bellies. A bloody small price to pay for an occasional smudge of soot on a fine gentleman's starched collar."

Conan Doyle let the Yorkshireman rant on until he, at last, paused for breath. "I'm afraid my friend misspoke. We have not come to discuss fog, but to discuss the *Fog Committee*."

For a moment, a look of fear flashed across Ozymandius's face before a fierce light burned hot in the gray eyes, a muscle quivered in the implacable jaw.

"Enough!" he barked, silencing Conan Doyle with a look. For the first time, he seemed aware of his draftsmen and a roomful of eavesdropping ears. He nodded toward a door at the end of the room. "Not here," he said and added curtly, "Follow."

They struggled to keep up with the industrialist, who walked with a distance-devouring stride, along first one corridor and through a door, followed by a second and then a third. With each doorway they passed through, the din of machinery grew steadily louder. Arkwright paused at a final door and flung it open. They stepped into a factory where the air vibrated with a percussive cacophony of pounding steam hammers, shrieking saws, and the roar of mighty steam engines turning enormous wheels, the brassy arms of their giant connecting rods pulverizing the air with each dizzy revolution. Dwarfed by the machines, men in overalls beetled about the factory floor, wrenching on giant beam engines, their faces runneling sweat, while women and children hunched over belt-driven machines with spinning wire brushes they used to polish shiny brass cogwheels. Once finished, they dropped the parts into baskets at their feet. When the growing pile threatened to overflow onto the floor, the baskets were hefted by other workers, loaded onto iron wheeled carts, and dragged away.

"Say what you have to say and be bloody quick about it," the industrialist snarled, as he strode quickly across the factory floor. "I'm a busy man who earned his fortune through hard graft. Not a *gentleman* who idles his day away over cups of tea and the day's newspapers. Time is money and I have none to fritter."

"The other night, you almost ran over our carriage on Piccadilly. Soon after, we encountered a strange man, more monster than man. That same night, Tarquin Hogg was assassinated."

At Conan Doyle's words, Ozymandius stopped short and glared at the two friends. "Who are you two? Who sent you to my door?"

But instead of answering, Conan Doyle drew out the shiny cogwheel from his pocket and held it up for Arkwright to see. At the sight of the cogwheel, the engineer's eyes widened, his jaw clenched. He looked ready to burst into a fit of histrionics, but instead his shoulders slumped and he growled, "Follow me."

They left the noise of the factory, weaved through a maze of offices, and finally stepped into a large and gloomy space lined with bookcases bowing beneath collapsing piles of engineering texts— Arkwright's private office. As they entered the room, the engineer crossed to his enormous desk and tossed a cloth over something he obviously did not want them to see. Conan Doyle hoped Wilde had also seen it, but the glimpse was so brief and the object so bizarre and out of keeping with the rest of the engineer's business, later on he could not be certain of what he had truly seen.

One large window, dimmed by years of soot, looked out over a grimy rooftop to a row of smokestacks billowing clouds of carbon black. The walls of the office were hung with photographs of past triumphs: giant locomotives, iron bridges, steamships, colossal beam engines. The Yorkshireman gruffly gestured for them to take a seat in the two chairs set before his hulking desk while he paced the room, a man in perpetual motion. After the third circuit, he paused long enough to take a cigar from a wooden box. Seeming to remember his manners, he grudgingly thrust the box at his guests. After each took a turn with the cutter, the three men shared a quiet moment as they puffed their cigars into life.

A large framed photograph hung on the wall behind his desk: two gentlemen in matching stovepipe hats posing before a giant steam locomotive. The men had their arms draped about each other's shoulders, a celebratory cigar clamped in their jaws. Ozymandius was the taller of the two, and shared a familial similarity with the shorter man—no doubt a brother. The photograph had been taken many years back, for both sported finely trimmed black beards devoid of a trace of gray.

Conan Doyle said nothing for several seconds. He took out the gearwheel and placed it upon Arkwright's desk and asked, "Is it something of your manufacture? I was told by an expert that only an engineer of considerable talent could fashion such a piece."

Arkwright stood looking down at the shiny metal gear, his jaw clenching. Finally, he could resist no longer and snatched it up, scrutinizing the object closely. He asked in an accusatory voice, "Where did you get this?"

"I found it in the house of Tarquin Hogg. It was part of a mechanical heart that had been implanted in the assassin's chest. Someone is reanimating executed prisoners using these infernal devices and programming them to murder key figures in the government."

"Whaaaaat?" The engineer exclaimed, his eyes widening. But then he shrugged it off and muttered, "Highly bloody fanciful!" and tossed the heavy metal gear back to Conan Doyle.

"So the piece is not of your manufacture?"

"I did not make it. It is not one of mine. Now good day to you *gentlemen*."

"What about your brother?" Wilde spoke up for the first time. "The chap in the photo with you. Your partnership is obviously dissolved, as evidenced by the statue you had amended. Could your brother not have fashioned it?"

"My brother, sir, is dead."

"Dead?" Conan Doyle echoed.

The industrialist seemed to go into a trance, his glassy stare fixed on something from long ago in the past. "An accident. Ten years ago. We made weapons back then: machine guns, cannons, bombs. My brother had an idea for a revolutionary new weapon: a steam torpedo. But no ordinary torpedo—a guided torpedo. A device possessed of a degree of autonomy. It was meant to be a war-winner—an unstoppable weapon that would seek out and destroy enemy ships from a great distance. We thought we had perfected it, but . . ." His voice shriveled and he shook his head scornfully. The engineer turned his back on them and stared fixedly at the framed portrait on the wall. "It worked flawlessly in tests. But on the day of the demonstration, in front of the queen, the admiralty, and all the bloody world, it went terribly wrong. The torpedo missed the target, ran ashore, and crashed into the reviewing stand." He shook his head at the painful memory. "Dozens were killed . . . including my brother's wife and son."

"Your brother was also killed in the blast?" Wilde asked.

Arkwright hesitated a long moment before answering, "My brother, Solomon, also died that day."

Conan Doyle pondered a bit and then calmly asked, "Do you mean he literally died, or that he died to you?"

The engineer drew a breath; his mouth opened, ready to answer, but then he caught himself and the iron returned to his voice. "Who are you to question me? Who the bloody hell are you two?"

"People interested in thwarting an assassination plot which I believe you are somehow involved with . . . however tangentially."

The engineer's nostrils flared; his lips compressed to a thin line. When he spoke, his voice shook with anger. "Get out. Bloody well get out of my factory." He stalked around the desk and Conan Doyle's heart quickened as it seemed Arkwright was about to physically attack them.

But instead he stooped over and bellowed in their faces. "GET OUT!"

* * *

"The grandly named Ozymandias need not fear assassination," Wilde said. "The man is likely to succumb to a fit of dyspepsia at any moment."

The two were once again in the hired hackney trundling back toward London. Conan Doyle toyed with the shiny gear in his hands. "Did you happen to see the object on his desk? When we entered the room, he hurriedly threw a cloth over it, but I managed to catch a glimpse. Did you?"

Wilde shook his head. "I saw the cloth and the rough outline of something beneath it. What was beneath it?"

"I cannot be certain, but it looked to me like a mechanical arm."

Wilde furrowed his brow. "You mean, a mechanical human arm?"

"Yes, a skeletal armature made of shiny metal. It looked as though it articulated in precisely the same manner a human arm would." He raised his own arm and flexed it to demonstrate. "The shoulder, the elbow, the wrist, and the fingers, down to the individual phalanges— all articulated."

"Quite a departure for Mister Arkwright, who seems to specialize in all things enormous and loud: giant steam engines, locomotives, ships. Perhaps he is pursuing a new field of endeavor."

"Having recently seen what I believe to be a mechanical heart, I find it an unsettling coincidence."

"There's that word again: coincidence."

"Yes," Conan Doyle agreed. He paused to remove his pocket watch and held it up to the light to check the time. Although it was scarcely three, the skies were darkening ominously.

The two fell silent. Contemplative.

Ahead, the road dipped in a long, downhill sweep of cobblestones. On the distant skyline hung the brooding silhouette of London. Monochrome. Colorless. A city formed of soot and shadow wrapped in a tattered gray shroud of clouds. From this elevated perspective, they looked out over housetops and chimney pots, factory chimneys, steamships churning the Thames and fiery locomotives chasing along steely rails, all of them releasing black plumes that rose into the hazy skies and were soon drawn up into carbonaceous clouds so bloated with soot and smoke they dragged their furry bellies across the church spires, unable to rise any higher.

"Good Lord, Arthur," Wilde breathed as the two friends observed the dark spectacle, "what are we doing to the world?"

And then, as sooty drops lashed the cab windows, the city melted and ran, one darkness bleeding into another, a charcoal sketch left out in the rain.

❦

CHAPTER 17

A DROWNED OPHELIA

The Mutoscope flutters and goes dark. The toy maker draws his face away, a hand clamped to his eyes. His shoulders heave. Noiseless sobs rack his body. He fights to compose himself. Abruptly, driven by a sudden resolve, he abandons the Mutoscope and strides across the empty toy store to the open trapdoor. His feet stomp down the bare wooden steps and he crosses the cellar workshop to the workbench set against the bare brick wall. He pulls the hidden handle and the door to an adjacent cellar springs open.

He takes a lantern from its hook and enters the space, passing the hulking restraining chair, and moves to a door at the far end of the space. He keys the lock and steps into a smaller room where his breath fogs the air. In previous times this was a larder for keeping meat; the thick walls are built from massive stones rendered smooth to hold in the chill. Large blocks of river ice sit stacked beneath a scattering of straw, and the flagstones underfoot shine wet from melt water. Dominating the center of the room are two tanks, one large, one small, like metal coffins clamped shut with iron straps.

He moves to the larger tank, unfastens the metal straps, and flings open the lid. The tank is filled to the brim with a glass-clear liquid that could be mistaken for water were it not for the astringent smell of alcohol rising from it. He lofts the lantern and stares rapturously

162 CR THE DEAD ASSASSIN

into the depths. The naked body of a young woman hangs suspended. Her eyes are closed as though lost in her dreams, and in the subtle eddies of the turbid liquid, her long blond hair writhes like underwater weed.

"My beloved," he whispers in words that fog the air.

He plunges an arm into the liquid. It is breathtakingly cold, but before his hand goes numb and loses all feeling, his searching fingers catch and cradle the slender curve of a neck. He carefully lifts and the face of a drowned angel surfaces from the liquid, the plastered hair streaming, the skin marble white and etched with a tracery of fine blue veins. As he draws the face closer, an arm floats up and a hand breaks the surface, revealing torn flesh and the chewed-off stubs of missing fingers.

"Our long years of separation are almost over. Soon, we will be reunited with our child, and we will walk together in the light."

And then he leans close and places a tender kiss upon the stiff, gelid lips.

CHAPTER 18

INVITATION TO AN EXECUTION

"Oscar! Oscar! Awaken at once!" A strong hand gripped Wilde's shoulder, shaking him awake. He reluctantly surfaced from sleep to find himself in his room in the Albemarle. Conan Doyle was standing over him, fully dressed in hat and coat, having just cabbed over from his own gentlemen's club, the Athenaeum.

"Dash it all!" Wilde moaned. "Why did you awaken me? I had just discovered a secret closet within my house that I did not know existed. The closet was filled with shoes. Thousands of pairs of shoes. And when I tried them on, they all fit perfectly. It was the most profoundly moving experience. It was so vivid." He sniffed the air. "I swear I still have the aroma of butter-soft leather in my nostrils. Have you ever in your life had such a dream?"

"We all have those dreams, Oscar. Now, I am sorry to awaken you so early, but I have shocking news."

"News in any way related to footwear?"

"I'm afraid not." Conan Doyle flourished the morning paper, opened it to the front page, and thrust it under Wilde's nose. The banner headline read: "Murderer of Lord Howell to Hang!"

The Irish playwright's mouth fell open. "How is that possible? Vicente was arrested but four nights ago!"

Conan Doyle was equally flummoxed. "Arrest, trial, and execution in a handful of days? The British judicial system has never in its history worked with such expediency."

The Irishman's eyes raced across lines of type, reading. "He's to be hanged at Newgate on Wednesday." Then realization stunned his eyes wide. "But . . . that's today!"

"Precisely."

"Tried and found guilty of treason by a special sitting," Wilde read aloud, poring over the words. "In less than a week? Such an excess of haste seems impolitic, even in the case of treason."

"I greatly suspect this execution has been rushed in order to silence Vicente before he can speak to anyone." He snatched the paper back. "We must endeavor to see this man, Oscar. Talk to him. Learn the truth. Before his voice is forever extinguished."

Wilde's expression betrayed a lack of enthusiasm. "But, Arthur, you know how executions are. Newgate will be swarmed by every scamp, scallywag, ne'er-do-well, pimp, whore, prig, and pie monger, not to mention the bad, the mad, the insane, and the morbidly curious. We shan't be able to even get within gawking distance."

"Our fame may prove a key to unlock Newgate." He tossed the paper aside. "Come, Oscar. Get dressed. We must leave without delay."

Wilde stared up at him, flabbergasted. "Now? Just like that? I shall require at least an hour to select a suitable wardrobe. Come to think, what does one wear to an execution? Black? A tad cliché. And rather morbid given what is already likely to prove a morose occasion."

Conan Doyle crossed to the armoire, snatched it open, grabbed a shirt at random and threw it at Wilde, who caught it and paused, struck by the color. "Burgundy? Really?" He laughed. "Rather a bold choice, don't you think? Bravo, Arthur. Burgundy: a color that is rich and yet appropriately circumspect." He held the shirt beneath his chin for Conan Doyle's approval. "What do you think, Arthur? This shirt with an ivory cravat? Please, I want you to be brutally honest."

"Being brutally honest, we need to leave now. Immediately. This instant. Newgate executes its prisoners on the stroke of nine and it is nearly eight o'clock."

"B-but, Arthur," Wilde sputtered. "Does a gentleman have time to wash? To shave? To break a crust? I am quite famished."

Conan Doyle snatched the silver hip flask from the bedside table and pressed it into Wilde's hands. "Here's your breakfast. Now be a good chap and drink it down quickly. The game's af—"

"Cease!" Wilde cried out, flinging up a restraining hand. "Please do not utter that phrase and I promise I shall hurry and never complain once."

* * *

Wilde kept his promise and did not utter a single complaint during the carriage ride to Newgate Prison. Instead, he uttered many complaints—about the lingering fog, about the traffic, about the potholed road, about the noisome air—in an ongoing litany until the long, squat, ominous hulk of Newgate Prison finally hove into view through the carriage windows.

"Ugh," he exclaimed upon seeing the stony shoulders of the prison (with the sepulchral dome of St. Paul's hovering weightless above like a memento mori). "Newgate: a prime example of *Architecture Terrible*, a style so repulsive it proclaims its dread function to all who see it. Just looking upon its hideous proportions is like a slap of reprimand."

Even though all executions were now carried on within the walls of Newgate, out of sight of gawkers, a mob of hundreds swarmed beneath the prison's grim façade: Fleet Street hacks, penny-a-line pamphleteers, firebrand priests sermonizing against sin, false beggars, shoeless urchins with filthy faces, reeling drunkards puking on their own shoes. And, of course, despite being literally in the shadow of the most feared symbol of the law's displeasure, the criminal classes, to whom the event wielded an attraction the way a magnet draws iron. And so dipsmen worked the crowd, brazenly rifling pockets while streetwalkers with rouged faces and overspilling bodices buffed men's eyes with their breasts, and sharp-dressed swells arm-in-arm with peach-cheeked courtesans and a faceless horde of thrill-seeking loiterers and ne'er-do-wells from all levels of society, each and every one summoned by the titillating spectacle of the suffering and death of a fellow human being.

The carriage trundled along Newgate Street until forced to a standstill by the press of bodies. Conan Doyle flung open the door and he and Wilde dropped from the carriage into the greasy jostle of the crowd. The two friends threaded a meandering path through the morbid carnival until they fetched up outside the prison's infamous black gates. Set within the hulking outer gate was a smaller, human-sized door. Behind a sliding lattice grille lurked a uniformed prison officer with a face like a clenched fist, snarling at every supplicant who wheedled to gain entry. Conan Doyle shouldered past them all and handed in a note. "This is for your warden. Tell him it is from Arthur Conan Doyle, the author of the Sherlock Holmes stories."

The guard snatched the paper and glared at it with a doubting scowl. He eyeballed Conan Doyle and Wilde up and down, and then banged the grille shut without speaking a word.

"That looked far from promising," Wilde observed.

"I concur."

"Although if I hired him to be my footman, I should seldom be bothered by creditors."

After a short wait, they heard the clunk of a heavy iron bolt being shot and the door-within-the-door swung open. The same surly guard beckoned them with a get-yer-arses-in-here wave. Wilde and Conan Doyle stepped through Newgate's infamous portal to a dread realm devoted to misery, suffering, and death. Without speaking a word, the grim-faced guard marched them along an echoing stone corridor to where a man in a gray suit with graying hair stood waiting. His face contained no glimmer of emotion, although the depth and severity of his frown lines suggested that he was a man with little practice in smiling.

"I am William Bland, warden of Newgate."

Conan Doyle nodded a bow and presented a small, leather-bound book to the warden. "I hope you will accept this collection of Sherlock Holmes stories, with my compliments."

The warden pointedly eyed the proffered book but made no move to take it.

The Scots author quickly added, "I have taken the liberty of signing it to you, sir."

Still, the warden kept his arms resolutely folded behind his back. "Your offer is noted, Doctor Doyle, but I cannot accept. I do not sully my mind by indulging in the fripperies and distractions of the day. The Bible is the only book I read."

To his mortification, Conan Doyle was forced to retract the snubbed offering, which he hastily secreted in a coat pocket. "Ah, I see," he muttered, stunned by the naked surliness of the warden's demeanor.

"The state is about to relieve a man of his life," Wilde said in his "lecture hall" voice. He had captured the entire North American continent with it, and had no doubt it would impress a lowly prison governor. "As two of the nation's leading scribes, we are here to interview the unfortunate party and draw a picture in words of his final hours upon the earth."

Bland seemed unimpressed by Wilde's grandiloquence. "And what will that accomplish?"

The Irish wit was lost for a comeback. "Why, it will . . ." He threw a glance at Conan Doyle. "Go on, Arthur, explain to the governor what our mission today will accomplish."

Put on the spot, the Scottish author threw a cutting look at his friend, but then forced a smile and said, "We are here as witnesses to history. To record the laudable efforts of the British penal system in preventing our nation from a descent into anarchy and lawlessness."

If the warden was any more impressed by Conan Doyle's speech, he successfully concealed it. "Newgate has been visited many times by scribblers such as yourselves, gentlemen. Mister Dickens himself toured the facilities here many years ago and wrote a very dour report of conditions inside Newgate."

"Really?" Conan Doyle blustered, although he had pored over *Sketches by Boz* many times and was well acquainted with the passages.

"Yes, very drab indeed. I hope your reports will be equally dark. For the world needs to know that Newgate Prison is the last place any man or woman should wish to visit."

As if to punctuate the remark, Bland turned his head and stared pointedly at Wilde, who visibly paled. And then the warden leaned forward, bringing his face uncomfortably close to Conan Doyle's—a headmaster about to scold a naughty pupil. "Those who enter Newgate leave broken men," he said, lavishing the Scottish author with breath that smelled as if a lead spoon had dissolved in his corrosive mouth. "And some do not leave at all, but are buried beneath the stones of the Bird Cage Walk, where they will remain prisoners of Newgate until the Resurrection. Bodies of the executed are taken there straight from the scaffold. A floor slab is pried up and the carcass dropped into the pit below. Final absolution is provided by a splash of water and a bucket of quicklime—to speed the dissolution of the skeleton."

Conan Doyle dared not breathe until the Warden finally drew his face away.

"Unfortunately, we have quite run out of room," Bland continued. "Nowadays, executed prisoners must be taken from the prison to be inhumed in a potter's field along with the indigent, the insane, and all the other useless detritus of society."

Conan Doyle swallowed a grimace and molded his features into an expression he hoped resembled affability. "I come purely in the interest of research, so that I may provide my readers with an accurate description of the rigors of prison to . . . to . . . provide a somber lesson for those who might be tempted to stray—"

"So, you wish us to leave?" Wilde interrupted. "It seems we have been invited inside Newgate simply to have the door slammed in our faces by you, personally."

But instead of taking affront at Wilde's remark, the warden shook his head mildly. Apparently, his countenance had only the one dour expression. "Quite the opposite, gentlemen. My prison is open for your inspection."

* * *

It soon became obvious that the guard escorting them had been drilled to provide an intimate tour of all of the very worst of Newgate's privations. First they visited the men's cellblock, a place gaggingly odiferous with the stink of unemptied slop buckets, alkaline sweat, and the tangible reek of lives wearing to the bone. Next, they trod a dark maze of corridors, passing along the way a shuffling prisoner being prodded along by a guard's wooden truncheon. The prisoner cut a nightmarish figure in his gray uniform, a cloth disk bearing the number 19 sewn onto the breast—the only identity permitted inside the prison walls. He wore the requisite cap with its large visor that projected straight down to hide the prisoner's face and allowed only a restricted view of his confines through a pair of eye slits.

They passed an open door to an exercise yard where men in striped prison uniforms trudged in aimless circles around a narrow quadrangle. Next they entered a dinful gallery where convicts trudged upon the giant wheels of wooden treadmills, while others labored at The Crank, a wooden box fitted with a handle that turned in a box filled with sand to provide a resistance. In all cases, the one and only goal of such punishments was futility: a cruel reminder to every captive of the state that their energies were squandered meaninglessly and produced nothing but sore muscles, racked bodies, and broken spirits.

"The poor wretches toil like Sisyphus," Wilde muttered sotto voce. "I could not survive a day in such a place."

The extremities they witnessed cowed Conan Doyle. He had

always been a staunch supporter of law and order, but the diabolical ingenuity of the punishments seemed out of proportion to any crime, perhaps short of murder.

Finally, they stepped into the condemned cell, a gloomy but comparatively large space created by knocking two cells together. The wan morning light filtered in through two barred windows. At one side of the cell, a pair of guards lounged at a pine table, playing cards. The only other stick of furniture was a low cot covered by a thin cotton pallet and a worn woolen blanket. The Italian valet, unshaven and wretched in his prison uniform, slouched on the end of the cot where he stared at the rectangle of sky caged by the barred window. He was not alone. A handsome man in his early thirties, with a noble mien and head of ash-blond hair that had enjoyed the benefit of curling papers, sat at his side, a black Gladstone bag nestled on the floor at his feet. He was busy unwinding the dressings on the condemned man's arm. Conan Doyle surmised that the handsome man must be the prison doctor. He rose from the cot when Conan Doyle and Wilde entered and addressed them in a challenging voice. "Who are you? Might this man not be allowed to compose himself unmolested in his final hour of life? What are you, newspaper reporters?"

At the comment, Wilde sucked in an audible gasp and pressed a hand to his breastbone, pantomiming umbrage.

"I, sir, am Oscar Wilde, playwright and raconteur. My companion is the esteemed author Arthur Conan Doyle, and I can safely vouch that neither of us has ever been so insulted in our lives. Newspapermen, indeed! Do I look like a newspaperman? Do I dress like a newspaperman? Do I display the sunken posture of a man who spends his life on all fours, grubbing about in the unhappiness of human suffering?"

The prison doctor lowered his eyes. "I apologize. I am Doctor John Lamb, the only physician here in Newgate. It is my lot to attend to the poor souls walled up within this place. I do what little my meager skills permit to alleviate the suffering of the men and women here.

Yes, even those who are condemned. For I believe that even the lowest in society deserve to sip from the cup of human dignity before the state strips away their soul."

Conan Doyle stepped forward and gently took the Italian's arm. The condemned man sat passive and silent—a man shaken from a dream only to awaken into a nightmare. The Scottish author inspected the physician's work. A ten-inch incision, beautifully stitched, showed where the doctor had performed a miraculous repair of the arm.

"This is most artfully done, sir," Conan Doyle observed. "The bone was shattered by a bullet, and yet he can raise and move his arm with little discomfort. I am a doctor myself and have stood in attendance at some of the best surgeons at my medical school in Edinburgh." He carefully lowered the valet's arm and reached out to shake the doctor's hand. "I congratulate you, sir, and am curious to know how you performed this minor miracle."

Doctor Lamb shook the proffered hand and acknowledged Conan Doyle's praise with a nod and a modest smile that betrayed his satisfaction at the obvious pride he took in his work.

"As a prison doctor, the pecuniary advantages are scant," he spoke in a cultured voice as mild as his demeanor. "My reward comes in the freedom to practice my technique. Including, what some would consider, *experimental* procedures." He added somewhat ruefully, "I have an advantage over other doctors in that my patients do not complain much. And in the case of poor souls condemned to die, have not the means to do so. And so I am free to practice a form of healing whose orthodoxy might be questioned elsewhere. As you correctly noted, the bone was shattered into fragments. I straightened the ends using a bone saw and then held the ulna together using screws and metal straps."

"Screws and metal straps?" Conan Doyle repeated. "I have never heard of such a thing! Surely, metal will corrode inside the body and cause infection?"

"Precisely why I used a special iron-free alloy that does not corrode. The strap is affixed to the bone with brass screws so that stabilizes the bone until it knits together naturally. In addition, I have concocted a salve that alleviates the swelling typical after surgery and promotes rapid healing. The incision was then sewn up in the usual manner."

"Exemplary stitching, if I say so," added Wilde. "I wish the woman who did my shirts had hands as skilled as yours."

"Thank you, Mister Wilde." The doctor paused to glance at his pocket watch. Reminded of the time, he hefted his Gladstone and stood up to go. "I must take my leave of you gentlemen. As always, I have an infirmary full of patients to attend to."

Dr. Lamb bowed to them both and nodded to the two warders as he left the cell.

Throughout the conversation, the Italian valet remained placid and dazed. Wilde finally spoke his name, "Vicente," and the man looked up with hollow, unfocused eyes dripping with mortality.

In fluent Italian, Wilde told the valet who they were and why they had come. "To hear your side of the story, which I believe has not been heard." He perched on the edge of the cot beside the condemned man and laid a comforting hand on his shoulder. "Tell us," he purred in Italian. "What really happened that night?"

Vicente took a deep breath and shuddered from the horror of casting his mind back to that dreadful evening. At first, he stumbled over his words, and then spoke in rapid bursts of Italian, which Wilde translated for Conan Doyle.

"It was late. My master dined at six thirty and then I dressed him. He had a meeting."

"With who?" Conan Doyle interjected. "Ask him if he knows who Lord Howell was meeting?"

Wilde translated the question, but the handsome valet shook his head.

"I no know. I no know. Important man. Someone high up. Lord Howell was upset . . . agitated. After dinner he dismissed the cook and the maid-of-all-work. Gave them money and sent them away."

"And you've no idea what he was worried about?"

The Italian shook his head. "Something serious. Something bad. I know because Lord Howell took money from the wall safe . . . and a loaded pistol."

Conan Doyle and Wilde exchanged a look.

"He tell me to go away, too. He says there is much danger. But I would not leave. I said I would stay and face the danger standing at his side. And then a gentleman came to the door. He and my master had words."

Wilde leaned forward and asked in Italian, "Did your master and the gentleman argue?"

"Yes. No. Not an argument. But they spoke too loud. I think the visitor also knows of the danger. He left quickly."

"What did the man look like?" Conan Doyle queried. "Can you describe him?"

Vicente covered his eyes with a hand, thinking. "A man of past middle years. Big whiskers." He mimed sideburns with his hands. "A man of wealth, but I could tell he had no servants."

"How could he tell that?" Conan Doyle asked.

A wan smile crossed the Italian's face. "Because his clothes were rumpled. Not pressed. And he wore a very ugly hat."

"What type of hat?" Wilde asked.

The Italian used both hands to mime a tall hat rising from his head.

"A top hat? The man wore a top hat?"

"Like a top hat, but taller. Too tall. Ridiculous."

Conan Doyle felt an uneasy stirring. "Ask him how the gentleman arrived. Did he come by hansom, or carriage?"

Wilde put the question to the Italian, who responded by acting out a man seated behind a steering wheel and making a hissing noise that needed no translation.

"He arrived by steam car!" Conan Doyle said. "How many people in London wear a stovepipe and drive a steam car? Only one I know of: our Yorkshire friend, Ozymandius Arkwright."

"And you think such a man is somehow involved in an assassination plot?"

The Scottish doctor's face projected mystification. He shook his head. "I cannot say, but I am now convinced he is the blurred figure in the photograph of the Fog Committee." He nodded at the valet. "Ask Vicente what happened next."

Wilde relayed the question and the Italian grew visibly upset. "After the gentleman visitor left, the master had me order a carriage. He said we must both leave. But the carriage was late because of the fog. I went out into the street to look . . . and that's when I saw him."

"Saw who?"

"A man made of shadows, standing in the fog. When he does not move, I shout at him: 'Who are you? What you want?' The man steps forward. He walks like this . . ." Vicente got up from the cot and shambled up and down the confined cell, his face sweating and manic. "I shout again. 'Who are you?' And then he comes on through the fog until the streetlamp—whoosh—lights up his face and I see it is not a man. It is . . . the devil." Vicente dropped heavily on the cot and buried his face in his hands, his breath squeezing out in an agonized wheeze.

"The devil?" Conan Doyle repeated. "What does he mean, the devil? Ask him what he means, Oscar."

Wilde put the question to the valet, who finally peeled his large hands from his handsome face. "He was a man. But he was not. He moved. He walked. But his eyes were dead and a boneyard reek hung about him. I scream and run. My master comes out as I run past him, back to the house, the dead man chasing me. Lord Howell draws his pistol and shoots. BANG! BANG! BANG! Three times. The devil man flinches. Blood spurts. But still he keeps coming. We slam the door. Turn the key. Throw the bolts. Then BOOM! A sound like thunder as the dead man flings himself against it. We back away and then BOOM! The hinges break and the door crashes down. The dead man bellows like a bear and shambles into the house. Lord Howell raises his pistol and fires, but the bullet hits me in the arm. I scream. The pain so bad. I fall down. The devil comes on. Lord Howell runs into the parlor. Slams the door. Locks it. I think I am dead, but the devil steps over me. He smashes down the parlor door. Then, BANG! I hear a shot. And another, and then click, click, the gun has no more bullets. I stagger to the parlor in time to see the devil grab Lord Howell by the throat, lift him off his feet, and then . . . and then . . . he twist his neck all the way around. I hear bones snap and crack . . ."

The Italian's words dissipated and a silence heavy as syrup poured into their ears.

Wilde nudged the Italian on by saying, "And what happened next?"

By now the Italian was sweating, shivering—a man in a fever. "I faint. I faint away. When I awaken, the devil is gone. My master . . . Lord Howell . . . is dead. He is dead. I crawl into a cupboard to hide— in case the devil comes back for me. I find a bottle and drink. I fall asleep and into this nightmare, from which Vicente cannot awaken."

The Italian began to weep and smite his chest with his own hands. "I did not kill my master! I did not kill my master!"

Conan Doyle was listening intently and heard Vicente quickly mutter something that Wilde did not translate, but which made the Irishman visibly rock back.

"What did he say, Oscar? My Italian's very limited. Something like: 'I love my master'?"

Wilde hesitated before answering. Fidgeted. Shot his cuffs. Finally, he leaned close and spoke in a low whisper so the guards could not overhear. "Not precisely. He said he would not kill his master because . . . because he and Lord Howell were lovers."

Conan Doyle sat in stunned silence, mouth agape. Finally, he swallowed and said, "Y-you're quite sure, Oscar? You're sure he meant—"

"I am quite sure, Arthur. I am quite sure he meant that he and Lord Howell were lovers in the manner of the ancient Greeks."

Neither man spoke for a full minute. The only sound was the Italian's soft weeping.

"Well," Conan Doyle finally managed to say. "That explains why the wheels of British justice turned so quickly for once."

"Yes," Wilde agreed. "It simply wouldn't do for it to become common knowledge that the war minister, a decorated hero of the Crimea, practiced the Uranian way of love. And, most unforgivably, with his valet, a man of the lower classes."

Both looked up at the approaching tread of heavy feet. A group of sober-faced men crowded in through the cell door: Prison Warden Bland, a black frocked priest, Dr. Lamb, and two uniformed prison warders. It was a few minutes before nine. They had come for Vicente.

The hour of execution was nigh.

The young Italian saw them, too. Realizing that his death was but moments away, his face turned ghastly white. He pulled something from beneath the woolen blanket and stared at it for one last time: a square of folded paper and a small photograph. He kissed the photograph, muttering in Italian, and then looked up at Wilde with tears in his eyes and pressed them into his hands.

Wilde glanced at them: a photograph of a young woman, by resemblance a sister or cousin, along with a tightly folded letter damp with tears and tattered from many readings.

The valet muttered something to Wilde, and even though Conan Doyle could not completely understand the meaning, he fully understood the intent: the valet was pleading for Wilde to write to the woman in the photograph, informing her what had become of him.

"Gentlemen," the prison warden announced. "The hour is at hand. Please go. We must make the prisoner ready to face his sentence."

* * *

"I want to leave this wretched place at once," Wilde said in a taut voice. "I do not wish to witness what is about to happen."

"Nor I."

But to their surprise, instead of returning to the front gate, the thuggish guard led them into an open quadrangle milling with newspaper men, civic officials, the idly curious, and, most shockingly, a few well-dressed society women, all attending on the pretense of fulfilling some form of civic duty in witnessing an execution, and not at all idle thrill seeking.

"You fail to understand," Conan Doyle explained to the guard, "we wish only to leave."

The guard did not attempt to conceal his amusement. "Too late to get squeamish now. The gates are locked. No one comes or goes until the execution is over." He flashed them a Marquis de Sade grin. "Sorry, gents."

Trapped.

"What in God's name is that?" Wilde said, pointing at something.

The corner of the yard featured a strange construction with a steeply pitched roof complete with a glass skylight to allow daylight in. A low fence screened the lower half from view.

"The execution shed," Conan Doyle answered. "It contains the gallows and the trap door."

"Surely not?" Wilde said in a tone of utter revulsion. "It resembles a macabre Punch and Judy theater!"

The two friends were pinned against a wall, helpless to escape. The restive crowd fell silent as the condemned man, his arms pinioned at his sides, was led out onto the gallows platform. Dr. Lamb and a chaplain preceded the executioner, with Prison Warden Bland following at the rear. As the chaplain wobbled forward to give the prisoner last rites, he tripped and nearly sprawled full length.

"Wonderful," Wilde said. "As at any good execution, the chaplain is drunk. Could this get any more delightful?"

The crowd of gentlemen began to push and jostle, subtly scrumming for a spot with the best view of the gallows.

An elderly man stepped to his right and Conan Doyle glimpsed the back of a head with long fiery red curls tumbling down about the shoulders. The redhead looked at something to his right and Conan Doyle instantly recognized the face. "That is the Marquess of Gravistock, Rufus DeVayne! He companioned the Prince of Wales to your play the other night."

"Really? Are you sure?" Wilde said, squinting at the figure. "I doubt I would have forgotten meeting a youth so handsome."

"You didn't, Oscar. You were in your dressing room, sulking."

"Ah, yes." Wilde remembered, rather sourly.

A raffish young swell in a white silk topper also clapped eyes on the marquess and called out to him, "Rufus, you young fiend, is that you?"

The marquess turned to look and unleashed a wicked smile. "Hello, Bunky," he replied. "It *is* I, manifested in the flesh."

"What drags you from your rooms to this pest hole? Are you an enthusiast for executions?"

"Don't be dull, Bunky. Everyone here is an enthusiast for executions, you included. I am here because a taste of death fires the blood. And in the hopes of gaining a trinket." He flashed a pair of scissors. "I hope to snip a lock of hair, an earlobe, anything. Such talismans are imbued with great power."

The young swell barked a laugh and said, "Just like at school. Still worshiping the devil, eh?"

"You've got it wrong, Bunky. It is he who worships me!"

The marquess seemed impervious to the scandalized stares launched at him by everyone within earshot of the remark. Conan Doyle harrumphed his disapproval and commented, "The young marquess seems rather a cad."

But Oscar Wilde did not answer. He was staring fixedly at the young aristocrat in a pique of rapture.

On the gallows, the chaplain meandered to the end of his prayer and made a rather sloppy sign of absolution. Vicente was shuffled forward onto the trap by a warder gripping either arm. One dropped to his knees out of sight behind the wooden palisade as he bound the Italian's ankles together.

"I refuse to witness this," Wilde said, turning his face away.

The executioner stepped forward and drew a white hood over Vicente's face, the fabric of which sucked in and out with each quickening breath. A warder handed the executioner the thick hawser with its heavy noose, and he slipped it over the young man's head. Vicente's knees visibly quivered as he took the weight of the rope.

The crowd's subdued murmuring drained away. From somewhere, the execution bell began to toll the hour. *Clong . . .*

At the bell's first strike, a flight of grubby pigeons burst up from the rooftops, wings creaking as they flapped around the courtyard, once, twice, three times, and then fled away.

. . . clong . . . clong . . .

The executioner gripped the long handle of the trap release.

. . . clong . . . clong . . .

Wilde's head, against his volition, turned back to look.

. . . clong . . . clong . . . clong . . . clong. The bell tolled nine times and stilled. A resonating silence spread out in all directions.

The executioner yanked the handle, a catch released, and the double doors of the drop fell open with a guttural sound. Vicente seemed to hang suspended for a moment and then plummeted from view with a dreadful suddenness. The rope snapped taut and quivered with tension. All breath sucked from the crowd. Silence reigned. Some looked distraught. Some smiled. Others held a mystical look upon their faces, as if savoring the lingering taste of death.

A slow murmur began at the front of the crowd and swept back to where Conan Doyle and Wilde stood. For a moment they were puzzled, but then they understood why. The hanging rope was jerking from side to side and a sudden realization swept the crowd.

The executioner had botched the job.

The drop had not broken Vicente's neck, and he was strangling to death. His muffled screams, though faint, rose from the drop pit. They continued for several long moments, the rope penduluming back and forth with its dread weight, until it shivered and stilled.

Conan Doyle's mouth filmed with bile. The death had been neither clean nor instantaneous.

"Oh, badly done!" a voice chortled—unmistakably that of the marquess.

A chorus of boos went up, and suddenly apple cores, crumpled newspapers, and every missile that came to hand began to soar from the crowd, aimed at the bungling executioner. The chief warden, the executioner, and the prison guards cowered beneath the fusillade and looked from one to the other with dismay.

"I—I f-feel . . . r-rather . . . ill . . ." Wilde stammered out. His brow beaded with perspiration. His wan complexion had grown clammy and waxen.

"Take a deep breath. Fill your lungs. Breathe man, breathe!"

Wilde's knees quivered. Conan Doyle gripped his friend by the arm and began to push him through the booing crowd toward an exit. The Scottish author was a large and strong man, but Wilde was over six foot and weighed several stone more. If the Irishman fainted in the press of the crowd, he would prove an immovable object.

"Come, Oscar. Keep walking. It's just the shock. You'll be all right. Breathe deep. Fill your lungs with—"

"Going dark . . . can't see . . ."

"A few feet more," Conan Doyle grunted through clenched teeth as he strained to hold his friend up. "Just a few feet more."

"I f-fear . . . ," Wilde gasped, ". . . it . . is . . . rather . . . too . . . laaaaaaaayyyte . . ."

Wilde's knees buckled and he sagged to the ground, dragging Conan Doyle down with him.

CHAPTER 19

RIGHT COFFIN, WRONG CORPSE

"Stop thrusting that dagger into my brain, Arthur, I am quite recovered!"

Wilde flailed a clumsy hand, trying to push aside the smelling salts Conan Doyle was wafting under his nose.

They were seated once again in the sanctuary of Wilde's carriage. Conan Doyle reached over to let down the window and tried to guide the Irishman's large head outside.

"What on earth are you doing?" Wilde demanded, firmly resisting.

"You need air. Take a good lungful."

"Are you mad? The air is dangerously fresh. What I require is a cigarette."

Against Conan Doyle's repeated urgings, Wilde insisted on lighting up one of his Turkish cigarettes. Despite all logic, after several long, lung-tingling drags, he seemed to revive and was finally well enough to look about and take note of where he was. The driver had drawn up a little ways from the prison gates. Having slaked their blood lust, the mob was dissipating, as revelers repaired to alehouses and brothels to satiate other appetites.

"I'm afraid we're trapped here until the crowd thins," Conan Doyle said. "Plus, you still look a little green." He tried again with smelling salts, but Wilde pushed his hand away.

"I am Irish. Those of us who hail from the Emerald Isle are given to mossy complexions." He dug in his coat pocket and drew out a hip flask. "This is what I require to revivify body and soul." He uncapped the flask, took a long swig, and offered it to his friend. "A nip for the doctor, too?"

"A tonic I fully concur with." Conan Doyle took a swig and gasped out a liquorish breath as high-proof brandy burned down his throat, kindling a fire in his belly.

Wilde eyed the milling crowd with distaste and said, "I do not wish to tarry in this insalubrious place. Have you seen enough, Arthur? Why do we loiter?"

"I am struck by the presence of the marquess. A strange coincidence. First he is at the theater, bosom companion of the Prince of Wales, and now here."

"When it comes to *bosom* companions, Prince Edward's current mistress has few equals."

"Yes, very droll, Oscar. I see you are fully recovered."

"The marquess's attendance at one of my plays is fully understandable—genius attracts the attractive—but I cannot imagine why such an elegant young aristocrat would frequent something so horrid as a hanging."

"You heard what he said to that young swell. Plus, I noticed the other night that he wore a pendant about his neck—a pentacle."

"A pentacle? Then perhaps he truly is an aficionado of the occult."

"He seemed quite boastful of the fact when his friend 'Bunky' recognized him."

"I thought that was a jest. How very odd." Wilde mused a moment and said, "Still, it is the meek and mild Doctor Lamb that intrigues me."

"How so? He struck me as a noble man. He has renounced monetary gain to volunteer his talents to the least fortunate in society."

Wilde's mouth puckered skeptically. "Yes, he said as much, and yet his clothes argue volubly against his claimed state of penury. You did notice his attire?"

Despite being the author of Sherlock Holmes, Conan Doyle was embarrassed to admit he did not share his fictional creation's powers of observation. He shook his head, abashedly.

"Our poor-as-a-church-mouse physician was kitted out in fawn doeskin trousers, a very fine shirt of Irish linen with French cuffs, and a beautifully tailored waistcoat from a gent's haberdashers I only frequent when I am feeling at my most self-indulgent. The prison doctor may indeed receive a pittance of a yearly stipend, but he obviously enjoys someone's patronage when it comes to procuring his wardrobe."

"Perhaps he supplements his income by other means."

"A darker, but entirely credible possibility."

Conan Doyle frowned. "Of course, bodysnatching is largely a thing of the past, but medical schools still require fresh corpses for students of dissection."

"And as prison physician of Newgate, the selfless Doctor Lamb would be in a most convenient position to procure the very freshest of pickings."

"I am curious to witness the fate of the body. The executed are left hanging for a full hour to ensure death. We will just have to wait—"

He was interrupted as the prison's smaller gate-within-a-gate flung open. A cadre of uniformed prison guards jogged out and began to drive the crowd back with threats, curses, and the occasional jab of a truncheon in the ribs. The main gate opened behind them and a hearse drove out drawn by two black horses with plumed heads. The well-heeled spectators that had been allowed inside the prison now also spilled out of the main gate, joining the mob.

"But there's the hearse now," Wilde pointed out. "Surely an hour has not elapsed?"

Conan Doyle's mouth dropped open in surprise. "No, it has not. Clearly they are not following protocol."

With jeers and cheers, the waiting rabble surged forward to greet the hearse, a sea of upraised hands, all jostling for a single touch of the dread black carriage.

"What are they doing?"

"A morbid tradition. They all seek to lay a hand upon the hearse . . . for luck."

"Ugh!" Wilde had had enough and was about to insist they depart when he spotted a mane of fiery red hair among the scrum of figures darting dangerously close to the turning wheels.

The Marquess of Gravistock.

Meanwhile, Conan Doyle's attention was fixed upon the driver's seat of the hearse. The noble Doctor Lamb rode alongside a funeral groom in a top hat draped in black crepe: a man with a familiar port-wine stain.

Conan Doyle suddenly flung open the carriage door and dropped to the cobblestones. "I will leave you now, Oscar."

"What? Wait! Where are you going?"

"To follow the hearse. I want to see the body placed in the ground. I suggest you return to your club until you recover."

Without waiting for a reply, Conan Doyle plunged into the milling crowd and soon vanished from sight. Wilde strained to keep his eyes on the long mane of fiery red curls amongst the river of bobbing top hats. He followed the marquess's progress along Newgate Street until he climbed into his personal carriage.

A very distinctive carriage, as it turned out.

Wilde rapped his knuckles on the carriage ceiling.

"Yes, sir?" his driver called down.

"Gibson, I want you to follow that carriage."

"Which one, sir? I see a number of carriages."

"This one is hard to miss. It's a rather handsome yellow landau . . . and it's being drawn by four zebras."

*   *   *

Feeling slightly foolish, Conan Doyle trotted along behind the hearse, in the coma of a comet's tail of whooping and skipping street arabs. But as the crowd thinned, the hearse gained speed and began to draw away and Conan Doyle feared it would leave him behind. Fortunately, he was able to steal a hackney cab someone else had bribed to wait behind, by offering the driver a bribe of a larger denomination, and resumed the pursuit. Soon the ominous hulk of Newgate fell behind the hearse and its following cab.

It proved to be a short trip. A brief trot up Farringdon Road ended at Spa Fields, London's most infamous burial ground, a barren two-acre plot of unconsecrated mud where the poor, the indigent, and the corpses of executed prisoners were interred at a minimum expense to the state. Separated from the surrounding tenements by only a tumbledown wooden fence, a stench of putrefaction hovered about the place, released by the eructations of gas from corpses ripening like vile fruit beneath a thin skimming of mud. Conan Doyle watched as the gates opened and closed behind the hearse and instructed his driver to pull up a dozen feet beyond.

He stepped down from the cab and, removing his top hat and coat to be less conspicuous, tossed them back onto the seat. "Wait here," he called up to the driver.

"Wait 'ere?" the incredulous driver replied. "With the stink of contagion shiverin' in me lungs? I'd be like to catch me death!"

Conan Doyle dug in a pocket and tossed up a half crown. "Another if you stay." And with that, he ducked through one of the many holes in the dilapidated fence.

Although he knew of Spa Fields's reputation, he was not fully prepared for the blasted vista that greeted him: a churned field of muck, trampled flat of grass and trees. Here and there, a few tilting gravestones, like a mouthful of crooked teeth, marked the most recent burials. In places the ground appeared to be moving and alive, swarmed as it was by fat bluebottles and shabby crows rooting amongst the broken clods for a greedily gobbled morsel.

Stumping across the landscape like damned souls wandering in purgatory were the gravediggers: lumpen golems conjured from grime and filth; although, to call them gravediggers was part misnomer, for they spent as much time digging up as they did digging down as Spa Fields recycled graves with unseemly haste to make room for new interments.

Rising from the blasted ground like a black tumor swelling upon a diseased face was a bone-house crematorium with a brick chimney belching human ash. This was the place where coffins and rotted corpses—after an indecently brief sojourn amongst the worms—were burned to make space for more.

Conan Doyle was in time to watch the hearse rattle across the rutted ground to where the black maw of a freshly hewn grave yawned. Dr. Lamb jumped down and strode toward the waiting grave, the Gladstone bag swinging at his side. Four funeral grooms unloaded the cheap-deal coffin and lugged it to the scandalously shallow grave where it was lowered belowground without care. In place of a formal ceremony, Dr. Lamb dropped to one knee, grabbed a clump of soil, and lobbed the clod onto the coffin. He stood for the briefest of moments, head bowed, as if murmuring a prayer. The perfunctory ritual performed, the doctor settled the top hat upon his crown of blond curls and strolled back to the hearse.

A pair of rumpled gravediggers leaned on their spades as they watched, and now they stirred into action, kicking and shoveling dirt into the grave. The hearse driver shook the reins and the ominous black carriage jounced across the rutted field back toward the gates. Conan Doyle had barely time to spring back into the shadows of the fence to avoid being seen. The hearse clattered through the gates and swung left, heading in the opposite direction by which it had arrived. Conan Doyle vacillated, torn by the urge to follow the doctor and hearse, but finally succumbed to the stronger instinct of staying to ascertain what exactly was in the coffin.

"You there," he shouted, striding across the muddy ground toward the shoveling figures. "Stop this instant."

The two gravediggers ceased their labors and looked up with eyes startling white against the blackened grime of their filthy faces.

Conan Doyle reached the graveside and commanded, "Dig it up. Immediately."

The two grubby fellows answered with gormless stares.

Just then a door in the bone house banged open and a squat figure emerged and stumped toward Conan Doyle with a strange, attenuated gait: a dwarfish man in a full-sized frock coat whose long tails dragged through the mud.

"What is this? What's going on?" the man demanded in a querulous voice. Up close, his appearance was startling. The stumpy body supported a large head with a prominent, domed forehead. The man also had a clubfoot, as evidenced by the hugely built-up sole of his right boot.

"I must insist you open this coffin."

"What? Who are you? I am the sexton here. By whose authority—?"

Conan Doyle found himself at a loss for what to say, but suddenly burst out: "I am William Bland, Warden of Newgate Prison."

The pronouncement widened the dwarf's eyes. Conan Doyle did not know where the words had come from. He had not consciously chosen to lie, but he would not stop until he had discovered the truth.

"William Bland? Here? Prove it."

Conan Doyle ground his molars. He did not expect to have his bluff called. But then a sudden inspiration struck him. "Proof? If it's proof you want—" He dug in his pocket and pulled out the small leather volume of Holmes stories he had unsuccessfully tried to present to the real Warden Bland. "This is one of my most prized possessions: a signed volume of Sherlock Holmes stories. I carry it everywhere with me." He slipped off the red ribbon, opened to the frontispiece, and thrust the small volume in the dwarf's hands. "See. Read for yourself: It was presented to me, personally, by the greatest writer of our times, Doctor Arthur Conan Doyle."

The small man snatched the volume. His eyes crawled across the dedication over and over again. Placated, he handed the book back and spoke in unctuous tones, "My apologies, Warden Bland, but you must understand my caution." And then he added, with no shred of self-awareness, "There are those *unscrupulable* types wot do not show the dead the respect they is deserving thereof. As you might have noticed by my execrable vocabules, I am a great reader myself, for I believe it felicitates the brain corpuscles."

"I quite agree," Conan Doyle said, adding, "But I must have you open the coffin. I believe a terrible error has been made."

"Error? I fail to perspicate your meaning. Wot error?"

"I believe the coffin you are currently burying . . . is empty."

The sexton made a spluttering sound. "Empty? But surely my men would have noticed the faultability in weight—"

"Most likely lead ballast, added to the coffin to counterfeit the weight of a corpse."

The sexton looked at the gawping gravediggers who showed no signs of having comprehended any of their conversation. "Wot are you waiting for?" he shouted. "You heard Warden Bland. Dig it up. Now! Sharpish!"

Whipped up, the gravediggers set to with gusto, and within seconds their spades were scraping against the coffin lid. Ropes were tossed down into the grave and looped under the coffin, which was hauled up from the ground with ease. Conan Doyle sensed that his supposition was correct. With the coffin aboveground, the blade of a spade was driven beneath the lid, which pried open with a loud crack revealing . . .

. . . a green-faced corpse in a thin white shroud.

The dwarf glared up at Conan Doyle, who stood openmouthed. "Empty coffin, eh? Not so empty after all, eh, Warden Bland? If that's who you really are!"

"No . . ." Conan Doyle shakily admitted, ". . . not empty. But that is not the body of the man I saw hanged this day at Newgate."

CHAPTER 20

AN ENCOUNTER IN A PORNOGRAPHIC BOOKSHOP

Wilde followed the marquess's carriage across London until it turned onto the ironically named Holyfield Street. Given its many bookshops, those ignorant of the street's reputation might mistake it for a place of learning. However, the readers who ventured inside these premises were mostly enthusiasts in search of a very different kind of *literature*. Wilde instructed his driver to follow the marquess's carriage from a greater distance, so as to avoid detection.

Drawn by four African zebras, the yellow landau drew open-mouthed stares from Londoners prowling the narrow pavement. It slowed to a halt at the curb, pausing only long enough to discharge the marquess, who ducked into the nearest bookshop before the landau rattled away.

Wilde rapped on the ceiling of his carriage and called up, "Here, Gibson."

The carriage drew up. Wilde studied the shop sign: COOPER'S BOOKS. An unremarkable name, but enough to stir the vapors of recollection somewhere in the far back reaches; Wilde felt sure he'd visited before. He stepped down from his carriage, instructed Gibson to return in half an hour, and followed the marquess into the shop. As he stepped through the door, he suddenly recalled a previous visit and remembered precisely which type of books were for sale here.

Pornography.

The small shop was neatly arranged with low tables displaying volumes varying from the vaguely naughty to the cheerfully saucy to the throbbingly visceral. He could not restrain his eyes from wandering the covers. (Some illustrated books had even been propped open to display the quality and filthiness of their engravings.) A study of titles revealed tomes to suit the gamut of erotic tastes and sexual peccadilloes, including an inordinate number (such as *Lady Bumtickler's Revels*) dedicated to the peculiarly English vice of flagellation. Wilde pried his eyes from the books with some difficulty and scanned the small space. Several well-dressed men browsed the tables, all studiously avoiding eye contact with one another. Mysteriously—although Wilde had watched him walk into the shop—the marquess was nowhere to be seen. He quickly surmised there must be another room where even stronger, perhaps illegal, reading matter was secreted.

Defending the shop counter was a muscular man with a regulation moustache and a martial bearing that suggested a former occupation in the military. Conspicuously positioned on the countertop close to his elbow was a stout wooden bat, presumably to discourage patrons who might mistake the business for a lending library. He noticed Wilde eyeing the other clientele and cleared his throat in a warning growl, scorching him with a hostile glare.

The Irishman instantly dropped his gaze and affected to be browsing. He snatched up a volume at random and flipped it open. Inside he found photographs of sun-bronzed youths striking poses in classical settings with Greek columns, their slender torsos loosely draped with togas that, despite yards of flowing material, somehow failed to conceal their virile nakedness. Heat flashed through Wilde's veins. Suppressing a thrill, he set the book back on the table and wandered casually to the counter—as casually as one can wander to the counter in a pornographic bookstore—and instantly had the clerk's full attention.

"Might I help you, sir?"

"A friend of mine recommended your shop."

"Did he now, sir?"

"A young gentleman with the most exquisite mane of red hair. Perhaps you might recognize him?"

"I'm certain I wouldn't. I don't recognize none of the customers. It's my job not to."

"My friend said I might find something *special* here?"

"Did he indeed, sir?"

"Yes. You see I'm looking for something, how would one put it, out of the ordinary."

"Not sure I follow you, sir."

"My friend said this was the place."

"Did he now, sir?"

"Yes. He said you specialize in unusual tastes."

Wilde left the insinuation hanging in the air. The clerk met the Irishman's gaze levelly, his face sphinxlike and inscrutable. For a fearful moment, Wilde suspected he was about to receive the unhappy end of a club in the face. But after a lengthy pause, the brusque clerk cleared his throat and answered enigmatically: "You might try that booth against the wall, sir."

"Indeed? The booth? Thank you."

Wilde sauntered over to the solitary wooden booth, swept aside a black curtain, and stepped inside. The booth was small and featureless: a cubbyhole containing nothing. He stepped to the back of the cubicle and drew aside a second curtain to discover a door.

Of course.

His hand grasped a brass knob tarnished from the grip of many sweaty palms. It turned without effort and the door sprang open.

He stepped through it into quite another realm.

He found himself in a dark and shadowy space of indeterminate size, sketchily lit by quivering gas jets turned down low: a bookshop-within-a-bookshop. Heady incense uncoiled in the air. Vaguely human shadows browsed the low tables. He picked up a book at random:

Black Magic, Forbidden Knowledge. He set it down and gazed at other titles. *Necromancy: The Art of Raising the Dead.* As he reached for it, another hand also grasped the book and he found himself in a minor tug of war. Surprised, he looked up into the face of a depraved saint.

"And so is it true, Mister Wilde, you can resist everything except temptation?"

Rufus DeVayne stood before him. His face was long and thin with an aquiline nose and wicked cheekbones. Most notable was the hair, which affected the long, flowing ringlets of a civil war Cavalier. Although he was of slighter build, the two men were equal in height so that Wilde gazed directly into the marquess's jade-green eyes, which were belladonically dilated.

Wilde's stomach danced. His knees quivered.

"Could this be magic?" the marquess said in a high, breathy voice. "For years I have wished to meet the famous Oscar Wilde. And now you have materialized before me . . . in the flesh."

Knocked momentarily off kilter, the world's most famous wit quickly recovered his balance. "I have the honor of addressing the Marquess of Gravistock, do I not? My apologies for failing to greet you personally the other night. I'm afraid I was rather out of sorts." He offered his hand. "Charmed."

"I sincerely hope you shall be," the younger man replied, taking it.

The marquess's handshake was weightless and insubstantial, like clutching a handful of mist.

"You are clearly on a quest, Mister Wilde. Did you come to this bookstore seeking knowledge . . . or did you come here seeking me?"

Wilde turned up the mantle of his languorous charm. "Oscar Wilde is always seeking beauty. Therefore, I must count our meeting here as a fortunate accident."

"An accident? Truthfully? Your carriage is very handsome, Mister Wilde. In fact, I could not help but notice it following mine all the way from Newgate Prison."

Wilde suddenly found himself lost for words—a rare occurrence.

"Do I make you uncomfortable, Mister Wilde?"

"It's a trifle claustrophobic in here. In such confined quarters, there is scarcely room for two personalities as large as ours."

DeVayne's fiery curls bounced as he tossed back his head and unleashed a shiver of girlish laughter.

"If you led me, Marquess, it was to a place I already wished to go. I have a great interest in the occult. I drew upon it whilst writing *The Picture of Dorian Gray*."

"Indeed, it is my very favorite novel."

Like a magician performing a trick, the marquess reached into the tails of his cloak and conjured up a small leather-bound copy of the book. Wilde blinked with surprise.

"I carry it with me at all times," DeVayne explained. "It is my touchstone. Indeed, it has been the model for my existence. In a way, it created me, so I should be honored to have it signed by its creator."

The younger man held out the novel, and Wilde received it with trembling hands. He set it down upon the nearest table, drew a fountain pen from his breast pocket, and stooped to sign the title page. His hand shook as he scribbled his signature, so that *Oscar Wilde* read as if it had been signed during a minor earthquake. As he handed the volume back, DeVayne was standing much closer than social norms obliged English gentlemen to do. His liquid eyes shone lambent. His breath smelled of flesh—a carnivore that had dined recently.

DeVayne caressed his beardless chin with the spine of the novel. "Now I have your name. Written in your own book. Written in your own hand. It is as if I possess a spark of you. Therefore, I think a fair exchange is required." DeVayne handed Wilde the copy of *Necromancy: The Art of Raising the Dead*. Wilde's eyes skimmed the title and for the first time he noticed the author's name.

"*You* wrote this book?"

The marquess replied with a smile and a hand-on-heart bow.

Wilde paused a moment, before commenting as mildly as possible, "And are you practiced in the art of raising the dead?"

DeVayne stifled his smile with difficulty and the room dimmed as though a candle had been snuffed. "Quite easily the most extraordinary question I have been asked this day. But then you are a most extraordinary man, Mister Wilde. But I thought your attentions had turned to drawing room comedies of late. Are you penning a new occult novel? Or is Doctor Doyle also involved? I noticed he companioned you in the crowd at Newgate."

Wilde swallowed. He and Arthur had been standing at the back of the crowd, far behind DeVayne. He could not guess how the young man could have noticed their presence.

"Arthur and I were recently summoned to a murder scene. Somewhat unusually, it appeared that the murderer was a dead man. Usually, death proves a major inconvenience in the commission of such crimes. I was wondering if you could shed some light."

"I'm afraid I am only in the habit of shedding darkness," the marquess japed. "Although, if it is illumination you seek . . ." He drew a glass phial from the folds of his cape, "this ampoule contains all the light you will ever need."

"What is it?"

"A mental stimulant. The blood of the Inca gods rendered into crystalline form."

"Cocaine?"

"Yes. It is quite the rage now. Oh, but do not worry. Unlike heroin it is not at all addictive." The marquess tugged free the stopper with his brilliant teeth and sifted white powder onto the back of his glove. He brought his face close and snuffed the powder, pinching his nose. When he looked up at Wilde, DeVayne's eyes were all pupil.

"Would you care to try? I promise it will blow the cobwebs from the darkest corners of your mind."

Swayed by the beauty of the young man and his closeness, Wilde found himself incapable of refusing. "I should love to indulge."

The marquess sifted another line of cocaine onto his glove. Wilde stooped and held the young man's hand as he snuffled up the white powder, a curiously intimate gesture. Immediately, a blizzard swept Wilde's mind. Suddenly, everything seemed clearer. Sharper. Better.

"Why did you attend the execution this morning?" Wilde asked.

"I had hoped to touch the dead body, to snip an eyebrow, perhaps."

"My dear boy, why ever for? As a ghoulish memento?"

"As a talisman. Such artifacts are used in many powerful spells."

"Indeed?"

"Indeed. Plus there are many aspects of executions that entice me. Have you heard of *angel lust*?"

"I'm quite certain I have not."

"Did you know that hanging produces an instant erection and a powerful ejaculation?"

"Really? How . . . interesting."

"I have an erotic print in my rooms: a hanged man in a chamber of the Inquisition. He has a huge erection and a powerful arc of fetch is spurting forth from it."

Wilde's smile buckled at the edges. The conversation was taking a strange turn. "I prefer my erotica sans execution."

"Oh, but it is the most erotic combination conceivable. The seed of life gushes forth even at the moment of death."

"Not to my taste, I'm afraid. I worship youth and beauty."

The marquess smiled coyly at the implied compliment. He produced a calling card and handed it to Wilde.

"I should very much like to become friends with you, Mister Wilde."

"Oscar, *please*. If we are to be friends, you *must* call me Oscar. Only creditors and bank bailiffs call me *Mister Wilde*."

"Oscar it is, then. Here is my card. I am having an event this very evening."

"A dinner party?"

"Of sorts. A bacchanal. A feast for all the carnal appetites. I should love it if you came. I could show you so much."

"You may count upon my attendance."

"Eight o'clock, Oscar," the marquess said, turning to leave. "I do hope to see you. Until then I hope my book makes for fascinating reading."

"Alas, I fear it could never be as fascinating at its author."

The marquess smiled craftily, and snapped a curt bow before leaving by the same hidden door he had entered. Dizzied by more than just narcotics, Wilde stood for some time, clutching the book, his mind awhirl. He did not remember leaving the shop. He did not remember walking miles through the crowded streets of London. He did not remember the instructions he had given to his driver, Gibson, who returned to the bookstore with the carriage and found him long gone.

Oscar Wilde was besotted.

CHAPTER 21

BEFORE RIGOR SETS IN

Once again, the story plays out in a dreamy riffle of black-and-white images: the vaporous mist tendriling up from the loch's glassy surface. The young woman with her hair of white fire strolling toward the camera, her bare feet paddling the shallows. A lock of hair falling loose across her lovely face. Her coy smile, as if she feels the greedy eyes pressed up against the glass of the Mutoscope. She looks back at the golden child in the sailor suit. The tinplate boat with its windup propeller churns circles about the chubby legs. . . .

Somewhere, ten years into a future they will never know, a shop bell jangles.

The hand continues cranking. The images cascade. Then the hand slows. Stops. Turns the crank backward. Time reverses in a way that life cannot. The toy warship churns in retrograde circles about the boy's legs and then leaps back into his arms.

Ring . . . ring . . . ring . . . Someone is yanking at the bellpull with such vigor the jangling bell threatens to rip loose from the wall.

Jedidiah draws his face away from the Mutoscope, glances up to notice that it is not the shop door. Someone is at the cellar door behind the premises.

The Mutoscope swallows his coin and the cyclopean eye dims

into blindness. He abandons the machine, strides across the shop, and tugs at the rope dangling from the ceiling. The trapdoor in the floor flings open. Ducking his head, he tromps down the wooden steps into a workshop lit by hissing gas jets.

Maddeningly, the bell jangles and jangles.

"Yes, yes," he shouts. "I'm coming, damn you!"

Jedidiah moves swiftly across the workshop to the far wall. He pauses at a bench strewn with half-made toys. The wall above is lined with tools hanging on hooks. One hook, however, is conspicuously empty. He reaches up and pulls on it. At his tug, the hook pivots downward. Somewhere within the wall, a hidden catch releases with a dull *thunk*. A section of the wall splits open and swings wide, taking half the workbench with it.

He steps through the dark opening into another space, a workshop for a decidedly darker form of work. A restraining chair dominates the central part of the space. Behind it, a smoked glass screen. Directly in front of the restraining chair a white sheet has been hung on the wall—an improvised screen to catch a magic lantern's projected image.

The bell jangles frantically.

He steps behind the smoked glass screen and tugs at a large handle. At the far end of the room, a tall metal door springs open.

"Why make us wait?" an impatient voice calls as its owner, the handsome Dr. Lamb bustles in, Gladstone bag gripped in one hand. Four funeral attendants dressed in black crepe stagger in behind him, lugging a cheap-deal coffin.

"How long?" Jedidiah asks.

"Less than an hour has elapsed," Lamb answers. "Still, we must hurry . . . before rigor sets in."

The funeral attendants thump the coffin to the floor and hurriedly tear loose the lid, revealing the still-cooling body of the Italian valet in his burial shroud. The kinked neck bears a purpling rope burn. The engorged face is cyanose blue, the tongue hanging loose. The funeral attendants struggle to lift the limp corpse from the coffin and drape it atop a scarred wooden operating table. Dr. Lamb drops his Gladstone beside the corpse, snatches it open, and extracts a scalpel and a bone saw. He looks up at Jedidiah. "You have the heart mechanism ready?"

"Of course." Jedidiah brings forward the slim metal box, brassy and precisely machined.

Dr. Lamb draws up liquid from a smoky brown bottle into a horse-sized hypodermic. He raises the needle and squirts a fine jet into the air.

"What is that?" Jedidiah asks.

"Adrenaline . . . along with a powerful coagulant of my own devising. This time, if an artery is cut with a knife or severed by a bullet, the blood will instantly coagulate upon touching the air."

"So this one won't bleed out? How do you know it works?"

"The prison infirmary has many inmates lingering at death's doorway. We had an elderly prisoner afflicted with typhus. Mere days to live. I gave him an injection of the drug. Within seconds, I was able to slice through his femoral artery. It should have produced a gushing fountain but the blood coagulated instantly. I next tried the carotid artery in the throat. The same result."

"And the prisoner still lives?"

The doctor looks at the toy maker with puzzlement. "Certainly not. He died within minutes. The coagulant is so powerful it effectively turned his blood to stone. Of course, with the blood pressure so high, we will not have the same difficulty."

And with that, he plunges the needle of the hypodermic into the corpse's neck and depresses the plunger all the way. That accomplished, he sets the empty syringe aside and snatches up a huge scalpel. "Make ready with the device," he says to Jedidiah. "My technique is advancing with practice. This one should not take as long as previous."

He drives the scalpel into the corpse's thorax until the blade bites into the sternum below, then draws the blade down the chest with the zeal of a butcher slicing a rump roast for an impatient customer. Moments later he has the chest cavity peeled open and the small space resounds to the bone saw's monotonous rasp.

⚜

CHAPTER 22

CAKES AND CORPSES

When the whirling carousel of Oscar Wilde's mind finally groaned to a shuddering standstill, he found himself sitting at a small table in the window of the Corner House teashop on the Strand. Evidently he had been there for some time, for crowding the table in front of him were no fewer than four towering sandwich stands with each of the three tiers crammed with battalions of tea sandwiches and every description of confectionary, both sweet and savory: deviled eggs, fairy cake, potted shrimp, sticky buns, mince pies, chocolate truffles, sponge cake, lemon bars, macaroons, gâteaux, malt bread, Viennese whirls, and of course, that most English of artery-clogging indulgences: Devonshire clotted crème and scones. He balanced a hot cup of tea upon a saucer. On the table before him stood two teapots, one he had already emptied and another one waiting, fully brewed and ready.

Wilde looked dozily about, fighting the peculiar sensation that his mind had gone out for a wander without him and had only just returned. The surrounding tables were fully occupied, mostly by elderly ladies taking tea. The chatter of hot gossip and the clatter of teacup against china saucer were positively clamorous. Just then, a very weary Conan Doyle trudged up to the table and collapsed in the chair opposite.

"Been looking for you all over. Fortunately, a large Irishman in the window of a teashop is quite conspicuous. I thought perhaps they were trying to raffle you off."

Wilde spoke around the cucumber sandwich he was munching. "You look beastly."

"I am exhausted," Conan Doyle admitted. "I have had quite the day."

Wilde raised his extravagant eyebrows and paused to dab butter from his lips on his napkin and wash down his mouthful with a sip of Lapsang souchong.

"I have the most extraordinary news to share."

"Although you thought I was idling at my club, I too have news to share," Wilde mumbled around the mouthful of sandwich he was chewing feverishly. His actions seemed manic, sped-up. Conan Doyle detected a lack of focus about his friend's eyes and, for the first time, noticed the huge spread of food on the table.

"Good Lord, Oscar! Are you catering for a church fête?"

"I cannot stop eating the cucumber sandwiches. They must put something in them."

Conan Doyle ogled the celebration of sandwiches and confectionaries. He was a large man whose muscular frame required regular fueling, and the aroma of whipped cream and pastry sugar set him to salivating. Wilde noticed his friend eyeing the feast and said, "By all means, Arthur, feel free to indulge. Even from here I can hear the Doylean stomach growl like a ravening beast."

"Most kind," Conan Doyle said. He snatched up a cucumber sandwich and inhaled it. Then followed suit with a chicken curry, and then another cucumber.

A waiter approached. "Pot of tea for you, sir?"

"Earl Grey, please, and a pot of hot water."

The waiter whisked himself away. Conan Doyle fixed his friend with a stern gaze, leaning over the table as he spoke in a low voice. "I have some shocking news to relate to you concerning our friend Doctor Lamb."

Wilde waved a hand. "Please can we not mention that ghastly business whilst we are dining."

Conan Doyle snatched another sandwich and crammed it in his mouth. "Theeere wurf no bobby in the coffee."

Wilde responded in kind: "I'm furry, whash did chewsay?"

Conan Doyle swallowed his mouthful and said. "There was a body in the coffin, but not the right one. Vicente's corpse had been substituted with that of an older man. Judging by the man's wasted appearance, I'd wager another denizen of Newgate."

Wilde paused mid-chew, his long face a parody of itself. He swallowed noisily, wiped his mouth on a napkin, and said, "Oh dear. That *is* a very disturbing turn of events."

"And your news?"

"After you abandoned me at Newgate, I followed the marquess." Wilde saw the question framed in Conan Doyle's eyes and added, "I suspected it was no coincidence he attended the execution this morning."

"And what happened?"

"I did as your Sherlock Holmes chappie would do. I *followed* him," Wilde announced theatrically.

"Whatever do you mean?"

"I followed his carriage. He went straight from Newgate to Holy-field Street, where he stopped in at a bookshop."

"So he is an avid reader. What of it?"

"A bookshop on *Holyfield Street*."

Conan Doyle shook his head blankly.

Wilde sighed. "How may I put this delicately? I am referring to a *gentleman's* bookshop."

Realization sparked in Conan Doyle's eyes. "Good lord! You mean a *pornographic* bookshop." He had spoken a little too loudly, attracting disapproving glares from the matrons chatterboxing on the next table. He lowered his voice and continued: "You didn't go inside . . . did you?"

Wilde made a pained face. "No, I went home and breakfasted on goose pâté and toast points and therefore have nothing to report—of course I went inside, Arthur! That is what *following* means!"

Wilde then relayed in detail the story of his bookshop encounter. At first Conan Doyle shifted uncomfortably at the description of the pornography, but then his eyes widened at the description of Wilde's discovery of the secret bookshop-within-a-bookshop.

"Your Holmesian observation of the marquess's pentacle necklace was astute. He claims to be an acolyte of all things occult. In fact, we made an exchange."

Conan Doyle's frown drooped his moustaches comically. "An exchange? What kind of exchange?"

"I signed his copy of *Dorian Gray*. In exchange he gave me a copy of his own book."

Wilde reached across the cake trays to hand his friend a small leather volume.

"*Necromancy: The Art of Raising the Dead?*" Conan Doyle read aloud. "You mean he claims he can—"

"Raise the dead, Arthur. Yes, I thought the title rather gave it away."

"You cannot believe he truly possesses such abilities?"

"If not the marquess, then apparently someone in London does. How else do you explain the restless noctivigations of Charlie Higginbotham, who maintains a very busy social calendar for a dead man?"

"You honestly believe this young man can raise the dead?"

"I honestly believe he believes so."

Conan Doyle flipped open the small volume and scanned a few lines. It seemed pretentious gobbledygook. "Have you read it?"

"I read the first sentence. It contained a semicolon. I could read no further. The semicolon is unquestionably the ugliest piece of punctuation in the English language. It is neither full stop nor comma, and as such a mongrel construction. Furthermore, no one from

206 CR THE DEAD ASSASSIN

Jonson forward can agree upon its use. I ceased reading. Such an early appearance of a semicolon did not portend for a pleasant read."

Conan Doyle snapped the book shut and traced a finger across the gold pentagram embossed upon its cover. "I would like to share this with my new acquaintance."

"Your lady friend, the medium?"

"We are having dinner tonight. She is conversant in matters of spiritualism, the occult, witchcraft, necromancy."

"What well-educated lady in English society is not?"

"I suppose you could join us."

Wilde shook his head. "I, too, have a dinner invitation. I am to journey to Hampstead, to the ancestral seat of the DeVaynes. What the evening holds for me I cannot guess at."

CHAPTER 23

A DINNER DATE TO REMEMBER

They drew the usual stares, but Conan Doyle no longer cared. He sat across the dinner table from Miss Jean Leckie, whose lovely head floated buoyantly on the exquisite curve of her long neck. They had returned to the scene of their first assignation, the Tivoli restaurant, and in the welcoming glow of the Palm Room's electric lights, the young woman's hazel-green eyes sparkled with delectation. After a dinner of watercress salad, oysters, and champagne, they had desserted on truffles drizzled with chocolate. Now he watched the tip of her pink tongue lick the chocolate from her spoon. She noticed his stare and stifled a guilty smile beneath her napkin.

"I must apologize, Doctor Doyle. Most unladylike. I assure you, my mother brought me up to have better manners."

"Arthur," he scolded gently. "You must call me Arthur."

She rested the hand gripping her spoon upon on the table. Quite unconsciously, he reached out and placed his hand atop hers. "It gives me great joy to make you happy, Jean."

He gazed into her eyes, a little too deeply. She looked down and drew her hand away.

He knew his behavior was appalling. Ridiculous even. He was a public figure. A well-known author. People were staring. *Damn them,* he thought. *Let them stare.*

"I do have a question for you, Jean."

She looked up, her eyes brimming with hope. "Yes?"

Conan Doyle drew the small leather volume from his inside pocket. "I thought I might make use of your encyclopedic knowledge of the occult."

Her expression faltered, but he failed to notice. She smiled gamely and said, "I would hardly compare myself to an encyclopedia, but perhaps I may be able to help."

Conan Doyle handed the book across the table to her. She opened to the title page. Her eyes swept the gothic type and she looked up in surprise.

"Necromancy! How very dark!"

"You are familiar with the term?"

"My father had a comprehensive library. As a young girl I was expressly forbidden from reading certain books." She flashed a wicked smile. "Of course, those were the books I read first."

She dropped her eyes to the page and began reading. Conan Doyle contented himself to watch as she read the first page and then the second. At the third page, her eyes flickered as she scanned a line over and over. She closed the book and looked up at him, her expression unreadable.

"What do you make of it?"

"Is this something you are reading for research? A new book you are planning?"

"Ah, yes," Conan Doyle fibbed. He could not endanger her by going into the details of his current adventure.

"Very heady stuff."

"The book purports to have knowledge of a ritual to raise the dead."

"Yes," Jean replied. "It requires the sacrifice of a virgin."

"Ah!" Conan Doyle replied, suddenly embarrassed.

The young woman reached across the table and placed her hand on his. "Fortunately, I have a brave, strong man to protect my virtue."

Conan Doyle was struck speechless. From the sparkle in her eyes, it seemed clear she was offering him a gift.

* * *

It was fully dark by the time Wilde's carriage rolled up to the gate-house of the walled grounds encompassing the DeVayne estate. The gatekeeper who emerged from the tiny cottage proved to be a feral-looking man dressed in antique garb complete with knee britches and a leather tricorn hat. Wilde dropped the carriage window to speak to him and was alarmed to see a huge blunderbuss balanced in the crook of his arm.

"Good evening. My name is Oscar Wilde."

"Arrrr," the gateman replied as he scratched a bushy sideburn with long, horny fingernails.

"You have, no doubt, heard of me."

"Arrrr," the gatekeeper replied, by which Wilde could not tell if he meant yes or no.

"I am here at the personal invitation of the marquess."

"Arrrr."

"Might I inquire . . . why the weapon? Are you expecting armed raiders?"

"Arrrr. Ye know about the marquess's menagerie?" the man asked in an accent so rustic it was practically sprouting stalks of corn.

"Menagerie?"

"Animals. He collects 'em. Running loose on the grounds." The gatekeeper patted the blunderbuss fondly. "That's why oi got this."

"Indeed?" Wilde's eyes flickered up from the man's face to the pri-mal darkness crouched beyond the gates. "And do you have a spare we might borrow?"

The gatekeeper chuckled. "Arrrr, ye'll be all roit. Just keep to the droive and stay in the carriage and you'll loikely come to no harm."

The gatekeeper stepped to the double gates and swung them wide with a shove. As soon as the carriage passed through, Wilde hurriedly flung up the window and scooted back on the seat cushion, sitting as far from the glass as he could.

The house could not be seen from the front gate for the gravel drive ascended a steep grade. But as the carriage crested the low rise, the ancestral seat of the DeVaynes' rose into view: a palatial, two-story manor with a Georgian façade. Amber light blazed from the tall windows. Struck by the sight, Wilde drew down the carriage window and leaned out. The chill night air pooled in his lungs and was only part of the reason why a premonitory shiver danced down his spine.

The circular driveway fronting the mansion was busy with fine carriages dropping off partygoers. "Draw up here, Gibson," Wilde said, choosing a spot on the periphery. The driver climbed down from his seat, lowered the metal step, and Oscar Wilde descended. Despite the bitter chill, he chose to leave his overcoat behind, preferring to enter wearing only his formal black evening suit, a fresh green orchid pinned to his lapel. Earlier, he had spent hours at his toilette: bathing and shaving and brilliantineing his chestnut hair, then dousing himself with French cologne, reasoning that, if he could not erase the marks of time, he would at least tie them up in a pleasing package. Girding his loins for battle, he lit a Turkish cigarette, swept back his auburn waves, cinched the knot of his tie, shot the cuffs of his evening jacket, and strolled toward the blazing entrance in shoes buffed black and gleaming.

But as he crunched across the drive, the darkness around him irrupted with a cacophony of jungle sounds. He looked about nervously. Then something screamed. Loud and close. His polished shoes skidded to a halt. A large, unfathomable shape floated toward him from the darkness, which resolved itself as a strutting peacock. The bird unfurled its extravagant fan of feathers and gave them a shake. Relieved, he let out a breath and smiled at his fear. But then a lithe blur on four legs rushed from the night, snatched up the peacock in its jaws, and gave the bird a fierce shake to break its neck.

A huge lioness.

Noticing him, it growled a warning and trotted away with the bird in its jaws.

Wilde dropped his cigarette and hurried toward the safety of the house, scuffing the toes of his shoes as he kicked gravel. He reached the colonnaded entrance and flung himself through the open front doors.

The entrance hall was a grand vault of marble lined with tall Grecian urns and classical busts on columns. Overhead, giant chandeliers bedecked with candles flooded the space with light. Waiting to greet guests were two life-size golden statues of naked youths—a faun and a naiad—each posed holding a silver tray. Wilde was pleased to see that they were honestly nude, and did not comport with the English prudery of fig leaves or conveniently arranged drapery. He dropped his calling card atop the growing pile on the naiad's sterling tray, at which point the female statue came alive, smiling and bowing to him.

Wilde started and laughed with delight. *"Tableau vivant!"* he crowed, and bowed in response to the two young people, who were clad only in gold body paint and laurel crowns.

The naked faun stepped forward and offered up a tray of Venetian masks.

"Would sir care for a mask?"

"No, thank you," Wilde replied, "the one I am wearing usually suffices."

He stepped into the wide hallway and was met by a bewigged servant, anonymous in a white porcelain mask. The servant presented him with a tray of champagne flutes effervescing with an intriguing emerald concoction.

"What on earth is this libation?"

The servant, who was apparently mute, answered only by miming lifting a drink from the tray and imbibing. Wilde had never seen a drink quite so green in color, a luminous shade of jade. He snatched up a glass, nodded his thanks, and continued on. The first sip set his palate alive with a premonition of rapture. On his second sip, his tongue parsed a giddy dance of gin, champagne, and botanical infusions commingled with a fatal undertow of absinthe that gave the drink its lethal green tinge.

Suddenly, a flock of sheep appeared, crowding the hallway as it surged toward him. He forded through the wooly mass like a man wading through deep water, struggling to keep his feet as the mindlessly *baa*ing creatures pressed around his legs. Following the flock was a comely young wench with her long blond tresses tied up in pink ribbons and ponytails. She carried a tall crook and was dressed in a shepherdess's costume that could have been lifted from a child's storybook, except that the front of her dress had been cut deliberately low to expose a pair of buxom breasts. She flashed Wilde an impish grin as she passed, and he looked back to find that the rear of her Little Bo Peep dress had likewise been cut high so as to frame the ripe apple of her naked arse.

The marquess had promised Wilde a revel. Now it seemed he had received a foretaste of things to come. He followed the hallway and soon reached a landing where a short flight of steps climbed to an open set of doors. He summited them and found himself on the threshold of a great hall resplendent with battle flags and suits of armor. In the middle of the hall, lit by the glow of a huge fire roaring in the fireplace, a different kind of war was taking place—a struggle involving an army of naked flesh. Men and women of all shapes and sizes and ages copulated on cushions and couches amid rapturous groaning and ecstatic moans.

The bacchanal, it appeared, had started without him.

He stepped into the hall, crashing through a curtain of hashish smoke. A small Indian boy in a dhoti and turban sat cross-legged before a huge hookah and now offered up the pipe. Wilde set down his glass and then took the pipe and clamped it between his lips. He drew in a deep lungful of smoke that funneled straight into his brain where it swirled in curling arabesques, dissolving his thoughts and any lingering inhibitions with it.

As he watched the orgy from the sidelines, a sudden revelation struck him. Although the participants wore Venetian masks, their identities were easy to guess at. Wilde was astonished to note that they comprised many from the upper echelons of English society, including cabinet ministers and their wives, members of the House of Lords, and even a number of high-ranking clergymen.

Just then a couple sauntered past on their way to join the torrid love pile. The woman, naked apart from rhinestone-spangled nipples and a black leather mask festooned with ostrich feathers, held a riding crop in one hand. The other hand gripped a leather leash by which she led a middle-aged man. The gent, bearded beneath the black leather mask, had a Buddha belly, flabby buttocks striped with red welts, and a flaccid penis that waggled sadly as he was led into the hall. Despite the disguise, Wilde instantly recognized the portly figure of the Prince of Wales and almost greeted him as such. Fortunately, he still possessed sufficient presence of mind to hold his tongue.

In the midst of all the nakedness, more of the masked house servants circulated, offering up salvers of sweetmeats and more of the exotically colored elixir to those orgiers who reclined on cushions at the side of the love pit, watching as they recuperated from their efforts. One servant noticed the lone Irishman and glided toward him bearing a tray of drinks. As he silently bowed and offered up the tray, Wilde could not help but notice the port-wine stain that ran from beneath the mask and down one side of the servant's neck. Unfortunately, it was an observation his mind would not retain a moment later. The Irishman helped himself to another glass of the emerald cocktail and asked aloud, "What on earth is this sublime drink?"

"Nectar of the gods," answered an elderly lady who wore a mask and a sparkling tiara in her gray hair and nothing else. From her excruciatingly posh drawl, Wilde recognized the lady as none other than the dowager Dame Helen Montague-Hunt. She was sipping a glass as she reclined on a pile of cushions, her spindly legs thrown over the shoulders of a muscular young man who was enthusiastically rogering her.

The green liquid glided down Wilde's throat like molten gold. He felt his body changing state from solid into gas, as if he were sublimating, an atom at a time, into the surrounding air. While he was still able to form a cogent thought, he stopped a passing servant and asked, "The marquess?"

The masked servant pointed upward to the hammer-beam ceiling.

As if on queue, a woodwind of Middle Eastern origin wheedled an insinuating tune. The bacchants paused in their exertions to look up, calling and applauding as something extraordinary was lowered from the rafters of the great hall. At first, Wilde could not make out what it was, but as it descended from the shadows, he descried the shape of a giant cross, hung inverted. Lashed to the cross by ropes binding his arms and feet was the slim figure of a man, naked apart from a ragged loincloth, his tumble of red tresses capped by a crown of thorns.

Rufus DeVayne.

The orgiers parted as the cross touched ground. A bevy of servants rushed forward to catch it and turn it right side up. Amidst applause and cheers, the marquess was unlashed and stepped down from the cross blowing kisses. A smile lit his face as he noticed Wilde, and he moved forward to greet him, his slender body flushed, his eyes spilling stars.

"Oscar, my new friend. You came!"

"Dear boy, where beauty summons, Oscar Wilde must follow."

The marquess shrilled a delighted laugh. He snapped his fingers and a servant scurried to offer up a tray of green cocktails. The marquess snatched one up, tossed it down, and snagged himself a second. A pair of servants came forward to draw his arms into the sleeves of a silk gown embroidered with hierophantic symbols and tighten the sash. He threw a slender arm about Wilde's shoulders and whispered, "You must come up to my rooms." He semaphored a vulpine smile. "I have something very special prepared for us."

Wilde leaned his head toward the younger man, drunk with the liquor of longing. For a brief moment, he saw himself with a terrible acuity, and he knew that, if he followed the young man, he would leave his old life behind forever. He grasped that "Oscar Wilde," the persona he had spent a lifetime crafting, would be utterly annihilated. He would be mad to succumb to such a risk. The cliff edge yawned before him and Rufus DeVayne beckoned him to step off into the abyss.

"Lead on, sweet youth," he heard himself say, "I would follow you into oblivion."

As the younger man led him from the hall, the marquess noted, "I see you chose not to wear a mask."

"Yes, I came as Oscar Wilde. I could think of nothing more apropos."

DeVayne laughed as they reached a grand staircase and began to climb. "Come, Oscar," the marquess said, taking him by the hand. "We must ascend to Elysium." At the top of the stairs they turned onto a long corridor. Although his feet still trod the earth, Wilde's mind was a helium balloon tugged along by a string.

Their promenade along the hallway could have taken seconds or days. Suddenly, Wilde found himself inside a huge and sumptuously appointed bedchamber hung with paintings and lithographs that shared a common theme of nudity and torture. As DeVayne had promised, one wall held a giant canvas: a lithograph of a torture chamber of the Inquisition: a hanged man dangled from a gibbet, an arc of semen jetting from his huge erection.

"Do you like my art, Oscar? I have my own personal torture chamber close by should you wish to indulge."

A premonitory jolt of anxiety swept through Wilde. "Perhaps another time," he said, his lips dry.

The room was opulent with soft pillows and low sofas. An impossibly huge four-poster dominated one side of the room. Lying atop the bed were two children, a boy and a girl of perhaps six or seven. Their eyes were heavy-lidded and possessed only a smear of focus, suggesting both had been drugged. The children were naked apart from cherub's wings strapped to their backs, and had been posed stretched out upon the bed, head to head. Each rested upon an arm that was in turn pillowed upon a human skull. A leather strap dangled loose about their throats. A short wooden stick lay close by.

Wilde scrambled to catch hold of the bobbing balloon of his mind and reel it back in. "What is this?" he asked.

"Do you not see? One for you. One for me. You may take either the girl or the boy. In truth, I am not particular."

"What in God's name are you proposing?"

The marquess chuckled. "Nothing we do here tonight is in God's name. I presume you read the book I gave you? The ritual of immortality requires the sacrifice of a virgin."

Wilde's face turned to stone. "What? You mean the stick? The leather strap?"

"A garrote." DeVayne's face loomed close. Warm, carnivore's breath washed Wilde's cheek. "You will find strangulation far more intimate than sex. To stare into the eyes of your sacrifice and watch the soul slip from its fleshy prison gives you not just immortality, but eternal youth. I have read *Dorian Gray* a hundred times. Is that not your deepest desire? Eternal life? Beauty that time cannot wither? But while you can only write about it, I can manifest it."

Wilde's tongue was thick and clumsy in his mouth as he struggled to speak. Suddenly his intoxication was a leaden blanket he wished to shake free of. "B-but these are innocent children!"

"Yes, quite innocent. Guaranteed virgins. The boy cost me five pounds. The girl was ten pounds." DeVayne giggled. "I think the family thought I was purchasing her for a brothel, hence the higher price. Fortunately, there are many parts of London where life is a commodity cheaply purchased."

"Surely this is all a tasteless joke!"

DeVayne misread the look of horror on Wilde's face. "Do you doubt me? Do you doubt my abilities?" He reached in the pocket of his robe and drew out a small pistol: a two-shot derringer with an up-and-over barrel. He pointed the gun at the Irishman's chest and for a terrible moment Wilde thought he was about to die. But then the marquess flipped the gun in his hand and extended it, grip-first to Wilde, who accepted it numbly. The marquess seized the barrel and drew the muzzle to his own chest.

"Put a bullet through my heart and I shall resurrect myself before your very eyes. Do it, Oscar. Shoot."

Wilde's finger trembled on the trigger. For a giddying moment he knew that, in that instant, he was entirely capable of murder. That nothing would give him greater pleasure than to end the life of Rufus DeVayne.

"Go on." A mad smile quivered upon the marquess's lips. "I can see from your eyes that you lust to kill me. Do it! I have heard you say that you can resist everything except temptation. Why begin an unpleasant habit now, when you stand upon the threshold of immortality?"

Wilde dithered. "I imagine the pistol is a stage prop. Or loaded with blanks."

DeVayne shook his head. "Oh no. It is as real as I."

The Irishman was seized by a sudden resolve. "Then we will see if your imagined immortality can withstand a real bullet." DeVayne's smile buckled as Wilde's finger tensed on the trigger. But at the last second, he whipped the pistol aside and pointed the muzzle at one of the plump bed pillows. The gun fired with an ear-ringing BANG and the pillow exploded. Feathers and white down floated down from the ceiling, settling on DeVayne's fiery hair and shoulders.

"Never doubt me, Oscar. Never doubt—"

Gripped by a mad impulse, Wilde lunged forward and gave the slighter man a vicious shove. The marquess reeled backward several staggering steps and sat down hard upon the floor. Seizing the moment, Wilde grabbed the boy by the arm and tugged him off the bed. DeVayne stumbled to his feet and stood wavering, held at bay by the derringer leveled at his chest. He watched, powerless, as the Irish wit scooped the little girl from the bed and tossed her upon his shoulder.

"I am leaving now. And taking the children with me."

"You're being very rude, Oscar. Are you trying to make me cross?"

"You must excuse me, Marquess, but I find that this room reeks of excrement, and I do not think it is from something I've trodden in."

"Mister Wilde, you have spoiled my evening. However shall I redress this insult?"

"I suggest a strongly worded letter to *The Times*. I find them most efficacious."

And with that final riposte, Wilde turned and fled the room, dragging the boy behind. The rush of adrenaline had momentarily burned off the fog swirling in his mind, but his bloodstream was still awash with narcotics and he struggled to navigate the labyrinthine hallways. Finally reaching the grand staircase, he stumbled down it several times only to find himself back at the top of the landing. On the third attempt, as he rested on the middle landing, he accosted someone coming up the stairs. The man wore a pair of fine boots and a shirt, but had carelessly misplaced his trousers somewhere. A Venetian mask concealed his features but could not hide a fine head of blond hair, tightly curled. Although he seemed familiar, the man was bleeding light trails and strangely colored sounds, which made further identification impossible.

"Excuse me," Wilde said, addressing the stranger. "I am attempting to descend this staircase, but it appears to go up in either direction. Would you be so kind as to point the way down?"

The man gestured and stepped aside and Wilde followed his point and finally tripped off the stairs onto the ground floor. He noticed that he still held the derringer in one hand and, anxious to be rid of it, deposited it upon the silver tray of a passing servant. As he dragged the children past the open door to the great hall, he could not help but glance inside. The bacchants still writhed in the pit, and their sweating bodies, in the gleam of firelight, resembled a scene from *The Inferno*.

At last he reached the entrance hall, where the living golden statues had abandoned their posts and were trying to shoo the panicking herd of sheep out of doors. He pressed through their *baaing* mass, and was relieved to finally stumble down the marble steps into the night. The shock of cold November air scourging his lungs revived him somewhat, although as he hurried to his carriage, a pair of long-necked giraffes lollopped across the circular drive. Wilde could not be sure if they were real or a vestige of the volatile chemicals roiling in his brain. When he reached his four-wheeler, Gibson stirred inside the carriage, tossing aside the heavy blanket he had wrapped himself in. "Mister Wilde? What? Why do you have those children?"

"The evening began as an indulgence and quickly devolved into a rescue," Wilde explained as he flung open the carriage door and loaded the children inside. "Quickly, Gibson, fetch a blanket to wrap these babes before they catch their death."

"Are we going back to your club, sir?"

"No," the Irishman said, hauling himself inside the carriage and collapsing onto the seat cushion. "We must find an orphanage to provide a safe haven for these waifs, and then I want to go home. To Tite Street. I have been a neglectful father of late and wish only to reside in the bosom of my family. After this evening I am done forever with drinking and carousing."

The children were bundled under a pile of blankets and promptly fell asleep. Soon the carriage was rattling back up the drive, away from the house. As the Irishman looked out the window, a pack of something with sharp claws and razor teeth gazed back from the darkness with luminous eyes. He suppressed a shudder and slipped a hip flask from his pocket.

Well, perhaps just the carousing for now, Wilde thought to himself as he quaffed a mouthful of brandy.

CHAPTER 24

USELESS FRIENDS AND DANGEROUS DRUGS

As the maid conducted him into the parlor of number 16 Tite Street, Conan Doyle caught Constance Wilde standing compromisingly close to Robert Sheridan—much closer than two casual friends should stand, and one a married lady at that. They sprang apart upon hearing him clear his throat. Sheridan moved to the window and stood gazing out, clearly embarrassed. Constance, in full blush, rushed over to greet the author.

"My dear, Arthur. It is so good to see you," she said, gripping his hand solicitously. "With Oscar forever at his club, we have become strangers of late."

Conan Doyle was still recovering from the shock of catching her in a moment of indiscretion and had not yet composed his face.

"How is Louise?" she asked. "Her struggle for health continues?"

He nodded gravely. "She abides."

"You must be so very lonely. Still, I understand you have a new friend? Several of my acquaintances have seen you dining with a most attractive young lady."

The thinly veiled threat was not lost upon Conan Doyle. Apparently all of them, Arthur, Oscar, and Constance were engaged in some degree of infidelity. Still, Conan Doyle was distressed to hear that he was already the subject of gossip.

"I have many friends amongst *the Society*. Miss Leckie has been assisting me with my research on the occult . . . for a book I am writing."

Constance Wilde was a striking woman with an intellect to match. "Research? Is that what it is called now?" She smiled. "I wish you both much success with your . . . research."

Conan Doyle brushed his walrus moustache with agitation. "Is Oscar at home? I stopped in at his club, but he did not spend the night."

"Yes, my husband did grace us with his presence last night. He arrived home in the early hours, rather the worse for wear. I cannot imagine what he'd been up to, but he was in quite a mania. He insisted upon waking the children and lavishing them with hugs and kisses. He promised that he would never stray and that his children were the dearest thing in the world to him." Constance smiled ironically. "Of course, Oscar promises many things when he is feeling . . . poetic . . . as you no doubt know."

Conan Doyle felt himself being drawn into a confidence about the Wildes' marriage he did not wish to share. His own personal life was tangled enough.

"Is Oscar awake?"

Something in Constance's eyes drew back, realizing she had crossed a line. "He is in his study with the boys. I'm afraid he is still somewhat discomposed."

* * *

When Conan Doyle entered the study, his Irish friend was slumped in a chair, an ice bag balanced on his head, a lavender mask blindfolding his eyes. The boys, Vyvyan and Cyril, were marching about the room like soldiers, Vyvyan blasting on a tin trumpet while Cyril banged a toy drum with the kind of hateable fervor only a child can manifest.

Wilde moaned beneath the lavender mask and called out, "Is that you, Arthur?"

"Yes!" Conan Doyle shouted to be heard above the racket. He dropped into the armchair opposite Wilde's.

The Irish wit paused to remove the eyeshade and display eyes that resembled bloody marbles. "As you can see, I had quite the evening." He turned to the end table and sifted a spoonful of white powder from a paper packet into a glass of water and agitated it with a spoon. He glugged down the glassful and shivered with disgust.

"Is that a nerve tonic?"

"So the chemist claimed, although I am certain the man is an amateur poisoner in his free time. I confess it is doing precious little to soothe my nerves, which are frazzled beyond repair. Ugh, my head is bursting. Do you have any laudanum?"

"Certainly not!"

"Are you sure? You are, after all, a doctor."

"I'm quite sure, Oscar. I do not have my medical bag with me."

"And you don't carry any on your person? For emergency purposes? Because, I assure you, my headache constitutes an emergency."

"I am not in the habit of carrying laudanum about on my person. It is a dangerous drug."

Wilde released an exasperated sigh. "What is the point of being a doctor if you cannot dispense dangerous drugs to your friends? Always remember, Arthur, the synonym for friend is *useful*. One has no useless friends. Uselessness is a trait reserved for one's relatives."

Vyvyan thrust the bell of his trumpet within an inch of Wilde's ear and sounded a window-rattling BLAAAAAAATTT!

"Ohhhhhh . . . Vyvyan!!" Wilde moaned. "Do not sound that horn in Papa's ear, lest it prove the trump that announces his departure from this mortal coil."

"Did you not purchase these instruments for the boys?" Conan Doyle asked with barely suppressed glee. "You specifically asked for the noisiest toys in the shop."

"Hoist by my own petard. Gloat if you must."

Conan Doyle reached into his pocket, drew out DeVayne's slim tome on necromancy, and pushed it into Wilde's large hands.

"I have startling news to share about this book."

Wilde glanced blearily at the slim volume. He casually leaned forward and tossed it onto the coal fire. The leather cover puckered and shriveled, and then the book crackled into flames and was utterly consumed.

"I have news to share about its author, and your news cannot possibly be as startling as mine. But let us not discuss these matters within hearing of the *grande dame*." Wilde tottered up from the chair, wincing, both hands clamped to his head as if holding together the cracked halves of a broken china bowl. "Come children. Cease your musical torture. Let us go into the garden and play cricket, before Papa suffers a paroxysm."

After the children had been suitably muffled up for the chill day, the two writers stood in the garden, sharing confidences as they supervised the boy's cricket game. Vyvyan defended a miniature set of stumps with a child's cricket bat while Conan Doyle bowled to him with a soft rubber ball. Cyril fielded the balls that rolled into the far corners of the yard. Wilde smoked a cigarette, pretending to play wicket keeper, but whinged every time he had to stoop to pick up the ball.

As the boys ran about, Conan Doyle shared his story of Miss Leckie's revelations about the book. Then Wilde launched into a heavily censored version of his encounter with the marquess. Conan Doyle was scandalized by the description of the orgy, but when Wilde described what happened in the marquess's bedchamber, the Scotsman dropped the ball he was preparing to bowl and stood in openmouthed horror. "A sacrifice, you say? Two children? You cannot be serious, Oscar. Please assure me you are making all of this up!"

Wilde wearily dragged upon his cigarette and released a pluming breath into the November air. "I am happy to confess that even I lack sufficient imagination to invent such depravity. I once told you that

Rufus DeVayne was Dorian Gray." He shook his head ruefully, his gaze fixed upon something a thousand miles away. "I was mistaken. He is Caligula."

Conan Doyle was about to question Wilde further when Constance stepped from the house. "Oscar I think it is time the children came inside, before they catch their deaths."

Wilde placidly assented, watching as his wife scooted the boys back into the house.

When the two friends were at last alone in the garden, they exchanged a grim look.

"Terrible things are happening in this country, Arthur. I have witnessed a level of decadence, wickedness, and depravity—practiced by some of the highest in the land—which I could not even guess at. Perhaps we do need a revolution. Perhaps it is time to sweep away an old order grown corrupt."

Conan Doyle shook his head. "I for one do not intend to choose sides. I intend to choose my own values. But I believe that we cannot afford to remain ignorant, nor to ignore a palpable evil and hope it will not reach out and touch our own families." He reached into a pocket and drew out a sheet of tightly wadded paper, unfolded it with care and handed it to Wilde.

13/13
The Revolution is Upon Us.
Join the struggle for workers' rights
Meeting: St. Winifred's
Friday, Dusk

Conan Doyle continued, "The meeting is to take place tonight at a derelict church in St. Giles. We must attend that meeting, although it will not be without considerable danger. We will need to dress in disguise. It will require a good deal of bravery. Are you willing to risk everything? Are you willing to try and make a difference?"

"I abhor bravery," Wilde said, drawing deeply from his cigarette. He exhaled and continued, "Bravery is a desperate act made necessary by a failure of the human imagination. But I am afraid I have no choice." He dropped the cigarette to the grass and ground it out beneath the sole of his shoe. "You may count upon Oscar Wilde."

CHAPTER 25

DESCENT INTO THE UNDERWORLD

"You're not wearing *that*?"

"I was about to say the same thing about your attire, Arthur, only I was too polite."

Wilde had just tripped down the front steps of number 16 Tite Street to join Conan Doyle, who stood waiting at the curb with a cab. Earlier, they had both decided that Wilde's fine new carriage was too conspicuous, and so Conan Doyle had hired the services of Iron Jim and his hansom for the night. The Scottish author was dressed in an outfit he wore when exploring the rougher parts of London doing research for his Sherlock Holmes stories: a heavy wool pea coat and a shabby peaked cap of the type worn by stevedores on the docks, tough canvas trousers, and iron-shod clogs. To his horror, Wilde was kitted out in a bottle-green coat and black velvet knickers, silk stockings, and buckled shoes.

"Oscar, we are slipping into the lion's den. I thought we agreed that we must blend in? Dress down? Counterfeit the attire of a working man?"

"You said 'dress down,' Arthur, and these are my oldest and shabbiest clothes. If you notice, the cuff of this sleeve is visibly worn and the shirt has a stain upon the collar. Possibly caviar. Possibly red wine.

What's more, my face has not enjoyed the kiss of a razor since this morning. I feel positively slovenly."

Conan Doyle released a sigh and threw a suffering look up at the cabman seated on his perch atop the hansom. They had not even set off, but the Scotsman was considering abandoning the entire venture. However, there was no choice, they had to be at the meeting.

"Where to, Guv'nor?"

"St. Giles, Jim. And take your time. We wish to arrive after dusk."

A look of fear flashed across the cabby's face. "St. Giles? After dark? Are you quite sure? It's dodgy enough in the daylight."

The cabbie had a valid point. Slums such as St. Giles were lawless enclaves ruled by criminal gangs. Even the police were reluctant to enter such places unless armed and in great numbers. Two gentlemen going it alone at dusk smacked of suicide.

Conan Doyle had been fingering a crown coin in his pocket. He let it loose and probed deeper, finding a coin of higher denomination. "Here you go, Jim." He handed up a golden sovereign. "There's another for you on the return journey."

The cabbie eyed the proffered coin dubiously, his weather-beaten face a mask of reluctance. But finally, he reached down and snatched the sovereign. "Right you are, Gov. I'll get ya there and back, safe as houses."

Wilde peered up at ominous skies. "Scarcely half past three and the fog is already rising."

"Yes," Conan Doyle agreed, "but let us hope it is a pea-souper. We may need to slip away under its cover."

* * *

Both men were quiet and thoughtful during the cab ride. Both knew the danger of what they were about to undertake. Wilde chain-smoked as usual, and when he reached into a breast pocket, Conan Doyle thought he was searching for a fresh box of lucifers, but instead he drew out a tightly folded piece of paper.

"What is that?"

"The photograph and letter entrusted to me by the late Vicente. I finally had a chance to read it. The young woman in the photograph is Vicente's sister, his only surviving relative. The letter was from her, describing the death of their mother. When this madness is over, I shall mail the letter and photograph back to her and include a note informing her of her brother's sad demise."

The trapdoor in the ceiling opened and Iron Jim's rugged face appeared framed in it. "We're here, gents. Best be on your guard. It don't look none too friendly."

Conan Doyle had naïvely imagined they would simply cab up to the front doors of the abandoned church of St. Winifred's and be dropped off. But as the hansom approached the lawless slum of St. Giles, they found the streets blocked by heaped-up barricades of paving slabs, broken furniture, and scavenged debris. Manning them were gangs of club-wielding toughs who stood idly about, puffing clay pipes, swigging from bottles, and warming themselves on open trash fires. And everywhere the ominous black flyers:

The hansom stopped a hundred feet shy. "I reckon that's it," Iron Jim called down. "I daren't go no further."

"Well, there you have it, Arthur. We tried. I suggest we go for supper at the Ritz—"

"No, Oscar. We didn't come this far to turn back at the first obstacle." Conan Doyle ruffled his moustache, thinking. "We shall just have to dismount and walk in."

"Walk in? Those chaps look less than friendly. What happens if there's trouble?"

"Then we shall just have to walk back out . . . hurriedly."

"Dear me," Wilde pouted. "This has all the hallmarks of an extremely poor idea."

The two friends alighted from the hansom and set off walking. The two toughs manning the barricade watched them approach.

"And who are you two?" asked a man whose face had been zigzagged by the jagged end of a broken bottle.

"Me and him are lads from downriver," Conan Doyle said, affecting a Cockney drawl.

The other tough was holding a shillelagh and spoke with an Irish accent so thick as to be barely intelligible. "We're here lookin' for police spoiz. You boiz wudna be plainclothes coppers, wudcha?" He smacked the club into his open palm menacingly. "Only we'd be lookin' to kill yuz if ye wur." He chuckled darkly and his friend joined in.

"Me name's Jim," Conan Doyle improvised. "I works on the docks."

"Oh you work the docks, do ya?" The scarred man nodded to the orange glow of the trash fire. "Step into the light then, and let's see yer hands."

Conan Doyle quailed at the demand. He had the smooth, immaculate hands of a writer. In an attempt to disguise their condition he had blackened his fingers with a lump of coal from the fireside scuttle, and then pulled on a pair of fingerless woolen gloves. But they were devoid of the cuts, welts, nicks, and calluses that a real stevedore would have. As soon as the toughs saw their immaculate condition, the lie would be revealed. The game was up before it had even begun.

Apparently Wilde guessed the same thing, because he stepped forward and addressed the Irishman in Gaelic. The man listened to Wilde's banter, sharing a laugh, and then the Irish tough clapped a hand on his comrade's shoulder and said, "Deese lads is all roit. Lettem true."

With a nod and a friendly wave, the two friends passed unmolested through the barricade and entered St. Giles proper: a slumland warren of semi-derelict houses, grimy courtyards, open sewers, and stinking alleyways glued together by poverty and filth. When they were safely out of earshot, Conan Doyle glanced at Wilde and asked in a tight whisper: "I thought our goose was cooked back there. What on earth did you say to him?"

"I told him I was a senior commander in the Fenian Brotherhood and that you were my Scots bomb maker."

"Good Lord," Conan Doyle said. "What are we mixed up in?"

The higgledy streets were rapidly filling as shadowy figures drifted out of every alleyway and side road, joining the hordes marching toward the church. The meeting was attracting followers in the hundreds—rough men, and slatternly women—who cursed and spat worse than the men—some bouncing babies on their hips or dragging behind ragged and complaining children. As their numbers grew, the narrow streets resounded to the tromp of clogs on cobblestones, spiked with snatches of laughter and brayed curses.

By the time they reached the church, the two friends were part of a huge cohort. Although St. Winifred's was little more than a gutted shell, shafts of light shot from its glassless windows and the hubbub of voices from within testified that hundreds were already in attendance, with more arriving by the second. They filed inside in a shuffling lockstep. Unevenly lit by a scatter of lanterns and burning torches, the once-sacred building had long since been stripped of its pews and any religious artifacts. A battered pulpit still commanded the center of the nave, but now its sides were plastered with 13/13 flyers.

Conan Doyle guided Wilde toward a spot in the far recesses, where he had vainly hoped they would have the space mostly to themselves; however, the church was rapidly filling to capacity. Rough working types: navvies, dockers, mudlarks, ratters, and casual laborers—the working poor of London—filed in from either side. The two writers soon found themselves crammed shoulder-to-shoulder, hopelessly hemmed in. A ferret-faced man in a crumpled top hat and a grimy topcoat, reeking of gin, stumbled into Conan

Doyle with bruising force but did not apologize. He shot the author a quick up-and-down glance and then moved his penetrating gaze to Wilde, whose choice of attire sprang a suspicious frown to the drunkard's greasy lips.

Conan Doyle's heart clenched with fear. If the drunken brute kicked up an uproar, he and Wilde would be lucky to get out of the church alive.

The drone of conversation drained away as a well-dressed figure crossed the aisle and sprang up the steps of the pulpit. As he stepped to the railing, torchlight swept aside the shadows, revealing a familiar face—Dr. John Lamb, the stylishly dressed doctor from Newgate Prison.

Conan Doyle and Wilde shared a look of disbelief.

"Friends! Friends! Friends!" Dr. Lamb began, raising his hands for attention and tamping down the last dregs of babble. "Many of you already know me, for I use my skills as a physician to assuage the suffering of the poor, of the lame, of the sick. I do so without concern for my own purse, for I believe in the commonwealth of man. We are here tonight to speak of revolution. Every revolution needs a general. A Wat Tyler. A great man who will lead that cause. That man is here tonight. That man is ready for the struggle. That man will stand by you to the death. Please greet the leader of our brave revolution."

The doctor tripped down the stairs as another man vaulted up. He wore a long cape with a hood that hid his features. As he stepped into the pulpit, he drew back the hood and shrugged the cape from his shoulders. The vision of an effete young man with fiery red curls spilling to his shoulders shocked the space into an echoing silence.

"I am Rufus DeVayne, Marquess of Gravistock. I come before you—"

The rest of his words were drowned in a deafening roar of howls, boos, and catcalls that rattled the stone vaulted ceiling.

Conan Doyle shared an astonished look with Wilde. "Is he mad, coming here?"

Wilde shook his long face and agreed. "Surely this mob will tear him apart."

DeVayne stood patiently waiting, his face fixed in a serene smile. Each time he tried to speak, howls of derision drowned out his words. Finally, he leaned back from the railing and let the crowd roar on. Then a man stepped to the base of the pulpit and hawked a wad of spittle at DeVayne. A quivering silver oyster arced high into the air and splattered across his cheek.

The crowd boomed with laughter and the drum of stamping feet grew deafening.

For long seconds, the young aristocrat did not flinch, did not move. Then he carefully wiped the gleaming oyster from his cheek. He stood for a moment, looking at the contents of his palm, and then slowly, deliberately, and with apparent relish, licked the wad of spittle from his palm.

It was an act that shocked even the hardest man, and the church fell into stunned silence. The moment turned upon a pivot and now DeVayne commanded the mob's attention. He gripped the pulpit railing and leaned far over it, his eyes blazing as he addressed the crowd in his high, ethereal voice, a stiletto blade probing for the gap between ribs.

"A normal man might be cowed by jeers and boos. A normal man might flinch at being spat upon."

His pale face cracked a wicked smile.

"But I am no ordinary man." He swept the crowd with an imperial gaze. "Why? Because I choose not to be. And I suspect you—all of you—are men who would be extraordinary. Sheep need to be led. To be shorn of their wool. To be used as beasts of the field until the day their throats are offered up to the razor."

He paused to allow the echoes of his voice to subside.

"But I see no sheep in this place. I see only extraordinary men. Men who are ready to rise up from slavery. To shake off servitude and take what is rightfully theirs. My name is Rufus DeVayne. I am a cousin of the Prince of Wales. Fifth in line to the throne. To you, I am a toff. An aristocrat. But know that I am vilified as a traitor to my class. And with good reason."

He leaned far over the pulpit railing, the shifting torchlight twisting and contorting his features. And then he dropped his voice to a barely audible rumble that all ears strained to hear. "Because they fear me. They fear my beliefs. And I would make them fear you."

He had found his rhythm and now he leaned back. At ease. The crowd in his thrall. The mob murmured. No one stirred. DeVayne looked down upon a multitude of upturned faces. The sallow-cheeked faces of the working poor. People touched by the words of an exotic figure that looked like a man-child and spoke like a demigod. A figure that held all spellbound.

Conan Doyle threw a quick glance at Wilde, who also watched, mesmerized.

DeVayne continued, "I have a title. I am a marquess. I live in a fine house and eat from golden plates. Why? Because I am superior to the common man? Because of some divine right?" He sneered. "No. Because hundreds of years ago my ancestor killed another man and stole what was rightfully his. Likewise, the monarchy is nothing but a system of theft made legitimate by masquerade party dress and the trumpery of law. But I have no love for title or privilege. I would have all my brothers and sisters sit at the table and break bread with me. No man higher. No man lower. No man made to bow and scrape to another."

The crowd rippled with nodding heads.

"France had its revolution one hundred years ago. England's revolution is long overdue. But I warn you, my brothers and sisters, freedom can only be purchased with blood . . . with courage . . . with sacrifice . . . and loss. So, I ask you tonight, are you extraordinary men and women? Or are you sheep?"

Someone whispered in the back on the vestry and the whispers grew to murmurs that rolled across the pews in a wave of sound that finally broke at the foot of the pulpit Rufus DeVayne towered from.

"NOOOOOOOOOOOOOOOOOOOOOOOOOOOOOO!"

"On the thirteenth of this month, I will be there at the gates of Buckingham Palace. Ready to face the rifles and bayonets of the queen's army. Ready to scale the railings and pull them down. On that day, at one o'clock, Big Ben will chime thirteen times. That is our signal to rise up. Together we will storm the palace. Together we will take back the birthright of the common people that was stolen long ago. My brothers and sisters. My equals. My comrades in arms. Will you be there with me? Will you rise up? Will you strike a blow for freedom?"

DeVayne hurled the challenge into the room like a stick of dynamite with the fuse lit and fizzing. Then he stood back, relaxed, and waited, a strange smile upon his lips.

For a moment the walls of the church seemed to suck inward in one collectively drawn breath, the premonitory silence before the thunderclap, and then the air split with a thunderous roar of voices loosing a cry of "YEEEEEEEEEEEEEEESSSSSSSSS!"

Clenched fists pumped the air. Iron-shod clogs stomped the flagstones and made them ring.

DeVayne acknowledged their cries like an emperor being showered with rose petals.

Conan Doyle jabbed an elbow in his friend's ribs and shouted above the roar, "This is a very dangerous man."

Wilde tore his eyes away with difficulty. "Yes, dangerous . . . and magnificent."

With applause crashing about him, DeVayne quit the pulpit, skipped down the steps, and joined Dr. Lamb waiting below. Barely acknowledging the cheering crowd, the two men strode up the aisle and out of the church. The audience surged to follow, and Conan Doyle and Wilde were swept up in the crush and carried from the building. Once outside, they ducked clear of the hurrying mob to pause a moment and confer.

"It appears there is even more to worry about from DeVayne that I at first thought," Wilde said, pausing to spark up one of his Turkish cigarettes.

"But he is clearly mad. A revolution will never take hold. He's just going to get a lot of people killed."

"Cadge a fag, mate?" a rough voice asked from Wilde's elbow.

"By all means," Wilde assented, and reflexively held out his silver cigarette case. Conan Doyle noticed it was the ferret-faced man in the crumpled topper who had lavished Wilde with a suspicious glare. He tried to warn his friend with a look, but it was too late.

The man took a cigarette from the case and rolled it beneath his gin-blossomed nose. "Thanks mate. What sort of fag's this? Smells a bit queer."

"They're Turkish. I buy them from a special shop on the Old Kent Road. I highly recommend them if you're in the city."

Conan Doyle nearly swallowed his own tongue.

"I thought as much," the man said, flinging the cigarette to the ground. "We got us a coupla toffs here!" he bellowed. "A coupla spies, I reckon!"

Heads turned to stop and stare.

Conan Doyle leaned into Wilde and muttered in a low voice. "We've been rumbled, Oscar. When I give the word, run for your life."

"Spies," the man shouted aloud, pointing. "We gotta coupla bleedin' spies in our midst."

All the shouting was grabbing attention. People stopped to look. They began to draw a crowd. Fearful of being encircled, Conan Doyle grabbed Wilde's sleeve and began to usher him away. But now a group of ten or more followed behind, dogging their steps.

"Barstards!"

"Kill the toffs!"

A rock whizzed past Conan Doyle's ear and then he snarled with pain as a second, much larger rock, bounced off his shoulder with bruising force. Instinctively, he knew that more, and much worse was about to follow.

"Now, Oscar, run!" The two men took to their heels, surprise momentarily stealing them a few yards, but then the mob took off in pursuit.

Up ahead, all the shouting had alerted the toughs guarding the barricade and they stepped forward to block any escape, cudgels at the ready. Conan Doyle noticed the dark opening of a ginnel to their right: a tight passage between buildings too narrow to be considered an alleyway. He pointed and veered toward it. "Quickly, Oscar. Perhaps we can lose them in there."

They ducked into a passage so narrow their shoulders scraped along the bricks on either side as they ran. The ginnel wound downward and emptied out on the lower street. They ran along the terrace and then ducked down a side alley and pressed themselves against the wall where they paused, sucking wind, straining to listen.

"I think we're safe," Conan Doyle panted.

"S-s-safe?" Wild gasped. "If they don't murder us first, you're going to kill us with all this running. You know my views on exercise and the dangers of healthy living."

"I told you we were going to a dodgy area, Oscar. Perhaps you could have dressed a bit more aggressively."

Wilde stiffened his posture. "What do you mean, aggressively? Silk stockings, a bottle-green coat and velvet knickers—if this is not an outfit that rings the shop bell, bangs its fist upon the counter, and demands in a brusque voice 'look at me.' I don't know what aggressive means."

"Shush!" Conan Doyle gestured for silence. From a nearby street came the scuffle of running feet, but it soon fell from hearing. "Quietly, then, let's go."

The two men crept farther down the alleyway, and had only gone fifty feet when a half-dozen bone-bruisers marched from a side alley and tromped toward them with a swaggering walk freighted with menace.

Conan Doyle looked about. The brick alley walls were ten feet high and topped with rusty nails and daggers of broken glass to discourage climbing.

"Much as I hate to criticize, Arthur, your escape plan leaves much to be desired."

"Is that all of you?" Conan Doyle called out to the looming figures. "Hardly seems a fair fight. If you like, we'll wait while you fetch more help."

A cackle of laughter. They turned to see four more figures advancing from behind.

Trapped.

"Now there's ten of us," one leered. "Is them odds more to yer likin'?"

"What now?" Wilde asked. "There's far too many to fight."

"I'm afraid we have no choice in the matter. My father always told me: if a gang confronts you, pick out the biggest and loudest. Knock him down first and the rest will scatter and run."

"My father's advice on such situations was to retain the services of a good doctor."

Conan Doyle shrugged the coat from his shoulders, dropping it to the alley, freeing his arms to fight. "I suggest you shed your coat, Oscar."

"Surely you jest. The alley is filthy. I shall take my beating with my coat on."

"You there," Conan Doyle said, nodding to the tallest figure. "Step forward and let's see what you're made of."

But the man who stepped forward wasn't just the tallest, he was also the widest. He barked a laugh and peeled off his overcoat to reveal the physique of a circus strongman. Although going to fat, the man possessed a barrel chest and arms bigger than most men's legs.

238 CR THE DEAD ASSASSIN

Atop the hulking shoulders sat a head like a battle-scarred cannon-
ball with cauliflowered ears and a nose that had been broken and re-
broken to a twisted snaggle of cartilage.

"Oh dear," Wilde said quietly. "It appears you have challenged
Hercules himself to a bare knuckle fight."

Conan Doyle stepped forward and dropped into a boxing stance,
fists up and ready. It was clear the strongman could weather a blow
to the face, so the Scottish author let him throw the first punch—a
wild full-out haymaker easily dodged by jerking his head back at the
last moment. Even so, the giant fist came so close he felt the breeze.
In response, he feinted a left jab, and as the man's hands instinctively
came up to protect his face, Conan Doyle danced forward and swung
a right hook into his solar plexus that sank to the elbow. It proved a
crippling blow. The strongman buckled in two around the punch, ex-
pelling air with a grunt, and sagged to his knees. He teetered for a
moment, arms hugging his belly, and then the light went out of his
eyes and he toppled face-first to the cobbles.

Out cold.

Stunned by the loss of their champion, the gang took a collective
step backward.

Wilde threw his friend an inquiring glance. "Arthur, at the risk of
being pedantic, shouldn't they be running away just about now?"

"Um, it doesn't always work."

The ferret-faced man in the broken top hat had been hanging
back in the shadows and now he hollered: "Get 'em, lads! Scrag 'em!"

Howling like beasts, the pack fell upon the two friends and a wild,
fist-flailing melee ensued. Conan Doyle fought off three and four at-
tackers at a time, sometimes taking two blows to deliver one of his own.
A number of the thugs set upon Wilde, thinking his prissy attire made
him the easier target. They soon found out, however, that although his
hands were soft, his knuckles were hard and the six-foot-one Irishman's
height, weight, and superior reach allowed him knock senseless anyone
foolish enough to come within range of his long arms.

Suddenly the gang found many of their toughest fighters sprawled unconscious on the ground as the apparently helpless toffs proved to be skilled fighters. Conan Doyle dropped another man with a one-two uppercut and advanced upon the rest, fists windmilling, eyes blazing with fight. Like jackals confronted by lions, the pack broke and took to their heels at a flat-out run, no man wanting to be the last one out of the alleyway.

Conan Doyle and Wilde suddenly found themselves alone, with five burly men knocked flat and groaning on the cobblestones. Though battered and bruised, both friends had emerged from the battle triumphant, and were charged with adrenaline and euphoria.

"Extraordinary!" Wilde said, indicating the fallen prizefighter. "How did you drop that behemoth with one punch?"

"I learned how to box at boarding school and was quite good. As a doctor, I learned about anatomy. The solar plexus is a point at which a great number of blood vessels come together. A hard, swift blow placed at a precise location causes the vessels to spasm, depriving the brain of blood. As you saw, unconsciousness quickly follows. But what about you, Oscar? I knew you had boxed some at Oxford, but you handled yourself exceptionally well. That last uppercut was brilliantly executed. Nearly took the blighter's head off!"

Wilde smiled modestly. "I was a passing fair boxer, but soon decided my face was far too large and pretty to be used as a punching bag. Thereafter I concentrated my martial efforts on the debating club, preferring repartee to fisticuffs."

Conan Doyle paused in pulling on his coat to give his snout an experimental tweak to ascertain that it was merely sore, and not broken. "Those louts were seasoned toughs. We are lucky to have escaped with a few cuts and bruises." He examined his friend. "Stand still, Oscar, while I look at you." Wilde's chestnut curls were severely tousled. Someone's knuckles had left a red scrape across his cheekbone.

Wilde saw his look of concern and said, "Tell me the truth. I'm horribly disfigured, aren't I? It's not me I worry about, it's the loss to the world."

"Just a slight abrasion on one cheek. A bit of rubbing alcohol and you'll be fine."

The Irishman fixed him with an abject look. "You may rub your alcohol so where you like, Arthur. I intend to drink mine."

Conan Doyle laughed and clapped his friend on the shoulder. "You're a Viking, Oscar! An absolute Viking."

"Thank you, my friend." Wilde conceded, preening a little. "I think we acquitted ourselves quite well."

"Damned well!"

"There's no need to swear, Arthur."

"Quite right. I apologize."

"Now what?"

"We must find our way out of this wretched place. Hopefully, Iron Jim will still be waiting with the hansom."

They emerged from the alley within sight of a corner business bursting with light and activity despite the fog. Just then the front door banged open, releasing a squawk of inebriation and a man staggered out, coat half on, half off. He weaved along the pavement, struggling to pull his arms into the sleeves of his coat, but then tripped and face-plowed to the pavement, where he vomited before rolling into the gutter.

"A gin shop," Conan Doyle said. "Let's stop in and see if we can find out where we are."

As the two friends pushed in through the door, the paint-stripping whiff of cheap booze scoured their sinuses. The place was a raucous mulligan of slack-faced men and cackling women singing, cursing, guzzling gin and then banging their empty glasses down on the tabletops for more.

The discordant duo of stevedore and aesthete garnered quizzical stares as the two writers shouldered a path to the bar. The barman was a small man hiding behind an enormous black moustache.

"What's yer poison?" he growled impatiently—other customers were already hammering their empty glasses on the bar to be served.

"Two mother's ruin," Conan Doyle said. "Best you got."

The barman set two grimy glasses on the counter and sloshed into each a clear liquid with the turbidity and bouquet of turpentine. "Tanner a piece," he grunted.

Conan Doyle slapped down a shilling and the barman disappeared to answer the braying voices of his importuning customers. The author clinked glasses with his friend and said, "Here's to us, Oscar, poets and warriors both."

"*Sláinte agus táinte!*" Wilde replied with a traditional Irish toast.

Both men took a sip and choked. When Wilde could draw breath again, he wheezed, "I am certain the dray horse that produced this elixir is far from well. Let us repair to my club. Another sip of this juniper poison and I shall be struck blind."

"It may not be drinkable, but it should prevent infection." Conan Doyle tugged a handkerchief from his pocket, dipped it in his gin glass, and pressed it to Wilde's skinned and swollen knuckles, causing him to wince and cry out.

"Enough!" he gasped. "It will only kill the germs by first killing me!"

Conan Doyle took a moment to assess his own injuries. The knuckles of both hands were badly bruised and beginning to swell. His throbbing ear felt as if it had swollen to the size of a dinner plate.

"Oi! You bastards!" a voice bellowed and the room fell silent.

The ferret-faced man stood in the open doorway; crowded behind were a gang of twenty or more. The louts had regrouped and fetched reinforcements with them, most armed with clubs and staves.

"Oh, dear!" Wilde said. "How do we escape this?"

"I am quite done running for one evening." Conan Doyle reached into a pocket and drew out a fistful of banknotes. "I shall buy our way out." He flourished the bills for all to see. Then he shouted, "Drinks on me!" and flung the money into the air.

Pandemonium ensued as drinkers fought to scrabble up the money and their pursuers were pinned in the crush. Wilde ducked under the serving hatch while Conan Doyle vaulted onto the bar and over. The two friends ducked through a doorway. They passed through a room stacked with crates of gin bottles and through another door that opened onto a cobblestone yard secured by a bolted wooden gate. Flinging open the gate, they stumbled into a gloomy alleyway.

But they were not alone. A carriage pulled by African zebras had drawn up and two figures stood waiting.

CHAPTER 26

A NICE NIGHT FOR A DROWNING

"You and your companion have a talent for survival, Mister Wilde," DeVayne said. "However, if our friends find you, it is likely you will both die a very unpleasant death." The slender aristocrat sauntered up to Wilde and caressed his chin with the back of a leather-clad hand. "And despite our misunderstanding of the previous evening, I should be sad to see anything happen to that long, lovely Irish face."

The four men stood in a frozen tableau. "You have the advantage of us, Marquess," Wilde admitted.

Dr. Lamb coughed into his hand discreetly. "The mob will be upon us soon."

"I can offer you gentlemen safe passage." DeVayne indicated the carriage with a nod. "My carriage is at your disposal."

Dr. Lamb held the carriage door open and stood waiting.

Wilde shot a glance at Conan Doyle, who shook his head. Should they step into the yellow landau they would place themselves utterly at DeVayne's mercy.

Shouts and curses from behind told them that some of the thugs had followed them through the bar and were spilling into the gin shop's cobbled yard.

Wilde suddenly broke from the spot, stepped to the carriage, and climbed in. Conan Doyle hesitated a moment and followed, his hands balled into fists ready to throw a punch. Fortunately, the carriage was empty and he bounced onto the seat beside Wilde.

Dr. Lamb and the marquess climbed aboard and sat opposite the two friends. The marquess rapped on the carriage roof and shouted, "Away!"

The carriage pulled out of the alleyway and turned left, passing the gin shop where a press of armed men choked the doorway as they tried to squeeze in. The landau passed by without slowing and Conan Doyle and Wilde released a pent-up breath.

The marquess's expression betrayed his amusement at their predicament. "Did you gentlemen enjoy my speech?"

"I found it greatly surprising," Wilde said. "I knew you were an acolyte of the occult, but I had no idea you also held political pretensions."

"I am a deeply complicated man. Many underestimate me. An error of judgment that shall soon cost them dearly." His face tightened in a feral smile, his eyes aglitter. "England is about to change, gentlemen. The glorious Empire is about to fall. You need to decide which side you stand on: the old, corrupt side, or the new, egalitarian side. When we come to power, those who have ruled for centuries will be swept aside. We shall establish a new order: a republic based on logic and reason, where gentlemen such as yourselves shall be exalted as gods."

The carriage swept past streets lit by burning barricades and soon left St. Giles behind. Conan Doyle kept darting glances out the window, casting about for a familiar landmark, hoping to catch a glimpse of Iron Jim and his hansom cab. But the fog was thick and he had no sense of where they were nor in which direction they were heading.

The marquess and the doctor leaned, heads together, chuckling over some whispered secret. Abruptly, DeVayne rapped on the ceiling and the carriage drew to a halt. Both men tensed as the marquess drew a small dagger from his sleeve. "I offer you one last chance. Swear a blood oath that you will stand with me. If you decline, I shall drop you here and you must take your chances when the revolution comes."

"I'm afraid I must decline your blood oath," Wilde said. "I swoon at so much as a paper cut."

"I also decline," added Conan Doyle.

DeVayne sat in silent contemplation, tapping the tip of the dagger against his pursed lips. "Very well, your choice is made. Your fate decided. I urge you to remain uninvolved in the events that are about to unfold. I know a great deal about both of you." He glared at Wilde. "I know about your two beautiful boys, and your tawdry diversions in the 'special' clubs of Soho." He slid his gaze to Conan Doyle. "I know about your consumptive wife and your ongoing dalliance with the young woman. Oh, and I know about that ludicrous little puppet Cypher. Be assured, gentlemen, none who stand against us shall be spared." He paused and then added, "Nor shall their families. Now get out." DeVayne, having said all he wished to say, reclined back into his own personal darkness.

Conan Doyle and Wilde stepped down from the carriage. The door banged shut, a whip cracked about the zebras' ears, and the landau lurched away, abandoning them to streets of rime and swirling fog. The two men looked about, baffled by what they saw, or rather failed to see. The only indications of civilization were the charcoal silhouettes of hulking brick warehouses. The mournful drone of a fog-horn sounded in the distance.

"Where the devil are we?"

"This is clearly not where we left the hansom," Conan Doyle observed. "He drew in a deep breath through his nose, scenting the air. "Judging by the thickness of the fog, the stink, and that steamer fog-horn, I'd say we're close to the Thames, but far downriver."

Both men looked up at the clop-clop of approaching hooves.

"We're in luck," Wilde said. "That must be the hansom now."

Both stared expectantly into the fog. Something large tore loose of the gray veil: a dark carriage drawn by two black horses with plumes bobbing atop their heads.

"A hearse!" Conan Doyle said.

"Hearse or hansom, I care not. Let's flag it down."

Both men shouted and waved at the oncoming hearse, which failed to slow or break rhythm. In fact, upon seeing them, the top-hatted driver whipped up the horses, which bore down on the two friends, forcing them to leap aside to avoid being trampled.

"Damn you!" Conan Doyle shouted after the driver. The hearse carried on and was swallowed up in the fog. The clopping of hooves suddenly slowed and stopped.

The two friends looked at each other.

"Did they see us?" Wilde asked. "Was it a mistake? Are they coming back for us?"

Conan Doyle shook his head uneasily. "I just realized something. I caught a glimpse of the driver's face. He had a port-wine stain down one cheek."

From somewhere in the fog, they heard a door creak open and slam shut. And then they heard a noise that filled them both with dread: *Wissssshhhthump . . . wisssssshthump . . . wissssssshthump . . .*

"Oh dear God," Wilde moaned. "Not again!"

Fog swirled and a shadowy figure lurched toward them. It stepped into the light of the streetlamp and showed its impossible face.

"Vicente!" Conan Doyle gasped. "But we saw him hanged!"

The once-handsome head sat upon a neck twisted by the hangman's rope. The face, bloated and ghastly, pulsed with swollen veins. The yellow eyes fixed upon them and the raggedy form slumped forward like something from a nightmare.

"RUN!" both shouted.

The two friends took to their heels, running away blindly into the thickening fog.

Wisssssshhhthump . . . wisssssshthump . . . wissssssshthump . . .

They came upon the wall of a warehouse and slid along it, hands groping the cinderous bricks. The wall abruptly ended and they followed the curbstone into another street. But in the blindfolding fog, every step was an act of faith.

"I have no sense of where we are," Conan Doyle said. "We could be walking into a cul-de-sac."

"Look," Wilde said, pointing. "I believe I can make out several streetlamps. If we go this way—"

Whooossh! An arm swung from the fog and grazed Wilde's face. He cried out in surprise. They hurried away, straining to follow the dull glow of streetlamps that seemed to recede before them. From behind came the *wissssshthump* and the scuffle of dragging feet.

"This is impossible," Wilde whispered. "Vicente was dead. We saw him hanged."

"He has been revivified. He is now some kind of monster."

Wissssshhhthump . . . wissssshthump . . . wissssshthump . . .

"Look!" Wilde said. "Up ahead. I think I see someone."

"No. We cannot go that way. We cannot endanger innocent people."

"Do we not number amongst the innocent, too? In fact, compared to the many scoundrels in London society, you and I are easily the most innocent!"

They hurried on, and soon beheld the comforting sight of two blue uniformed constables loitering on a street corner, chatting and laughing.

The officers startled as the two friends burst from the fog and ran up to them.

"Constables!" Conan Doyle said. "You must help us. We are being pursued by a monster."

The policemen took in Conan Doyle's stevedore clothing and Wilde's worn aesthete clothing. "You lads out slumming? Been drinking have you?"

"No!"

"I had a nip of brandy earlier."

"Oscar, shush!"

"He did ask."

Wissssshhhthump . . .

"Look!" Conan Doyle said, pointing at the ragged form shambling toward them. "That's him now!"

The two constables shared a knowing grin. "He's had a few from the look of him. Friend of yours, is he?"

"No! It's not a man at all! It's a killer. A monster!"

"Gets like that when he's had a few, does he?"

The dead man shambled into the glare of the streetlamp where the constables glimpsed the horrid face for the first time.

"Strewth!" the first officer said to his mate. "He don't look too good, right enough!"

The first officer stepped forward to meet the creature, brandishing his truncheon. "We ain't gonna have any trouble from you, sonny. Are we?"

In response, the monster swung a clublike arm that broke the constable's collarbone and forced him screaming to his knees. He grappled for a hold of the monster's ragged shirt, but it reached down, seized his helmeted head in both hands and twisted, breaking his neck. The monster let go and the constable slumped to the ground, dead and staring.

The second constable fumbled a whistle to his lips and split the silence with a sharp whistle blast. He leapt forward, truncheon drawn, and gave the monster a mighty whack across the head. It seemed not to feel anything and clamped a dead hand upon the constable's face, forcing the whistle down his throat. The policeman choked and writhed, struggling momentarily before the creature tore the jaw from his skull. A ragged scream peeled from the policeman's throat and he fell to the cobblestones, twitching and writhing.

The two friends cried out with horror and took to their heels, running away as fast as the fog would allow. The pavement underfoot was broken and heaved and Wilde caught a foot and sprawled on the ground. Conan Doyle grabbed him by the scruff and roughly dragged him to his feet.

Wisssssshhhthump . . . wissssshthump . . . wisssssshthump . . .

They hurried on, nearly colliding with lampposts that loomed unexpected from the fog. They turned randomly right onto one street and then left onto another. The warehouses fell behind. By now the air had grown noticeably chill and damp and soon they nosed the unmistakable reek of the Thames.

"The river," Wilde panted.

"Perhaps we are close to a bridge."

"Shush!"

Wisssssshhhthump . . . wisssssshthump . . . wisssssshthump . . .

"It's coming this way."

"How can it follow us in all this fog?"

"It is a reanimated corpse, neither dead nor alive."

Wisssssshhhthump . . . wissssshthump . . . wisssssshthump . . .

They hurried on, and soon reached the tidal foreshore of the Thames. The only structures hereabouts were creaking wooden hovels where the poorest of the poor lived. Built of scrap lumber salvaged from the river, they stood teetering on support poles driven into the mud. The vague glimmer of tallow candles in a few of the glassless windows suggested habitation.

"Should we seek shelter with them?" Wilde asked.

"We will only endanger more lives."

With thick fog cover and no streetlamps, the way ahead was unfathomably dark. But then, a gibbous moon, late rising above the river, lit the shifting panes of fog with light.

"Look," Conan Doyle said. "There's a boat." He pointed to a small rowboat drawn up on the mud flats.

"A boat? At this hour? In this fog and darkness? I tremble at the thought of taking a steamer on the sunniest of days."

"We merely have to row out a dozen feet and the thing cannot pursue us."

Wissssshhhthump . . . wissssshthump . . .

The monster was getting closer with each slumping step.

"Oscar, come. We must."

"No!"

"But it's our best hope."

"Out of the question."

"Why ever not?"

"I fear the water."

"More than the thing pursuing us?"

"I cannot swim, Arthur."

"What?"

"I never learned to swim. Shocking, I know. At last, something Oscar Wilde is not accomplished in. Gloat, if you must."

Conan Doyle laughed ironically. "Drowning is the least of our worries. One mouthful of Thames water is pure poison. You won't have time to drown." He grabbed Wilde's sleeve and urged him toward the boat. "Come along!"

They left the cobbled road, crunched across a gravel brake and onto the muck-slick foreshore, instantly sinking to the ankles. Feet slipping and sliding, they slogged through the shoe-sucking mire to the boat. Each grasped a side and heaved. Instantly, they discovered why someone had been careless enough to leave a rowboat in plain sight. The boat was ancient, its timbers waterlogged from years of service—too heavy to be stolen. They groaned and heaved and strained to drag it the short five feet to the water, but the rowboat proved immovable.

Wissssshthump . . .

"Push, Oscar, push!"

"Ugh, why did we have to choose the heaviest watercraft in history? I suggest we look for another."

Wissssshthump . . .

The dead thing raked the gravel with its feet and shambled onto the mud, feet slithering drunkenly before it found its footing and lumbered closer. Soon, it was mere feet away. It raised its arms and plunged toward Wilde, who was pushing at the stern of the boat.

"Pusssshhhhhhhh!"

Muscles quivering, both gave a final mighty heave. The boat sucked free of the muck with a *scccchhhlurrrrrp* and slid into the icy Thames. As it floated free, Conan Doyle sprang aboard, reached back, grabbed Wilde by the front of his coat and dragged him over the transom. He tumbled into the boat, which rolled alarmingly, almost tipping the pair into the water. As the vessel pitched and heaved, Wilde clambered to find a place on the seat while Conan Doyle scrambled to gather up the worn and splintery oars that had been left rammed beneath the seats.

They looked back. The thing that had once been Vicente stood at the water's edge, a silhouette of impotent rage, watching them drift away.

"We're safe . . . we're safe . . ." Conan Doyle breathed exhaustedly, reaching forward to clap a hand on Wilde's knee. Both men shook hands, gasping with effort, laughing with relief.

"You have paddles sorted out, Arthur?"

"Yes."

"Then I suggest you use them. The beast is following us into the water!"

To their horror, the monster waded out to its knees and stood watching the rowboat. Conan Doyle slipped the oars into the rattly oarlocks and began to row, pulling with all his strength. With each stroke, the heavy rowboat, riding perilously low in the water, plowed clumsily ahead. As they moved farther out, the monster and the shore disappeared in the murk. Soon Conan Doyle found himself rowing blindly into a featureless void. Finally, he ceased his efforts and raised the dripping oars, catching his breath as he strained to look around. "Can't see a blessed thing. I have no idea what direction I'm rowing in."

"We're in the very middle of the Thames. I fear we could be run over by a steamer."

"I doubt it. No captain is mad enough to venture out in this fog."

"And yet here we are, seasoned sailors, out for a moonlight paddle."

"Look about, Oscar. I need a point of reference. A church steeple. A streetlamp. Anything."

As if obliging, the moon slid from behind a scrim of cloud, lighting the circle of water about them.

"I still see nothing," Wilde said. "Do you know which direction we're heading?"

"If I keep the moon to my right shoulder, we should reach the west bank of the Thames."

"Or row all the way to the channel."

Conan Doyle fell to the oars and pulled with all his strength. Soon he lacked any breath to argue, locked into a rhythmic pulling at the oars. Overhead, the moon sailed through thickening clouds, vanishing and reappearing. Wilde crouched in the back of the boat, eyes sifting the fog. Finally, he announced, "Arthur! I see something! Keep going. Straight ahead."

Conan Doyle pulled until his arms and shoulders burned with fatigue; he lifted the oars momentarily to look for himself. "Yes. I see it, too. I think we've done it. I think we've reached the far shore!"

"And look, there's someone there!"

Wilde stood up in the rocking boat and waved both arms. "Hallooooo! Can you hear us? Hallooo!"

The boat drifted closer to shore and a moment later both men cried out in horror.

"It's him!"

In the drifting fog, Conan Doyle had rowed in a huge circle and brought them back to the precise place they set off from. Now he wrestled with the oars again, paddling backward with one and forward with the other to spin the boat.

"Look!" Wilde shouted.

As they watched, the dead man waded farther into the Thames.

Knee deep. Waist Deep. Chest Deep. A final plunging step and the gruesome face vanished beneath the black water.

The two men stared at the surface of the river with anticipatory dread.

Flat water. Calm. Silence.

"Thank goodness," Wilde exclaimed, "the thing has drowned itself!"

A sudden commotion of bubbles broke the surface. And then something burst up from the water, arms flailing like steamboat paddles, driving straight at them.

"My God," Conan Doyle said. "It can swim!" He snatched up the oars and heaved, rowing for all he was worth. Slowly, gradually, the swimming figure dropped farther and farther behind. Abruptly, the swimming stopped and the monster sank beneath the surface.

"It's gone under. Surely this time it has drowned?"

They watched the surface. A few stray bubbles broke here and there and then . . . nothing.

"I think you're right, Oscar. I think this time it has—"

Something exploded in the water beside the boat. A pair of hands latched onto the gunwale, tipping the rowboat precipitously as a waterlogged shape began to drag itself aboard.

"Look out!"

"It's climbing in!"

With no other weapon to hand, Conan Doyle struggled to wrestle an oar from its oarlock. As it came loose, the monster already had an arm and a leg inside the boat. He swung the oar with all his might. It connected with the creature's head with a hand-wringing WHACK but failed to slow it down. The sodden form flopped into the boat and struggled to its feet. Conan Doyle shifted to an overhand grip and brought the oar crashing down on the monster's head. THUD! It was a mighty blow and the creature staggered backward, off balance. Conan Doyle flipped his grip, holding the oar like a lance. Wilde guessed his intent and latched hold. With their combined weight, they speared the blade into the monster's chest and pushed with everything they had. The monster let out a bestial roar and toppled backward over the gunwale, cannonballing into the Thames and sending up a huge geyser of water.

The two friends stood trembling in the middle of the wildly pitching boat, looking at the dark water with dread anticipation.

Silence.

A few stray bubbles. And then nothing.

"I struck it two good blows about the head," Conan Doyle said. "Surely it's done for—"

There was a tremendous crash and a seismic shudder as something drove up through the rotten timbers of the hull and a hand clamped upon Conan Doyle's ankle with a bone-crushing grip. Water gushed into the boat through the hole.

Conan Doyle shouted with pain and tried to prise the fingers loose, but the iron grip was unbreakable. "Oscar, it has me!"

Wilde snatched up the dropped oar and swung at the monster's hand. The blade missed, smashing into Conan Doyle's shin, making him bellow with pain.

The heavy boat began to rapidly fill with water and Conan Doyle knew it would soon sink.

"We're sinking, Oscar. It will likely let go of me once we go under. You must swim for it. Cast off your coat, it will only drag you down."

"My coat? This coat? Never!"

"Don't be a fool man! Don't drown for the sake of vanity!"

"I can think of no nobler cause to die for!"

"Get ready to jump and remember to keep your mouth closed. The river here is rank with every form of filth and poison."

"I shall be sure to keep your sage advice in mind whilst I am drowning."

Conan Doyle and Wilde continued to grapple and pull at the monster's fingers, but its death-grip was inhuman.

Soon, black Thames water surged over the gunwales and the boat filled with water. At the last second, Wilde leapt and struggled to swim away from the sinking boat. He looked back to see Conan Doyle's agonized face as the boat dragged him beneath the water. Huge bubbles erupted for long moments, gradually thinning to a trickle, and finally stopped.

Wilde was suddenly and terribly alone in the water. Conan Doyle had drowned.

The water was stunningly cold. The Irishman flailed toward the shore but the heavy coat billowed out behind like a sea anchor, pulling him under. Reluctantly, he opened his arms, shrugged his shoulders and let the river take the coat. Wilde had not been completely honest: he could swim after a fashion. After ten minutes of flailing and splashing he slogged up from the river onto the mud and vomited up a gutful of vile water before collapsing to gag and choke.

"Arthur," he wheezed, lying in a waterlogged puddle. "My poor dear friend. Oh, Arthur."

He had been lying there, gathering himself for several minutes, when he heard a splash. He raised his dripping head from the muck and looked back at the river. To his amazement, something glimmered on the surface, a foaming of bubbles. And then he saw the head of a swimmer break the surface.

Wilde clambered unsteadily to his feet. The swimmer was moving slowly, methodically toward shore. But was it man or monster?

"Arthur?" he called out, both hopeful and fearful lest it not be. The swimming shape drew closer. "Arthur! Is that you? Please be you. It looks like you. Follow my voice! This way! Keep swimming! You can do it!"

The swimmer came on in a slow but steady breaststroke. The bobbing head intermittently vanishing as it sank and rose, sank and rose. But then Wilde suddenly had his doubts. He stopped calling. Took several nervous steps away from the water. By now the swimmer had reached the shallows and a sodden human figure dragged itself up-right, water streaming from its clothes.

"Arthur . . . is that you? Please, say something."

The shadowy figure staggered up from the reeking Thames and onto the muddy shore in a series of lurching steps and collapsed at Wilde's feet. Although barely recognizable, his hair matted with riverweed and filth, it was, indeed, Arthur Conan Doyle.

"Arthur!" Wilde said, falling to his knees and embracing his friend. "I feared you had drowned. The monster had you in its grip. How did you escape?"

Breathless and gasping, Conan Doyle opened his hand to reveal a tiny silver pocketknife. "My father gave me this on my tenth birthday. I keep it in my pocket at all times. It is very sharp. I held my breath as the boat went under. Then my knowledge of anatomy served me well. I reached down and, by feel alone, severed the tendons of the creature's fingers one-by-one. Even a monster with tremendous strength must have tendons to grip something. As I cut through the last tendon, the grip went slack. I broke free and floated to the surface, though I was on my last breath."

"Well done, Arthur. You have destroyed it."

Conan Doyle looked at his friend with sudden concern. "No, Oscar, I did not destroy it. The monster's arm was thrust through the timbers of the hull. I assumed the heavy boat dragged it to the bottom of the Thames."

"Then it's not dead?"

Both men looked up at the sound of splashing. The monster had also swum to shore, and now it stood up in the shallows, water sluicing from the ragged clothing. It paused a moment, as if gathering its dreadful inertia, and then shambled up the beach toward them.

"Apparently not," Conan Doyle said, dragging himself to his feet. He looked about for a weapon and snatched up a heavy lump of waterlogged driftwood and ran down to meet it, shouting a kind of battle cry. As the creature came sloshing up from the water, the Scotsman swung with all his might and brought the driftwood club crashing down on its head with a mighty thud. Vertebrae cracked, kinking the head upon its neck and staggering the monster. But then it snarled and lunged at Conan Doyle, grabbing him by the coat front and flinging him away a dozen feet. He crashed heavily to the ground driving the air from his lungs, momentarily stunning him. Before he could recover, the monster was upon him. One hand clamped about his throat and began to squeeze. The second hand fumbled to gain a grip, but the severed tendons had rendered the flapping fingers useless. Still the grip of the monster's single hand was crushing and Conan Doyle found himself being throttled to death.

WHACK! Wilde had recovered the chunk of driftwood and brought it down upon the monster's head. The blow would have killed a living man, but the creature scarcely noticed. Conan Doyle's face purpled as the relentless grip tightened and he struggled vainly to pry loose the fingers.

"Oscar!" he wheezed in a strangulated voice. "Hit him!"

THWACK! Wilde's club came down again, crunching vertebrae, kinking the monster's neck in the opposite direction.

Conan Doyle was gargling up froth. His vision began to darken and his fingers grew clumsy as his oxygen-starved brain began to sink into oblivion.

THUD! Wilde brought the club down a third time and the chunk of driftwood broke in two. The Irishman looked around and despaired. The foreshore was barren, with nothing left to use as a weapon.

Conan Doyle's heartbeat thundered in his ears. The world began to recede down a dark tunnel. A hundred miles away, his hands flailed uselessly.

Suddenly Wilde thrust something in front of the monster's face. The creature froze. A convulsion shook the large frame. The grip loosened as the fingers relaxed their hold on Conan Doyle's throat. It snatched the object from Wilde's hand, rose stiffly, and stood cradling the thing in its hands, brows hunched stupidly as it studied the object. And then the face grew soft. The posture slackened. The monster threw back its head, opened its mouth, and released a mournful cry of utter desolation.

Conan Doyle struggled to sit up, choking for air. He looked from the monster to Wilde in amazement.

"What . . ." he asked in a ruined voice ". . . what did you do, Oscar?"

"I showed it the photograph of Vicente's sister. Apparently, it still retains some human memories."

The monster stood gazing at the photograph, moaning, the mouth hanging slack and drooling. And then it turned and slouched away, howling like a beaten dog, its prey suddenly forgotten.

Wilde helped Conan Doyle stagger to his feet and the two friends slogged through the mud to a nearby road.

"What do we do now, Arthur? We are beaten, bruised, and soaked to the skin. We have no money. No carriage. And we have barely survived being attacked by a monster."

Conan Doyle watched the twisted silhouette shamble away in the fog and a spark lit in his eye.

"What else can we do? We must follow it."

CHAPTER 27

A PLEASANT NIGHT CRUISE
UPON THE THAMES

The pursuit went on for miles, Conan Doyle and Wilde shadowed the stuttering figure from a distance. Afraid to follow too close. Afraid to lag too far behind in the dense fog. They moved at a steady jog that kept their bodies warm, although now and then each would be racked with a convulsive shiver.

"Explain something to me, Arthur. We just barely escaped from that thing with our lives. Why are we now pursuing it?"

"In the hopes it will lead us to its lair."

The monster strode on, untiring and indefatigable, while the two friends struggled to keep up. Finally, under the grinding accumulation of footsore miles, both men began to flag as the monster gradually outpaced them. As they approached Westminster, it had shrunk to a tiny figure in the distance. And then the fog thickened and erased it from sight.

"Gone . . . it's gone," Conan Doyle admitted wearily. "We have lost it." The two stumbled to a standstill.

"What now?" Wilde asked. "There is another monster loose in London . . . and this time I refer to the mad marquess."

Conan Doyle looked around. A flyer plastered on a nearby wall caught his eye:

The Scottish author frowned. His shoulders slumped in resignation. "You and I have done our utmost, Oscar, but this is beyond us. I think this is a matter best handled by Cypher and his people." Remembering something, he fumbled in his top pocket and drew out the small envelope the little man had given him, thoroughly dampened from their dip in the Thames.

"What's that?" Wilde asked.

"Cypher gave this to me. He said to only use it in the direst situation. I think we have reached that juncture." He tore off one end of the soggy envelope and drew something out.

Conan Doyle looked at his friend with a sour expression.

"You appear far from happy, Arthur. What is it?"

"Two steamer tickets."

Wilde's face grew grief-stricken. "Dear God! Not the Thames, again? Not twice in one night!"

* * *

The paddleboat *Poseidon* was tied up at Lambeth Palace Pier, but the decks were deserted, the wheelhouse dark.

"No one about," Wilde said, and made to walk away. "We shall just have to try elsewhere."

"No. Wait. Look." Conan Doyle clapped a restraining hand on his friend's shoulder and pointed to the smoke purling from the flared smokestack. "The boilers are lit. That means someone is aboard."

Conan Doyle banged on the wheelhouse door with the meat of his fist. After a pause, the door flung open and a gruff bearded man in a salt-stained uniform leaned out, jaws working at the mouthful of tobacco he was chewing. He gave the two friends a wire brushing up and down with his flinty eyes. "Yeah? Watcha want?"

"From the faded salt stain on your uniform and the rum on your breath, I'd wager you are an ex-navy man and currently the captain of this vessel."

The man's head tilted back, warily. "What's it to you?"

Conan Doyle flourished the tickets under the captain's nose. He took one look and choked down his mouthful of 'baccy, sobering instantly. He turned and bellowed down the stairs, "On deck, you lot. We're casting off."

With its boilers constantly shoveled with coal, the boat soon made a head of steam. Minutes later, Conan Doyle and Wilde stood in a pair of smelly and scratchy uniforms the captain had rustled up. Both men had blankets around their shoulders and sipped at battered metal mugs that held Barbados rum spiked with a tiny splash of tea.

"I am nostalgic for sensation in my feet," Wilde said, shivering beneath his blanket. "I feel as waterlogged as that wretched rowboat."

Conan Doyle did not answer. He could not tear his gaze from the fog cleaving about the prow as the steamer churned ahead, shafts of light from its powerful carbide lights probing the fog ahead. "I feel as though I am sailing through the clouds in one of Jules Verne's aerial contrivances."

One of the steamer's crew moved to the prow of the boat. He was equipped with a signaling light and sent out a series of flashes into the darkness. Moments later he was answered by pulses of light emanating from the dark silhouette of Tower Bridge.

"What on earth is that chap doing?" Wilde asked.

"He is semaphoring a coded message made up of long and short flashes. If you notice, the message is acknowledged and then repeated on up the line, from bridge to bridge. Cypher will have word of our coming long before the boat arrives."

Finally, the skeletal shape of a jetty loomed from the fog. The captain shouted to the man in the wheelhouse, who threw levers back and forth. *Poseidon* roared and shuddered, releasing a whoosh of spray as one set of paddle wheels slowed, and then one reversed with the other paddle wheels powered forward, spinning the boat about so that it paralleled and gently snugged up to the dock. Waiting crewmen, agile as monkeys, leapt from the boat and cinched ropes around bollards.

A diminutive figure stood waiting on the dock's worn planking— Cypher. He was flanked, as always, by two large figures in black coats and bowler hats—Dandelion and Burdock.

The crew swung out the gangplank, bridging the gap from deck to jetty, and Conan Doyle and Wilde stepped from the paddle steamer.

"You have something to report?" Cypher asked. He had evidently been waiting for some time; his round spectacles were fogged into opaque disks.

"We have a great deal to report," the Scottish author replied.

The two friends related their story, Conan Doyle providing the narrative with Wilde jumping in now and then, chiefly to provide details of his fright, his physical discomfort, and the loss of his beloved green coat and the irreparable damage thereby done to his wardrobe. When the full story had spilled out of Conan Doyle, Cypher stood mulling in silence.

"Well," the Scottish author demanded. "What are you waiting for? The police must be dispatched. DeVayne must be arrested. This must be stopped, and stopped now."

"Thank you, Doctor Doyle for your efforts."

"What about *my* efforts?" Wilde peevishly added.

"*Both* your efforts. We knew something of the marquess's delusional plans for revolution. He bragged about elements of it to the doctors at the sanitarium. I had considered it the ramblings of a deranged mind, but apparently he has convinced others to participate in his madness."

"What about the monster that chased us across half of London? The reanimated corpses they are using as assassins?"

The puppetlike head nodded slightly. "Scarcely believable, but regrettable if true. It greatly concerns me when the state goes to the trouble and expense of executing a prisoner who then refuses to lie down and stay dead."

"What shall we do about it?" Conan Doyle demanded.

"We, meaning the Crown, will do what is necessary. You, meaning yourself and Mister Wilde, will return to your respective domiciles and do nothing further."

"Do nothing further?" Wilde burst out. "Surely you are jesting. The creature that pursued us is a ruthless killing machine. We looked on, helpless, as it butchered two constables. The people behind this abomination must be—"

"Thank you, Mister Wilde," Cypher interrupted. "But now is the time to remain silent. Our enemies lurk in our midst, from the lowest to the highest echelon of society. Even—it distresses me to confess—within the royal palace. But rest assured, I have an end game in place. For now we must remain silent, hidden, and allow the conspiracy to unfold. Once all the players have revealed themselves . . . then we shall strike."

"So that's it?" Conan Doyle said. "Oscar and I are simply to go home and do nothing?"

"Precisely that," Cypher said with a taut smile. "Nothing." And with that, he turned and walked away. But then, remembering something, he stopped and turned back.

"I have made a carriage available. It will take Doctor Doyle to the train station and then drop Mister Wilde at his house on Tite Street. You are both to remain at home, where it will be safest for you and your family. Her Majesty thanks you gentlemen for your efforts, but you are now released." Cypher walked on until the shadows drowned him.

* * *

After their long ordeal, both men were bruised, battered, and totally exhausted. Wilde fell asleep immediately during the carriage ride. Although weary with fatigue, Conan Doyle could not close his eyes. Once again, he felt his soul torn by two concerns: his wife and family in Sussex, and the safety of Jean Leckie, here in London. When the carriage dropped him at Waterloo station, he did not bother to wake Wilde to say good-bye, but let him snore on, mouth wide open, head lolled back on the seat cushion.

When Conan Doyle reached the ticket counter he found the Surrey train hissing at its platform, delayed by fog. He purchased a ticket and then bought a second, to be held in the name of Miss Jean Leckie. He then arranged for a telegram to be sent to Jean urging her to join him at his Sussex home.

"Won't be delivered until the morning, sir," the ticket counterman said. "What with the fog."

Conan Doyle nodded morosely and took his ticket. He could not imagine what he would say to Touie. How he would explain their need to play host to a beautiful young woman his wife already suspected him of having an illicit affair with. But he reasoned that the consequences could not possibly be as terrible as hearing of Jean Leckie's murder.

THE FOG DESCENDS

A great hall in a great house. A hammerbeam ceiling floated fifty feet above the stone flagged floor. Gargoyles crouching high among the shadowed rafters leered down with stony smiles. Family crests and ancient battle flags draped the walls. Suits of armor lurked in shadowy alcoves, gauntleted hands gripping the pommels of their swords, eye slits dark and menacing. All of it, however, was a sham, a fake; for despite the artful counterfeit of age, the artifacts were modern copies, as was the mansion that encompassed them.

A long feasting table commanded the center of the hall, around which assembled a group of gentlemen: distinguished ones judging by the fine tailored suits, gold stickpins, gleaming watch fobs, and polished shoes. Each of them smoked—fat cigars, deep-bowled pipes, cigarettes, so that their combined exhalations fugged the air about them and smoke rose in curlicues to the ceiling rafters. Although several chairs remained empty, the faces arranged around the table were instantly recognizable as the lofty echelon of politicians, bankers, industrialists, and business magnates collectively known as *The Fog Committee*. The men sat and smoked in dour silence. One fidgeted. Another sighed. All exhibited the exasperation of important men unused to being kept waiting.

The double doors at the side of the hall flung open and a tall, balding man entered, shoe leather squeaking as he strode across the flagstones—the Commissioner of Police, Edmund Burke. His adjutant, Dobbs, entered with him but remained standing by the door as his master folded his long body into the empty chair at the foot of the table. All eyes fixed upon him expectantly, but Burke took out a cigar and made the other members wait, watching in silence, as he snipped the end with a cigar cutter, struck a match, and puffed the cigar into life before turning his attention to them. "My apologies for being late, gentlemen," he said in his booming voice. "But I was delayed by the fog."

Several members snickered at the obvious irony.

"Where is our illustrious host?" George Hardcastle, the coal mine owner, bellyached. He was a short, broad man with the appropriately moleish physique of something evolved to live underground.

"No doubt sleeping off an opium stupor!"

The financier, Sir Lionel Ransome, fretted, "We are all fools to follow this man."

"He serves our purpose . . ." muttered the judge, and then added darkly, ". . . for now."

But the financier's comment had broken the dam wall of silence and a flood of doubt poured from the committee members.

"He is deranged, clearly."

"And one we do congress with at our peril."

"After we seize power, DeVayne must be done away with—swiftly."

"I agree."

The police commissioner leaned forward on his elbows and growled, "When this is done, we must wipe the slate clean, so that none of this business can ever be tied back to us."

The table buzzed with a collective murmur of *hear-hears*.

A scowl wrinkled the old admiral's face as he hissed at his neighbors, "Ssshhh! Lest you be overheard."

The police commissioner chuckled fatuously and countered, "Easy, old man, we are quite alone." He slouched back in his chair, puffed his cigar and blew a dilating smoke ring up toward the shadowy ceiling. "Only the gargoyles can hear us."

At that moment, the eyes of the gargoyle on the farthest wall went dark, as the face that had been pressed up behind it drew away, the listener having heard more than enough.

Moments later, a door at the end of the hall opened. Rufus DeVayne entered and walked toward his seat at the head of the table. "Good news, gentlemen," he announced gaily. "Our rally at St. Winifred's was a resounding success. I have inflamed the unwashed multitude." He settled into his chair. "And now to the business of this committee meeting. I refer, of course, to the fog. It needs to get worse, gentlemen. Much worse."

The industrialist came close to apoplexy. "But I am already burning twice the usual amount of coal in my factory furnaces. Are you trying to bankrupt me?"

"Forget the expense," DeVayne snarled. "You should be burning *three* times the normal amount of coal—no, *four* times. Consider it an investment in your future. The fog is our greatest ally in this endeavor. We are fomenting unrest. Sowing the seeds of chaos. Because of the fog, trains cannot run. Omnibuses are canceled. Carriages abandoned in the streets. Shops must shut early. Commerce shudders to a halt. Most importantly, the fog hampers the police. Even the army cannot move freely. Tomorrow is 13/13. The capital must grind to a standstill beneath a pall of smoke and fog. Then a mob will assemble outside the railings of Buckingham Palace. We have a confederate in the clock tower. At one o'clock Big Ben will strike thirteen. That will be the signal to storm the palace."

"How many and armed with what?" the old admiral asked.

"A mob of a few hundred," DeVayne speculated, "armed with knives, clubs, stones, cobbles dug from the road."

The coal mine owner grew agitated. "Against guardsmen armed with rifles and bayonets? They will be slaughtered in seconds!"

DeVayne laughed. "Oh, I have little doubt of it."

"What is the point of such a futile effort?" Burke sneered.

"The point, gentlemen, is to provide a cover, a smoke screen, a wall of fog such as you have created by burning coal in your factories morn and night. The mob has no chance of taking the palace, but their presence will allow us to enter unmolested. Yea, they will throw the gates open to me."

"How so?" the coal magnate asked.

"I will arrive in my carriage, an aristocrat seeking sanctuary. My landau is well known to the guardsmen. After all, who else in London has a carriage drawn by zebras?"

"Say you do manage to slip onto the palace grounds," the commissioner said with unconcealed skepticism. "What then?"

DeVayne took out the long-barreled derringer and set it on the table before him. It drew the eyes of most of the Fog Committee members, but Burke was not impressed.

"A pop gun? Is that your strategy? You'll never get close enough to the queen to use it. She'll be surrounded by armed guards."

DeVayne's smile couched both indulgence and threat. "I will not act as assassin. The rear of the carriage will contain the monster, concealed beneath a pile of blankets. Once inside the palace gates, I shall unleash the beast. No matter where the queen hides, no matter how many guards surround her, our assassin will seek her out unerringly. Our monster is now unstoppable, unkillable. The queen and the Prince of Wales will die on that day. With no immediate successor, the nation will descend into chaos and the people will turn to us to save them. Conveniently, I will be on hand, fifth in line for the throne, ready and willing to take the reins of power and return stability to a nation in chaos. My first act as king will be to dissolve Parliament, and then we shall sweep to power, unopposed. The remaining members of the so-called royal family will be rounded up and quietly dispatched. Then, once again, an *English* king will sit upon the *English* throne."

"And what of us?" the commissioner asked. "I trust you will not forget us once you wear the crown?"

DeVayne laughed. "You gentlemen know my passions. I desire only the trappings of royalty: the crown, the palace, the land. The nation I will leave in your infinitely capable hands. While you gentlemen steer us back on the path of industrial growth and prosperity, I will be busy redecorating the palace and moving in my menagerie. I can see my lions now, frolicking in the fountains and sunning themselves on the palace steps."

The double doors opened and Dr. Lamb entered with Jedidiah, the toy maker, following close behind. DeVayne acknowledged them with a nod, but by the severity of the doctor's expression, it was clear something had gone badly wrong. He sought to end the meeting quickly. "Thank you for attending, gentlemen. Our plan proceeds apace. We reconvene tomorrow for the final act."

The Fog Committee stood up from their seats and filed out of the great hall, muttering and chuntering. DeVayne remained in his seat, smiling confidently. But when the double doors closed on their backs, he jumped up from the table. "What is it?" he demanded. "I can see from your faces you have bad news."

By way of answer, Jedidiah drew off his scarf to reveal a neck purpled with five finger-sized bruises. "When the monster returned, it attacked me. Luckily, it had been gone for hours. I would have been throttled to death had it not run out of fuel at that very moment."

The marquess's face betrayed his shock. "I don't understand. How—?"

The doctor handed him a small square photograph of a handsome young woman.

"Who is this?"

"It is a photograph of Vicente's sister. I know, because while he was in Newgate he looked at the photograph a hundred times a day, rereading her last letter and weeping."

Jedidiah took up the story. "The monster returned with this picture clutched in its hand and only dropped it to choke me."

DeVayne thought for a moment and realization lit his eyes. "This is Wilde's doing; and that walrus-faced friend of his. That must mean—"

"They are still alive," Dr. Lamb said, finishing the thought.

"Impossible!" DeVayne shook his head. "How could they survive the monster?"

"There's more," Jedidiah said. "All the tendons in the monster's left hand had been severed as if by a scalpel. The knifework was precise, and must have been performed by a person with medical knowledge. No doubt Doctor Conan Doyle."

Dr. Lamb spoke out, "The monster was clearly affected by seeing the photograph of his sister." He glared at the toy maker and spoke in a voice strained with emotion, "You told me the thing had no soul. That it retained no memory of its former life."

Jedidiah shook his head dismissively. "A residual memory, that is all. A scrap of recollection. It is a dead thing."

"I heard it howl. Like a soul in torment!"

"Enough!" DeVayne spat. He turned away and stood tapping the photograph to his lips, deep in thought. "I underestimated our scribbler friends. We cannot afford to make that mistake a second time."

"So we try again to kill them?"

DeVayne shook his head. "I have a more reliable method. I know Wilde and Conan Doyle and their weaknesses. We will have the monster kidnap their loved ones: the young woman Conan Doyle is having a dalliance with, and one of Wilde's children. That will guarantee they stay out of the fray until our new regime is established. After which, they and their families can be collected and lawfully executed as enemies of the state." He looked to the young doctor. "The monster is repaired?"

Lamb nodded. "A few hours' sewing."

"Good. Load the creature in the hearse and go collect them. While they are guests in my dungeon they may provide me with a few hours' diversion."

CHAPTER 29

THE IMPORTANCE OF BEING IN DEADLY EARNEST

As the author of Sherlock Holmes stepped from the train onto the railway platform at Haslemere, the morning chill seeped through his clothes and left him shivering in the brittle dawn light. He thought of Jean Leckie back in London. Would she be safe? Had he run away to leave her to a terrible fate? The train whistled and chuffed away, leaving him a lone and lonely figure on an empty platform, torn between the desire to rush back to the ticket office and buy a return ticket and the need to protect his family. But in the end he turned and walked down the platform to retrieve his tricycle. He faced a desolate ride home.

* * *

The drumming snatched Conan Doyle from a horrid dream. He creaked open his eyes to find Kingsley's windup soldier, an inch from his nose, pounding its drum in a blur of mechanical arms.

"It works, Daddy. You mended it! You mended it!"

His little boy stood at his bedside, showing off his newly repaired clockwork guardsman. Conan Doyle pushed himself up from the pillow with a prolonged groan. The author was an athletic man, used to exerting himself in golf, cycling, cricket, even skiing, but after the previous evening's exploits, everything hurt. Everything ached. He tottered up from the bed, barely able to pull his arms into a dressing gown. He could only imagine how poor Oscar, who broke a sweat stirring sugar into his tea, was faring.

"Shush with your toy, Kingsley. You'll awaken the house."

"Silly Daddy. Everyone is already up."

Conan Doyle glanced at the clock and was shocked to find it was nearly twelve o'clock. Kingsley was right. He'd slept half the day away.

"There's a lady in the parlor who says she's your friend."

"A—a lady?"

"A pretty lady. She and Mummy are drinking tea."

Conan Doyle puzzled over what his little boy was talking about. Suddenly the realization hit him. Yanking open the wardrobe door, he began snatching out clothes. A clean shirt. A pair of trousers. A tweed jacket. There was only one pretty woman it could be. He trembled to think what Louise must have been thinking. Worse still, he dreaded to think what Jean must have been suffering.

* * *

Wilde was in the dining room of his Tite Street home, cracking the top off a soft-boiled egg with a butter knife (a physical effort that made him wince) when the boys marched in, Cyril banging his drum and Vyvyan blowing his trumpet. The playwright was still dressed in his silk pajamas and dressing gown having only recently staggered from his bed.

"Boys! Boys! Boys!" he remonstrated as they began their third circuit of the breakfast table. "Please, march in another room at a greater remove. Papa is feeling particularly delicate this morning."

Constance Wilde appeared at the open doorway, her eternal shadow, Robert Sheridan, lurking behind. Both wore hats and coats and were muffled up to go outside.

"Oscar!" Constance exclaimed, surprised to see him. "You did not spend the night at your club, after all?"

It was a remark he was expected to rise to, but Wilde felt as buoyant as an iron skillet. Rising was the last thing he was going to do. "Last evening I had a swimming lesson followed by a pleasure cruise down the Thames. I am still somewhat waterlogged."

His wife's expression betrayed her puzzlement, but she responded with an ironic laugh and said, "Robert and I are taking the boys to the park."

"Excellent," Wilde replied. "I suggest Hyde Park or St. James's park."

"Hyde Park? But that's miles away."

"Yes," Wilde said. "Far out of earshot, I would wager."

As he lifted his teacup, Constance noticed his bruised and gashed knuckles. "Oscar! Whatever happened to your hands? You look as if you've been fighting."

Wilde paused a moment in sipping his tea and said, "My new ingénue refuses to learn her lines. I'm afraid it came down to fisticuffs."

A stunned look swept Sheridan's face, but Constance merely laughed and said, "He is joking, Robert. One of the many joys of being married to Oscar is that I get to enjoy the Wildean wit all day long."

Constance and Sheridan left Wilde to his breakfast and went about the chore of squeezing two wriggling boys into winter woolens. The maid entered the breakfast room bearing the newspaper and the morning's correspondence on a silver tray. The Irish wit's digestion was not helped when he snatched up the paper and read the headline: "Anarchists to March upon London!"

The article was a catch-your-breath stream of hysteria detailing a planned mass march of socialists and their sympathizers scheduled to take place the very next day. He read as far as the second paragraph before tossing the paper down. He knew far more than the scattershot speculation of the *Times* reporter. A cream-yellow envelope caught his attention. It was addressed to him with no return address. When he slashed it open with a letter knife, a small photograph fluttered out and landed faceup on the table. It was the crinkled photograph of

Vicente's sister. Inside the envelope, he found a note scribbled in a crazed hand:

I cannot fathom how you are still alive. I warned you to stay away. Now I must make you unhappy.

The note was written in red ink and scrawled with a pentagram.

Wilde's stomach churned with queasy dread. The note did not require a signature: he knew DeVayne's mark when he saw it.

Constance, Sheridan, and the two boys were halfway out the front door when Wilde dashed from the breakfast room into the hallway.

"Stop!" he demanded.

"Whatever is it, Oscar?"

"You and the boys are to stay home."

Constance was accustomed to Wilde's role as casual, just-passing-through husband and father. Now, his adamant tone astonished her.

"Oh, you are joking again, Oscar—"

"I assure you I am in deadly earnest, Constance. You and the boys are to remain home. I forbid you to leave this house." He glared at Robert Sheridan, who was hovering in the open door. "And you, Robert, must go home."

"But, Constance and I—" Sheridan started to protest.

"Go home!" Wilde said and propelled him roughly across the threshold with a violent shove and banged the door shut in his face.

"Oscar! Are you mad? What is wrong? Have you forgot yourself?"

Wilde showed her a face she had never seen before in all their years of marriage. "No," he said in a voice pitched to a low rumble. "I had forgot, but now it seems I have finally remembered myself." He gripped his wife's hand with frightening force. "Things are happening, Constance. It is not safe to go out."

"Is this about last night?"

"I will not distress you by sharing the horrid details, but know this:

there is a darkness descending upon this country. For once you must do as I bid and keep the children and yourself at home. I have never demanded anything from you in this marriage." His eyes blazed with intent. "But now I am demanding this."

Constance Wilde's eyes grew wide. Her lips quivered. "Yes, Oscar," she replied in a torn voice.

Wilde turned to the waiting boys, recomposing his face into a fatherly smile. "But as you boys are all dressed up, Papa will take you into the garden and play cricket. And then we shall come inside, drink hot cocoa, and I will compose a new fairy story for you."

The boys cheered and jumped up and down with glee. "Smashing!" Cyril cried. "What will our story be about, Papa?"

"Yes," Vyvyan echoed. "What kind of story?"

Wilde considered a moment. "It will be a story about a beautiful young man who sins against nature . . . and becomes a monster."

✳ ✳ ✳

When Conan Doyle stumbled into the drawing room, still struggling to fasten the studs of his collar, his wife was propped stiffly in the corner of an armchair. Miss Jean Leckie perched upon the Doyles' excruciatingly uncomfortable horsehair couch. Both women had teacups sitting in their laps, but neither seemed to be drinking. Or chatting. Or making eye contact.

Or giving any indication they both occupied the same room.

"Arthur," his wife said. "You have finally bestirred yourself. I have been entertaining your city friend, Miss Leckie. I am afraid to say your description did her a great injustice, she is in no way a rather plain, or *spinsterly* type."

His wife drowned a cruel smile in her teacup. Jean Leckie fixed him with a look that pleaded *help me.*

Conan Doyle shifted his feet, dithering. Rather than take the unoccupied seat on the couch next to Miss Leckie, he drew up a hard-back chair and sat in the no-man's-land between the two. "Oh, I don't think I said any such thing, Touie."

"Yes, you did, Arthur. I remember it distinctly. Plain. Spinsterly. Those were your exact words. So when Miss Leckie showed up at our front door unannounced, bag in hand like a homeless vagrant, I could not imagine who this striking beauty was."

Conan Doyle colored. His wife was making them both squirm. Jean Leckie dropped her eyes to the rug, face burning with shame. The teacup in her trembling hand chinked against its saucer.

He could see where the situation was likely to lead and decided that candor was the only path. He rose and stood with one hand on the chair back. "I must explain why I asked Miss Leckie here. It is not for the reason you imagine. Nor could ever hope to imagine. I urged her to join us here because it is no longer safe in London. For her. For myself. For no one."

"Whatever do you mean, Arthur?" Louise Doyle asked.

"I mean that our nation teeters on the brink of revolution. Even as I speak, there is a secret struggle between opposing factions to assassinate the queen and replace our government with a new regime."

Suddenly both women's expressions mirrored each other's: mouths agape, eyes wide.

"And what has this to do with you and Miss Leckie?"

"Lately, a number of high ranking government officials and leaders of commerce and industry have been the target of assassins. I was recruited by an agent of the crown to investigate. My dear friend Oscar has been assisting me. Last night we ran afoul of some of the conspirators . . . and barely escaped with our lives."

His words drew gasps from both women and Conan Doyle beamed with a strange satisfaction. "Miss Leckie is quite the innocent party in all this. I invited her to dinner after our monthly SPR meeting. I did not know it at the time, but I was under surveillance."

Louise Doyle stiffened in her chair. "Surveillance? You mean . . . you were being spied upon?"

Conan Doyle nodded. "By agents of the crown, and agents hostile to the crown. My innocent invitation to supper inadvertently brought Miss Leckie to the attention of unsavory elements who may wish to do her harm."

Touie's eyes filled. "Oh, my dear Miss Leckie. I am so sorry to hear it. Of course, you must stay with us until the danger is passed." She looked up at her husband. "But what is to become of the country, Arthur? What is to become of us all?"

The Scottish author shook his head ruefully. "I cannot say." He walked to the window and gazed out. Beyond the front garden's swathe of green lawn, the hedgerows and farmer's fields of Sussex formed a vista of bucolic tranquility. "We live in parlous times. Oscar and I have been warned to lay low and let events play out as they may. We can only pray that our nation endures."

* * *

The hearse slowed as it passed number 16 Tite Street, and then the driver, anonymous in a black top hat and funeral frock coat (anonymous, apart from the port-wine stain running down one cheek), whipped up the horses. The hearse spun onto a side road and then turned hard left into a narrow alleyway and drew up directly behind Wilde's home. The funeral grooms jumped down and flung open the glass door at the rear of the hearse.

A man clambered out. Or rather, something that had once been a man. Dressed in rumpled clothing, the reanimated corpse shambled to the garden wall and stood looking up.

On the other side of the garden wall, Wilde puffed at one of his Turkish cigarettes as he watched his boys play cricket.

"I'm cold, Daddy. May we go inside now? You promised to tell us a fairy story about a monster."

"In a moment, Cyril. Papa has not yet smoked his last cigarette and you know how Mama disapproves of your father smoking in the house. And this despite the fact that Papa bought the house for Mama and pays all the bills."

"But, Daddy, why is it Mummy's say-so?"

"Men have been asking themselves that very question for thousands of years, Vyvyan. If you have the misfortune to marry one day it is likely you shall be asking yourself the same question."

Constance Wilde appeared at the back door, a shawl thrown about her slender shoulders. "Five more minutes boys," she called and went inside.

"Did you hear that, lads? The voice of authority has spoken." Wilde rummaged his pockets for a box of matches, but found none. "Vyvyan, let Cyril have a turn at bat whilst Papa pops inside. I'll just be a tick."

In the alleyway, the dead man crouched down and then sprang up, easily vaulting the ten-foot wall. He landed with a heavy thump in the corner of the yard, screened from sight by an overgrown wisteria bush.

In the parlor, Wilde called out, "Constance, do we have any matches?" as he rummaged drawers in the sideboard.

In the yard, Vyvyan bowled an easy underhand to Cyril, who whacked the ball and sent it bouncing.

"Third drawer down," Constance called back. "Are the boys still outside?"

"We're coming in after the last is over."

Constance entered the parlor. "You smoke too much, Oscar."

"Fortunately, I have you to remind me of that—ah, here we are." Wilde snatched up a box of lucifers and shook it. A faint rattle told him that it still contained a few matches. He smiled triumphantly and pocketed it.

Vyvyan scampered after the ball, which rolled across the grass into the far corner of the yard where it bumped into a pair of feet in battered leather boots. The young boy ducked under the dense branches of the wisteria in pursuit. When he bobbed up again, he found himself face to face with a terrible stranger. The man smelled horrid and looked very queer. His eyes were vacant and unblinking, the whites, a sickly yellow color. The man released a gurgling sound and plumes of steam jetted out both nostrils. Vyvyan went wide-eyed and rigid. His head tremored atop his neck. The boy opened his mouth and tried to scream but nothing came out. The grisly man raised his huge hands, showing nail beds blackened with filth. He rumbled a guttural moan and lunged for the boy.

Constance moved to the parlor window and looked out. The light was failing fast and the garden was steeped in gloom. "Where's Vyvyan?" she asked in a voice strained with motherly worry.

"He's bowling to Cyril."

"I don't see him."

"He's probably gone to fetch the ball."

Wilde joined his wife at the window and the two of them peered out. Cyril was standing at the wicket, shouting for his brother to come back and bowl. But Vyvyan was nowhere to be seen. Husband and wife exchanged a look and then rushed outside together.

They were just in time to see a tall figure lurking in the shadows at the bottom of the garden. From behind he resembled a shabby tramp.

"You there," Wilde shouted. "Who the devil—?"

The figure turned at Wilde's shout. It was the monster. He was clutching Vyvyan to his chest, a large hand clamped over the boy's mouth; Vyvyan's wide, terrified eyes sparkled with tears. And then, with the dreadful suddenness of a nightmare, the figure crouched low and leaped over the garden wall in a single bound, taking their eldest child with him.

Constance's scream shattered the air.

Wilde flailed out, grasping, but failed to catch her as she swooned to the cold ground.

* * *

Supper had been consumed in a strained, scrape-of-fork-upon-plate silence. Now the family had retired to the big parlor where the red coals of a fire throbbed in the hearth. As the Doyle family were entertaining a visitor, the children had been allowed to stay up and now sat on the floor flanking their mother's chair—as close as they were allowed to come, given her disease. Conan Doyle stood leaning upon the mantelpiece, smoking his pipe. This left Miss Leckie alone on the love seat, an item of furniture whose very name seemed so incriminating he dare not sit down upon it.

"Such lovely children," Miss Leckie said. "And so polite and well-behaved."

"Yes," Conan Doyle agreed, "Touie is a model mother."

"I should so like to have children of my own . . ." Miss Leckie said, and then realized she had strayed into a dangerous territory, adding weakly, ". . . someday."

"I'm sure you will soon meet a handsome *young* man," Touie said, and then twisted the blade. "Someone closer to your own age."

A movement outside the window caught Conan Doyle's eye. He moved to the glass, where he stood looking through his own reflection into the gathering twilight.

"What is it, Arthur?"

"I thought I saw a carriage on the road outside, but it's gone now. Vanished behind a hedgerow."

"Just a farm cart, perhaps?"

"Awfully late for a farm cart, and the road sees so little traffic."

"Someone lost, then?"

Conan Doyle turned from the window, puffing thoughtfully at his pipe. "Yes, I imagine you are right. Just someone lost."

The Surrey rental house was isolated. He had chosen the locale for its clean rural air, but it was remote. He didn't say anything, but at such moments he wished they had a dog to guard the house.

A large, ferocious hound. However, Touie's respiratory difficulties forbade the owning of pets.

Miss Leckie suddenly brightened. "Oh, but I quite forgot. I brought gifts for the children." She reached down and opened the bag at her feet, drawing out two packages wrapped in brown paper and tied with string. Conan Doyle instantly guessed where the presents had come from, but said nothing, biting down on the stem of his pipe to suppress a smile.

"Presents? How generous of you," Louise Doyle said in a peevish voice. Conan Doyle saw the flash of jealousy in her eyes. "Unfortunately, we must not allow our children to be spoiled. They already have plenty of toys."

"Oh please may we have them, Mummy?" Mary Doyle asked, looking up at her mother.

"Yes, we want our presents!" Kingsley importuned. "Please, Mummy, please!"

Faced with the prospect of breaking her children's hearts, Louise Doyle had no choice but to acquiesce. "I suppose," she said with obvious reluctance, "under the circumstances. Oh . . . very well."

The children pounced on the packages and tore them open with glee. Kingsley danced with glee at his windup monkey. He plopped down on the rug and instantly began to wind the key. The monkey made a comical chuttering sound as it backflipped and then flipped again, bringing squeals of childish delight from the young boy.

Mary tore open her present and gasped. She looked up at Jean Leckie, her eyes pooled to overflowing. "Oh, thank you! Thank you! Thank you! It is quite the loveliest doll I've ever seen."

"Show us your doll, Mary," Conan Doyle urged.

Mary held up the doll for all to see. It was the very one Jean Leckie had been so drawn to at Jedidiah's Emporium of Mechanical Marvels.

"But she has a secret," Jean Leckie said mysteriously. She gestured, and Mary brought over the doll and knelt at her feet. Jean Leckie lifted the doll's petticoats, causing a moment of embarrassment, but then all noticed the key dangling from its blue ribbon. She wound the key fully and handed the doll back. The music box whirred and began to play an aria. The silver notes touched Conan Doyle's heart. He glanced at Touie and saw that his wife was looking intently at Jean and the children gathered at her feet, her eyes liquid and gleaming.

Louise Doyle rose creakily from her chair, leaning on the arms for support.

"Are you quite well, Mrs. Doyle?"

"I am rather fatigued. You will excuse me, Miss Leckie, if I retire to my bed."

"Touie?" Conan Doyle asked in a concerned voice.

She recomposed her face and said, "I am fine, Arthur. Simply tired. It has been a trying day." She turned her gaze to Miss Leckie, and this time her smile, although pained, seemed genuine.

"Good night to you, Miss Leckie. And thank you for the gifts. Your kindness has made you a favorite with our children."

Louise Doyle shuffled from the room, leaning first on the back of a chair, the sideboard, and finally the doorframe. Conan Doyle dallied a moment, and then went after her. When he reached the hallway, his wife was trudging up the stairs in her slow, deliberate fashion, pausing after each laboring step to catch a ragged breath.

"Touie?" Conan Doyle called up to her from the foot of the stairs. "Are you quite well?"

His wife paused a moment before turning. She spoke with a hitch in her voice, but her words had gravity to them. "I have watched you all night, Arthur. The way you look at that young woman. And the way she looks at you."

Conan Doyle's heart fluttered. He raised a hand to protest, but his wife shushed him. "I admit I am jealous. What wife would not be? But I am a realist. We both know how tenuous my grip on life is. I would never willingly give you up . . . never . . . but I have watched how that young woman is with my children. I love you and the children more dearly than I love my own life. I despair to think of you lonely. I despair to think of my children growing up without a mother. It has long been my greatest fear. I do not seek to die readily. But neither shall I seek to linger. For once, I see happiness before me." Her voice broke. Tears trickled unashamedly down her drawn face. "Y-you have my blessing. You both have my blessing. . . ."

Conan Doyle said nothing as his wife labored up the stairs, but when he returned to the parlor, his heart felt so full he feared it might burst.

For the sake of decorum, Conan Doyle had surrendered his bedroom to their houseguest, while he slept on the day bed in his study. By the time all had retired for the evening and the house fell silent, night and its darkness crouched on the other side of the window glass. He sat at his writing desk, sipping a brandy and staring at his own reflection in the window.

He was a young thirty-six years old. His brown eyes were bright and clear. His hair was dark and glossy without a single gray hair. Thanks to a regimen of walking, riding his tricycle, and vigorous sports ranging from golf to cricket, he was physically in his prime. His life with Touie was approaching its end. Now he dared to entertain a new life, a second life, with the ravishing Jean Leckie.

A stir of shadows outside startled him from his reverie. Something had flitted past the window. An owl? A bat? Or something larger? Could an intruder be lurking?

He reached for the right-hand drawer of his writing desk, slid it open, and fumbled for a heavy object trussed in a black cloth. He drew it out—never taking his eyes from the window—and shook loose the wrapping, revealing his Webley revolver. His large fingers scrabbled in the drawer for a box of cartridges. Charged with adrenaline, his hands shook slightly as he pushed the fat bullets into the empty chambers, loading all six rounds. He stood up from his chair, banged the drawer shut with one knee, cinched tight the belt of his robe, and strode for the door.

He stepped from the house into a dark, moonless night. Damp

night air pooled liquid and chill in his lungs. The revolver held ready, his slippered feet silently trod the front path to the road, where he stood, peering this way and that, scanning the shadows. Something hunkered in the far distance, an amorphous blob of darkness. But it was too dark to make out any detail. He could be looking at anything: a stand of hedgerows, a random tangle of shadows. Was that a carriage of some kind parked atop the rise of the lane? And then, as if in confirmation, he caught the faint whinny of a horse in the distance. It seemed to confirm his deduction, but then he remembered that his farmer neighbor kept several horses. It could well be one of his. He looked down at the dirt road for wheel tracks, but he had not brought a lantern with him and the roadway was unreadably dark.

With his back turned and his attention fixed at his feet, he did not see the man-sized shadow slide from behind the bushes at the front of his house and step in through the open front door. Conan Doyle stood stock still for several long minutes, looking, listening. He drew in a deep breath, sniffing the air, which held country smells of manure and the tang of peat fires.

He had been imagining things.

He suddenly became aware of the weighty revolver in his hand and slipped it into the pocket of his robe, then turned and shuffled his slippered feet back toward the warmth and light of his open front door.

* * *

Conan Doyle was dredged up from a hideous dream by the *rapatatatatat* of tinny drumming. His mind bumped up against the membrane of sleep like a balloon bumping up against a ceiling it could not break through.

And then a piercing scream tore his eyes open.

He struggled to kick loose of the tangle of sheets wrapped about his legs and tumbled from the daybed onto the floor. Scrambling to his feet, he banged a knee painfully into a chair and limped toward the door of his study, only to turn back to snatch up the revolver from his desktop. By the time he left the study, the drumming had stopped. His heart galloped when he looked down the hallway and saw the front door standing wide open. Then a second piercing shriek drew his eyes up the staircase. A young girl's scream.

"Mary!" he uttered and bounded up the stairs two at a time. He reached the landing just as Louise Doyle staggered out of her bedroom, clutching the doorframe for support. Conan Doyle ran into his daughter's room only to find the bed rumpled but empty. For a horrible moment he thought she'd been snatched. But then the screams continued. He ran back onto the landing, noticing for the first time that the door to his own bedroom was ajar. When he and Touie rushed in, they found Mary wrapped in a cocoon of bedclothes, eyes wide, her small body convulsing with terror.

"Mary!" Conan Doyle said. "What is it? What ever's the matter?"

"A—a—a—a . . ." The young girl was near catatonic. ". . . a h-horrible man! He t-took the lady."

For the first time, Conan Doyle became aware of Jean Leckie's absence.

"What happened?" Louise Doyle urged. "Mary, you must tell us."

The young girl's eyes darted wildly. "A bad dream woke me up. I brought my doll to sleep with the nice lady. I fell asleep, but then a noise woke me up. A man was standing over us. A horrible, horrible man. She pushed me under the covers so he wouldn't see me. But then he grabbed the lady and carried her out. I screamed, but he didn't stop."

The full force of events hit Conan Doyle and his face prickled with pins and needles of shock. He turned and rushed from the room, thundered down the staircase and bolted outside. By now, dawn was a fiery stain on the eastern horizon. He reached the lane in time to see the figure of a man shambling toward the square hulk of a hearse parked in the distance. The figure carried a human form hanging limp in its arms. From the shambling walk, he instantly recognized that it was not a living man.

He set off running up the lane, sharp-edged stones cutting painfully into the soles of his bare feet. But the hearse was too far away and he would be too late to reach it. He stumbled to a halt and raised the revolver, drawing a bead on the back of the shambling figure, waiting for his pounding heart to slow before he squeezed off a round. But then he lowered the gun. In this light, at this range, he dare not risk a shot lest he hit Miss Leckie. Two men in undertaker's garb flung open the glass door and the monster clambered inside with his burden. Conan Doyle heard the coachman's shout and the crack of a whip and could only watch, helpless and impotent, as the hearse rumbled over the crown of the hill and vanished from sight.

Miss Leckie had been taken.

Stunned and despondent, he stumbled back into a house in uproar: the children crying, his wife screaming with terror, the maid and cook wailing and scurrying about. He stood in the hallway, cudgeling his brains. What to do? Who to call for help?

And then he noticed Kingsley's windup guardsman lying in the middle of the hall rug. Its drumming had been what awakened him, but the tinplate toy had been crushed, flattened beneath the monster's heavy tread. The metal seams had split wide and when he stooped to pick it up, something metallic and shiny fell out upon the rug.

A brass cogwheel.

It was an instantly recognizable shape. Conan Doyle suddenly knew who was behind the reanimated corpses . . . and where precisely he would find him.

CHAPTER 30

CHASING MONSTERS

Conan Doyle stepped through the main gates of Waterloo Station foot-sore and weary. Impossibly dense fog had stalled the train two miles from the station, forcing him to abandon the carriage and walk the tracks the rest of the way. He had a satchel thrown over his shoulder that contained his latest Casebook, as well as his Webley revolver and a full box of shells. Lost in his own turmoiled thoughts, Conan Doyle failed to spot the looming figure of a large man until it stepped from the fog in front of him.

"Arthur."

"Oscar?"

For once, Wilde was dressed in a rather ramshackle fashion. His wild mane of chestnut hair was disheveled. He had not shaved and his eyes looked bleary and bloodshot from lack of sleep.

"My boy has been taken," he said in dull and disbelieving tones.

"What?"

"Vyvyan . . ." His voice was utterly bereft. ". . . snatched before our eyes . . . by . . . dear God help me . . . by that . . . creature!"

At the news a giddy weakness flashed through Conan Doyle.

"Vyvyan, too?" He gripped Wilde's arm. "Miss Leckie was ab-ducted this morning. And by the same soulless devil we encountered the other night."

"What are we to do, Arthur?" Wilde fretted. "What are we to do? We must summon the police! We must contact your diminutive friend from the palace, Mister Riddle. I will roust the old biddy Victoria from her bed if need be. My darling boy has been kidnapped!"

"I'm afraid we cannot wait for the police. We must seize the initiative. Our enemies are ahead of us. Remember today's date and all that 13/13 business. The revolution, if there is to be one, will start within hours. The authorities will no doubt be overwhelmed."

"What shall we do? Where shall we find them?"

Conan Doyle dipped in a pocket and withdrew the cogwheel, holding it up for Wilde to see. "Does this look familiar?"

"The gear you found at Tarquin Hogg's home?"

"No, but its double. This fell out of Kingsley's broken toy—the one I had mended at Jedidiah's Emporium."

"I fail to understand."

"I now believe that our friend Jedidiah is behind the monster. If you recall we both gave him our calling cards. Cards that bore our home addresses. Very convenient for the kidnappers."

"Dash it all! You're right, Arthur. So what do we do?"

"We go looking for answers. Our first stop must be the Emporium of Mechanical Marvels."

"But however shall we find our way? This blasted fog has brought the capital to a standstill. The omnibuses do not run. I could not locate a hansom and was obliged to walk all the way from Tite Street. Since I arrived here the fog has been steadily thickening. I doubt I could find my way home in this miasma."

Both men stiffened at a jovial laugh that came from somewhere in the swirling gray.

"Foggy is it, gents?" a Cockney voice announced from the shadows beside the empty newspaper kiosk. "I wondered why it was so quiet about."

Although he was only a few feet away, Conan Doyle and Wilde had to step closer before they made out the owner of the voice. Standing in his usual spot beside the newspaper kiosk was the Crimean war veteran and his tray of pennants. Tendrils of fog swirled about him, licking the black lenses of glasses behind which no vision was ever perceived.

But in the face of blindness, Conan Doyle suddenly knew how they would see their way.

*　*　*

The Scottish author kept a hand on the veteran's epauletted shoulder while he and Wilde linked arms. With the veteran's cane tap tapping the curbstone, they navigated slowly but steadily through the murky maze of London roads in a fog so total that street signs were invisible from more than two feet away. Twenty minutes later, they fetched up outside Jedediah's Emporium of Mechanical Marvels.

"Well done, Sam," Wilde congratulated.

"Yes," Conan Doyle added. "Without your assistance we would have been lost after the first street."

The shop was locked up tight just like all the businesses they passed; a CLOSED sign hung in the window. Conan Doyle took the Casebook from his satchel, scribbled a note, and then tore the page out and pressed it into the blind veteran's hands.

"We need one more favor, Sam. Detective Blenkinsop lives close by, on Anglesey Street. We need you to deliver this note and then fetch him here. Do you think you could find the address?"

"Anglesey Street?" The veteran scratched his stubbly chin. "Wot's the number?"

"Forty-two."

"However shall he read the house number?" Wilde asked.

But the veteran didn't need to see, he had his own way of navigating the city.

"Number forty-two? The lady wot lives in the bottom flat has a yappy little dog called Bonzo. I usually tosses it a biscuit when it comes sniffing about me feet. Don't you worry, I can find it, no bother."

The veteran turned and began tapping his way toward Anglesey Street. He had gone barely ten feet when he vanished from sight.

Conan Doyle turned to Wilde. "I noticed from your walk you seem a little stiff."

Wilde grunted a laugh. "Stiff? After our adventure on the Thames the other night, a corpse in full rigor is more flexible."

The Scottish doctor unshouldered his satchel and opened it. He drew out a smoked glass medicine bottle and handed it to Wilde.

"Medicine, Arthur?"

"The laudanum you once asked for. Mixed with gin and cocaine."

"Sounds playful. But won't it make us somewhat . . . sedated?"

"Not with all the amphetamines I added. Go on, take a good swig, you will soon feel better. Probably better than you have ever felt in your life."

"Arthur, you dog!" Wilde smirked. "Am I at last being a bad influence upon you? You once said you didn't dispense dangerous drugs."

"Only in an emergency. And this qualifies. After all we've been through and have yet to endure, we both need a restorative. Now go on, take your medicine as the doctor orders."

Wilde uncapped the bottle and took a long, Adam's-apple-bobbing swig. He handed the bottle back to Conan Doyle, who did likewise. After a moment, Wilde commented, "Interesting, my face appears to have gone completely numb."

"It does have that side effect. Still, let us get on with the task at hand." The two friends studied the darkened shop front. Wilde thumbed the door latch experimentally, but to no avail. "Locked," he said, "and we have no key."

Conan Doyle reached into his satchel and drew out his Webley revolver. "Fortunately I brought a skeleton key with me."

"Good Lord! Won't that fetch the police?"

"A good thing if it did." Conan Doyle dropped into a wide-legged stance, aiming the muzzle an inch from the lock. Anticipating shrapnel, he turned his face away and squeezed the trigger. BANG! Up close the shot was a thunderclap that ricocheted from the doorway, fell into the arms of the fog, and was quickly smothered.

The bullet had neatly blown the lock out of the door. The shop bell tinkled as Conan Doyle shouldered his way inside. Wilde followed after, remarking, "I should think it's pointless announcing our entrance after that."

"Keep your wits about you," Conan Doyle warned. "Our resurrected friend might be lurking."

"Heavens, I wish you hadn't said that."

The two men split up and crept about the shop. Looking. Listening. The space between shelves was unfathomably dark. Wilde struck a match only to yelp as a wild-eyed, toothy visage loomed from the darkness—the painted face of a rocking horse. Both circuited the shop and met up at the far wall where a sliver of yellow light gleamed beneath the parlor door. They paused on the threshold, listening.

From within came a faint but steady *click-click* . . . *click-click* . . . *click-click* . . .

Conan Doyle threw Wilde a baffled look and the Irishman volleyed it back. The Scottish author stood back and raised his pistol, then nodded to Wilde, who twisted the doorknob and flung the door wide. They expected an armed assailant, or Wilde's kidnapped son and Miss Leckie tied to chairs. Instead, they found a domestic scene.

The blond-haired boy sat in his bath chair, a blanket draped across his lap. As before, his head turned to follow the movement of the toy train. However, the toy locomotive had toppled from its track and lay on its side, a puddle of water seeping from the tiny boiler. In the nearby rocking chair, the lady in the coal-scuttle bonnet furiously knitted away, needles mechanically working: *click-click* . . . *click-click* . . . *click-click* . . . The scarf she was knitting spilled in folds at her feet, perhaps ten feet long and steadily growing.

"I—I—I'm terribly sorry," Conan Doyle started to say, but then his words shriveled in his throat. He and Wilde exchanged a mystified look and stepped closer. He touched the woman's bonnet and it fell back to reveal an armature of wire forming a rough approximation of a human head. He lifted the blanket from the boy's lap and found no legs: only a clockwork mechanism where the lower half of a body should have been.

Both figures were lifelike automatons, robotically repeating the same action over and over again.

"Good Lord," Wilde breathed. "They are mere mechanisms, after all."

Conan Doyle picked up a framed photograph from an end table and showed it to Wilde. It was the photograph he had seen on their earlier visit: a pretty blond woman posed in front of a lake with her hand on the shoulder of a fair-haired young boy of perhaps four years old who stood clutching a windup battleship.

"I believe these were the real models," Conan Doyle said.

Wilde raised his bushy eyebrows. "And what became of the originals?"

"What indeed?" Conan Doyle shook his head grimly. "I suspect they are no longer with us. I believe these simulacrums are Jedidiah's attempt at a replacement."

"How grotesque."

"I fear we are only just beginning to understand how twisted the mind of Jedidiah is."

At his words, realization flashed in Wilde's eyes.

"What is it, Oscar?"

The Irish writer sighed and shook his head. "I am a complete fool!" He fixed Conan Doyle with a solemn look. "What was the name of Ozymandius's estranged brother?"

Conan Doyle thought a moment. "Solomon?"

"Precisely. As a student of the classics, I am mortified that I failed to tumble to it sooner."

"Tumble to what?"

"In the Book of Kings, Jedidiah is another name for Solomon."

"Ahhhhh! So after the accident with the torpedo, where his wife and son were killed—"

"He changed his name and seemingly his identity, from Solomon to Jedidiah."

A floorboard creaked behind them. Conan Doyle spun and aimed the revolver, finger tensed on the trigger.

"Don't shoot!" Detective Blenkinsop stood in the parlor doorway, the old veteran lurking behind.

"Detective Blenkinsop!" Conan Doyle exclaimed. "Thank goodness. You'd better come look at this."

"What is it, sir?" Blenkinsop asked. He had obviously dressed in a hurry, for the front of his coat was misbuttoned. "What have you found?"

Conan Doyle nodded and the young detective stepped forward and peered at the two automatons. "Strewth!" he exclaimed raising his homburg and scratching his head. "Proper lifelike, ain't they?"

"I believe Jedidiah is involved in a revolutionary plot that is unraveling at this very moment. I fear he is behind the kidnapping of Mister Wilde's son and my friend, Miss Jean Leckie. Moreover, I believe he is behind the dead men who are coming to life and assassinating key members of the government."

Blenkinsop let out a whistle. "All pretty serious charges. I mean, them big dolls is proper queer all right, but they ain't against the law. I can't go to Commissioner Burke unless we got something more substantial. Some proper kind of proof."

Conan Doyle sagged visibly. "You are correct, Tom. We shall just have to keep searching the premises until we find it." He thought a moment and said, "I believe a thorough probe of the cellar workshop should be next."

As the men stepped back into the toyshop, a crouching shape stirred to life in the shadows, luminous eyes aglow. Startled, Blenkinsop turned and fired a single shot. BANG! Silver smoke purled in the air as the men crept forward and discovered what it was. The bullet had struck the wooden head of the Automaton Turk cleanly between the eyes. Despite the injury, the Turk stared demonically as his wooden arm lifted the pipe to his carved lips, exhaled a tendril of steam, and then swept smoothly across the chessboard and tapped three times.

"What is this infernal device?" Conan Doyle asked. He started to snatch open the various doors, revealing the clockwork mechanisms within. At the heart was a metal box, warm to the touch. His fingers fumbled a latch and the door sprung open. No one was prepared for the horror they found within.

A pair of living eyes stared back at them like bloody marbles and below, glistening white fangs. The men recoiled, exclaiming in shock and disgust. What they had found was an abomination: a monkey's head, very much alive, although severed from its physical body. A metal collar encircled the stump of a neck. Rubber hoses pulsed with blood being pumped by a steam pump, leather bellows creaked up and down, pumping air, replacing lungs.

The ghastly secret of the Turkish Automaton revealed.

"Blimey! That's nasty, that is!" Detective Blenkinsop breathed. He covered his mouth with his hand and turned away.

"What is it?" the blind veteran asked. "What's he see?"

"A sin against man and nature," Wilde hissed.

Conan Doyle touched a hand to his friend's arm. They shared a look that acknowledged both were gripped by horrid speculation as to the well-being of their loved ones. "Come," he urged, "we must search the workshop."

The door in the floor flung open when Conan Doyle yanked the rope and the men peered down the precipitous steps. A light had been left burning as if someone or something down there waited for them. Detective Blenkinsop brandished his pistol and stepped cautiously forward. "I should be the one to lead the way," he said. "This is now police business."

They left the Crimean veteran to guard the top of the stairs and crept down the creaking steps, eyes probing the shadows. At the bottom they found a well laid-out workshop: half-assembled toys scattered atop workbenches, rolls of tinplate neatly stacked, tools hanging from hooks on the walls. There was nothing sinister about the place. No place prisoners could be held. No hidden cubbyholes.

"Nothing here," Blenkinsop said. "Not a sausage."

"Blast!" Wilde shouted, his voice cracking with disappointment. "Where can they be?"

Conan Doyle looked about the workshop. "Wait. There is something odd about this space."

"Odd?" Blenkinsop said.

"It is too small. The shop upstairs is quite large. This looks to be half the size."

He crossed to one wall, examining the bricks. "Note that the bricks on this wall are much newer than the bricks on the opposite wall." His eyes traced the brickwork until he found what he was searching for: a straight crack that ran from floor to ceiling. The workbench set against the wall bore a cut that ran at an angle and intersected the same crack. He studied the hooks projecting from the brickwork. Only one was not hung with a tool. He grasped it and gave an experimental tug. The hook swung down on an invisible hinge and the wall opened with a clunk, rotating smoothly on an invisible pivot. They crossed through into the resurrection chamber.

"Another workshop," Wilde said.

Conan Doyle looked around at the giant restraining chair, the laboratory tables, and the scarred wooden operating bench. "A workshop for evil. This is where they assemble their monsters."

Blenkinsop found the door to the old larder. "Wonder where this leads?" He opened the door and went in. Conan Doyle and Wilde waited. After what seemed a very long time, Blenkinsop reemerged. Only now his expression was dire.

"What?" Wilde asked.

"Everything's cold in there. On ice. And there's two metal coffins."

Wilde exchanged a look of dread with his friend.

Conan Doyle handed Blenkinsop the hissing lantern. "You open them, Tom."

The younger man nodded. "Yeah. Right you are." He stepped back into the larder and they heard the clang of metal lids being thrown open. Blenkinsop emerged moments later, his face ashen. He licked his lips, struggling to find his voice. "A young woman . . . pretty." He looked at Wilde. "And a little boy."

At the news, Wilde clamped a hand over his mouth to stifle a moan of despair. Conan Doyle stepped forward and said, "I must see for myself." He took the lantern and entered the larder. By the time he stepped back out, Wilde was shaking with dread anticipation.

"It's all right, Oscar. It's not Vyvyan, nor is it Jean. The two metal tanks contain the bodies of Solomon's young wife and son. Although preserved in chilled alcohol, the corpses have deteriorated quite badly."

Wilde shook his head. "Dear Lord, what demons are driving this man? Surely, he does not hope to revivify their corpses after so long?"

A terrible thought occurred to Conan Doyle. *Maybe he does not. Maybe that is why he has abducted Miss Leckie and Wilde's young boy. Perhaps he will somehow replace his missing family.* He made the mistake of looking at Wilde. As the two friends' eyes met, it was as if the thought was transmitted telepathically between them.

"Dear God, no!" Wilde breathed.

"Come!" Conan Doyle shouted as he hurried back across the workshop and charged up the wooden steps to the toyshop.

"What now, Doctor Doyle?" Blenkinsop shouted as he and Wilde hurried along behind.

"Our course of action is clear. All paths lead to one man: Rufus DeVayne, the Marquess of Gravistock. We must hurry to his family seat. I'll warrant that is where Jean and Vyvyan have been taken. And I'll warrant that is where we will find Jedidiah, or as he is really known, Solomon Arkwright. We cannot delay a moment longer, for fear of what is happening to our loved ones. Oscar and I will lead the charge."

"Sorry, sir," Blenkinsop said. "But I believe that is my job."

"I must differ with you, Tom. You must alert your colleagues in the police and then I want you to go to Buckingham Palace."

"To the palace? Me?" He laughed. "Copper or not, I doubt they would let the likes of me in."

"I will give you a note explaining everything. You must deliver it personally to a man named Cypher. Saying his name will open doors."

"A bloke named Cypher?"

"They will understand. Now Oscar and I must make haste."

"But how will you get there in this fog? The trains do not run. There's not a hansom to be had."

Conan Doyle pondered a moment, brows knit, but then something hanging on the wall caught his eye and a tight smile formed upon his face. "I think the evil genius Solomon Arkwright has provided the answer." He pointed to the steam motorcycle hanging on the wall.

After they wheeled it out of the shop and onto the street, it took Conan Doyle ten minutes of head scratching before he could puzzle out its operation. "The water goes in here," he said, patting the streamlined brass tank. "And the calcium carbide pellets go in here." He yanked the cork from a smoked glass bottle and tipped a stream of white pellets into a metal reservoir. "Now, I believe the boiler is lit using this striker." He depressed a spring-loaded plunger. There was a scratching sound and the *foop!* of a gas flame lighting. Within moments, the boiler hissed as it worked up a head of steam. He climbed astride the saddle, opened a petcock, and pistons began to drive up and down in their cylinders. And with that the machine came to life, throbbing between his legs, tendrils of steam wraithing about the engine. He had discovered two pairs of goggles hanging from a hook above the motorcycle and now he pulled on a pair and handed the spare to Wilde. "Here, Oscar, you will be needing these."

"Whatever for?"

"To keep the wind out of your eyes."

The Irishman chuckled ironically. "Oscar Wilde, ride upon such a contrivance? Surely you jest. Oscar Wilde does not ride bicycles or motorcycles. A hansom cab is the only two-wheeled vehicle I deign to ride inside."

"How did you imagine we were going to get there?"

"I imagined you would ride, whilst I perambulate alongside."

"Think of Vyvyan; we have no time."

"But how will we see? The fog is so thick one can barely walk in it."

Conan Doyle sparked a lighter and the steam cycle's huge carbide headlamp flared to life, hurling a dazzling beam before it.

"Good lord, you have awakened a cyclopean beast!"

"Hop on," Conan shouted above the clattering racket. "This way, we'll be there inside half an hour."

With great awkwardness, even for him, Wilde cocked a leg and straddled the bike, settling his backside into the bucket-like pillion saddle with the exaggerated caution of a hemorrhoid sufferer.

"Are you aboard?" Conan Doyle shouted over his shoulder.

"Only my most vulnerable appendages."

"Right, then. Here we go. Hang on tight."

Gears ground as Conan Doyle yanked levers, squeezed calipers, rotated handgrips, searching for a clutch. He gripped a small lever on the handlebars, pulled it back, and the motor revolutions climbed to a roar, the machine vibrating dangerously beneath them. A relief valve popped, jetting steam with a shriek. He threw more levers and then finally got lucky and found the clutch by slipping a toe beneath a foot pedal and lifting upward. Gears engaged with a *graunch* and the machine leaped forward. The cobblestones were greasy with fog and the back tire broke loose and spun madly. Conan Doyle snatched the handlebars left and right, fighting to stay upright. They veered across the road, mounted the sidewalk, careened off a wall and back onto the street. A lamppost loomed. Wilde shrieked and closed his eyes, hunkering behind Conan Doyle. Somehow they managed to swerve around it, although it clipped the Scotsman's elbow painfully.

Suddenly the bike was flying along Winchester Street at a mete-
oric ten miles an hour, a speed which seemed much faster because
of the fog and the necessity to dodge and weave around abandoned
carriages blocking the roadway. Like men straddling a spluttering
comet, they streaked through the streets of London and soon began
the long, slow climb to Hampstead, where the fog finally began to
thin. During the first five minutes of riding Conan Doyle attempted
to slow for a corner only to discover that the machine had yet to be
fitted with brakes. He decided not to broach the matter with Wilde
who, lapsed Catholic though he was, was frantically reciting the rosary at the top of his voice.

As for stopping, Conan Doyle reasoned that wouldn't be necessary until they reached the DeVayne family seat, at which point he
would just have to improvise.

CHAPTER 31

A TOAST TO DEATH

The Fog Committee sat convened around the long table in the great hall of DeVayne's ancestral seat for what they all hoped would be the final time.

DeVayne rose from his chair at the head of the long feasting table and addressed the assemblage of dour-faced members. "Gentlemen, we are mere hours away from writing our names in the history books." He raised his hand and snapped his fingers. The masked servants, who had been standing silently around the edges of the room, moved forward, bearing trays with crystal goblets and sparkling decanters filled with the green liquor. DeVayne seized a glass and bade the other members to follow suit. "Such a momentous occasion calls for a toast."

"A toast to what?" the judge asked.

"A toast to death," DeVayne answered, and added, "the death of the old regime and the birth of a new British republic."

"What is this concoction?" asked the old admiral, eyeing the deep jade drink with obvious doubt.

"The libation of the gods," DeVayne answered. "A drink for those who dare ascend the steps of Olympus. Come, join me in a toast to our great enterprise."

The others took up their glasses, but no one drank.

DeVayne noticed their reluctance and sighed in exasperation.

"Honestly, gentlemen, do you think I would poison you at this juncture? When we stand upon the threshold of victory?" To demonstrate, he quaffed his drink in one long gulp and thrust the goblet at the servant who quickly refilled it. "A toast, gentlemen. In just a few hours, the world will change for us all." He smiled. "A toast to the new republic."

All the members of the Fog Committee rose and reached across the table, to chink glasses.

"To the new republic!"

A WAGNERIAN DEATH

The steam cycle whooshed through the open gates of DeVayne's mansion, its scorching carbide lamp lighting up the eyes of a pack of jackals and scattering them. Conan Doyle shouted to his pillion passenger, "I thought those were dogs, but they look like jackals."

"Part of the marquess's menagerie," Wilde yelled back. "The beasts wander loose on the grounds. But don't worry about the jackals, I'm sure the lions will keep them at bay."

"Lions!"

As the steam cycle effortlessly sped up the steep drive, Conan Doyle eased back on the throttle lever, slowing the engine's revolutions and using the uphill slope for braking. They coasted to a standstill at the crest of the hill, and he put his feet down to steady the machine. Below them, the brightly lit pile stood waiting. Although the circular drive was empty of carriages, it was currently occupied by a pride of lions that sauntered lazily and drowsed together in tawny heaps.

"Good Lord!" Conan Doyle remarked. "I had thought you were joking and was about to suggest we abandon the motorcycle here and proceed on foot."

"Unless you can run faster than a gazelle, I highly recommend against that. The inside of the house is safe. There may be a few sheep wandering about, but the only carnivore roaming the halls is the marquess."

Conan Doyle eased on the throttle until the engine revolutions climbed to a roar, and then shifted into gear and released the clutch. The steam cycle sprang forward and they plummeted down the hill at breakneck speed and careened into the circular drive, spraying gravel. The intention had been to stampede the lions, but the pride seemed drowsily unimpressed by the hissing steam cycle. They orbited once and then a second time.

"You are merely succeeding in annoying the beasts," Wilde shouted, "and we are losing the advantage of surprise."

Conan Doyle ground his teeth with frustration. If the lions wouldn't move willingly, he'd force the issue. He let go of the throttle momentarily and fumbled the revolver from his overcoat pocket, pointing it in the air and pulling the trigger. BANG! The report of the gunshot slapped the limestone façade like a thunderclap and rebounded, rousing the lions into flight.

"Aha!" Conan Doyle triumphed. He fumbled to regain his hold on the handlebar while still clutching the revolver and inadvertently slammed the throttle lever hard against its stop. As the power surged full on, the steam cycle careened out of control. Suddenly they were pointing straight at the front steps. Conan Doyle barely had time to shout "Hang on!" as they rocketed up the marble staircase in a bone-shaking ascent and crashed through the great oaken doors. As the steam cycle shot across the marble entrance hall, the rear tire lost grip and the machine slewed from beneath them, spilling its riders. Carried by inertia, the riderless machine crashed into a heavy pedestal holding the bust of William Archibald DeVayne and toppled it, setting up a domino effect where one column slumped against its neighbor in a series of resounding crashes that ended with hundreds of years of DeVayne heritage scattered across the entrance hall in fragments.

The steam cycle came to rest in the middle of the entrance hall, where it lay spinning on its side in a widening pool of water, rear wheel turning madly, clouds of steam venting from a cracked boiler jacket. Conan Doyle and Wilde lay on their backs several feet away, winded but alive. Finally, both staggered to their feet amidst much grunting and groaning.

"Is there a chance they heard us?" Wilde asked.

Conan Doyle looked at his friend askance. "Heard us? A brass band and a firework display would have made less noise."

Miraculously, Conan Doyle had managed to hang on to the pistol, and now he waved it to indicate the way. "Come along, Oscar, there's no point in stealth now. We must rescue our loved ones. Time to beard the devil in his den."

Wilde nodded at the steam cycle, which sputtered and hissed like a dragon in its death throes. "What about that thing? I fear it may start a fire."

Conan Doyle pondered a moment. When the boiler ran dry it was entirely likely it would explode or catch fire. "Yes, I believe your concern is well founded. Still, a fire will give them something to contend with." He fished in a coat pocket and pulled out the glass bottle of calcium carbide pellets. The hall table boasted a solitary vase holding freshly cut flowers that had somehow escaped the mayhem. He snatched out the vegetation, tossed it aside, and emptied the full bottle into it. The white pellets hit the water and erupted in a fury of frothing bubbles.

"What are you up to, Arthur?"

"Mischief. Should we encounter Mister DeVayne and his cronies, this may provide us with some fog of our own."

A pair of masked servants ran into an entrance hall, mutely gesticulating with alarm.

"RUN!" Conan Doyle shouted at them. "RUN FOR YOUR LIVES! IT'S GOING TO EXPLODE!"

The servants needed no further persuasion, and bolted through the front doors, leaving the two friends to move unimpeded through the house. With a growing pall of steam following behind, the two authors tramped the empty hallway until they reached the open doors to the great hall where Wilde had witnessed the orgy. A quick glance inside revealed some kind of meeting under way. Conan Doyle held the pistol ready and whispered, "Prepare yourself, Oscar." And with that, the two friends burst into the hall, ready for anything . . .

. . . other than what they discovered.

Convened around a long table were all the faces they recognized from the newspaper clipping.

"The Fog Committee," Conan Doyle breathed.

"Yes. And all quite dead."

Shockingly, the cadre of high-powered politicos and industrial magnates, along with Edmund Burke, the commissioner of police, and the right honorable Judge Robert Jordan, sat slumped in their chairs, bodies relaxed in postures of death—heads hanging slackly, glazed eyes staring at nothing. Rufus DeVayne sat at the head of the table, host of the macabre dinner party, his head fallen to one side, eyes half-lidded, a trickle of green liquor dribbling from the corner of his mouth. Several of the Fog Committee had vomited in their last moments. Glutinous ropes of saliva trailed from the judge's open mouth to the green syrup puddled on the table before him. The coal mine owner alone had managed to rise from his seat, but sprawled dead a foot from his toppled chair. Many cold dead fingers still gripped a glass holding dregs of the fatal green cocktail.

Conan Doyle set the gun down upon the table and felt at the judge's throat. "Still warm. Death must have come upon them swiftly. The green liquor no doubt contains a poison of great efficacy."

"But why? And why would DeVayne drink his own poison?"

A bottled-up laugh burst from somewhere, and suddenly DeVayne jerked upright in his seat, the rictus grin relaxing into a wicked smile. Conan Doyle grabbed for the gun but DeVayne lunged first and snatched it up. "Too slow, Doctor Doyle!" DeVayne cackled. He rose to his feet while keeping the gun leveled. "I know you're asking yourself, how did he survive? Did he really take the poison? In fact, I drank two full glasses. But I have been taking small quantities of the poison for months to build up a resistance."

"But why kill your fellow conspirators?" Conan Doyle asked.

"Who can be trusted in a conspiracy? They wanted me only as a figurehead. In the days after the revolution, I knew I would prove obsolete, disposable, an embarrassing reminder of the regime they had just overthrown. After any revolution, there comes a time when the revolutionaries turn upon each other, as during the days of *The Terror*. Besides, I no longer need them, and a dictatorship is far less messy to manage."

"I care not what group of despots runs this country," Wilde said. "You or the current rogues' gallery. I came to get my boy back. Arthur came to get Miss Leckie. Return them to us and you can go about your sordid little revolution with no interference from us."

DeVayne dropped back into his chair, sitting sideways, one leg dangling over the chair arm. He waved the pistol carelessly as he spoke. "I'm sorry, but you two are far too deeply involved. I trusted these fools more than I trust either of you, and I just killed them all. Besides, I have a special use for both the woman and your pretty young boy. They are waiting in my private dungeon right now. Oh, but don't worry, I won't kill them immediately. The rite of immortality requires the sacrifice of a virgin, and you absconded with my last two."

"You monster!" Wilde spat. He lunged at DeVayne and Conan Doyle struggled to restrain him.

The marquess fixed Wilde with a pitying scowl. "Monster am I? Well, if it's a monster you want, it's a monster you shall have." He raised his voice and called out, "Gentlemen, would you bring in our Italian friend. Mister Wilde and Doctor Doyle are anxious to become reacquainted."

The double doors at the end of the hall opened and the two men entered pushing a wheeled version of the restraining chair. Conan Doyle recognized Dr. Lamb immediately, but gasped aloud when he saw the second figure: a frock-coated gentleman in a stovepipe hat. "Ozymandius Arkwright!" he hissed. "I knew he was somehow implicated in all this—" But then the words died in the Scotsman's throat. As the figure approached, he saw that it was not Ozymandius, but Jedidiah, the toy maker and owner of the Emporium, transformed by his attire into an eerie echo of his square-jawed brother.

"Evidently Ozymandius lied," Wilde muttered. "His brother Solomon clearly did not die that day."

Pinioned in the restraining chair was the corpse of the Italian valet, hanging slack and lifeless in its cage of iron bands. DeVayne left his seat and strode over to join them.

"I am the one who brought these two geniuses together. As I once said to you, Mister Wilde, in the new regime men such as these will be lauded as gods. Unfortunately, neither you nor Mister Doyle will live to see that day." He turned to the engineer. "Solomon, I believe our friends need a demonstration of our improved assassin."

DeVayne eyed both of them cruelly. "You were lucky to escape the first time. We discovered your little trick with the photograph. But this time I will ensure that the creature fully imprints upon you both. I shall tell it you murdered Vicente's sister. The animal drives of hatred and rage are far stronger than the weak human notions of love and sentiment, as you will discover when the monster's hand plunges through your ribcage and rips out your heart." He nodded at Solomon. "Begin the resurrection."

"One question, Solomon," Conan Doyle called out. "What do you hope to gain by all this death and destruction? Will killing the queen somehow bring your family back?"

The gray-haired man in the black stovepipe regarded Conan Doyle a moment and sneered with derision. "The queen, sir? Shall I tell about our beloved monarch? I created a war-winning weapon: a guided torpedo that could destroy a warship from a mile away. The nose of the torpedo was fitted with a glass window. Inside was a pigeon trained to recognize the silhouette of a warship and steer toward it by pecking at metal paddles. But on the day of the demonstration, some fool released a flock of doves to welcome the queen. The pigeon saw the shadow of the doves on the surface of the water. Instinct took over from training and the pigeon turned to follow the flock. Dozens were killed. I saw my wife and beloved child go down before my eyes." Solomon Arkwright's chin quivered; his eyes filled with hot tears that melted before a glare of burning hatred. "But you know what the irony is?" He shook his head bitterly. "The accident fnished us as weapon makers. But not because of the people killed. Not because of the death of my wife and child. But because of the pigeon. The great animal lover Victoria was horrified that a weapon designed to save countless lives of British seamen required the sacrifice of a single bird. And so we were stricken from the list of weapons suppliers."

Conan Doyle briefly wondered what was happening in the entrance hall and whether the servants had all fled the house. He decided to play for time. "Solomon," he called out. "We have met your brother. We know what happened those many years ago. You suffered a terrible loss. But is what you are doing true to the memory of your loved ones?"

The engineer looked at Conan Doyle as if he were stupid. "Everything I do is for my family. I will revive their bodies . . . not just their memory." Solomon's head shook with a violent tremor.

Conan Doyle suddenly remembered the photograph of the Fog Committee. He had surmised that the figure in the stovepipe hat had deliberately turned his head to blur his own image. Now he understood the truth: it was the nervous tic the man had no doubt been left with after that tragic day when he saw his wife and child die before his eyes. Solomon Arkwright was a deeply traumatized man, but he might yet be reasoned with. "We have seen the bodies of your wife and son. They have deteriorated too far be revivified, no matter how clever your heart pump is."

"The marquess's magic will take up where our science leaves off." Solomon's words were raveled with desperation. "He has given me his solemn oath that we shall walk together again in this life."

"Walk together? What, like that thing?" Wilde said, pointing to the dead man in the chair. "You will revive them as shambling monsters?"

"Shut up!" Solomon bellowed. "Shut up!"

The engineer spread open the monster's shirt, revealing the brassy metal box. His fingers found and depressed the recessed plunger, which scratched a inner striker plate and ignited the carbide fuel. Soon they could hear the ascending hiss of water coming to a boil.

DeVayne and his two cronies stepped back behind the restraining chair, out of the monster's field of view. The heart pump's telltale sound filled the hall: *wisssshthump . . . wissssssshthump . . . wissssssshthump . . .*

Within minutes, the corpse began to quiver as hot blood pumped through cold flesh, dormant nerve endings fired, and limbs twitched. Then the creature stirred. It drew in a ragged breath and released a plume of steam.

DeVayne smiled as he watched. "Solomon has increased the steam engine's output, raising the blood pressure to six times that of a normal human, bestowing the creature with unstoppable power."

As the tissues engorged with blood, the thing in the chair seemed to inflate. Huge veins plumped on the face and neck and the skin darkened to the color of a sanguine bruise. Then, with a blood-chilling scream, the grizzled head rose up and the yellow eyes startled open.

The marquess leaned close to the gruesome head and purred into its ear: "The men you see before you are the cause of your suffering. They murdered your sister. Your soul will never know peace while they live. You must destroy Oscar Wilde and Arthur Conan Doyle. Tear off their arms. Smash them. Peel the flesh from their bones. Crush and rend them utterly. Only then will you know peace. Only then will you be released from this prison of corrupt and stinking flesh you now inhabit."

The monster began to writhe violently in the chair, an engine fueled by hatred. One iron band restraining an arm broke with a loud snap, and then another. The chair creaked and groaned as the monster rose to its feet, snapping the heavy timbers as if they were matchsticks. The monster stood erect, pausing a moment as if gathering momentum, the yellow eyes fixing upon the two friends, and then took a lunging step forward.

"Kill them!" DeVayne urged. "Kill! Kill! Ki—"

KAA-BOOOOOOOOOOOOOOOOOOOOOOOOM!

His words were drowned by a thunderous explosion that blew in the doors and snuffed out the gaslights. Suits of armor toppled and crashed. A pall of dust fell from the rafters and mixed with the smoke and steam swirling in through the doorway to form a blinding fog. When the pall of dust and smoke finally cleared, Conan Doyle and Wilde had vanished.

So had the monster.

Dr. Lamb looked terror-struck. "What was that explosion?"

A masked servant ran by the doorway.

"Wait!" DeVayne shouted, but the servant had already vanished.

"What do we do now?" Solomon asked. "The two meddlers have escaped and the house is on fire."

DeVayne thought a moment and said, "We must proceed with our plan. Wilde and his friend are as good as dead. The monster will track them unerringly." He turned to Solomon. "You must find the creature and bring him back." He handed over Conan Doyle's revolver. "In the unlikely event he hasn't already killed them, use this and make sure they're dead. The doctor and I will be waiting in my landau. We cannot delay. We must be inside the gates of Buckingham Palace before Big Ben strikes thirteen."

Meanwhile Conan Doyle and Wilde were running pell-mell through the hallways. "I told you to shut that steam thing down, Arthur."

"Yes. It worked rather better than I'd hoped." But in the next instant he was struck by a dread realization. "We must find the dungeon where Miss Leckie and Vyvyan are being held, before the fire becomes a conflagration!"

They paused at the foot of the grand staircase.

"Only stairs going up," Conan Doyle said. "None going down."

"This is a mock Tudor manor. It only has two floors."

"Then where would the dungeon be?"

Wilde thought a moment and said, "When we were in his rooms, DeVayne said his dungeon was nearby."

"Where are his rooms?"

"Somewhere on the upper floor. I'm not sure exactly."

From down the smoky corridor came a dreadfully familiar sound: *wissssshthump . . . wissssshthump. . . .* Through the swirling smoke, they glimpsed the monster, stumping toward them."

"Quickly, Arthur, up the stairs!"

The two friends vaulted up the staircase with Wilde leading the way. They turned right and hurried along the corridor.

"Which room?"

"Alas, I cannot recall."

"So many rooms. So many doors. How shall we ever find them?"

"Perhaps they are somewhere near. Close enough to hear us if we shout."

Both men began to shout aloud: "JEAN! VYVYAN. JEAN! VYVYAN!"

Conan Doyle paused to look behind. Smoke was chimneying up the staircase and spreading along the upper landing. The smoke swirled and the monster stepped out of it and slouched after them.

"The creature's following us."

They loped on, shouting at the top of their lungs. "VYVYAN! JEAN!"

Wilde grabbed Conan Doyle's arm and dragged him to a standstill.

"What?"

"I hear singing," Wilde said. He looked at Conan Doyle with a mystified expression. "It sounds like . . . an aria?"

Conan Doyle instantly recognized the singer. "It's Jean. She is a classically trained mezzo-soprano. That's her singing."

"How apropos. I suppose, if I must die, at least I shall have a suitably operatic death. Here I am running through a burning manor pursued by a raging monster. And all to the accompaniment of an aria. Even Wagner could not stage such a drama."

They followed Jean Leckie's soaring voice to a large set of double doors and crashed through them.

"These are his rooms!" Wilde said. He dashed about, searching amongst the elaborate furniture and the four-poster bed; however, Vyvyan and Jean Leckie were nowhere to be seen. Conan Doyle slammed the bedroom doors shut and bolted them.

"I'm afraid that won't keep it out for long."

"Hardly."

"Jean!" Conan Doyle shouted. "Keep singing."

The silvery aria started up again.

Wilde pointed. "It's coming from the wall, behind the print."

He pointed to the print DeVayne had so lovingly described in the bookshop. Conan Doyle examined it and speculated, "It must conceal a door."

"Then there must be a catch or handle somewhere," Wilde said, hands exploring the edges of the frame.

"Don't bother!" Conan Doyle pulled the small silver penknife from his pocket, swung out the sharp blade, and slashed through the canvas in a giant X pattern. He and Wilde tore loose the flapping canvas to reveal a dungeon door, massive and heavy, bound together with iron straps and dozens of black rivets. Wilde grabbed the black iron ring and yanked, but to no avail.

"Damnation! It's locked. We must batter it down."

"With what?"

Wisssshthump . . . wissssssshthump . . . wissssssshthump . . .

The double doors suddenly burst inward from a blow. The stench of decaying flesh preceded the monster into the room. It paused a moment to fix them both with its ghastly, yellow-eyed stare.

Conan Doyle grabbed the statue of a small bronze satyr from a nearby table and brandished it like a club. But to his surprise, Wilde pushed him aside and stepped toward the monster. He dropped to his knees before it and clasped both hands together in a gesture of sup- plication. The beast stumbled toward him and raised a clublike arm, coiled to smash. But then Wilde addressed it in fluent Italian, speak- ing in an impassioned voice, smiting his own chest from time to time. The beast stood frozen. It seemed to be listening, its facial muscles rippling with an inner struggle as the last fragments of Vicente's hu- manity warred with the resurrected monster he had been fashioned to be. Wilde finally finished and the monster looked down upon him, as if unsure what to do.

"What did you say to it?"

"I asked him to save my little boy. I implored him in the name of his sister and all the loved ones in Italy he will never see again."

Suddenly, the monster lowered its arm. It looked from Wilde to the door and back. And then the face tightened into a snarling gri- mace; a rising growl roared from the lungs. Wilde reared back, antic- ipating a deathblow. But instead the creature shambled forward and struck the door a resounding blow. The great door shook, but held. Another blow and another. An iron strap tore loose and clanged to the ground. More blows. The wood cracked and split in places. The monster backed away and then charged the door, smashing into it with such force that the hinges tore loose from the frame and the door toppled inward. The monster backed away and Conan Doyle and Wilde rushed into the chamber.

The room inside resembled the dungeon in the print, although the cell was faux-painted plaster, not stone. Torture devices hung from the walls. Gaslights disguised as torches illuminated the windowless space.

Jean Leckie sat on a simple straw pallet in the corner, cradling Wilde's boy in her lap. And now both cried out in relief.

"Papa!" Vyvyan croaked in a dry voice.

"My beloved child!" Wilde cried, scooping up his son and hug- ging him to his chest.

"Papa . . ."

"Yes, Papa came to get you. All the monsters in the universe could not have prevented it."

Conan Doyle took Jean Leckie by the hands and drew her to her feet. Her lips trembled as she fought to control her churning emotions. Her eyes sparkled with tears. Conan Doyle drew her into his arms and they shared a long, soul-quaking embrace. Suddenly remembering the monster, he flung about to look. But the bedroom was empty. The creature had gone.

As the four stumbled back down the long hall to the grand staircase, the smoke was chokingly thick.

"Shall we never be free of this blasted fog in one form or another?" Wilde complained. They hurried down the staircase to the ground floor where dense smoke swirled. By now fire had climbed up the fine paneling and flames were licking across the ceiling, leaping from room to room.

"Quickly!" Conan Doyle urged. "We must reach the entrance hall before the fire cuts off our only exit."

But as they ran along the hallway past the grand hall, they found their way blocked by a solitary figure in a stovepipe hat.

Solomon Arkwright.

He brandished the Webley revolver, threatening them. "You and Wilde may save yourselves, but the young lady and the boy must remain."

"You had a wife and child of your own once," Wilde said. "You know full well the pain of loss. Would you inflict that upon others?"

But there was no pity in Solomon's eyes. "Yes. I would burn the world to ash to be reunited with my family. Now send the woman and boy toward me and leave, or I will shoot them down before your eyes."

Wilde and Conan Doyle shared a look. "What shall we do?" Wilde asked. "We are trapped between an inferno and a crazed man with a gun."

But then something slouched into view behind Solomon, a gory figure that limped steadily along the burning hallway, unaffected by the scorching heat. Conan Doyle saw that it was bearing down upon Solomon and sought to distract him.

"Solomon. It's not too late. Abandon this madness. The house is lost."

In response, the toy maker raised the gun and aimed it at Conan Doyle's heart. "I am a man already burning in hell. My soul will be damned for what I have done. And what I have yet to do. But I would pay that price willingly to have another second with my family. Would you not do the same?"

Solomon's finger was tightening on the trigger when the creature stepped from behind and threw its arms about him, pinning his arms in a crushing embrace. As the monstrous grip tightened, the gun went off: BANG!, firing a bullet into the floor. And then again: BANG! Solomon choked for breath. His face purpled. Eyes bulged. A rib snapped with a sharp *pop!* He moaned, feet kicking, but the deadly embrace squeezed ever tighter.

The monster's face convulsed as it fought to control its lips and tongue long enough to summon a particle of the man who had once been Vicente and articulate a final clutch of words. *"Pregate per me."*

"It spoke, Oscar! What did it say?"

"Pray for me," Wilde answered in a breathless voice.

And with that, the monster stepped backward into the flames and ignited like a roman candle, and the thrashing form of Solomon Arkwright, imprisoned in its arms, also caught fire. His piercing shrieks were terrible to hear and the friends looked away.

"Quickly," Conan Doyle urged, "we must get away. The monster's steam boiler will likely rupture in the great heat."

The group stumbled on, plunging into thickening smoke.

"Get down on all fours," Conan Doyle urged. "The smoke will be less intense."

They all dropped to the rug and groped blindly along the hallway.

"It's getting hotter!" Jean Leckie cried.

"Surely we are crawling into the flames?" Wilde fretted.

"Just a bit farther," Conan Doyle shouted. "The entrance hall is mostly marble. What little can burn has likely already been consumed."

Conan Doyle had one arm about the waist of Miss Leckie, while Wilde held Vyvyan to his side. But even at floor level, the smoke was choking and the heat dizzying. The Scottish author could feel Jean's trembling body beginning to falter as she crawled beside him. For a dreadful moment he feared he had made a fatal miscalculation and considered turning back, but by now all visibility was lost. Coughing and choking, hot sparks singeing their hair and faces, they inched along in a tedious crawl. Conan Doyle, sweating through his clothes, began to feel nauseous and woozy. Abruptly, the hall rug ended and he felt cool marble beneath his fingertips. The smoke brightened and suddenly he could see the diamond pattern of the marble tiles. Ahead, smoke swirled, revealing patches of sky. "Up," he shouted. "Get up!" The four of them finally reached the double doors and staggered out of the burning building into fresh, clean air.

Waiting for them on the circular driveway were dozens of blue-uniformed constables with two black Mariahs and several horse-drawn wagons. Detective Blenkinsop stood in the middle of the melee, shouting orders. DeVayne's servants sat in a knot on the grass lawn, their hands in manacles. Several had lost their masks, among them the man with the port-wine stain and others who had manned the hearse.

"Thank gawd!" Detective Blenkinsop said, rushing forward to greet them. "I had a horrible feeling you'd all burned alive in there."

"DeVayne!" Wilde cried out. "Do you have DeVayne?"

Blenkinsop shook his head grimly. "No. Looks like he scarpered. Don't you worry, though, we'll track him down."

"But he's going to lead an armed revolt at the palace. We have to—" Conan Doyle stopped short as a carriage appeared coming from the stables: a yellow landau drawn by four African zebras.

They all watched, dumbfounded, as the zebras trotted toward them. Suddenly, Detective Blenkinsop gathered his wits and shouted, "Stop that carriage! It must not pass!"

Stirred into action, a dozen constables ran onto the gravel drive, linking arms to form a solid blue cordon. Conan Doyle feared the driver would spur the zebras and trample them, but the yellow landau drew to a halt. Suspecting a trick, Blenkinsop, Conan Doyle, and Wilde rushed over to see if the carriage was occupied.

The Marquess of Gravistock, Rufus DeVayne, lounged on the carriage seat, showing little concern for his situation. He was dressed as if for his own coronation in an outlandish getup: a plumed Napoleonic hat and a plush red military uniform with a white sash slashing across his breast, the jacket jangling with obscure medals he had no doubt awarded himself.

Detective Blenkinsop snatched open the carriage door and jerked a thumb at its lone occupant "Right you, out!"

DeVayne picked at bit of imaginary fluff on his sleeve and appeared not to hear. "There is no need to shout, officer. As a condition of my surrender, I insist that I travel in my own carriage." He did not look at anyone as he spoke. "Royalty does not travel in conveyances used to transport common criminals."

Detective Blenkinsop unleashed an angry snarl as he reached in, grabbed the front of DeVayne's uniform jacket, and dragged him out of the carriage. The marquess juggled to keep the admiral's hat upon his head, but seemed in denial of his situation.

"Is that it?" Conan Doyle said in a voice husky with anger. "You who are responsible for so much anguish, for so many deaths, surrender so meekly? Without a struggle?"

DeVayne answered with a foolish grin. "You sad little man. I am of the aristocracy. Cousin to the Prince of Wales. Fifth in line to the throne of England. They dare not try me in the public courts or imprison me in a common jail. Thanks to my little *soirees* I know too much about the peccadilloes of the rich and powerful: Which cabinet minister likes little girls. Which bishop prefers little boys. Which knight of the British Empire thrills to the sting of the lash. I especially know what cousin Bertie likes. If the British public found out about the Prince of Wales and his rather *peculiar* tastes, he would never ascend the throne. No, they dare not try me. They cannot jail me and they will not kill me. As before, I will be confined to a nice quiet sanitarium somewhere peaceful and rustic. I do hope it has a well-stocked wine cellar."

At the remark, a howl of outrage tore from Wilde who balled his hand into a fist and drove it into DeVayne's mocking face with all his might. The force of the blow broke the aristocrat's nose and drove him to the ground. "You are everything vile! A murderer, a kidnapper, and you dare boast about it! You are the reverse of Dorian Gray. You are a portrait of disease hiding a stinking corruption within!"

DeVayne actually smiled as he looked up at Wilde, his nose crookedly twisted and dripping blood. From his madly dilated eyes, it was clear he had taken a massive dose of the green liquor.

"My creator!" he laughed. "Know this, Oscar: your downfall—when it comes—will be farther than mine. Perhaps they will let you visit me in my madhouse. We can stroll the grounds and reminisce about our magical time together."

"Not this time, Marquess."

All looked around at the strangely familiar voice. The ranks of police officers parted and the diminutive figure of Cypher stepped through, his hulking minders shadowing close behind. "This time you will not be sent to a sanitarium," Cypher said with relish. "I have picked out a very special place where the Prince of Wales and all your highborn friends won't find you. Where you are going has a cold climate and six months of darkness every winter. And I'm afraid this time you will not enjoy clean sheets and a soft bed. None of the locals speaks English, so you will be unable to send a message to your friends lurking in England. But you will be kept busy. The governor believes that long days of hard labor are beneficial for the character.

I hope you like turnips, because that is all you will eat. And yet you will be rich in one thing: solitude. During the long winter nights you will have hours to reflect upon your wretched existence." Cypher nodded to his two men. "Shackle him hand and foot. If he attempts to talk to anyone, gag him. No, on second thought, gag him anyway."

For a delicious moment, DeVayne's formidable hauteur collapsed in a wide-eyed, lip-trembling look of despair. And then he was scruffed by the hulking minders and dragged away to be slung into the back of a waiting Mariah.

Blenkinsop looked at Jean Leckie. "You all right, Miss?"

Jean Leckie stifled a cough on the back of her hand. Her pretty face was smudged with dirt and smoke. "Yes, quite well, thank you." She turned and looked to Conan Doyle and Wilde. "Or rather, thanks to these two brave men." Even though they had reached safety, Vyvyan obviously felt safe with Miss Leckie, for he still clung to her skirts. Blenkinsop reached down and ruffled the little boy's hair.

"How you doin' young 'un?" he asked.

"I was jolly frightened," Vyvyan said, shyly, "but the nice lady said my daddy and his friend would come for us."

"And they did, didn't they, son?" Blenkinsop said.

Conan Doyle turned to Cypher. "Could you find someplace to keep them safe, until this business is over?"

"My pleasure," Cypher replied, and nodded to his two minders. "These gentlemen will be their personal bodyguards." At that moment, a four-wheeler appeared, coming from the direction of the stables. Cypher waved and it drew up before them.

"That carriage looks like Commissioner Burke's black growler," Conan Doyle said.

"He shan't be needing it anymore," Wilde noted.

The ginger minder Conan Doyle had nicknamed Dandelion opened the carriage door for Jean Leckie. Wilde picked up his little boy, hugged him extravagantly, and kissed him on both cheeks. "Vyvyan," he said, "Daddy will take you home to Mummy soon, but first he has some grown-up business to see to. Your auntie Jean will look after you." He handed his boy up to Burdock, who saw him settled on the carriage seat and pulled the door shut behind him. Jean Leckie quickly let down the carriage window. Conan Doyle moved forward to take her hand as she leaned out. "In spite of everything, I want you to know, Doctor Doyle, that I have greatly enjoyed making your acquaintance." She flashed him a heart-crushing smile, and then her eyes moved to Wilde. "And you, too, Mister Wilde."

Despite being disheveled, his mane of hair wildly mussed, his jacket marred with scorch marks and burn holes, the Irish wit straightened his posture and threw her a bow with a courtier's flourish. "Oscar. You must call me Oscar. Only bank bailiffs and deranged madmen call me Mister Wilde. And you have my most utmost, heartfelt thanks for looking after my precious child."

And with that, the growler rattled away.

Conan Doyle watched the carriage disappear over the top of the rise and then turned to face the others. "It just struck me. There is one rogue still unaccounted for."

"Who is that?" Cypher asked.

Conan Doyle turned and studied the servants, who were being questioned where they sat upon the grass. Only one servant still kept the porcelain mask in place. Although it concealed his face, it could not disguise the extravagantly curled blond head of hair. The Scottish author stalked over and ripped off the mask, revealing the handsome features of Doctor Lamb. "Another one for you, Blenkinsop."

Minutes later, Dr. Lamb and several of the surviving undertakers were hauled away in manacles. "You're too late to stop the revolution!" Lamb shouted as he was goaded along by the prodding of nightsticks. "The people shall rise up and throw off their shack—" His final words were interrupted by a large policeman who clamped a hand over his face and shoved him into the back of a Mariah.

"Now what?" Oscar Wilde asked.

"We must return to the palace posthaste," Cypher said. "There is still danger."

From behind came a loud crack and the sound of shattering glass. The men looked around as a large section of the building's façade collapsed in upon itself in a tumble of bricks and broken masonry, sending up huge tongues of crackling smoke and flame.

"Should I send for the fire boys?" Blenkinsop asked. "Seems a shame. Such a grand building. It might still be saved."

Cypher shook his head, his lip curled in disgust. "No. Let it burn. There is nothing worth preserving here."

* * *

Cypher rode with Conan Doyle and Wilde in the marquess's zebra-drawn landau, which led the procession of Black Mariahs and police wagons on the trip back to London. When the strange cavalcade entered a dim and foggy Trafalgar Square, demonstrators were already massing, dozens clutching banners bearing the 13/13 symbol. As the demonstrators caught sight of them, many stopped to scream invective or hurl rocks and apple cores, but most just gawped at the spectacle of a carriage drawn by four zebras.

The mariahs and wagons turned off to take their prisoners to holding cells in nearby police stations, leaving the yellow landau to carry on unescorted. As it turned onto the Mall, the carriage was forced to a crawl by milling crowds of grim-faced men and women, all of them marching to lay siege to the royal palace. Disturbingly, many were armed with iron rods, pitchforks, and long wooden staves. Conan Doyle and Wilde shared an uneasy look. Their carriage could easily be overturned and all in it dragged out and set upon by the mob. But behind the wire-rimmed spectacles, Cypher's bland countenance seemed unperturbed.

As the gates of Buckingham Palace came into view, Conan Doyle saw the red tunics of guardsmen ranked behind the tall iron railings, bayonets fixed to their rifles. He also noticed several hastily erected wooden towers on the palace grounds, their tops draped with tarpaulins, and his stomach churned with dread at what he guessed they might conceal.

"This will end in sorrow," Wilde whispered.

Slowly, slowly, the landau managed to suck loose of the glutinous mass of humanity. At its approach, guardsmen threw wide the palace gates and the carriage rattled through them. The crowd surged behind, attempting to rush inside, but the gates banged shut in their faces. Conan Doyle turned and glanced back. They were safe behind the iron railings, but the restive mob was growing by the minute.

The carriage drew up in the shadow of the palace, and the three men clambered out and took up a position behind the wall of soldiers. Cypher produced a large brass pocket watch and flipped it open.

"Four minutes before one," he blithely noted.

Conan Doyle and Wilde cast nervous glances back and forth as the minute hand ticked slowly toward the hour. And then the fateful moment arrived. The air seemed to tighten. In the ranks of soldiers standing to attention, many licked nervous lips. In the final seconds, even the crowd fell silent.

At last, the hour struck as Big Ben chimed once: CLONG.

The struck chime resonated outward across the capital . . . only to dissolve into silence.

Anxious glances passed around the crowd.

"It only struck once," Conan Doyle said. "It only struck once!"

Cypher, who stood rocking back and forth on the balls of his feet, allowed himself a cruel smile.

Minutes passed. The crowd grew restive and surged this way and that in a great, dark swarm. Shouts and angry voices called out as it became obvious that something had gone badly wrong. They had been lied to. Deceived. Big Ben had not chimed thirteen times as promised. A few rabble-rousers in the crowd began to shout and gesticulate, trying to jump-start the revolution without the agreed-upon signal. The mob grew restive and surged forward in a great wave of bodies. Those who were not ready were crushed up against the ironwork, pinned and helpless, while others began to scale the railings.

At that moment Cypher gave the slightest of nods to a nearby uniformed sergeant, who drew his sword and raised it high in the air. At the signal, soldiers atop the wooden towers threw aside the tarpaulins, revealing Gatling guns. The sergeant bellowed a command and the guardsmen massed in the palace yard raised their rifles, pointing out at the mob.

Conan Doyle's stomach lurched. The British army was about to open fire on its own citizenry.

Several of the protesters had reached the top of the railings, with more scaling behind them. Cypher nodded a second time and the sergeant drew his sword down in a slashing motion.

A cry of protest started to rise from Conan Doyle's throat, only to be drowned by a cacophonous din as the Gatling guns opened fire with a deafening, percussive CHUNKA-CHUNKA-CHUNKA, firing over the heads of the crowd, lacing the air with a deadly blur of flying lead. Hot shell casings showered down from the towers and rang metallic upon the parade ground.

Outside the railings, panic ensued. Banners toppled as the crowd turned and surged away. Many fell and were trampled in the mob's mad, terrorized flight. Then the palace gates were thrown wide and ranks of soldiers marched out behind a thicket of bayonet points.

The revolution, which should have begun at one o'clock, had dissolved into chaos by three minutes past the hour. The army swept unopposed into the square where only a few unfortunate souls lay dead upon the ground, felled not by machine-gun fire, but trampled to death in the crowd's panicked rush to escape. Minutes later, the only evidence, besides a scattering of corpses, were abandoned banners crumpled upon on the ground and the odd ownerless shoe.

Cypher turned to Conan Doyle and Wilde with a self-satisfied smile on his small face. "Now, gentlemen, you truly are relieved. You may go home to your families, safe in the knowledge that the British monarchy will endure for another thousand years."

But as the two friends settled themselves back in the landau, Conan Doyle muttered to Wilde in a low voice, "I am no longer certain that is a good thing."

A SUMMONS TO THE PALACE

Three days later, the weather trough that had been stalled over England gathered its skirts and swept out into the Atlantic. Gusting winds from the Continent snapped the flags atop Marble Arch and scoured the last tendrils of fog from London's alleyways and thoroughfares. It was on a blustery, blue-sky day that Conan Doyle debouched from the echoic vault of Waterloo Station to find Wilde's private four-wheeler drawn up at the curb waiting to collect him.

He clambered aboard to find Wilde in a characteristic pose: legs crossed, an elbow cupped in one hand, the smoke from a Turkish cigarette curling up about his face.

"Oscar." Conan Doyle nodded in greeting and dropped onto the seat cushion. He drew off his top hat and settled it next to him. Both men were dressed in their finest. Conan Doyle noticed Wilde's own top hat on the seat beside him, although it was a choice of headgear he rarely favored.

"Did your family not accompany you?" Wilde asked. "The pulchritudinous Miss Jean Leckie?"

"They are coming up from Surrey on the next train."

"Ah."

"Are you still residing at your club these days, Oscar?"

Wilde exhaled a drowsy lungful of smoke and gave an insouciant wave. "You will be gratified to know that I spent the entire week in the domestic idylls of Tite Street indulging in the comforts of hearth, home, and family."

"Glad to hear it."

Wilde rapped the carriage ceiling with his walking stick and the carriage set off. Conan Doyle noticed the fine envelope on the seat beside his friend.

"I see you have been perusing your invitation."

"I have read it six times since breakfast," Wilde replied, picking at a fleck of tobacco on his tongue. "It seems to promise much, but says little."

"It is vexingly vague as to what we are summoned for. You don't think . . ."

"Think what?"

"Oh, nothing."

"Is that a new suit, Arthur?"

"Yes. And I note you have your topper with you. A touch formal for you?"

"I thought it appropriate. We are going to the palace, after all."

"Yes, of course. I am sure it is just an interview, to hear, once again, the details of our side of the story."

"I am less certain. Everything Mister Cypher does is *sub rosa*, I doubt he would send out a secret missive using the official stationery of Buckingham Palace. It even has the royal seal upon it."

"So you think it possible—?"

"I definitely think it possible."

"That we might be recognized—"

"Rewarded . . . for our contribution."

"We did play a vital role in thwarting an assassination plot."

"Yes," Conan Doyle agreed. "But, still, it is highly unlikely."

They rode on in disingenuous silence, each pretending to take an interest in the sights of London rolling past the carriage window.

Conan Doyle took out a journal from his leather satchel, flipped it open, and began to scribble.

"One of your Casebooks?" Wilde inquired.

"Yes. And I believe I am about to write the final chapter." Conan Doyle set to scribbling, his pen filling the blank pages with his neat handwriting in blue ink.

But after several minutes, Wilde could not hold his peace and said, in a musing voice, "Sir Oscar Wilde. It has a certain ring to it, does it not?"

"It does, Oscar, it does. Likewise, I had rather thought that *Sir* Arthur Conan Doyle would look splendid on the spine of a book."

Both men luxuriated in the daydream of knighthood for a moment longer and then the Scotsman shook himself back into the real world and returned to his Casebook. "Best not to speculate."

"You're absolutely right."

"It is unlikely."

"Highly unlikely."

"Yes."

"Impossible."

"Oh," Wilde objected, "I would never say impossible!"

* * *

At the palace, the two colleagues were conducted into a plush antechamber close to the throne room. Cypher was waiting, sans his companion brutes. Conan Doyle was gratified to see that Detective Blenkinsop was already there. Upon receiving his invitation he had written to Cypher insisting that the young detective be recognized for his contribution.

"Tom!" Conan Doyle said, warmly shaking the man's hand.

"Just wish the wife and nipper coulda been here," Blenkinsop said, beaming with pride. "But, I know it has to be kept hushed up and all." The young detective wore his mop of hair parted in the middle and slicked down with hair oil. He was kitted out in his very finest suit; his shoes, although worn at the heels, were polished to a luster.

Cypher smiled superiorly. "At your request, Doctor Doyle, I had the detective reinstated in the police . . . and he is to be promoted."

"Marvelous!" Conan Doyle beamed. "Simply marvelous." His demeanor suddenly waxed cautious. "And, ah, where is the Prince of Wales? I assume he will be attending."

Cypher shook his head, looking like an unhappy puppet. "He will not, although it pains me to admit that his exact whereabouts are unknown. The prince somehow managed to evade the men I had following him. I believe he has absconded to Paris. Miss Bernhardt is performing there, and he has evidently rekindled his fondness for her."

Conan Doyle ruffled his moustaches in an irritated fashion and shared a worried look with Wilde.

Cypher consulted his watch with a frown, and then turned to the men. "The time has come. Are we all ready, gentlemen?"

The men nodded, even while making frantic, last-second adjustments to their dress, cinching ties, combing moustaches.

"Your audience will be brief. I must warn you not to approach Her Majesty. Also, do not speak unless the queen speaks to you. When the audience is at an end, you will bow and take several steps backward, head lowered, before turning and leaving the royal presence. Do you understand?"

They all nodded and mumbled yeses.

Cypher led the way, and the rest of the party followed close behind.

Conan Doyle leaned toward Wilde and muttered sotto voce, "Be prepared, Oscar. Her Majesty is greatly ailing. You may find her appearance quite shocking."

They crossed the hallway and entered the gilded fantasy of the throne room. Victoria Regina, as ever dressed in mourning black, waited upon her throne. Cypher led them to a spot a cautious distance from the monarch, where they stood in a line and bowed from the waist, although, once again, Conan Doyle had to fight the urge to drop to one knee.

From this distance, Victoria resembled a crumpled doll a child had clumsily arranged in a grown-up's chair. Her glassy eyes fixed them with a spaniel's gaze as she regarded them over her many chins. Her chest rose and fell fitfully. The head moved stiffly as Victoria swept her gaze across them and then raised a palsied hand in acknowledgment. When she spoke, her faltering voice could have been coming from a hundred miles away.

"Gentlemen," she said in a breathless, asthmatic wheeze. "We are informed of the great service you have done for your queen and your nation."

"We are here to serve, Your Majesty," Cypher said in an obsequious voice.

But then Conan Doyle caught a whiff of cigar smoke and heard a fruity voice announce, "Ah, there you are, Mother." He turned to see the Prince of Wales saunter into the room. Edward was not alone, and it took a moment for Conan Doyle to register the slender shadow pacing at his shoulder.

Rufus DeVayne.

"I heard that cousin Rufie has been a naughty boy again," the prince said. "This time I had to spring him from a madhouse in Latvia."

Across the room, jaws dropped, eyes widened. The next few seconds of shocked disbelief were to prove fatal.

Before Cypher could scream for the palace guards to seize him. Before Conan Doyle could shout a warning. Before anyone could move, DeVayne snatched something from his cloak—the two-shot derringer he had once offered to Wilde—and aimed it point-blank at the prince's head. Mistaking it for a prank, the Prince of Wales drew the cigar from his mouth and said, "See, here, Rufie, that's taking the joke a bit too far—"

"SILENCE!" Rufus DeVayne screamed. The derringer trembled

in his hand as he fixed the room with a look that dared anyone to test his resolve.

"Drop the pistol," Cypher threatened. "Or be cut down where you stand."

DeVayne merely smiled. "The revolution lives so long as I draw breath. Kill me and I will resurrect myself in three days. But by this act I shall live forever." He took a step away from the prince and spun around, aiming the derringer straight at Victoria. "So dies a tyrant!" he screamed. The gun fired with a percussive BANG! The bullet struck Victoria in the forehead. She startled. Her head lolled slack and she slumped upon the throne, eyes dead and staring. Blood trickled from the small bullet hole in her forehead and ran down her face.

DeVayne shouted in triumph and then swung the gun back to point it at the Prince of Wales' heart. His finger was tightening on the trigger when Detective Blenkinsop, who was standing the closest, lunged forward and wrapped his arms around the young aristocrat, smothering his arms. They staggered across the room, grappling. But then BANG! a second shot rang out. Detective Blenkinsop flinched, a sickening tremor shook his frame, and then he relaxed and slumped at DeVayne's feet.

In the next instant, one of the Beefeaters rushed forward and thrust the point of his halberd into the marquess's back, running him through so that the spear point burst through his chest. DeVayne's eyes widened. He staggered forward and looked down in disbelief at the metal shaft skewering his chest. He coughed, shooting out a spray of blood, and slowly crumpled to his knees. His eyes sparkled with tears. His long lashes fluttered. A weird, tremulous smile chased about his lips. Blood, frothy and arterial, trickled from the corners of his mouth. And then, incredibly, he seemed to rally, and spoke in a gurgly voice: "In three days, I shall rise again . . ." But then the light went out of his eyes and with a prolonged and weary sigh, as if sick of life, he relaxed into death and slumped backward until the spear propped him up, his arms falling akimbo.

The room broke into chaos. Cypher screamed at the Beefeaters, "Make sure he's dead!"

Conan Doyle and Wilde rushed to Detective Blenkinsop's crumpled form. When they turned him over, the front of his best suit was soaked in blood. Conan Doyle fumbled for a pulse in his neck. Finding none, his head dropped resignedly.

"Dead?" Wilde asked softly, laying a hand on his shoulder.

Conan Doyle looked up with a stricken expression, but could not summon the words and merely nodded.

"How terrible," Wilde breathed. "How terrible . . ."

Conan Doyle shook his head and croaked, "If it had not been for me, he would not be here today. And so I have caused his death."

"Nonsense, Arthur. You acted from the very best of motives. You could not have known."

"The queen!" The Prince of Wales wailed. "Fetch a doctor. The queen has been shot!"

Even through his shock, Conan Doyle realized he was the only doctor in the room. He rose to his feet and numbly approached the slumped form of Victoria. The bullet had struck her squarely in the forehead and a stream of sticky black blood runneled down her face. Her spaniel's eyes were wide open and staring. But then Conan Doyle frowned at something and reaching out, touched his fingertips to the blood, and examined them, releasing an astonished gasp.

"What?" Wilde asked.

Conan Doyle turned to his friend. "This is not blood. It feels like . . . oil! Dark red oil." Still not believing, he reached down and gently tilted the queen's head. The back of the skull was missing, blown apart, and he expected to see brains and gore. Instead, he found that the shattered skull case contained brassy cogs and a speaking tube that emerged from a hole in the wall behind.

It was suddenly clear they had all been deceived.

"An automaton!" Wilde gasped.

"Yes, another ingenious mechanism."

At that moment, a door hidden in the paneling opened and a short, stout figure stepped out:

Victoria Regina, this time in the flesh.

Following behind her was a man in a stovepipe hat, the engineer Ozymandius Arkwright.

"Mama!" the Prince of Wales cried out. He rushed over to her, wringing his hands. "I—I—I had no idea. I—I'm afraid I've been a fool again, ma'am."

"A role you are familiar with," Victoria noted sourly, "and play to perfection."

She looked about the throne room disapprovingly. "Where is this would-be assassin?"

The Beefeater who had run the marquess through mutely pointed. As she stepped over to inspect DeVayne's body, Cypher tried to prevent her. "Majesty, this is not a sight fit for royalty—" She silenced him with a wave. The aging queen threw a scowl of disapproval down at DeVayne's astonished face. "My assassin now lies dead. Traitor to your queen. Your nation. Your class. Your family name. Little man, with your trumped up ambitions, it would take someone far greater than you to slay a queen."

She looked up at the assembled courtiers and friends, her eyes blazing with self-righteous fury. Despite her tiny stature, despite her advanced age, she cut a formidably regal figure. She turned to the yeoman of the guard and commanded, "Your sword, sir." The yeoman quickly slid the blade from its scabbard and presented it to her, pommel first. She hefted its steely mass and addressed the room. "We have much thanks to give today. To our loyal servants of the crown. To our fearless subjects who placed the life of their sovereign above their own."

She focused her stern gaze upon Ozymandius Arkwright. "Step forward and kneel before your queen." He dropped to one knee and removed his stovepipe hat. Victoria touched the blade to one shoulder, lifted it, and touched the other shoulder. The queen smiled mildly and said, "Arise, Sir Ozymandius Arkwright."

Conan Doyle's eyes met Wilde's and both men wore an expression of deep vexation.

* * *

"What did Mister Ozymandius do that made him so deserving of a knighthood?" Wilde bellyached to his friend as they walked across the palace courtyard to his waiting carriage. "We were nearly torn apart by a monster. Drowned in the Thames. Shot. Stabbed. Poisoned by conspirators. All he did was build a giant doll. A mechanical puppet. A—"

"Decoy," Conan Doyle interrupted. "A very clever decoy that fooled an assassin and saved the monarch's life." He looked sagely at his friend. "This whole adventure—all of it—has been about the true face of evil hiding behind a mask. But now a good man is dead and I bear the full weight of guilt." He looked away into the far distance, despair crouched in the corner of his eyes.

"Mister Wilde, Doctor Doyle," a fruity and fatuous voice called from behind. "I would speak with you a moment."

The two friends turned to look. The Prince of Wales strode toward them trailing smoke from the cigar clamped in the corner of his mouth.

They both bowed, but for once the prince had dropped his air of condescension and seemed uncharacteristically bashful, even ashamed. "I must apologize to both you gentlemen," he began. "This has been a most regrettable business . . . most regrettable. Our man Cypher has told me of your role in this matter and I now realize that you two have been key to saving the queen's life, my life, and our nation."

But Conan Doyle found himself unmoved by the prince's words and spoke out in a fashion that surprised even him. "I am more concerned about Detective Blenkinsop than accolades for myself. He leaves behind a wife and young child, who through *your* interference have lost a husband, a father, a breadwinner . . . everything."

Wilde visibly cringed. Upbraiding a prince of the realm was unthinkable. He laughed politely and said, "Of course, my friend is suffering from a shock to the nervous system, aren't you, Arthur? He is not *literally* blaming you." He leaned close to his friend's ear and whispered sotto voce, "Think of Newgate Prison, Arthur. Think of the dark, dank cell that Burke promised us."

But the prince did not take umbrage. Instead, he seemed positively contrite. "Of course, you are right to speak out. Quite right. I know what you must think of me. I know what the world thinks of me. And I am ashamed. The death of this brave young man is rightfully laid at *my* feet, not yours. You are correct. He is the true hero. But I give you my word as a gentleman. As a prince. As your future king, that I will see to it that his wife and child receive the full beneficence of the crown and are taken care of for the rest of their days."

The prince's candor did much to disarm Conan Doyle's anger, but the heir apparent had not finished. "It has not been easy, growing up in my mother's shadow. I am cognizant of my many failings. Indeed, for much of my life I have rebelled against my station in life. But after this dreadful episode, the scales have fallen from my eyes. When I finally sit upon the throne, trust that I shall be a changed man. Perhaps I could even prove worthy of a hero such as Detective Blenkinsop." The prince shifted his feet. "Now if in the meantime there is any favor you wish to ask of me. Any. No matter how grand. Please name it."

Although not fully placated, the prince's self-abasement did much to assuage Conan Doyle's wrath. As both men muttered their thank-yous and bowed, a clatter of hooves announced the approach of a carriage. They were surprised to see Rufus DeVayne's landau, complete with its four zebras, draw up before them.

"What will happen to the carriage?" Wilde asked.

The prince shook his head vaguely. "I understand the zebras are to find a new home at London Zoo. I'm not sure what will become of the landau."

A sudden notion occurred to Conan Doyle. "Your Highness mentioned a favor? I wonder if I might beg a small indulgence . . ."

❀

THE SUN BREAKS THROUGH

Conan Doyle found his children, Kingsley and Mary, tossing crusts to the swans gliding the periphery of the circular pond in Hyde Park. His wife, Louise, was ensconced in a bath chair. The day was bright and breezy, but chilly. Pushing the bath chair was a tall, graceful young woman of striking beauty: Miss Jean Leckie.

"Arthur?" Louise Doyle called out as the Scottish author strode across the grass lawns to join them. "Is it still Arthur? Or must I now curtsey and call you, Sir Arthur?"

Conan Doyle smiled sheepishly. "I'm afraid I remain just plain Arthur for now." He laughed at their disappointed faces. "But not to be sad—the role Oscar and I played has been recognized. And now I have a happy surprise for you all."

"A surprise?" Jean Leckie asked. "What kind of surprise?"

"A carriage ride," Conan Doyle answered, and added, mysteriously, "A very special kind of carriage ride."

When the family emerged from the gates of Hyde Park, the yellow landau drawn by four zebras waited at the curb, where it was rapidly drawing a crowd of curious onlookers. As they caught sight of it, the Doyle children shrieked with glee and ran to pet the zebras. Conan Doyle held the carriage door open for Jean Leckie, and then put his arm about his wife and lifted her into the carriage. Both women were delighted to find Oscar Wilde already ensconced inside.

"Hello, Touie. Hello, Miss Leckie."

"But whose is this wonderful carriage?" Miss Leckie asked. "And the zebras?"

"A princely favor," Conan Doyle explained. "We have use of the landau until nightfall."

Wilde patted a straw hamper on the seat next to him. "Arthur and I stopped at Fortnum & Mason's on the way here." He hefted it from the seat and set it down upon the carriage floor to make room for the children. "It's a tad brisk out, but we thought the occasion called for a ride through the park followed by a picnic."

And so on the first fogless day in weeks, the friends set off on a long, lazy circuit of Hyde Park, drawing stares of wonder and stopping traffic wherever they went.

* * *

A gray morning where dawn was slow arriving beneath a pall of winter clouds. A crowd stood assembled in the courtyard of Newgate Prison. The doors of the execution shed had been thrown open and now, at precisely three minutes to nine, a grim procession filed out: a black-frocked chaplain (whose faltering gait suggested he had, once again, been sampling the communion wine), a balding physician, a pair of uniformed guards, and the dour prison warden, William Bland, bringing up the rear. As usual, Dr. John Lamb accompanied the party, only this time he walked with his hands pinioned at his sides, a burly warder gripping either arm. Without ceremony, he was led onto the trap, where one warder dropped to a crouch as he pinioned his legs. The chaplain stumbled through the prayer of benediction, and then Warden Bland asked if the prisoner had any last words.

Dr. Lamb's hair had clearly not enjoyed the application of curling papers, and had instead been chopped into spiky clumps by the prison barber's dull shears. Yet, he stood tall, wrapped in the tattered rag of his former dignity, as he addressed the crowd in a clear, un-wavering voice, devoid of fear.

"I believe in the Resurrection," he said, but then added with a sick smile, "the resurrection of the Marquess Rufus DeVayne. For he will rise aga—"

Warden Bland's gray face turned black, his frown lines crevassed. At a nod from him, the executioner stepped forward and roughly snatched a white hood down on the doctor's head, silencing him. With unseemly haste, he looped the heavy hawser about Lamb's neck, stepped smartly from the trap and gripped the release lever in his gloved hands. The hour began to sound: CLONG . . . CLONG . . .

And as the final bell tolled, the executioner yanked the lever, the trap dropped open, and Dr. John Lamb plummeted from this life into the next.

* * *

After a brief religious ceremony (which he would have despised), the Marquess of Gravistock, Rufus DeVayne, was quietly interred in the family crypt at the DeVayne family seat, the underground remains of which were the only part of the house not to have been razed by the fire.

Three days later, a gardener found the bronze tomb door wrenched loose from its hinges and the crypt empty apart from a torn burial shroud.

Although the grounds were searched, the mortal remains of the late marquess were never found.